Cabin

6

P. L. WELLISLEY

Cabin 6

Copyright © 2025 P. L. Wellisley

All rights reserved.

Cover design by P. L. Wellisley

ISBN: 979-8-9994875-1-3

Printed in the United States of America

First Edition

To anyone who's ever needed to leave in order to find their way home again.

1

This is for the Birds

Kinsley

Just two more days, I remind myself, scraping my three-inch stiletto across the cement. "What kind of asshole spits gum in the middle of the sidewalk?" I already feel the weight of the day pressing on my shoulders. My patience is thin, my nerves frayed, and if one more thing goes wrong, I might lose it right here on the street.

I step into the same mundane coffeehouse in downtown Seattle. I've been coming here nearly every day for eight months. It's two blocks from my office, the coffee's mediocre and the line's always too long, but I need caffeine.

The place has an industrial feel: White walls, a black ceiling and a constant hum of noise. A few tables sit beneath the windows, catching the morning light. The gray counter is lined with cups, each marked with a handwritten name waiting to be claimed.

As I stand in line, my mind drifts to the long list of tasks waiting for me. I started my law firm eight months ago, and I'm exhausted. It's starting to show. Today's my last day in the office. Tomorrow, I'll work from home, close up my apartment and pack for a much-needed month-long vacation.

The line shifts, but my head is still tangled in meetings. I take a step forward right into a man rushing for the exit, coffee in hand. Yes, I know the so-called "rule" about not wearing white after Labor Day. But come on, it's one day after for Christ's sake. Now, iced coffee is soaking into my white wide-leg pants

"I'm so sorry, sir. Please let me buy you..." I begin, but he cuts me off with a stubby hand raised in dismissal. He glares at me, trying to be intimidating.

"Are you stupid? I don't have time to wait in line again," he spits through his teeth. I might only be five foot two, but I won't cower from his words. He stomps off, his short square frame clad in a shit-colored brown suit disappearing into the street.

I glance down at my pants, reminding myself I have a change of clothes at the office. Why? Because this happens at least twice a week. No, it's usually not my fault. But today, my mind is on overdrive, scrambling to get everything in place before I take time off. I'm burnt out.

With a huff, I step out of line, abandon my morning fix and head out. I round the corner and walk two blocks to my office. It's only eight thirty in the morning. What else could possibly go wrong?

The city sidewalk is crowded, and the streets are choked with stop-and-go traffic. Tall buildings rise around me, blocking the view of Elliott Bay to the west of downtown Seattle. Not that I have time to enjoy it. Everyone in this city seems to be in a rush, and today, I'm no exception.

I open the door to Brighton Family Law. The office is sleek and modern, white marble floors and slate-gray walls. A small seating area sits to the left with dark gray chairs and a kids' table stocked with coloring books and crayons. The walnut reception desk stands ahead, just in front of a set of frosted glass doors leading to several offices and conference rooms.

Mel, my receptionist and longtime friend, looks up from her computer, her standard customer service smile already in place. But when her dark brown eyes land on my pants, the expression shifts from polite and professional to barely contained amusement. Trying not to laugh, she raises a perfectly manicured finger. "Seriously? White pants?"

"It's just one day after Labor Day." I square my shoulders and pretend to be pissed. I'm not actually mad and she knows this, so when I call her a "bitch" under my breath, she laughs out loud.

She really is the glue that holds this place together. Just last week, she calmed down a client in the middle of a hallway meltdown, scheduled three emergency consultations and still remembered to grab my favorite pastry on her coffee run. Without Mel, I'd be completely lost most days.

After stifling her laugh, she reminds me of a meeting I have in twenty minutes. Mel is runway-model beautiful, the kind of woman who turns heads without trying, the type who makes you feel underdressed just by breathing the same air. And yet, she's completely unaware of the effect she has on people, which makes her both infuriating and endearing. Her chestnut brown hair is cut in layers just past her shoulders, framing a perfect little nose. "Double bitch." Mel is a bit of a people-pleaser, which doesn't always sit well with me, but she's damn good at her job.

Once in my office, I quickly change, plop into my brown leather chair and get to work. Pulling up my schedule, I remind myself: *Last full workday for the next month. Just get through it.* Twenty minutes later, Mel walks in with my first appointment of the day, newly scorned Mrs. Perry, seeking a divorce after eight years of marriage.

"Hello, Mrs. Perry. I'm Kinsley Brighton." I rise from my chair and gesture for her to take a seat across from my desk. She's an older woman with dyed black hair and hunched shoulders beneath a multicolored knit sweater. Tears cling to the corners of her light brown eyes. With a heavy sigh, she drops into the chair and lets her oversized purple tote bag fall at her feet.

Mel softly closes the door as she exits the office. I slide a box of tissues across the desk to Mrs. Perry. For the next two hours, I

3

listen to what a complete and utter ass Mr. Perry is for cheating on her with...yup, you guessed it...her sister. I recommend splitting their assets evenly. That's when she throws a curveball at me.

"I also want child support," she spits.

"I'm sorry, Mrs. Perry, I wasn't aware there are children involved?"

"There's not. I want it for my parakeets, Bonnie and Clyde," she says with complete seriousness, as if this were the most obvious request in the world.

For about five seconds, I'm struck dumb. Regaining my composure, I tell her, "I'm sorry, Mrs. Perry, no judge in their right mind will grant the request for child support for pet birds."

As Mrs. Perry launches into another rant, I discreetly wiggle my wireless mouse, bringing my computer out of sleep mode. I message Mel, asking her to move my next two meetings to one of the other associates. She quickly replies with an eye roll emoji and a "you got it, boss."

After another forty-five minutes with Mrs. Perry, I stand, hoping she gets the hint, and slowly walk toward my office door. I reassure her Mr. Perry will pay for his infidelity. Opening the door, knowing Mel can hear us, I announce a little louder than normal, "Thank you for trusting Brighton Family Law. Mel will be happy to print out your paperwork."

Mel's head pops around the corner, lips pursed with mock annoyance, though the glint in her eyes betrays her amusement. I know I just threw her under the bus, and I'm not mad about it. Smirking, I return to my office and close the door. *One more day.*

I spend the rest of my day playing catch-up. I work through lunch, responding to emails and drafting paperwork that needs to be signed and tasks I'll leave for Mel to complete tomorrow. By late afternoon, I'm almost back on schedule when my cell phone buzzes, snapping me out of work mode. I answer without checking the screen.

4

"Hey, sexy. How have you been?" Ben's voice comes in, loud and clear.

Trying to sound as professional as possible, I respond, "I've asked you not to call me that, Ben. We haven't been together in over eight months."

"I know," he whines. "But I miss you. We should get together for lunch and talk about this."

Ben has always struggled with hearing the word 'no.' He's good-looking, sandy blond hair, sky-blue eyes, about six feet tall with a decent build. Once he told me our relationship was one of convenience, I was done.

Still, I can't blame it all on him. After years of working as a divorce attorney, watching marriages crumble and hearts break, I settled. Ben felt safe and reliable. But I want more. I want what my parents have. I want the thrill of being in love.

"I'm sorry, Ben. I don't think that's a good idea. I want more, and we both know you're not capable. I have work to do. Bye, Ben."

I hang up quickly, cutting the conversation short before he has the chance to spiral. Ben and I were co-workers at my last law firm. After our breakup, he started pressuring me to get back together. So, I left. In a way, I should thank him. If it weren't for his "What are you going to do without me?" attitude, I wouldn't have had the push to start my own family law firm.

Losing myself in court documents again, Mel pops her head into my office. "Ms. Brighton," she whispers. Glancing up, I see her tapping her watch, silently telling me it's five o'clock.

"Mel, for the love of God, call me Kinsley."

She laughs, stepping fully into the room and taking a seat across from me. "I can't help it when we're in the office."

"Save it for the clients. We're the only ones here." I grin.

5

She grins back. "Tell me about this big vacation you've been working so hard to keep a secret. Are you going somewhere tropical? Maybe a beach with smoking hot men playing volleyball, getting sand in all their good spots?"

She chuckles at her own joke, and I can't help but laugh, too.

I smile shyly. "No. I've booked a cabin on a private lake in Cranberry Ridge, a small town near Colville National Forest. It's about a six-hour drive from Seattle."

She looks at me like I've lost my mind. "You know that sounds like the setup to a horror movie, right?"

I laugh again, realizing she might have a point, but it's already booked. "I get what you're saying, Mel, but I just really need some peace and serenity."

"I totally understand. But please send me the address to this place. Ya know, just in case."

"I can do that. And... thanks for caring. Seriously, you're the best."

"Of course." She smiles. "Let's go home."

Gathering my coffee-stained pants and laptop, Mel and I step out the front door and lock it behind us. The sun has already started to set, casting a warm orange hue over the street. I give Mel a longer-than-usual hug, and then we go our separate ways.

I wave down the first taxi I see. After giving the driver my address, I settle into the seat and stare silently out the window, watching as the city grows darker and the streetlights flicker to life one by one. The driver pulls up in front of my seven-story, red brick apartment building. I thank him, pay the fare and step out. The cracked cement sidewalk leads me to the front door where I punch in my code on the keypad.

It's good to be home but not really. The familiar creak of the elevator, the soft hum of my fridge, even the scent of my lavender candle, all of it feels hollow, like I'm living in someone else's space.

6

The boxes still stacked in the corner whisper of things left undone, and the silence reminds me that I haven't really made this place mine. I've lived here for eight months, and with my hectic schedule, I still haven't unpacked all the boxes. It feels more like a hotel than a home. I take the elevator to the fourth floor, unlock my door and step inside, locking it behind me. Kicking off my heels, I make a beeline for the kitchen.

My kitchen has top-of-the-line appliances that rarely get used. White cabinets and beige and white granite countertops match the island. I open the refrigerator to find yesterday's leftover Thai takeout, a few bottles of water, milk three days past its expiration date and a handful of condiments. I throw the container of leftovers in the microwave and wait for the timer. I grab a bottle of water, sit on the stool next to the island and eat alone. I really do enjoy cooking, and I'm good at it. Finding time to grocery shop and cook every night is a pipe dream though.

I haven't even started my vacation, and I'm already feeling restless. Maybe it's the unfamiliar feeling of having nothing urgent to do or maybe it's the quiet creeping in after months of constant motion. I'm not used to stillness and, for some reason, it's making me uneasy.

I heave myself off the stool and head for the bathroom for a much needed everything shower. I stay in the water for so long my fingers wrinkle. After drying my hair, I slip into an oversized T-shirt and shorts, crawl into bed and set my alarm. I only lie there a few minutes before I'm out cold.

***

My alarm buzzes loudly, jarring me awake. The sun is shining as I draw back the curtains and remake my bed. Standing in the bathroom brushing my teeth, I glance in the mirror. I look a lit tle more rested than usual. I pull my auburn hair into a messy bun and give myself a pep talk.

"You need this vacation. You worked hard to build this life. Go enjoy yourself. Maybe get laid. Okay, that's another pipe dream. Where am I going to find a man in the middle of nowhere?"

I throw on a pair of black leggings and a white crop top that says, "Not today, Satan. Try again tomorrow." Barefoot, I pad into the kitchen and start a pot of coffee.

I receive yet another text from Ben. I swear that man has a hard time understanding what 'ex-boyfriend' means. I don't even bother opening it. Instead, I toss my phone onto the couch and head to the kitchen. If I give him attention, he'll think there's still a door cracked open. There's not. That door is sealed shut, boarded up and padlocked for good.

The next several hours I work from home. I remember to send Mel an email with the address and phone number for the cabins. When I booked the cabin, a very lovely woman named Judy assured me they do, in fact, have Wi-Fi and that check-in is at noon. She also informed me they don't get many guests this time of year. Renting in the fall is at a discounted rate. I'm a sucker for a good deal, so I opted for a month-long stay. I definitely need it.

When I finish work, I order pizza and make a to-do list:

1. Eat leftover pizza for breakfast.

2. Pack.

3. Overpack.

4. Vacuum.

5. GET RID OF THE MILK.

6. Take out trash.

7. Lock the door.

For the rest of the night, I make my way down the list, checking them off as I go. I pack three full suitcases and one duffle bag. I've lived in Washington my entire life, so I know the weather is unpredictable. I might need a swimsuit one day and snow pants the next. The rental car will be delivered in the morning. I don't drive much, so I kept it simple and selected a compact SUV.

8

Before I turn in for the night, I give my mom a call. She picks up on the second ring. "Hi, Mom."

"Hello, Kinsley. How's my favorite child doing?"

"Mom, I'm your only child." I chuckle.

"No, honey, your dad is acting like a man-child as we speak. He has a cold." She deadpans, and I can't help but laugh.

"I hope he's feeling better soon. Give him a kiss for me. I wanted to remind you that I leave for vacation tomorrow. And yes, I'll text you while I'm gone, and yes, I'll send you pictures."

She giggles. "You're such a smartass."

"I love you too, Mom."

"Kinsley, on a serious note, I'm not comfortable with you staying in such an isolated place so far from home."

"Mom, I'm thirty-two years old. I'm independent and smart. I'll be fine. If it makes you feel better, I'll check in every couple of days."

"It does, thank you. I love you."

"I love you, too. Bye."

"Tomorrow's the day," I tell myself while brushing my hair. My reflection stares back, wide-eyed, tentative, almost unrecognizable in its vulnerability. There's a weight behind my eyes, not from exhaustion, but from everything I'm about to leave behind. The quiet hum of the city outside feels different tonight, like something is waiting just around the corner.

2

The Great Calico Chase

Miles

I dodged right, then left, then right again, arms flailing like I was in some kind of Olympic fencing match against a four-legged opponent. "I've got you cornered now, you might as well give up." I puff, bent over like a man twice my age, sweat trickling down my back as I glare at Miss Dashworth with mock seriousness.

"I've been chasing her around the yard for fifteen minutes because of you." I huff at my brother.

Reed laughs. "Sorry, man! I didn't know she'd make a run for the door."

I playfully punched him in the chest as I walked past with Miss Dashworth, my long-haired calico cat, safely tucked under my arm. Two years ago, I found her as a kitten on the side of the road. I couldn't just leave her there. She was scared, shivering and a little feisty. I like that she's feisty. It gives her character.

"You could've helped me catch her."

"And miss watching you act like a lunatic? No chance." Rubbing his chest, he tries to suppress his laughter.

I'm thirty-three years old, and I don't think our brotherly banter and playfulness will ever get old.

"You're a dick," I grumble.

I place Miss Dashworth back in the house. "Will you be home for the Farmers Potluck?"

My parents bought the property in the early seventies. They lived in a small cabin for two years before building the farmhouse. The property borders the Colville National Forest and features a twenty-acre lake right in the center. My mother, Grace, loved the cabin life so much she had five more built overlooking the lake. Every year, she'd rent them to out-of-towners looking for a peaceful retreat. She used to say, "It's a place for city folk to go to fall in love." She was a hopeless romantic. Me, not so much.

Reed pulls his phone out, checking his calendar. "When's the potluck?"

Reed is two years younger than me. We both have walnut-brown hair, but his eyes are golden with hints of brown, while mine are a darker shade of brown. He also stands two inches taller than me at six foot four. Sure, he's got the height, but he's never beaten me in a fight. Although he'd remember differently.

"Two weeks from Saturday." We head toward the barn to tackle the long list of things that need to be done before winter sets in.

Every year, I harvest the fields, winterize the equipment, make repairs to the buildings and close down the cabins for the season. Normally, I have plenty of time, but this year I'm also hosting the annual Farmers Potluck. And it's not just your run-of-the-mill potluck, it's an EVENT.

All the local farmers take turns hosting, and over the years it's turned into a full-blown competition. Even though I don't really have the time to spare, I'll be damned if I let Old Man Floyd beat me.

11

Floyd's another local farmer who hosted last year. He's a grouchy old man, but he does a lot for the community. At almost eighty years old, I guess he's earned the right to be cantankerous. I don't dislike Floyd; I actually appreciate his competitive spirit when it comes to the potluck. In the end, it's for the community.

"I leave for Canada tomorrow morning. I'll be back in a week," Reed says, eyes on his phone. "I can help on the farm when I get back."

"Thanks." I shrug. Reed's a firefighter at the local fire department in Cranberry Ridge and volunteers to help fight wildfires in Canada. This summer, he spent most of his time up there. Now that the fires are nearly contained, this should be his last trip.

"I talked to Aunt Judy this morning. She said you're expecting a new cabin guest tomorrow." Reed tells me this like I don't already know.

"Yes, for a month." I huff trying to keep the annoyance out of my voice. It's just one more thing on my overflowing plate. I can't winterize a cabin when someone's staying in it. I don't like making assumptions about people, but seriously, who rents a cabin in the middle of nowhere for an entire month in the off-season?

As I slide the barn doors open and prepare to stack bales of hay in the loft, Reed grabs gloves for both of us. There's no conversation, we just do it, like it's second nature.

We grew up on this farm, and our dad taught us everything we know. He died in an auto accident when I was fifteen. Determined, my mom pulled herself together and worked even harder to keep the farm. I knew then I wanted to keep the farm in the family. Reed followed his dreams and became a firefighter, and I took over the farm when my mom died five years ago. She fought hard for a long time but in the end, cancer took her anyway. I renamed the farm to Davison Farms after in honor of my parents.

After we make quick work of the hay, we head back to the house for lunch. It's a two-story classic farmhouse. I've updated both the bathrooms and kitchen along with the windows and siding, keeping the outside the original white, with a large wraparound porch.

Reed grabs two waters from the refrigerator. "Do you have any big plans for the potluck?"

I answer while making us ham and cheese sandwiches. "Yeah, I'm adding bounce houses for the kids this year."

"I can come a couple days early to get give you a hand."

"Aunt Judy's been on a mission with all the details, but I might need help with setup."

Aunt Judy moved here when mom got sick. She stayed in the farmhouse with her right up until the end. After mom passed, Judy couldn't bear staying there. It held too many memories. Instead, she chose to live in the original cabin, the one my parents stayed in years ago.

Aunt Judy's the type who challenges what most people consider "normal." She's never had kids, and now that I think about it, I've never seen her with a man or a woman. Not that it's any of my business, and I've never asked. I offered her the cabin rent-free, of course, but she wouldn't hear of it. She insisted on pulling her weight. So, she's become our unofficial "cabin manager." She keeps all six cabins spotless and handles every reservation like it's a five-star resort.

Reed pushes his chair back, finishing his last bite. "I'll be here Thursday to help out with the potluck setup. Have you talked to Luke lately?" he heads toward the door.

Luke's been our best friend since we were kids. We grew up playing ball together, spending damn near every summer day side by side. When my dad passed, Luke stayed on the farm and helped with chores. He's more than a friend. He's like a brother to us.

"Yeah, I talked to Luke yesterday. He'll be home for the potluck." Luke is on a business trip about two hours away in Spokane and has been gone for two weeks, which is normal for his

13

job. He keeps what he does for a living to himself. I know he owns his own business, something to do with security. I'm not sure exactly, but Luke has always been a private kind of guy. I trust Luke with my life, so if he feels the need to keep this to himself, I don't push it.

Reed and I say goodbye the way we always do, as typical brothers. He flips me off, and I punch him in the shoulder. We put our parents through hell growing up. Sure, we fought now and then, but we always had each other's backs. Reed's a lot like our dad, short-tempered and stubborn. I'm more of a mix, A "joker's blend" of both Mom and Dad. I'll bring home a stray cat like Mom, and I'm just as overprotective as Dad.

Around noon, Colby shows up to help out on the farm. He's seventeen, and dead set on becoming a farmer one day. Two years ago, the local high school reached out asking if students could come by a few times a week to get hands-on experience. I don't really need help, but it was for the kids, so I agreed. I give them tasks, teach them what I can. Figure if even one of them sticks with it, it's worth it. He still has a lot to learn, but he's a hardworking kid.

I've only got one horse and six chickens, so the work's not too demanding. After a quick rundown of the morning chores, Colby gets started mucking out the stall and spends some time with Rocket before getting started on the coop.

Rocket is a dark brown American Quarter Horse who's been on the farm for twenty years. He's reached an age where he can no longer be ridden.

I officially retired him last year, and now he enjoys a peaceful life as an honorary "lawn mower." He's kept in a fenced pasture with a small stable attached, giving him shelter from the occasional wildlife that wanders out of the forest. I keep the chickens in a coop for similar reasons, though I let them roam freely under supervision a couple of times a week.

"Hey, Colby, I'm heading over to the cabins to get some work done. Can you manage the farm?" I gesture around as I ask.

14

"Yes, sir."

He's a shy kid. I'll get him to open up eventually but not today. There's too much to do. Trusting in Colby's ability, I give him a quick wave and head over to my pickup truck parked near the house.

I make my way around the lake to the cabins. Parking, I see Judy pulling weeds out of the flower bed in front of cabin number two. The cabins are numbered one through six and sit in a neat row just off the lake. cabin one, the only one with two bedrooms, is where Judy lives. Each cabin features a rustic exterior, its own patio and a brick firepit facing the water. They're all fully furnished and include modern amenities like Wi-Fi and cable. The lake itself has two small fishing docks, one on each side, with a canoe tied to each.

"Hello, darling," my aunt sings as she stands to hug me. I pretend like I hate affection, but I don't. Truth is, I haven't had any real affection since my last girlfriend over a year ago now. Well, except for Miss Dashworth, who shows her love by stepping on my stomach at 3:00 a.m.

Reed and I don't hug. That would be weird. We might throw a pat on the back now and then, but that's about it. My Mom was the most affectionate one in the family, something she and my aunt definitely had in common.

"Hi, Aunt Judy." I turn to grab my toolbox from the truck. "I just stopped in to fix the leaky faucet in cabin three."

Judy is in her late sixties with short gray hair framing her round face. Small crows' feet at the corner of her eyes. When she smiles you can just make out her dimples. She's a curvy woman about five foot five inches tall.

"Oh, that reminds me! I have a list of things that need tending to." She reaches into her garden smock handing me a slip of paper.

Setting down my toolbox, I read the list out loud.

1. Leaky faucet cabin 3

2. New lock cabin 5

3. Empty firepit cabin 4

4. Get married, have kids cabin 6

5. Kitchen light bulb cabin 2

"Haha, very funny Aunt Judy. I'll get right on it."

She waves her hand, giggling. "Okay, sweetheart."

After finishing my to-do list "except number four," I knock on Judy's door to let her know I'm leaving. But Judy has other plans. "I just made a big pot of chili. Why don't you come in for a bite to eat?"

Knowing when to pick my battles, I go inside. "Thanks, how could I pass up your chili?"

We have dinner together at least once a week. She reminds me so much of my mom, I have a hard time saying no. She's told me several times, "I just hate to think of you eating all alone." A part of me stays for dinner because I think she's the one that's lonely. But I don't mind it.

"Have you had a chance to call the rental company about the tent and tables?" I scoop up another bite of the best damn chili I've ever had.

"Oh yes, I almost forgot." She grabs us a beer from her refrigerator and pops them open. "They should be here to set everything up three days before."

"That's perfect. Thanks for helping me out."

"Anytime, honey. All you need to do is ask."

"What would I do without you?"

"Probably throw the worst Farmers Potluck in history and let Old Man Floyd beat you."

I know what she's doing, and it works. I immediately go into defense mode. "I'll bring the circus to town before I let that fucker one up me." She laughs until tears run down her cheeks.

"I think adding bounce houses for the kids is a great idea. They'll be delivered and set up the morning of the potluck," she reminds me.

"Every year something new gets added for the adults, and I don't know, I guess I thought the kids needed something, too."

She reaches out for my hand and gives it a squeeze. "Your parents would be so proud of you. Just like I am."

Her words hit harder than I expect. For a second, I see Mom standing at the edge of the lake, apron dusted with flour, calling us in for dinner with that soft smile of hers. I nod, not trusting myself to speak. The lump in my throat says more than words ever could.

"I was also thinking maybe we should go on one of those dating web sites and find you a good girl." She stares, not breaking eye contact.

The alarm in my head sounds. *Red alert, red alert, think quick.* I stand taking our bowls to the sink and use her words against her. "While we're at it, we could set one up for you, too. If I'm going down, I'm taking you with me." My attempt to deter her works.

Judy swats me with a kitchen towel. "I'm too old for any of that nonsense. Just think about it, Miles."

I help clean up the mess and our conversation switches back to something safe. "I'm surprised we have a guest coming tomorrow."

17

"Well, when she called and asked for the month, I thought this poor girl really needs a break. How could I say no?" Judy frowns.

"Do you know anything about her?"

"No, just her first name. It's Kinsley. I'd have to look up her last name on the forms. Do you want me to find it?"

"No, it's fine. It's just strange someone staying this late in the season and a little inconvenient. But it's fine, really."

She walks me to the door. "Good. It might be nice having someone stay for a while. Mix things up."

"It might be or maybe she's crazy and likes pineapple on her pizza," I add in mock disgust. That earns me another swat from Judy as I walk out the door.

She yells from the open door. "You should stop by tomorrow and introduce yourself since she'll be with us a while."

"I can do that. See you then."

When I open the door, Miss Dashworth is already waiting for me. The living room flows into the kitchen where a small breakfast nook sits near the stairs. The place is simple, white walls, high ceilings, and oak floors that creak in a few spots. A black leather couch faces a white brick fireplace with a TV mounted above it. The kitchen's been updated, appliances match, and there's an island with three stools that no one ever sits on. Off to the right, the dining room holds a big oak table, enough room for eight if needed.

I carry Miss Dashworth into the kitchen, her soft purr vibrating against my chest. She hops down gracefully when I set her near her food dish. With a scoop of her favorite salmon kibble, she's content, tail flicking in lazy appreciation. I grab the bookmarked novel from the coffee table and stretch out on the couch, settling into the familiar grooves of the cushions.

I've always preferred reading over watching TV. There's something about getting lost in someone else's world that quiets my own. Except during baseball season. That's non-negotiable. Reed, Luke and I have a standing tradition. Beers, wings and the game. Sometimes a few of the other guys from town join us, turning it into a full-blown gathering. But most times, it's just the three of us, trash-talking the opposing team, arguing over stats and sharing the kind of laughter that only comes from years of knowing someone.

I must've fallen asleep on the couch, book still open across my chest. Sometime in the middle of the night, I'm yanked out of a dream by the gentle but persistent pressure of tiny paws. Miss Dashworth is perched on top of me, kneading biscuits like she's working dough for a county fair bake-off. I groan and throw an arm over my face. "If I had a dollar for every biscuit you've made, I could retire," I mutter. She responds with a satisfied purr and a tail flick to my nose.

I groan and crack one eye open. "You couldn't wait until morning?" I sigh, giving her a half-hearted scratch behind the ear. She purrs like she's proud of herself. I scoop up the biscuit-making pain-in-the-ass and carry her upstairs, her purring not letting up for a second.

The primary bedroom is the last door on the left. A walnut-frame king bed sits in the middle, with a matching dresser and nightstands on either side, each with a small lamp. His-and-her closets sit on either side of the dresser. I crawl into bed, and Miss Dashworth curls up by my head. Her steady purring keeps me up for a bit, but eventually, I drift off.

3

BBQ Chips and Boundaries

Kinsley

It takes me an hour to cram all my bags into the rental. There's barely any trunk space, so I end up shoving my carry-on into the front seat. I should've gone with the full-size SUV, already regretting that choice. As if that's not enough, Ben's called three times this morning. I keep sending him to voicemail, but I know he won't stop until I either answer or block him. I'm trying to be nice, but damn, he makes it hard.

This morning, I dressed comfortably for the long drive: light gray joggers, a matching sweatshirt and white sneakers. I pulled my hair into a messy bun and put on just enough makeup to hide the fact that I barely slept. After double-checking my apartment one last time, I'm finally ready to go. I set the GPS, Davison Farms in Cranberry Ridge, and a few minutes later I merge onto Highway Two.

The city slowly fades in the rearview mirror. I've always liked city life, but lately, the thrill has worn off. Maybe I'm just tired. Maybe this trip will help me fall back in love with it.

As the skyline disappears and the roads grow quieter, I feel more relaxed than I have in years. About an hour into the drive, a nagging thought tugs at me. I've forgotten something. I grab the list off the passenger seat and scan it. "Fuck," I mutter. I forgot the milk.

Too late to turn around now. I'll text my mom when I arrive and ask her to swing by my apartment and toss it. Since she and my dad retired, they've been living in a quiet little subdivision just outside Seattle, only about thirty minutes from me if traffic's light.

For the next hour I listen to music at deafening levels to drown out my own singing. I haven't felt this carefree since I was a teenager. The song playing reminds of the time my best friend Raelynn and I snuck out of my parent's house to go to Ashley Marquette party. We drank vodka and danced all night long. That's the night I got my first kiss from Josh Stanton, the hottest boy in school. We got caught the next day with massive hangovers. Back then, it felt worth it. My stupid teenage mind lived on the "high" of that kiss for months, about the same amount of time I was grounded.

Silencing the music, I call my best friend, Raelynn.

She answers. "Hello BFF." The hum of a blow dryer is faint in the background.

"Hey girl, how's it going?"

She laughs. "Same shit, different day. How about you? Have you left for your not-so-paradise vacation?"

"I'm doing great actually. I left about two hours ago. How's married life treating you?"

Raelynn married her high school sweetheart, Jacob. They live just outside of Seattle in a cozy house. She runs her own beauty salon after graduating from cosmetology school, and she's damn good at it. Raelynn has the "girl next door" type of beauty with golden blonde hair always done to perfection, big brown doe eyes and a killer rack.

"Jacob and I are doing good." Her voice is cheerful, too cheerful. I immediately know something's wrong.

"What's wrong?"

She sighs. "We haven't been getting along lately, you know the pressures of being an adult."

21

I can sense she doesn't want to talk about it, so I respond like any best friend should. "That son of a bitch."

She laughs with a snort. "Oh my God, stop."

"When you're ready to talk about it, I'll be here."

"Thanks." That's all she says.

For the next hour, we talked about everything, except her marriage. That's one of the things I love about her. There's no judgement, no shame. Just best friends supporting each other.

She sighs. "I have a client in five minutes, so I better get off this phone."

"Ok, I'll talk to you soon. Love your face bye." I hang up and replay the conversation in my head. She sounded tired and defeated. I have the feeling I'll be talking to her sooner rather than later.

Hungry, I stop at the first gas station I find. It's a small building with only two gas pumps. Walking through the door, I see the snack aisle, pick my favorite BBQ chips and head to the counter. The attendant appears to be around fifty, his greasy black hair and stained uniform catching my eye for all the wrong reasons. Something about the way he moves makes my skin crawl, and a cold prickling unease washes over me before he even speaks. My stomach twists, not from hunger this time, but from the discomfort crawling up my spine. The stains on his employee-issued T-shirt only added to the unease. As I approach, he slowly but obviously looks me up and down, and then this fucker licked his lips. Ignoring him, I set my chips down to pay, and the creep says, "When you're done eating these BBQ chips, you mind letting me lick your fingers."

My response is quick. "Only if you want me to throw up, you fucking pervert." Turning on my heel, I abandon my chips and leave before the "finger licker" can respond.

I merge back onto the highway, still hungry and a little cranky. The unsettling encounter lingers in my mind like a bad aftertaste, but I force myself to focus on the road ahead. As the

22

Colville National Forest comes into view on my left, the tension in my shoulders begins to melt. It's breathtaking. The leaves are beginning to change with flecks of yellow and orange scattered across the dense tree line.

I crack the window, letting the wind rush in. The cool breeze tickles my skin, and the scent of turned-up dirt fills the car. Yeah, I definitely made the right choice for this vacation.

Pulling into a long driveway surrounded by trees, I'm starting to question if my GPS knows where it's going. That's when I see the lake, and I know I've found the right place. It's a small lake, but the way the sun reflects on the water makes it one of the most beautiful sights I have ever seen. The lake is so clear I can see the reflection of the trees and clouds on it. It's picturesque. A large white farmhouse with a covered wraparound porch sits on the opposite side of the lake. Next to the farmhouse is a large red barn, a small horse stable and a little chicken coop.

Parking, I see a group of charming rustic cabins. They all have their own back patio facing the water with outdoor furniture and a brick fire pit. The front of each cabin has a small picture window with a flower bed underneath. Every cabin has a stone chimney and a small foot path that leads to the front door.

The email I got when I booked the cabin says the office is in cabin one. Stepping out onto the gravel drive, I look around and notice the cabins are numbered one through six. That's where I see an older woman standing next to a flower bed with her hands on her hips, admiring her handy work. *This must be Judy, the Cabin manager*, I think to myself.

The woman turns when she sees me approaching. A smile spreads across her face, showing off her dimples. She has short gray hair, ivory skin and dark brown eyes. She wears denim overalls and a garden smock around her waist. Tucking her gloves into her smock, she extends her hand. "Well, hello, you must be Kinsley. I'm Judy. We talked on the phone."

I take her outstretched hand. "Yes. It's nice to meet you."

"Come on, let me show you around." She starts toward the cabins. "There are six in total. I'm in cabin one, and you'll be in cabin six. If you need anything, just holler." Her smile is warm, her voice even warmer.

"Thank you, that's very welcoming of you." And I mean it, Judy's a "peach."

"My nephew, Miles, owns Davison Farms. If I'm not around, I'm sure he'll be more than happy to help you." She winks. "You can find him at the farm most days."

I wonder what she meant by the *wink*. I shake the thought away as she hands me a key. Then she places her hand on my shoulder. "Welcome to Cranberry Ridge." She's so freaking sweet; I immediately like her.

I thank her again, retrieve my bags from the car and walk up the path to cabin six. Opening the door, I'm surprised by how spacious it is. It smells like vanilla, and I don't see a speck of dust anywhere. The inside has oak shiplap walls complemented by matching hardwood floors. The living room is furnished with a dark brown leather couch and a large matching armchair, both facing a stone fireplace. The kitchen is equipped with modern stainless-steel appliances and has an island with seating for two. Heaving my bags in the bedroom, I start organizing my belongings in the dresser and closet. The queen-sized bed is adorned with a handmade blue and white quilt and matching pillows. *Damn they look inviting.*

After I finish unpacking, I text my mom to let her know I arrived and ask her to please throw away the milk. She responds back telling me she'll take care of the milk and have a good time.

I also text Mel to check on how things are going in the office and let her know if she needs me to call. She response telling me, Everything's fine, stop texting her and have fun..

Stepping out the back door onto the patio, there's a clear view of the farm across the lake. The forest is within walking distance. Not that it matters. I sleep with a night light. There's no way I'm going in the dark. *What kind of animals live in such a dense forest?* I wonder. A quick internet search reveals a few dozen "mostly" harmless animals like deer and squirrels, and a couple that would scare the shit out of me like black bears and cougars. Shaking off the new fear I just unlocked, I continue taking in my surroundings.

After a few minutes of sightseeing, my stomach growls, reminding me I need to go to the grocery store. The idea of cooking my own meal for once excites me. I skip back into the cabin and make a menu for the week on a note pad I brought from home. By the time I'm done, I'm so hungry I could eat my own arm. I grab my keys and walk out the front door, locking it as I go.

Judy is standing next to her cabin as I walk up the path. I approach her, her wide smile returns. "Excuse me Ms. Judy, can you tell me how to get to town? I need to pick up a few groceries."

"Oh, sweet girl, please just call me Judy. And I can do better than that, just give me a second," she says, walking into her cabin.

When she returns, she hands me a piece of paper with a hand-drawn map that'll lead me to town. And just like that, my heart melts, right there outside cabin one.

"This is perfect. Are you always this hospitable?" I ask with a grin, hoping she knows I mean it as a compliment.

"No." She smirks. "Only to the guest I know will be around a long time."

"Yes, I guess a month can seem like a long time."

"I put my nephew's phone number on the back of the map in case you get lost," she says with a toothy smile.

"I better get going. I'm excited I get to cook tonight. Thanks for the map."

Turning toward my car. I don't know why I said that. Usually, when I meet someone for the first time it's a little awkward. But with Judy, it's different, like I've known her forever. She's so warm and easy to talk to, I'm half-tempted to dump my entire life story on her.

According to Judy's map, the farm is about ten miles from town. I'm humming along with the radio, thinking about what I'll cook for dinner, when a loud pop makes me jump. The car jerks violently to the left, making my heart slamming against my ribs. Panic claws at my throat as I grip the steering wheel so tight my knuckles turn white. I manage to guide the car to the shoulder and hold my breath as I get out to investigate. Rounding the front, I find the front left tire completely shredded, the rim sitting low on the gravel, looking just as defeated as I felt. Frustrated, I open the passenger door and retrieve my phone along with the map Judy made, with her nephew's number scribbled on the back. Just as I begin to dial, an old blue pickup truck pulls up beside me.

A man shouts through the open window. "You need some help?"

"I have a flat tire." I shift nervously, trying to sound more confident than I feel.

He doesn't even get out, just stares from the driver's seat, voice sharp. "Do you know how to change it?"

"I was just about to call for help," I admit, staying right where I am.

"No need to call, I'll fix it."

I watch as he pulls his truck onto the shoulder and retrieves a jack from the back. He looks around eighty years old with short gray hair and reading glasses low on the bridge of his nose. He's wearing a light blue button-down shirt tucked into denim carpenter pants. Setting the jack down next to my car, he says, "I'm Floyd. What's your name, girl?"

"Kinsley. Thank you for helping me, Floyd," I say no longer feeling nervous.

Floyd just grunts without saying another word until he's finished changing my tire. "That'll do it." He brushes the dirt from his hands.

"Please, let me pay you," I offer, reaching in my pocket.

He dismissively waves a hand at me. "Nonsense. Are you new around here? I've never seen you in town before."

"Yes, I'm staying at Davison Farms, and I was on my way to town," I answer.

Floyd is a little rough around the edges, but I have the feeling he's as soft as a pillow.

"Well, I got stuff to do. I better get going." He grabs his jack and heads for the truck.

"Thanks again for all your help, Floyd."

He waves. "No problem kiddo."

Yep, he's a pillow.

Forty-five minutes later, I turn onto Main Street. I take notice of some of the stores and shops in town and make a mental note to spend a day walking around. There are a two of places that stand out the most.

One is a coffee shop called Main Street Brew. It's a small red brick building with several white bistro tables set up in front. Green and white striped awnings hang over a large window and glass front door.

The other place is a used bookstore named The Second Chapter. The bookstore's exterior is decorated with a mix of red, yellow and blue paint. Benches line each side of the front door, creating a space to sit and read.

It's nearly three in the afternoon by the time I pull into the parking lot of Cranberry Ridge Grocery. It's a large white building with a variety of potted plants for sale outside. I parked near a cart corral, just about to open the door when my phone rings. *Of course, Ben again.* I feel the irritation creep in as I answer.

"What do you want, Ben?" My tone makes it clear I'm not in the mood for games.

"I just wanted to talk," he says, like that isn't the excuse he always uses. "You've been ignoring my texts."

"That's not an accident. We broke up for a reason, remember?" *And I'm not about to pretend otherwise.*

"I just, I miss you, Kinsley. Can't we at least be friends?"

I sigh, leaning back in the seat and pinching the bridge of my nose. "Friends don't make you feel guilty for moving on," I say, surprised by the steadiness in my voice.

There's a pause on his end before he finally speaks. "So, there's someone else."

I laugh once, dry and humorless. "Even if there were, it wouldn't be your business."

"Wow." He says it like I just insulted him. "I just thought maybe we could…"

"Ben," I cut in sharply, tired of the back-and-forth. "We are not getting back together. You're the one who said our relationship was one of convenience and I deserve more. Stop calling me!" I hang up before he can reply.

Staring at my reflection in the rearview mirror, I let out a slow breath. *I don't owe him anything, not anymore.*

I grab a cart and walk toward the entrance not wasting any time. I have a feeling I'm about to regret walking into a grocery store on an empty stomach.

4

Pickles and Apple Pie

Miles

While eating breakfast in the kitchen, I check the weather on my phone to decide where to start my day. Since Colby, my farmhand, isn't working today, I'll begin in the stables. Rocket, my old horse, greets me at the gate. He loves his daily head rub, and, of course, feeding time. While I muck out his stall, I let him roam freely in the pasture.

After putting out Rocket's feed, I move on to the damn chickens. Judy convinced me to get them for fresh eggs, which I do like. One of the few things I actually know how to cook. But they're a mess. I don't need another animal to chase. Miss Dashworth is more than enough.

As I approach the chicken coop, the flock gathers at the door, clucking in anticipation. I scatter feed on the ground to keep them distracted. Anything to avoid another chase around the farm. After cleaning the coop and collecting the eggs, I shoo the chickens back inside. It works on all but one. The moment I reach down to pick her up, the chase begins. She runs in wide circles for five solid minutes, then ducks under my truck. I kneel and stretch out my arm, and she runs to the other side. We repeat this dance for another five minutes

29

until she finally gives up. "Aha!" I shout, scooping her up triumphantly. I carry her back to the coop and close the door behind her. "This," I say to the chickens, "is exactly why I have Colby deal with you."

Opening the barn door, I grab my toolbox and crawl under the tractor to fix the axle. I'm under the tractor for hours and forget to eat lunch. My phone rings, and I roll out from underneath the tractor, grab it and check who's calling.

"Hey, Aunt Judy."

"Miles, honey. Can you do your old aunt a favor?" she asks sweetly, not bothering to say hello.

"Of course, what do you need?" She doesn't ask me for much, so when she does, I don't hesitate.

"Could you run to Cranberry Ridge grocery, and grab a couple things for me? I'll make you dinner."

"I can't say no to that." Frankly, my cooking skills are limited to pancakes, scrambled eggs and tacos, so I gladly accept her dinner invitations when she offers them.

"Let me get cleaned up, then I'll go. Text me your list." I'm almost done repairing the axle on the tractor anyway, so I don't feel bad abandoning it to help Judy.

"Ok, I will. Thanks. I'll see you soon."

Three seconds later, I receive her list; milk, rice, tomatoes and bread. She must have already prepared it. Her texting speed is usually as slow as molasses. It amuses me she knew I'd go to the store for her.

It's almost three in the afternoon, so I need to hurry if we want dinner at a reasonable time. I quickly shower, put on distressed jeans and a white T-shirt. Skipping the shave, I leave my five o'clock shadow for tomorrow. My hair is faded on the sides and longer on the top. I run my fingers through it, leaving it messy. I'm done and walking out the door in under twenty minutes.

I park in the parking lot of the grocery store and check Judy's list one more time. Entering the store, I noticed Colby is working today. Colby works at Cranberry Ridge grocery on the days he's not at the farm. As I walk past him, jokingly I say, "I spent the better half of my morning chasing chickens. No more days off." Colby chuckles and continues ringing up the next person.

As I turn down the aisle to grab the rice, I stop dead in my tracks. A woman is climbing the shelving unit, trying to reach something from the top shelf. Her back is to me as I walk up and offer my help. "You want me to grab that for you?"

She didn't see me coming. Startled, she lets out a yelp and loses her balance. Her outstretched arm hits the shelf on the way down. I quickly step forward and catch her by the waist, setting her gently back on her feet before stepping back. Clutching her arm, she turns to me with the most adorable scowl I've ever seen. Her gaze flicks to my chest, lingers on my arms and finally meets my eyes. A blush creeps up her neck. She's maybe five-foot-two with auburn hair and striking green eyes that could stop a man in his tracks. A light dusting of freckles dots her nose and cheeks.

"You scared the hell out of me," she hisses. It takes everything I have not to smile. I can tell she's not really mad. The look on her face makes me think she's embarrassed and maybe even a little curious.

"Sorry, I was just trying to help." I hold my hands up in mock defeat.

"I do this all the time. If you hadn't snuck up behind me, I'd have my pickles and be gone by now." She scowls, stomping her foot. *Did she just stomp her foot? Fuck, that was cute.* Wanting to see where this conversation goes, I decide to "poke the bear."

I tuck my hands in my pockets. "So, you don't need help then?"

"Do I look like I need help?" She tilts her head, waiting for my response.

31

"Yes. You ARE vertically challenged." I raise my hand to knee level to indicate something short. That earns me scowl number two. I'm hoping for at least two more scowls before the end of this conversation.

She puts her hands on her hips and fires back. "Really? That's the best you got? The air up there must be thin. Let's see you get something off the bottom shelf."

She steps aside, pointing down dramatically at the rice. *Scowl number three is on its way*, I think to myself.

"You just want to look at my ass when I bend over." I press my hand to my chest in fake horror. Her jaw drops but she quickly recovers and scowls at me. *YES! Three down, one to go.* I bend down and grab the rice I needed anyway.

"Oh, your ass isn't that nice." She realizes her mistake, and a blush spreads across her face.

"That's not what your eyes are saying." I can't hide my smile anymore. My gaze drops to her full pink lips, and I can't stop my eyes when they sweep over the length of her perfect body.

"Your eyes just raked over my whole body. You have room to talk." She smiles at her own comment.

When I step closer, she looks up and our eyes meet. She keeps eye contact and doesn't move away as I reach over her head and grab the jar of pickles from behind her. I linger for a moment before I respond. "I'm not ashamed I checked you out." I slowly inch away in time to see her breath catch in her throat.

"Thanks, I could've gotten it myself."

I hand her the jar, noticing the welt on her arm. "I know, but that's what we do around here, and you're welcome."

She grips her overflowing cart. "I better go."

"Okay, you go first. I don't want you staring at my ass when I turn around," I say as straight-faced as I can.

32

"You wish." She laughs, walking out the aisle.

Then it hits me, she still owes me one more scowl. The thought alone makes me grin as I quickly grab everything I need and rush to the checkout line. She's unloading the last of her items onto the belt when I approach.

I toss a bag of frozen peas into her cart. "You forgot something."

"What are these for?"

I point at her welt. "For your arm." I was only joking, but I hope she uses it. It looks like it hurts.

Scowling one last time she mouths "asshole." Her face then shifts into a smile followed by a laugh.

I laugh as I head to the express checkout. While I wait in line, I watch as she walks to the door. Just before she's about to step out, she looks over her shoulder at me, and my heart skips a beat. I don't look away; I want her to see me looking at her. I quickly pay for my items, bag them myself and head to the parking lot. I look around for her, but she's already gone.

Getting in my truck, I chastise myself for not asking her name. All I know about her is that she really likes pickles, but that's not enough for an internet search. Trying to erase her from my mind, I turn the radio on to my favorite sports podcast. But it doesn't work. All I keep thinking about is the way her eyes met mine when I got close to her, and the way she smelled like lilies and a hint of mint. Her laugh was so intoxicating, I'd pay to hear it again. I think about our conversation for most of my drive to Judy's. *Let it go, it's too late.*

As I pull in, I notice another car parked next to Judy's rarely used one and remember our guest has already checked in. I take Judy's ingredients to her door, knock twice and let myself in.

The living room has a vintage flower print couch facing the fireplace with an end table on each side. The kitchen doesn't have an island like the other cabins. Instead, it features a four-person oak

33

table with fresh flowers in the middle. Judy's sitting in her recliner reading another romance book.

She stands, checking the bag. "Great, you got everything."

I chuckle. "It was only four items."

"Yes, but you took longer than usual. Did something happen at the store?" She stops, giving me her full attention.

"Not at all. Just long lines at check out," I lie. Judy has been pushing me to settle down with someone, and I don't want to get her hopes up. I'll probably never see the girl from the store again, so there's no point talking about her.

"Dinner's almost ready. How does pot roast sound?" She lifts the lid to check.

"Sounds great. Wait…if dinner is almost done, why did I need to go to the store today?"

She waves her hand like it's nothing. "Oh, I just needed that stuff. I never said it was for tonight."

"How was your day?" I ask, changing the subject.

"My day was great! This afternoon I made two apple pies I thought would go good with dinner."

"That sounds awesome, but what are we going to do with two whole pies?" I love desserts, any sweets really. Judy knows this. I have a feeling she's trying to butter me up for something. I just don't know what yet.

"You're right. That is a lot of pie. I have an idea! You could drop one off to our guest in cabin six after dinner," she says, like she just solved a riddle.

"Sure, I guess I can drop one off since I still need to introduce myself." *This is going to be awkward. What am I supposed to say to this stranger? Hi, I'm Miles, I have a pie. Damn it Judy, why do you always put me in these situations?* Then I remind myself that Judy always means well.

Judy places our plates on the table, pats my shoulder and sits across from me. We have dinner with little conversation, giving me time to think about the girl from the store. Now I keep wondering who she is. Maybe I'll see her around town again. I can't get those green eyes out of my head. God, what if she's married or has a boyfriend? That's it, no more mystery girl. *She's married.* I try to convince myself.

"You ready for dessert?"

"That's the only reason I'm here."

Laughing, she hands me a small plate and calls me a heathen. Chuckling, I take my first bite. The pie is perfect. The apples are soft with the perfect amount of cinnamon and a golden crust. Apple pie is my second favorite dessert next to mint chocolate chip cookies.

"That was perfect. Thanks for dinner."

"You're welcome, I'm glad you liked it." She smiles sweetly. "I'll grab the other pie for you."

With a quick kiss on her cheek, we say our goodbyes. And I walk along the path towards cabin six with a pie in hand.

5

I'm Not Flirting, I Swear

Kinsley

Did that really just happen? I pull out of the grocery store parking lot. Using Judy's map, I follow the winding road back to the cabin, but focusing is nearly impossible. All I can think about is the ridiculously handsome man who accused me, accurately, of checking out his ass. For the next ten minutes, I replay our whole interaction in my head on a loop.

When I lost my balance on the shelf, I was sure I was going to faceplant on the linoleum. But I didn't. Instead, I landed in the arms of a strong, smoking-hot stranger. And how did I respond? Like a brat. Because I was tired, hungry and completely flustered by the human embodiment of a jawline. Ugh. I'm such an asshole. If I ever see him again, I owe him an apology, maybe even two. One for the scowl. And one for the "not-a-nice-ass" lie. Then he called me "vertically challenged." The nerve. But somehow, that one line completely flipped my mood. Who doesn't appreciate a man who can make you laugh even when you want to stay annoyed? The way he teased me, it felt strangely familiar, like we'd known each other for years. But I don't even know his name. And still when he stepped closer, something in me shifted. There was a spark, like electricity skating across my skin, and for a second, I forgot where I was. It was like getting caught in a spider's web but warm, magnetic and way too tempting to escape. And the worst part? I didn't want to escape.

I nearly missed my turn twice, so I refocused my attention on the map. When I get back to the cabin, it takes two trips to carry everything in. My empty stomach convinced me to grab things I didn't really need. While I'm putting everything away, my arm starts to really hurt. I grab the stupid frozen peas out of the bag. I shake my head at the memory of his smug face when he threw it in my cart and carefully drape it around my arm anyway, despite him being right.

I put everything away except the ingredients for spaghetti. Pouring a glass of wine, I toss the peas in the freezer, turn on my cooking playlist and get to work. Soon I'm dancing around the kitchen, chopping onions and stirring my homemade sauce. I sway to the beat, singing along while I slice vegetables for the salad. The smell of simmering tomatoes and garlic fills the cabin, wrapping the space in warmth. Leaning against the counter, I take a sip of wine and smile. I remember why I love cooking so much.

Every night, my mom used to cook dinner while I sat on the counter, watching her with wide-eyed anticipation as she sang and danced around the kitchen. When I was old enough to help, our evenings turned into kitchen dance parties. Cooking with her was always full of laughter and music. It's still one of my favorite memories.

Once dinner is finished, I sit at the island and enjoy my first home-cooked meal in months. With every bite, my mind drifts back to when man from the store said, "I'm not ashamed I checked you out." Yeah, the words were hot. It wasn't what he said, it was how he said it. That quiet confidence in his voice, the way his dark eyes never left mine. The subtle flex of his arms as he reached for the jar. And God, the way he smelled, like clean laundry and smoked wood. It was enough to short-circuit my brain.

After eating, I decide to forget about him. I'll probably never see him again anyway. I wash the dishes and wipe everything down, letting the rhythm of the familiar chore calm my racing thoughts. My arm is starting to hurt again, so I grab my wine and the frozen peas and head for the couch to watch tv. As soon as my butt hits the couch, someone knocks on the door. It's probably Judy. Who else would visit me here?

When I open the door, my brow furrows, and I'm speechless for a moment. It's him. The man from the store, staring at me with the same confused expression.

"What are you doing here? Oh my God, are you stalking me?" I'm a little scared but way too curious to slam the door.

He runs a hand through his hair. "Uh, it's a little hard to stalk you when I own the place."

"You're Miles? Judy's nephew?"

"I am. And you're Kinsley. The guest in cabin six." He shakes his head in disbelief. Then his eyes drop to my arm where the frozen peas are still draped.

I glance down at my arm. "The peas were a good idea. Thanks. I'm sorry about earlier. I wasn't myself."

His eyes lift to meet mine again. "You don't need to apologize. How's the arm?"

"It still hurts, but it's getting better." I lift the peas to check. He leans forward slightly as if to get a better look. I'm surprised by how genuinely concerned he seems. And I can't stop staring at him.

"Judy asked me to bring you this pie when I came to introduce myself." He stands upright, handing it over.

"Are you going to introduce yourself, or should I start?" I tease, hoping to break the tension.

He chuckles. "I'm Miles Davison. Nice to meet you."

I take his outstretched hand. "Nice to meet you, Miles Davison. I'm Kinsley Brighton." We hold on for a second too long, and butterflies flutter in my stomach. He must sense my nerves because he gently lets go and takes a step back.

He grins. "Well, Kinsley Brighton, I hope you like apple pie."

"Thanks. I love apple pie, Miles Davison," I reply, emphasizing his name.

He jerks a thumb over his shoulder. "I gotta go. I need to put Rocket in the stable. I'll see you around."

"Have a good night, Miles," I call after him as he walks away. I stand in the doorway and watch him walk all the way back to the driveway. *I lied. He does have a nice ass.*

I softly close the door and lean against it, still holding the pie. Taking a moment to regain my composure, I eventually set it on the counter and peel back the lid. Apple pie is one of my favorites. I don't even bother with a plate. I grab a fork and eat it straight from the tin.

For the second time today, I find myself surprised by this man. His name is Miles Davison, and he owns this farm, but that's all I know. Yes, he's hot. Rugged with broad shoulders, sun-kissed skin, eyes so dark you could lose yourself in them and a smile that radiates pure confidence. But beyond all that, who is Miles Davison?

I sit on the stool, shoveling forkfuls of pie into my mouth while my inner lawyer kicks into high gear, cross-examining everything I know about Miles Davison. He caught me before I hit the floor and checked on my arm. Maybe he's caring or just being a good neighbor. He's funny and quick-witted, playful or possibly immature. His aunt lives on his property, so maybe he's a family man or someone who exploits sweet old ladies. Basically, I know nothing about him.

I shake the thought, reminding myself I'm only here for a month, so it doesn't matter who he is. After covering the pie, I go to the bedroom, change into a tank top and shorts, and get into bed. It's quiet in the country, so it doesn't take long for me to fall asleep.

***

The next morning, I make coffee and sit on the patio, enjoying the view. Fog still hovers over the lake as the sun rises, casting a majestic glow on the farm across the water. I take a picture and send it to my mom with a quick text message letting her know I'm fine.

As I stand to head inside, I look around once more and notice a large black bear on the far side of the lake. The bear bends its head to drink from the lake and then looks up in my direction. I take out my phone, snap a picture before going inside, not wanting to attract the bear toward me.

I take my time getting ready. It's a little colder today so I chose a tan sweater and skinny jeans. An hour later, I'm dressed and ready to head into town. I close the door behind me and check to see if the bear is still hanging around. It's not, but I do see Miles walking out of his house heading towards the barn. When he looks my way, I quickly turn and start walking to my car pretending I don't see him.

I use Judy's map to get me back to town. Today I decided to visit the used bookstore, The Second Chapter, and grab a cup of coffee from Main Street Brew. I enter through the colorful front door of the bookstore, and I'm greeted by the scent of old books, reminding me of my elementary school library.

The store has thousands of books on its walls. The seating area at the front has a few people reading in large royal blue loveseats. The woman behind the large dark wood counter looks like she's stuck in the sixties. She has on a tie-dyed T-shirt with a matching headband. She waves at me as I make my way towards the sign that reads Romance.

When searching for a new book, I avoid reading the back cover. I feel it reveals too much of the story. Instead, I read the first two pages to decide if it's interesting. This process takes me around forty-five minutes to find two books I want. Ready for coffee, I pay for my books and thank the woman. I walk next door to Main Street Brew.

Walking past the white bistro tables outside I can already smell the fresh coffee. When I reach the door, I notice a for-sale sign. When I step in, it couldn't be more different than the coffee shop by my office. On the long white counter, there's a variety of coffee makers, espresso machines and other equipment. I'm not sure what they're used for. I prefer to drink plain coffee with cream and sugar. A dozen tables with floral covers are scattered around the open area, and most are occupied. There's no one in line when I step up to the counter. Older woman with a tired smile on her face is ready to take my order.

"What can I get you today?"

"I'll take a large coffee, cream and sugar, and a turkey sandwich, please."

The woman behind the counter smiles as she rings me up. She looks to be in her late sixties, with kind eyes and a name tag that reads "Margie." There's a calmness about her, the kind that only comes with years of early mornings and knowing most of your customers by name. She moves a little slower than most, but with purpose, like she's been doing this forever. Maybe that's why there's a "For Sale" sign in the window.

I thank her, take my coffee and step outside to one of the small café tables lining the sidewalk.

The town square stretches out before me, quaint and full of life. Kids skip along the brick-lined sidewalks while their parents stroll behind them, holding hands or balancing iced drinks. A group of older men gather near the barber shop, swapping stories I'm sure they've told a dozen times already. Laughter carries from somewhere down the block.

It's nothing like the city. No one's in a rush. People hold doors for each other and smile when they pass. They talk, really talk, right there on the sidewalk, like time's not something they're racing against. I wrap my hands around the warm cup, taking it all in. For the first time in a long time, I get it. The pull of small-town life. The way it slows you down, reminds you to breathe. It's heartwarming to know places like this still exist.

Clouds are starting to fill the sky, and I don't want my new books to get wet, so I quickly head back to the car. I don't need the map to find my way back now. When I pull into the driveway, I see Judy sitting in a rocking chair reading a book outside.

Closing her book she looks up. "Well, hello Kinsley. How's your day going?"

"It's great! I just spent a few hours in town." I hold up my books proudly.

"I just love a good book. Which ones did you get?" She pats the rocking chair next to her. I take a seat and hand her my books. She examines the first one then reads the back.

"This one looks interesting."

"I thought so, too, but I only read the first couple of pages," I confess. I watch her eyes light up looking at the second book.

She taps the book cover with her finger. "I've read this one. It's a good one."

"You like romance books, too?"

"Oh yes, there's nothing better than love." She looks up at the sky, and I have a feeling she's missing someone. It would be rude to ask, so instead I change the subject.

"I saw a black bear by the lake this morning," I tell her using my finger to point where I saw it.

"That's scary. Do you know much about them?"

I see a concerned look on her face. "No, I've never seen one that close before. Are they as mean as everyone says?"

"Absolutely! Never get close to them and never run. Let me show you how to scare one away."

Judy sets the books on the table, stands up and steps in front of me. Without warning, she spreads her arms and legs wide and screams at the top of her lungs. I yelp, nearly flipping out of the rocking chair. "What the hell, Judy?!"

She calmly sits beside me, totally unfazed. "See? It worked on you." I gape at her, half in shock, half in admiration. The woman has guts. Now we're both laughing, tears springing to our eyes.

Not a minute later, a pickup truck flies into the driveway, kicking up dust. Miles jumps out, sprinting toward us. His eyes dart around, wild and alert.

"What's going on? Are you okay?" He scans the porch like he's ready to throw down with a mountain lion.

"Judy was just showing me how to scare off a bear," I say, still laughing. Judy chuckles beside me, proud of herself.

Miles stares at us like we've lost our minds, but I can see the relief wash over him.

"She saw one by the lake this morning," Judy explains, before excusing herself to go make dinner. Miles' gaze snaps back to me, his expression now serious.

"If you see it again, call me. Do you have my number?"

"Yes, Judy gave it to me yesterday."

A smirk tugs at the corner of his mouth. "Good. If you need anything, call. Day or night. I'm always available."

A blush creeps up my neck. He knows exactly what he's doing.

Okay, I'll play your game, Miles.

"I'll consider that. Thanks." I walk away knowing full well he's watching. I let my hips sway a little more than necessary.

43

"Day or night!" he calls out as I reach my door. I glance back to see him still standing there, grinning like a fool.

"You couldn't handle day or night," I shout back, stepping inside with a smile, making damn sure I get the last word.

Once I'm inside, I let out a breath I didn't realize I was holding. "Okay, you're only here for a month. Stop flirting with him," I mutter to myself. I head to the kitchen to make dinner. Chicken parmesan takes about an hour, but it keeps my hands busy.

After I eat, I hop in the shower, twist my wet hair into a messy bun on top of my head and throw on a tank top and shorts. I grab the first book in my stack, curl up on the couch with a throw blanket over my legs and start reading.

About eight chapters in, I realize this isn't a romance novel. It's horror. Real horror. And it's getting scary. But I'm too invested to stop now.

A sharp bang cracks through the silence, snapping me out of the story. My heart jumps. I freeze, gripping the blanket tighter. I sit completely still, straining to hear past the pounding in my ears. *Was that outside the window?* I freeze, slowly close the book and peel the blanket off my legs. I stay completely still, listening. Nothing. "It's all in your head. Get it together," I whisper. Trying to shake it off, I set the book aside and head toward the bedroom. But just as I stand, I hear it again, closer this time. Cautiously, I move to the window and peek outside. A pair of glowing eyes stare back at me.

I yelp and stumble back, scrambling for my phone. My hands are shaking as I rush into the kitchen and snatch Judy's map off the counter, frantically scanning it for Miles's number. As soon as I find it, I bolt to the bedroom and dive under the covers like I'm ten years old again. "This is not happening. This is not happening," I whisper, trying to catch my breath. With fingers that won't stop shaking, I punch in Miles' number.

6

Late-Night Lies

Miles

My phone rings, yanking me out of sleep. I groan and roll over, eyes barely open. "Who the hell is calling this late?" I blindly reach for it. The number's unfamiliar, but I'm too tired to care. I answer anyway.

"Hello?"

"Miles, it's Kinsley. There's a bear outside my door," she whispers. The fear in her voice snaps me fully awake.

"Where are you?!" I shout, already throwing off the covers. I yank on my jeans, skipping the shirt and shoes.

"I'm hiding in the bedroom," she whispers again.

"Stay put. Stay quiet. I'm on my way."

I fly down the stairs, grab my keys off the table and sprint to the truck. The second I'm in, I throw it into gear and take off around the lake, heart pounding like a war drum.

I pull into the driveway, slam the truck into park, kill the engine, and jump out. I don't run. I'm not about to spook a bear.

As I get closer to the cabin, I spot a pair of glowing eyes near the porch. My whole-body tenses. But when I take another step, I see it clearly. A raccoon. I let out a sharp breath, somewhere between a laugh and a groan. Of course it is. I Shake my head, half relieved, half annoyed. I head up and knock on her door. No answer.

Worried she might be too scared to respond, I open the door slowly and step inside. I leave it cracked behind me, not because I plan to leave quickly but because I don't want her thinking I've come to corner her. After everything she's been through, the last thing I want is to make her feel trapped.

"Kinsley." I call out.

"I'm in here." Her voice is soft and shaky.

I follow the sound and stop at her open door. Just when I thought this girl couldn't get any cuter, I see her curled up under the blanket, the glow of her phone lighting the fabric. Something in me tightens, this fierce unexplainable need to protect her.

"It's safe to come out." I keep my voice gentle.

Slowly, the blanket lowers, and wide, anxious eyes peek out. "Is it gone?" she whispers, trembling. That look guts me. I walk to her bed and hold out my hand. She takes it, her fingers cold in mine, and I help her sit up. With my other hand, I gently clasp hers, guiding her attention back to me.

"Yes, it's gone. You're safe now." Her shoulders drop slightly, and I see her exhale. I let go and step back to give her space.

She swings her legs over the edge of the bed. "Are you sure? Was it a bear?"

I hesitate. I don't want her to feel silly, but I won't lie. "Yes, I'm sure. No, it wasn't a bear."

"I saw eyes. What was it then?" She presses the question, walking toward the living room.

I follow, trying not to stare. Her shorts are barely hanging on, the worn cotton clinging to her hips in a way that tugs at my attention, even as I try to keep my thoughts in check. I catch a glimpse of the bottom curve of her ass, all golden skin and tempting shadow. *Fuck, look away.*

I linger near the kitchen. "It was just a raccoon. It bolted when I got close."

She crosses the room and shuts the front door, then turns around and I nearly forget how to breathe. No bra. Her tank top clings like a second skin, nipples tight against the fabric. Damn. I tear my eyes away, landing on the book lying on the couch.

"Oh my God, I'm so sorry," she blurts. "I got you out of bed for a raccoon. I was reading, then I heard a noise, and I saw eyes, and, ugh, I'm so stupid." She buries her face in her hand, clearly mortified.

"Kinsley, really, it's fine. I told you to call." I walk over, drop onto the couch and casually pick up the book she left behind. When she shut the front door, I took that as an unspoken invitation.

She walks to the other end of the couch, tucks one leg under herself and leans into the armrest, facing me. I shift, mirroring her, resting my arm along the back of the couch.

"I didn't take you for a horror book fan." I glance at the cover, then back at her.

"I'm not." A half-laugh slips out as she picks at her nails. "I thought it was a romance."

"That explains a lot. No wonder you freaked out. I've read this one. It's intense." I set the book on the coffee table, catching her gaze trailing across my chest.

"Yeah, I'm burning that book tomorrow." She giggles, and I smile.

"Do you even know how to start a fire, City Girl?"

47

She smirks. "No. That's what the internet's for, Country Bumpkin."

I tilt my head, grinning. "What the hell's a bumpkin?"

"It's a…you know, a…I don't know," she stammers, realizing she has no clue. We both crack up and reach for our phones.

"Really?" I read the definition aloud, eyes narrowing. "You think I'm a simpleton? I'm offended." I slap a hand over my heart like I've just been mortally wounded.

Her jaw drops as she reads, then she bursts into laughter. "I'm sorry! I thought it meant, like, a pumpkin boy or something!"

She stands and heads to the kitchen, grabbing a wine glass. She glances over her shoulder, still grinning. "You want wine or beer?"

"I'll take a beer, thanks."

I watch as she pours a generous glass of wine and pops the cap off a beer. As she walks back, my eyes stay glued on her. She's feisty, classy and sexy as hell. She could probably make flannel look like lingerie. But she's vulnerable right now. Scared. So, I keep it in check.

"Thanks. You're not trying to get me drunk, are you? We barely know each other," I tease as she hands me the beer.

She grins, settling into her spot across from me, legs tucked beneath her, wine glass in hand. She doesn't say anything, but the look in her eyes, curious, teasing, with a flicker of vulnerability, says enough.

"Let's play a little game. It's called Two Truths and a Lie. That way we can get to know each other better, just in case you get drunk off one beer." She chuckles, and I catch it, the way her eyes slowly drift down my bare chest, then snap back to meet mine.

I still sense the nerves beneath her confidence. Maybe she just doesn't want to be alone. Either way, I'm not leaving. And I'm always up for a challenge.

"You do know games are meant to be won, right? What's the wager?"

She tilts her head, thinking. The kitchen light catches her green eyes, freckles lit up like stars.

"If I win, you have to give me a tour of your farm. If you win, I'll cook you dinner. Anything you want."

Deal. I'd agree to a hundred rounds if it means more time with her.

"Okay I'm in." I shake her hand. Her skin's soft, warm. I hold it a second longer than I should. "So, how do you play?"

"It's simple. I tell you three things about myself. One's a lie, you guess which one's the lie. Person with the most right wins."

"Easy enough. You go first, since you know more about me than I know about you."

I watch as she straightens her back and puts on her best poker face before beginning.

• I'm thirty-three.

• I'm a lawyer.

• I'm an only child.

I study her. "I think the lie is...you're thirty-three."

"Damn it! You're right! I'm thirty-two," she says with a playful pout. She sips her wine. "Your turn."

"Alright, Little Miss Lawyer. Here goes."

• I actually am thirty-three.

• My favorite color is pink.

• I have a cat named Miss Dashworth.

She taps her chin. "I don't think you're a pink type of guy."

"You'd be right. My favorite color's green."

Her eyes light up. *Worth it.*

"Okay, one point each. My turn."

• I'm from New York.

• I'm afraid of the dark.

• My favorite ice cream is chocolate.

"That's tough. I think chocolate is the lie. You strike me as a strawberry kind of girl."

"Nope! I love chocolate. I'm actually from Seattle."

That was fucking adorable.

"My turn. You won't get this right," I challenge.

• I have three brothers.

• I played baseball in high school.

• I love mint chocolate chip cookies.

She doesn't even blink. "Easy. No sane person likes mint chocolate chip."

"WHAT? Take that back! Mint chocolate chip is elite!" I joke, throwing a hand over my heart.

"Eww, that's disgusting!" She laughs so hard she snorts.

I laugh just because she snorted. I eventually admit I only have one brother.

We play a few more rounds, trading confessions and playful jabs between sips and laughter. She ends up winning by a slim margin, of course. But it doesn't feel like losing at all.

"It's late. I better get going." I stand and stretch, lingering for just a second, letting her eyes take me all the way in. "Thanks for the game."

Her eyes flutter toward the door, trying to avoid looking longer. "Thanks for saving me from the raccoon."

We walk to the door, and I hesitate. Shake her hand? Hug? I waver. She opens the door. I step out, then turn back.

"Thanks again for tonight."

She steps forward and hugs me. Quick. Warm. Disarming.

"You can give me that tour whenever you're ready."

Our eyes lock.

"Good night, Kinsley."

"Good night, Miles."

I head to my truck. Would I have stayed if she asked?

All. Night. Long.

Driving home, the quiet gives me time to think. Her voice, her laugh, the way she felt beside me, it replays on a loop.

Here's what I know so far: she snorts when she laughs. Blushes from her neck up. Tilts her chin and stares at the ceiling when she thinks. She trusts me. Enough to believe I can keep her safe. She's confident enough to admit she's scared of the dark. And she's badass enough to build a law firm from scratch. She's smart. Funny. Gorgeous. Brave. She's everything. And that's exactly what makes this so complicated, because the more I know her, the harder it is to accept that she's just passing through.

I freeze the second I walk through my door. *What the hell am I doing?* She's only here for a month. Then it's back to Seattle. Back to the life she's worked her ass off to build. I can't be the reason she gives any of that up.

51

7

The Abs Heard 'Round the Cabin

Kinsley

I wipe my sweaty palms on my shorts, watching Miles walk away, staring until he reaches his truck. Feeling like some lovesick teenager, I quickly duck back inside, hoping he didn't catch me watching.

As the door clicks shut, the last few minutes replay in my head. I think about everything I've learned, enough to call him a friend now. But friends don't look at each other the way he looked at me. Friends don't make your chest ache, and your stomach do flips at the same time. So how do I feel? The million-dollar question. And the answer? I don't know. I'm confused. Knowing I'm not going to figure out the mystery that is Miles Davison tonight, I crawl into bed, pull the covers up and try to shut my brain off.

It's been an hour since he left, and I'm still lying here, trying to convince myself he was just being friendly. But come on, I saw the way he looked at me. I felt it. That wasn't just friendly.

He didn't have to stay, but he did. I'm not even surprised we had a good time. He's got this magnetic, playful energy that just pulls you in. I didn't want him to stay just because I was scared. I wanted him to stay because I'm curious. Drawn to him.

Before tonight, I wasn't totally sure who he really was. But now? I'm sure. He's a good man. Maybe even a great one. Which just leaves me wondering, how the hell is someone like him still single?

I finally give up on sleep and head to the kitchen for a snack. I grab an apple and flop onto the couch. Doesn't matter where I am, he's completely taken over my brain. And the worst part? I'm not even trying to stop it. Maybe I should. Because if I fall any deeper, I don't know how I'll pull myself back out when this ends. It's ridiculous. I'm ridiculous. I should be thinking about how temporary this all is, how messy it could get. But I'm not.

He rushed to help me in the middle of the night. Didn't bother putting on a shirt or shoes. And that image? Burned into my brain, along with the fluttery chaos it left in its wake.

Honestly, I should be thanking the raccoon. During that game, all I could think about was tracing my fingers down those washboard abs. If I close my eyes, I can still see him standing shirtless in my bedroom doorway like a centerfold from a sex magazine, advertising orgasms.

It's been almost a year since I've had sex. Not because I haven't had the chance, but because I haven't wanted to, not really. Not until now. That realization hits me harder than I expect. And tonight? Tonight, my body remembered everything it's been missing. I'm not a one-night-stand kind of girl. I have a life in Seattle. A real one. A busy, carefully built, no-time-for-men kind of life. This? This thing with Miles, whatever it is, can't be real.

Around three in the morning, I finally fall asleep. With him still on my mind.

***

I'm shocked when I wake up at ten. I haven't slept in like that since I was a teenager. I toss a bagel in the toaster, load it up with cream cheese and head out to the patio with an oversized coffee. Wrapped in a blanket, I sink into a chair and watch the ducks glide across the lake while squirrels dig around for their breakfast. It's quiet. Simple. Peaceful. I could wake up to this every day and never get tired of it. And when I go back home, yeah, I know I'm going to miss this. All of it.

"Good morning, Kinsley." I hear Judy call. Looking around, I spot her walking toward the lake, a wicker basket swinging from her arm.

"Good morning, Judy. How's your morning?"

"It's wonderful!" She beams. "I'm on my way to feed the ducks. Want to help?" She lifts the basket slightly, giving it a shake.

"I'd love to. Let me just grab some shoes. You want a cup of coffee?"

"No thanks, honey. It keeps me up all night." She chuckles.

I hurry inside, slip on my shoes, and top off my coffee before joining her. We walk together down to the edge of the lake.

Four ducks paddle over the moment we stop, as if they know what time it is.

Judy tosses a handful of feed in the water. "Are you enjoying your stay?"

"I am." I watch one of the ducks dive after a sinking carrot. "I needed time away from the city. It's incredibly peaceful here."

"It is lovely." She nods. "Have you had a tour of the farm yet?"

"No. Not yet." I answer simply, avoiding eye contact.

I'm not ready to talk about Miles. Especially after last night. I left the ball in his court, and now I'm stuck wondering if he'll call or if I imagined everything.

54

Judy's cheerful voice gently pulls me out of my thoughts. "There's a walking path around the lake if you're interested. Miles won't mind."

Before I can start overthinking it, two more ducks gracefully land on the water. Judy holds the basket out, and I grab a handful of feed. "Thanks. I'll definitely keep that in mind."

Once the basket's empty, Judy brushes off her hands and turns to me.

"I better get back. My favorite game show's about to start." Then she pauses, glancing at me with a little grin. "Do you have any plans for dinner tomorrow night?"

I really do enjoy talking to Judy. She's easy to be around, kind, thoughtful, the type of person who makes you feel like you've known her forever.

"No, I was just going to stay in and cook."

"That's perfect!" She claps her hands together with delight. "You can come over for dinner then."

"Okay, but only if you let me bring dessert. Is there a bakery in town?"

"Yes, near Cranberry Ridge Grocery. It's called Sweet Spot. They make the best mint chocolate chip cookies," she says with the biggest smile I've seen yet.

Must be a family thing to like mint desserts, I think to myself, smiling at the memory of Miles' grin when he mentioned those cookies. The smallest things are starting to remind me of him, and I'm not sure if that excites me or terrifies me.

"I'll pick some up. What time would you like me there?"

"Does five sound good?" she asks, already heading back to her cabin.

"That's perfect. I'll see you then."

She waves a hand over her shoulder. "See you then." I linger by the water for a few more minutes, watching the ducks float peacefully before heading inside to get dressed.

***

In the afternoon, I stop at Sweet Spot Bakery. It's a quaint brick building with large flowerpots flanking the glass door. Inside, the sugary scent of fresh doughnuts greets me instantly, warm and inviting. The small dining area has a few cozy tables, each adorned with a simple flower arrangement.

A large display case sits front and center, brimming with baked goods. Behind it, the open kitchen hums with activity, a wide prep table, a commercial oven and racks lined with cooling pastries and cookies.

A woman in a black apron, dusted with flour, greets me. She's striking, with glowing skin and long black hair pulled into a high ponytail. But it's her smile that steals the moment; bright, warm, and impossible not to return.

"Welcome to the Sweet Spot. Can I help you find something?" Her megawatt smile makes me feel instantly at home.

"Yes, do you have mint chocolate chip cookies?"

"I sure do. Just pulled a fresh batch from the oven. They're cooling now." She nods toward the racks. "How many would you like?"

"I'll take a half dozen mint chocolate chip and a half dozen peanut butter, please." Peanut butter cookies are my absolute favorite.

She picks up a white baker's box, slips on gloves and heads to the back. While retrieving the cookies, she calls over her shoulder, "Are you new in town?"

"Yes, I'm staying at Davison Farms. Judy sent me."

"I love Miss Judy! She stops in at least once a week." She smiles fondly and returns to grab the peanut butter cookies.

"Judy's amazing. She's been so welcoming since I got here."

"My name's Naya." She offers the box with a warm smile.

"I'm Kinsley. Nice to meet you, Naya. How do you stay so thin with all this around you? These lemon tarts are calling my name."

"Thanks. I'm at the gym four days a week, strictly to keep my ass big and my stomach small."

"In that case, I'll take two lemon tarts and hit the gym later." We both laugh.

We hit it off instantly, talking like old friends. Somewhere between the cookie talk and shared laughs, I find myself relaxing in a way I hadn't in a long time. Before I know it, nearly an hour has passed.

Just before I leave, we exchange numbers and make loose plans to grab drinks next week. I leave the bakery with a new friend, a dozen cookies and tonight's dessert: two perfect lemon tarts.

When I return to the cabin, I change into comfortable clothes and pour myself a glass of wine. The oven timer dings, signaling my homemade pizza is ready. I eat on the couch while watching videos on how to start a fire.

According to the video, I just need to form a teepee with the logs, place kindling inside, light it and voilà! A fire. "Okay, sounds easy enough," I mutter, feeling more confident than I should.

After dinner, I wash the dishes and head to the patio, determined to prove I'm not entirely helpless. I follow the steps exactly, sacrificing the horror book as kindling. My mother would die if she found out I burned a book, but after what it did to my sleep, it deserves it. With the long grill lighter I found in the kitchen, I ignite the torn pages. A small flame flares to life. I sit back, hopeful. Three minutes later, it fizzles out. Forty minutes pass. I rewatch parts of the video. I rearrange the wood. I relight the cursed book. Again and again, the flames sputter and die, like the fire gods are laughing at me.

"What the fuck am I doing wrong?' I whisper to myself, frustrated. On my last attempt, it works, and I do a victory dance back inside to get my wine and lemon tart to enjoy by the fruits of my labor.

"City Girl" is what Miles called me when I told him I was burning the book. Joke's on him. I'm a little surprised he didn't call or text me for the tour. I've only been here a few days and somehow, I've seen him every day. I decide to call Raelynn for advice.

She answers on the first ring. "Hey girl." I know she's alone in the evenings. Jacob, her husband, works third shift for the local police department.

"Hey, you have time to talk?" I'm not sure if Jacob has the night off. It's like a secret code, if she says no, he's home and we won't have privacy. If she says yes, the coast is clear.

She chuckles. "Yes, all night."

"Bitch, there's a guy here and I need to talk."

"Bitch, tell me you didn't sleep with him already? You whore!" She mocks me playfully, shocked and excited.

I scoff. "Oh my God, no! I haven't slept with him! I barely know him."

"Okay, tell me everything. Wait! Let me get some popcorn first. Hold on." She puts down the phone and returns a minute later with her mouth full of popcorn. "Okay, I'm ready. Spill your guts!"

I tell her everything, from our encounter at the store to playing a game last night. What he looked like without a shirt. I even tell her about Naya at the bakery. I don't leave out a single detail. She asks questions, trying to understand and absorb my words. I wrap it all up with a sigh. "So…what should I do?"

"Wow, that's a lot in just a few days. Okay, let me get this straight. He's smart, funny, caring, sexy, has a job and loves his family."

"Yep, that sums it up." I walk into the cabin to get out of the cold and refill my wine.

"Make the first move, Kinsley! What's the worst that can happen?"

"What if he's not interested? What happens if it gets serious between us, and I have to go home?"

"He'd be a fool not to be interested in you. If he is a fool, why would you want him anyway? You're a bad bitch, own it! If it does get serious, cross that bridge when you get there." This is why I love her. She doesn't sugarcoat anything.

"You're right. Okay, I'll do it. I'll make the first move and text him tomorrow." I proudly remember, I AM A BAD BITCH.

"I want all the details. Call me tomorrow. I'm so freaking excited for you. I love your face."

"I promise. I'll call you tomorrow after I have dinner with Judy. Love your face, too."

I can do this. I'm pretty sure he felt the same. Raelynn's right. What have I got to lose? I'm going to text him tomorrow and ask about the tour he owes me. I need to look fantastic without it looking obvious that I'm trying too hard.

I head into the bedroom and start digging through my clothes and shoes, trying to pick the perfect outfit for tomorrow. After a quick shower, I roll my hair up in no-heat sleep rollers and climb into bed. Tucked under the covers, I give myself one last pep talk. "You've got this. Just put yourself out there. What's the worst that could happen?"

8

Ambush Dinner & Emotional Damage

Miles

This morning, I watched Kinsley and Judy feed the ducks from the barn. They didn't know I was there, felt a little like stalking, but I couldn't help it. She was wrapped in a blanket, and damn if she didn't look cute. But it wasn't just that, something about seeing her like that, soft and unguarded, hit me low in the gut. It stirred something I didn't want to name, something dangerous. Now I'm watching her again. She's sitting by the fire, the flames throwing a soft orange glow across her face. Her hair's come loose in a few spots, little tendrils framing her cheeks. I'd bet money she looked up a video on how to start a fire. I know the wood's damp. It must've taken her forever to get it going. But she did it. She's not a quitter. Somehow, that just makes her even more attractive.

I stayed away from her today. But I saw her across the lake, outside her cabin. I told myself not to look. Swore I wouldn't. Didn't matter. My eyes found her anyway. I don't want to be the reason she gives up everything she's worked for; her dreams, her life in the city. She's built something real, something important. But last night, I felt something. I know she did, too. And that's the problem. If I let myself get too close, look too long, I'm afraid I'll fall. And falling for her? That would mean risking everything. For both of us.

I saw what real love looked like. My parents had it, the kind that wrapped around you, steady and unshakable. Watching them, I thought love meant safety. But when my dad died in the accident, that safety disappeared. It taught me that love can turn on you in an instant. That kind of loss scars you. Now, every time I feel something real start to form, a voice in the back of my head warns me not to go there. Not unless I'm ready to lose everything. They loved without fear. But when my dad died in the accident, it shattered my mom. Her world collapsed. She was still young, still beautiful, but suddenly alone with two boys and a broken heart. The depression took over fast. She stopped eating right. Stopped calling her friends. The family tried to help, but she wouldn't let them in. She still did the basics, kept the farm running, fed us, but she wasn't really there. Just a shadow of the mother I remembered. She moved through life like it hurt to breathe.

Until Luke came. His parents had gotten themselves into trouble, the kind that meant Luke was headed for foster care. My mom wouldn't let that happen. She opened our home to him, just like that. And somehow, having Luke here gave her purpose again. She had to be strong for him. Helping him through the hardest time of his life helped pull her out of hers. That's when she started to come back to us. Not just for us but for herself.

I went to bed not bothering to eat dinner. I thought about the reasons I've avoided relationships. My ex-girlfriend, April, is the longest relationship I've had. She wanted me to sell the farm and move with her to Florida. I cared for her but in the end, I couldn't go. This is my family home. I love my life here. Or maybe she wasn't the one.

***

This morning, I woke up with a purpose. I cleaned the house and ate breakfast in silence at the kitchen table. My goal today? Don't think about the girl in cabin six. To keep my mind off her, I'll stay busy. I've got more than enough chores to keep me occupied. First stop: the hardware store. I need chicken feed and some wood to fix the dock. Both docks could use new boards, but I'll just focus on the one on my side of the lake today.

When I pull into the Gladwin Hardware parking lot, it's packed. *Great*, I think to myself. Inside, the familiar chime above the door announces my arrival. Dylan looks up from the counter and gives me a nod. He's the owner and one of the guys who comes over for beer and baseball on the weekends. We played ball together in high school. He also owns Gladwin Construction.

"Hey man, how's it going?"

"Hey, Dylan. Not too bad. You?" I take his outstretched hand.

"What brings you in today?" He waves to a customer on their way out.

"Need some chicken feed and three two-by-eights."

"I'll have Micky grab that for you." He calls over one of his employees.

"Thanks. You coming to the potluck?"

"Yeah, I haven't missed one yet. I heard you've got a hot guest staying in one of the cabins." He lifts a brow.

I want to punch him in the face, for two reasons. One: it's only 9:00 a.m. and now I'm already thinking about her. Two: he's talking about her like she's fair game, and she's not. I clench my jaw and give him a look. "Yes, I have a guest."

"Okay, okay, I get it." He laughs, holding up his hands in mock surrender. I'm not even sure why I'm acting so territorial. I hardly know her.

"When Reed and Luke get home Friday, we should all grab a few beers. I've got some stuff to burn in the pit," I say, shifting the conversation away from my hot guest.

"For sure. I'll be there. It's been a while since we all hung out." He waves at another customer walking in.

"Gotta go. See you then." I head to the checkout just as Micky brings up my supplies.

"Later." Dylan turns and is already chatting up the next person. That's Dylan for you, he could spend a whole day just talking to people, always with that same easy charm.

I loaded up the truck, drove home and got to work on the dock. The extra wood went into the barn for later. Just before I fired up the mower, I got a text from Kinsley.

Kinsley: Hey. I had a really good time the other night. Since you owe me a tour, are you free tomorrow?

I stare at the screen longer than I should. I want to see her. Hell, I've been thinking about her all day. But it's better if I don't. I'm not sure how much longer I can trust myself to stay in control around her. I tap out a short reply.

Me: I can't, sorry.

I tell myself it sounds safe, not cold, not a jerk move. Just honest. A few seconds later, her next message pops up.

Kinsley: I get it.

That's all she says. No emoji. No sarcasm. Just those three words. It's probably for the best we don't get too close, even if everything in me wants to. I just hope I didn't hurt her.

By the time I finish mowing, around three in the afternoon, I can't feel my ass anymore. I park the mower in the barn and crawl underneath it to clear out all the built-up grass clippings. It's hot, sticky work, but it keeps my mind off the girl in cabin six. My phone dings from the workbench. A missed call from Judy. I wipe my hands on a rag and call her back.

"Oh good, you're done mowing the lawn," she says, skipping right past hello. She must've looked across the lake and spotted me mowing.

"Hello, Aunt Judy. Yeah, sorry, I didn't hear my phone ring."

"You mowed it all at once this time. That's a lot for one day."

"Yeah, it's been a long day, but I wanted to finish it," I lie. Truth is, I just needed to stay busy enough not to think about Kinsley. Mowing forces you to focus on just you, the lines and the engine noise drowning everything else out.

"You must be starving. Why don't you clean up and come over for dinner around four-thirty?"

Damn. I really didn't want to be anywhere near the cabins today. But she knows I won't say no. And yeah, I'm starving.

"Sure. I'll be there at four-thirty." I give in with a sigh.

"Wonderful! I'll see you then," she chirps, clearly pleased.

"See you then."

After finishing up with the lawn mower, I close the barn doors and check the time. Thirty minutes until dinner. Just enough to shower and pull myself together. I scrub the sweat and grass off in record time, then throw on a pair of faded jeans and a plain black T-shirt. Simple, comfortable.

I arrive at Judy's cabin and let myself in. The savory scent of baked chicken and roasted asparagus hits me instantly, wrapping the room in warmth.

"You're right on time. It's almost done." She casts a glance over her shoulder as she tosses a few more cherry tomatoes into a bowl of greens.

I step further inside. "Need a hand?"

"I'm just waiting on the chicken now. Go ahead and have a seat. Tell me about your day."

64

"Dinner smells amazing. I'm starving," I admit, lowering myself onto the couch. "The lawn's finally finished. Ready for next week's potluck."

"Good. The tents go up Wednesday, remember." She watches the oven like it might spring to life.

"Yeah, got it. Reed and Luke will be home Friday."

"I can't wait to see them." Her smile is genuine, but there's a nervous energy in the way she opens the oven, like she's bracing for something to go wrong.

"Are you sure you don't need help?" I offer again, watching her fidget with a potholder, her movements oddly nervous.

She looks at the clock. "It should be done anytime now." One minute later she pulls the chicken out, placing the glass dish in the middle of the table with the sides.

Suddenly a knock echoes from the door. She practically skips toward it.

"You're right on time," she says with a little too much cheer. *That's the same shit she said to me*, I think, narrowing my eyes. My gut twists. Then I hear her voice.

"Thanks for inviting me." Kinsley steps through the door, holding a white bakery box and freezes the second she sees me. We both stop. Frozen in place. Caught completely off guard.

She looks incredible. A navy-blue cap sleeve dress hugs her figure perfectly, her brown strappy sandals clicking softly against the wood floor. Her hair is down, long, soft waves that fall to the middle of her back. I try to remember that I'm avoiding her. But fuck, she looks good. Too good. I whip my head toward Judy, shooting her a sharp look. She meets it with practiced innocence.

"Oh, let me take that and put it in the kitchen." She turns to Kinsley, completely ignoring my silent protest. *Kinsley*. Just hearing her name in Judy's voice makes something shift inside me.

"Miles!" Then, sugary sweet and not at all subtle: "Kinsley brought mint chocolate chip cookies. Isn't that thoughtful?"

"Yeah," I mutter, still refusing to look in Kinsley's direction. I keep my eyes locked on Judy like she's the damn culprit in all this, which, of course, she is.

"Dinner smells amazing, Judy." Kinsley's voice is as poised as ever, but I hear the question in it. The hesitation. She knows something's off.

"Let's eat!" Judy enters the room with three plates balanced in her hands like she's hosting a game show instead of a dinner ambush.

I step forward and take the seat furthest from Kinsley without a word. She gives me a look. Not angry, not confused, just quietly searching. Judy sets the plates down and takes her seat, acting like this whole situation is completely normal. It's not. Not even close.

Judy starts passing the food around the table. Starting with me, I passed it to Kinsley, making sure not to touch her hand.

"I met Naya yesterday. She's great." Kinsley's voice is light.

"Naya's a sweet girl, don't you think?" Judy looks at me.

I nod, barely glancing up. "Sure." I move my food around with my fork while they both start eating.

"This morning, I saw Floyd at the grocery store." Judy's fishing now.

"Did you?" I keep my tone flat, still not biting.

"Floyd?" Kinsley lifts her head. "The older gentleman with the blue truck?"

"Yes. Have you met him?" Judy turns to her, intrigued. I pretend I'm not listening, but I am.

"Yes, I met him the first day I got here. I got a flat tire on the way to the store, and he helped me fix it."

Judy looks at her plate, then up at me, like she's waiting for a reaction. "That was nice of him." Her tone is careful.

"It was." I give her nothing else.

"He's a very nice man." Kinsley's comment catches both of us off guard. Judy and I look at her surprised, and I glance away quickly.

"Floyd's normally a little cranky. He must have really liked you," Judy says with a knowing smile.

I stay quiet. I hate this. I hate the way I want to know everything about Kinsley. I hate how much I want to wrap my arms around her when she walked through the door. And I hate even more that I'm making her uncomfortable now. But it's for the best. At least, that's what I keep telling myself.

Once we finish dinner, Judy clears our plates and takes them to the sink. She grabs the cookie box and brings it to the table. She and Kinsley each reach for a peanut butter cookie. I pause. Peanut butter is Judy's favorite. Did Kinsley know that? She knew what my favorite was. But Judy hates mint cookies. That doesn't make sense. A knot tightens in my stomach. *Did she know I'd be here tonight?* Before I can chase the thought further, Judy snaps me out of it.

"Do you want a cookie? They're your favorite."

"No, thanks." A lie. I want one. I really do. But I'm already starting to crack. Judy gives me a pointed look and the smallest shake of her head.

"I can help clean up if you'd like." There's a hint of hesitation, but Kinsley's offer is sincere.

Judy opens her mouth to respond, probably to accept Kinsley's help, but I cut her off, trying to end the night before it gets worse. "No. I'll stay and help."

I look up just in time to catch the flicker of something on Kinsley's face. Hurt. Disappointment. It disappears as quickly as it comes, but it's there.

"Thanks, Judy, for the lovely dinner." Kinsley stands to leave. Her voice is light, but I can tell it's forced. "Next time, I'll cook."

Judy stands, too, shooting me a sharp look that says, "We're going to talk about this later." She walks Kinsley to the door while I stay rooted to my chair, waiting for the fallout I know is coming.

"That would be great. And I'll bring dessert." Judy wraps Kinsley in a warm hug, then closes the door gently behind her.

When the door closes Judy turns on me. "What was that all about?" she hisses. I don't think I've ever seen Judy this upset, at least not with me.

"I don't want to talk about it." I focus on the floor, avoiding her eyes.

"Then don't! But you ARE going to listen! I have watched you avoid loving someone just because you're afraid of getting hurt. Well, let me tell you, I would rather risk pain every single day than to live without love." Her finger gabs the air, sharp and deliberate. "You think your mother wished she never loved your dad? No! She would've gone through that pain over and over just to have loved and been loved."

"I…I just...I can't." My voice falters as I try to defend myself, but Judy cuts me off before I can explain.

"You're letting an amazing girl walk out that door because you're scared. And maybe that fear is justified, but what are you protecting yourself from? Heartbreak or happiness? You'll never know unless you try. Don't let her walk away without knowing you gave it a chance. How are you going to feel when she leaves and you never tried?" she asks, her voice growing softer.

It doesn't take me long to pull my head out of my ass. I might not be in love, but I can't ignore this any longer. I need to see where it goes, even if it scares the hell out of me. I'm still hesitant. I know she won't be here long, but I can't keep fighting these feelings. "You're right." I stand and rush to the door, pressing a quick kiss to Judy's smiling cheek before hurrying toward cabin six.

9

Definitely Wearing Pants

Kinsley

He's not interested. I heard you loud and clear, Miles, I think to myself, shaking my head as I step into the cold night. I'm not mad. I have no one to blame but myself. I should've known he was just being friendly. "Way to read the room, Kinsley." The words barely leave my lips. Why was he even there? Judy never mentioned he was coming.

Defeated and cold, I wrap my arms around myself and walk slowly toward my cabin. It's not a long walk, but I take my time, punishing myself for the mistake. *You're a lawyer. You read people every day. How did you miss his intentions?* I shake the thought away. As I reach the cabin door, I hear him.

"Kinsley." His voice is desperate. Urgent.

I turn to see him striding toward me, fast. His shoulders are tight, his eyes full of something I can't quite read. Tension? Regret? *I won't be rejected twice in one night.* I turn back toward my cabin, heart pounding.

"Kinsley! Stop!" His voice sharpens, louder now, more demanding.

I sigh and slowly turn around. But I don't look at him. I don't want him to see the hurt in my eyes. He steps closer, leaving only inches between us. I can feel the warmth radiating off his body, his breath brushing against my chilled skin, sending shivers down my spine. His jaw tightens, then loosens. Again. And again. He's searching for the right words. I brace myself, wondering if he'll say something that confirms what I imagined. That I made a fool of myself. But he says nothing.

"Good night, Miles." I reach behind me for the door handle.

"Look at me, Kinsley." He gently lifts my chin with his finger.

My hand stays frozen on the handle, stunned by his touch. When our eyes meet, little fireworks shoot through me, racing down my body.

His thumb brushes slowly along my jaw, grounding me just as I start to drift.

"Miles, I'm confused," I admit, my voice soft, my head giving a small shake.

He inches closer. I swallow hard as his mouth hovers just below my ear. God, he smells good, like pine and something darker.

"So was I. But not anymore." His eyes stay on me, steady, watching as my breath hitches.

"Oh," is all I can manage.

"You still want that tour tomorrow?" He moves closer, his breath teasing my skin.

Remembering I'm a bad bitch, I pull myself together. I open my door, and he instinctively takes a step back. His eyes lock on mine, waiting, quiet and intense.

I shrug one shoulder and smirk. "I guess I can stop by. I don't have anything else going on."

"I'll see you in the morning." With a half-smile, he turns. But then he stops, turning back, a more serious expression settling on his face. "You looked beautiful tonight. Make sure to wear pants tomorrow. I can't be held responsible if you don't." And with that, he turns and walks away.

I'm about to have a total girl moment, so I wait until he's far enough away. Once he disappears into the night, I step into the warm cabin and close the door behind me. Then I start giggling like a teenager and dance my way to the couch. I plop down, heart racing, and immediately call Raelynn.

She answers quickly. "Tell me everything."

"You will not believe what just happened." I giggle, then launch into the whole story: the text message, dinner with Judy, his behavior at dinner, what he said afterward, and how close he got to me outside my cabin.

"Holy shit, that's hot. He's going to blow your mind, probably make you forget how to breathe." She sighs dreamily.

A little ashamed, I cover my face with my hand. "Would I be a total slut if I wanted him to."

"Yes! Do it anyway!" She bursts out laughing. Now we're both laughing.

"I'm really nervous about tomorrow. He's a bit hard to read."

"You're nervous? Please. The way he asked you about that tour. He's already into you."

"I know he asked me over, but the way he was at dinner...I don't know. It felt off."

"You've got nothing to lose. If it's weird, make a quick exit. If not, ride him out...oops, I mean ride it out." She laughs at her own joke.

"Tempting? Absolutely. But I'm keeping it classy. For now." I remember the way his jaw clenched and the warmth of his breath on my neck. This man is a work of art I'm afraid to touch. Because letting myself reach for something that perfect feels reckless. What if he doesn't reach back? What if I fall and he doesn't catch me? But I won't show weakness in front of him.

"Let me know how it goes tomorrow. I've got a client in the morning, I gotta go."

"I will. Talk to you soon. Thanks, you're the best."

With everything that's happened over the past couple of days, Especially the way he basically blew me off at dinner, I know I need to play it safe tomorrow. Sure, Raelynn and I joked about him, but wearing pants is the obvious choice. Figuring out what that attitude was all about? That's the real mission.

Slipping into some warm pajamas, I know I'm not ready for bed just yet. A quiet walk by the lake might be exactly what I need to clear my mind. I grab my jacket and step out into the chilly night, hoping to burn off some of the restless energy buzzing through me. Something about Miles always seems to ignite a spark inside me.

As I near the lake, I catch my breath. The stars reflect in the moonlight, scattered like glitter on the still water, quiet, beautiful and just out of reach. It mirrors exactly how I feel right now. Still on the surface, but everything inside me is shifting, stirring, uncertain. It's mesmerizing. I stand there for a long moment, letting the view calm the chaos in my head.

Eventually, I make my way to the dock. It isn't lit, but the moon gives it just enough glow. I spot a tiny frog right before it jumps into the water with a quiet splash. For a moment, I consider taking the canoe out. But I stop myself. It's late. Not exactly the safest idea. And the truth is, I've only been in a canoe once when I was a kid. Still, the thought of drifting across the lake under the stars would feel magical.

As I head back to the cabin, all I can think about is Miles. I wonder what it would feel like to be touched by him. Kissed by him. Would I even remember how? What does he really want? To be friends? Friends with benefits? Something more? My life is in

Seattle, my work, my family, everything I've built. Could I walk away from all of it if something real started between us? My family dinners, my career wins, my Sunday morning routine with overpriced coffee. Could I trade all that for a chance at something I barely understand but desperately want? Maybe it's not a good idea. Maybe it's impossible. But somehow, I don't think I could stay away from him.

Greeted by the warmth of the cabin, I pour myself a glass of wine, sink into the couch and open a new book. I get lost in the romance on the pages, a story of true love. The kind I'm not sure I'll ever have. And yet, I've never felt a connection like the one I feel when I'm around Miles. I'm not saying he's my true love. Hell, I barely know him. But I crave the thrill. The spark. The possibility. He excites me in ways I haven't felt in a long time not just mentally, but holy shit, physically.

Stifling a yawn, I head to the bathroom, brush my teeth and crawl into bed, still thinking about him and just how confused I really am. As sleep begins to pull me under, one thought settles in my mind: Before I can even think about all the deep stuff, I need to know more about him.

***

The next morning, I wake up early. The sun is still rising, casting long golden streaks across the farm. I wrap my hands around a hot cup of coffee and step out onto the patio, letting the quiet settle around me. I wonder what today will bring. What will it be like spending time with Miles? I don't do well with surprises. Yet here I am, heading into the unknown with no clear expectations. Well, maybe one. Sex is definitely off the table. For now, anyway.

As I finish my coffee and head back inside, I know I need to pick the right outfit, something practical for a long tour of the farm, but maybe a little flirty too. Definitely not a dress. But something that might make him look twice. I take my time with my hair and makeup. Just enough, not overdone. A high, simple ponytail. Light eye makeup. A soft pink lip stain with a touch of gloss. Rummaging through my suitcase, I realize I didn't exactly pack for casual flirtation. But the forecast says it'll be warm today, so I settle on a pair of cut-off shorts with just the right amount of distress. Not too short, not too long. Casual. With a bit of edge. I pull on a fitted V-neck t-shirt in forest green, his favorite color, over my best push-up bra. At almost nine, I slip on my shoes, take one last look in the mirror and head out the door with a to-go coffee in hand.

The path Judy told me about starts just behind her cabin. It's wide enough for a truck, though almost hidden by overgrown grass and wildflowers that sway gently in the breeze. If I wasn't so damn nervous, I might actually enjoy the peacefulness of it. Birds chirp somewhere in the trees above me, and the scent of warm earth and wildflowers fills the air. It's the kind of path that would make someone feel calm. Grounded. But not me. With every step, my heart beats a little faster. I keep replaying last night in my head, his voice, the way he looked at me, the heat in the space between us. And his parting words: "Make sure to wear pants." God. I tug down on the hem of my shorts instinctively, regretting nothing, but maybe also kind of everything. Why am I nervous? I've handled disgruntled spouses in court without breaking a sweat. But this, walking down a quiet trail to see a man I barely know, feels infinitely more dangerous. Not in the literal sense. In the "what if he changes everything" kind of sense.

I stop just before the trees thin out, standing at the edge of the clearing. From here, I can see the barn more clearly now, weathered red wood, big double doors propped open and the early sun glinting off the metal roof. A few chickens peck near the edge of the coop. I press my palm to my chest, like it might steady the pounding there. *Just breathe. This is not a date. It's just a tour.* He invited me. I didn't force my way here. I'm allowed to be curious. I'm allowed to want answers. And I'm allowed to want him. I close my eyes for just a second, grounding myself, letting the breeze dance over my skin. The smell of fresh hay and something faintly sweet drifts in the air.

When I open my eyes again, I spot movement. He's there. Not close enough to speak yet, but close enough that the sight of him sends a ripple through my body. What if he regrets inviting me? What if this is the moment everything shifts, one way or another? I know once I take that next step, I'll be stepping into something I can't undo. My stomach twists, not with fear, but with anticipation, the good kind, the terrifying kind. My breath catches. My hands are clammy. Everything in me is screaming to move, to stay, to run, to leap. I don't know what's waiting for me over there, but I know I want it. God help me, I want it. I take a deep breath, trying to calm my racing thoughts. The trail curves gently through a small grove of trees, and just beyond them is a gravel driveway. Almost there. I take a slow, steady breath and step into the clearing. Gravel crunches lightly beneath my shoes. He hears it.

Miles turns toward me, wiping his hands on a rag. He's wearing dark jeans, boots and a gray T-shirt that clings to his chest and shoulders like it was made for him. A streak of dirt runs along one arm, and somehow it only makes him hotter. His eyes land on me and stay there. His gaze skims from my shoes to my ponytail and lingers at the curve of my hips. When our eyes meet, something flickers in his expression. Surprise, interest and something else I can't quite name.

"Morning." His gravel-rich voice sends a warm pulse through my spine.

"Morning," I manage, hoping my smile doesn't look as nervous as I feel.

He tosses the rag onto a nearby bench. "You found the path."

"Hard to miss when Judy gives very specific directions." My tone's light, trying to ease the edge in my chest.

He chuckles softly and steps toward me, closing a bit of the space between us. For a moment, neither of us moves. The space between us feels electric. Thick with everything unspoken.

10

The Chicken Was My Wingman

Miles

I hear the crunch of gravel before I see her. My head lifts, and there she is stepping out of the path like some kind of daydream brought to life. She's wearing a soft expression. She's stunning. She smiles nervously, and something inside me shifts, part relief, part panic. Seeing her again reminds me just how much is riding on today. I want to say the right thing, to make this moment matter. But mostly, I just want to earn that smile again. Maybe it's because of the way I acted at dinner. I know I'll have to explain myself. I don't blame her. We keep dancing around whatever this is.

She says something about Judy giving directions, and I laugh. Not because it's funny, but because if I don't, I might do something reckless. This woman has been running circles in my head since the night we played the game. Now she's standing right in front of me like a damn magnet, pulling me in. I want to peel her clothes off. I want to get lost inside her, to feel her body wrapped around mine, all softness and heat. I want her vulnerable when I'm inside her, but not because of doubt or confusion. I want it to be because she trusts me, because she wants it just as much as I do.

Shaking away the thought of sex with Kinsley, I clear my throat and try to get my head straight. I can't keep looking at her like this, not if I want to make it through the next few hours without doing something I WON'T regret.

"Ready for that tour?" I shove my hands into my pockets to keep them from doing what they want.

"Yes, lead the way." She nods, with a small smile. She steps beside me, her arm brushing mine, and I pretend it doesn't feel like a lit match against my skin. I motion toward the gravel path that cuts between the driveway and the barn.

"This way." I keep my pace slow so she can walk beside me. "I'll show you the barn first."

She glances around, taking in the landscape like she's trying to memorize it. "It's beautiful out here."

"Yeah, it is." But I'm not looking at the trees or the lake. I'm looking at her.

We reach the barn, the big red structure towering over us. Walking through the open doors, the familiar scent of hay and wood fill the air.

"This is where most of the work gets done." I show her through the barn, and the loft's carvings from when Reed and I were kids. I tell her about my parents and when the farm was built. She listens, asks questions and smiles like she's not just being polite but actually interested. Stepping out of the other side of the barn, there's a full view of the cabins. I watch as she takes in the view from my side of the lake.

"It's different from this side." Her eyes soften, as if she's seeing something she hadn't noticed before.

"Yeah, most people only see the cabins up close. But this..." I gesture to the view. "This is the heart of it all. Mom's dream."

She glances at me then, something flickering in her eyes. Curiosity maybe. Or something deeper.

"You grew up here with this as your back yard? That's amazing."

I nod. "I did. It's something isn't it? I've lived here my entire life. What about you? How long have you lived in Seattle?"

"My entire life." She echoes my words. I study her for a second before I continue.

"Do you like it?" I turn to face her.

She hesitates. "I used to. I liked the noise, the movement, the fact that nobody knows you unless you want them to. But lately, it feels wrong, like I'm missing something," she says thoughtfully, turning in my direction. "You're lucky."

"Why's that?"

She looks at me, her gaze soft but steady. "Because you belong somewhere. That's rare. Most people spend their whole lives searching for that, and some never find it."

Her words hit deeper than I expected. I've never thought of it that way, that this life would be something others might envy. It's always just been mine. Ordinary. "Maybe you're not missing something. Maybe you're just starting to figure out what you really want."

She doesn't answer right away, and I don't press her. The silence between us isn't awkward, it's thoughtful.

Then she gives me a small smile. "Maybe." I can see she's struggling with the heavy topic. I decide to distract her.

"Come on. I'll show you the coop. The chickens get pissed if I don't feed them on time."

She laughs softly, the sound light. A grateful look, like I did exactly what she needed without her having to ask. I start walking, and she follows beside me. Our arms brush once, and neither of us move away.

As we reach the chicken coop, the hens cluck and shuffle inside the fenced area like they've been waiting for me all morning. I grab the feed bucket and shake it once, the universal signal that breakfast is served.

"Alright, ladies," I call, unlocking the gate. "Let's not be dramatic about it." Kinsley leans against the coop, watching with amusement as the chickens swarm my boots.

"Are they always this aggressive?"

"Only when they see someone new. They think you're bringing treats."

She lifts her brows. "But I don't have treats."

I glance over my shoulder at her, smirking. "I'm the treat." She laughs.

"Here, take a handful." I know full well what's about to happen. But wanting to lighten the mood even more, I roll with it. As soon as she pulls her hand out of the bucket, all six hens zero in and charge. Her eyes go wide. She lets out a squeal, flings the feed and bolts, arms flailing. The sight nearly knocks the breath out of me. God, she's beautiful like this. Unfiltered. Alive. And she's running straight to me. I'm doubled over laughing when she makes a full circle around me, clinging to my back like I'm some kind of human shield. A few seconds later, I toss some feed on the ground to distract the feathered mob.

She's still clinging to my back, even after the hens lose interest and start pecking at the feed. I can't help it; my back slowly flexes under her grip. Her hands are warm, and the moment stretches out longer than it probably should. I reach around and touch her hand, gently curling my fingers around hers, guiding her around until she's facing me.

Our bodies are nearly pressed together, just a breath apart. Her eyes lock onto mine, and everything else fades. I watch as she slowly licks her perfect pink lips, and my jaw tightens instinctively.

I have to clench it just to keep from closing the space and claiming her mouth right then and there.

"You did that on purpose." Her voice is barely above a whisper.

"I did. If I'd known it would lead to this, I would've done it a hell of a lot sooner." Needing to break the moment before I lose it, I take a slow breath. "Want to meet Rocket?"

"Sure." The word barely forms on her lips, like she's forgotten how to speak.

I'm so tempted to touch her again, to close that space, but instead, I gently slip my hand from hers and gesture toward the stable.

As we start walking, I glance over at her. "Colby should be here soon to help get the chickens back in the coop."

She looks at me curiously, and I go on. "He's a good kid. Part of a school program. Comes out a few days a week to help around the farm. He'll be here for the next couple months, then I get a new apprentice." I catch the way she listens, the way her eyes soften a little.

"Colby will feed and brush Rocket," I say as we near the stable. "I'll leave that part to him, but I did want to introduce you." She perks up, light in her eyes. "He's older now, not really a riding horse anymore. But he still loves face rubs."

Her whole expression brightens. The kind of smile that sneaks up on you. "I can touch him?"

"Yeah," I grin. "He'll love that."

The stable smells of hay and old wood. Rocket lifts his head as we approach, ears twitching, soft brown eyes watching us with lazy interest.

"There he is." I pat the stall door. "Hey, buddy." He snorts softly, stepping closer, and I open the gate. "Come on in. He's gentle."

She steps in slowly, a little hesitant, but her curiosity outweighs her nerves. Rocket lowers his head toward her, and she reaches out, tentatively at first. When her fingers brush his muzzle, he leans into the touch. Her face lights up, wide-eyed and smiling. "He's so soft."

"Told you he likes face rubs." I watch her with more interest than I probably should. She runs her hand along his cheek, and he closes his eyes in pure contentment.

"I think he likes me." A little laugh slips into her voice.

"Yeah, I think he really does."

Me too, Rocket. The way she runs her fingers along his face, I can't take my eyes off her. Every movement, every soft word she speaks to him. I lean against the stall door, arms crossed, keeping my hands busy so I don't reach for her again. *Get a grip, Miles,* I scold myself.

Rocket huffs with content, head tilted into her palm like he's known her forever. And me? I'm standing here trying not to fall apart over a woman rubbing a horse's nose. I draw in a slow breath, hoping it'll settle something inside me. It doesn't.

Just as I'm about to give in to the urge to touch her, I hear the crunch of gravel outside. I push off the stall door and see Colby's truck. I straighten, drag a hand down my face and try to smooth my expression into something neutral. Something that doesn't give me away. "Sounds like backup's here."

A moment later, the stable door creaks open, and Colby steps in, ball cap pulled low. "Hey, Miles." He gives me a nod before his eyes shift to her. "Didn't know you had company."

"Colby, this is Kinsley." *The woman who nearly broke my self-control.*

She smiles and lifts a hand. "Hi. Nice to meet you." Colby gives a polite wave.

"Well, we'll leave you to it, Colby. Make sure to put the chickens back when you're done in here. I already fed them."

"Got it." He replies without looking up, scraping the pitchfork on the ground.

I gesture to the door, and Kinsley falls into step beside me. As we walk out into the golden light of the early afternoon, she doesn't say anything right away and neither do I.

As we walk toward the lake, she breaks the silence. "What do you harvest?" She nods toward the empty fields on the other side of the driveway.

"Field corn. I finished harvesting just before you arrived. I wanted to get ahead of it with the Farmers Potluck coming up."

"Farmers Potluck?" she echoes, brows lifting.

I grin at her expression. "Yeah, small-town tradition. End-of-season gathering. Everyone brings food. One of the local farms hosts each year. I figured Judy would've mentioned it."

"No. Tell me what it's like."

"Well, it's not your average potluck." I glance over at her. "It's a full-on community event. Live music, dancing. They set up party tents and haul in a dance floor. Each year, the hosting farm tries to outdo the last by adding something new. It starts in the early afternoon and ends around ten at night."

She raises a brow, interested.

"Last year, Old Man Floyd brought in a mechanical bull. Year before that, someone did a chili cook-off with judges and everything. It gets a little wild, in a very wholesome, rural kind of way."

She laughs. "That actually sounds amazing. What are you adding this year?"

"It's a blast. I'm adding bounce houses for the kids." I shrug. "I thought the kids needed something, too."

She smiles, clearly picturing it. "That's actually really thoughtful."

"You should come."

She looks at me, a little surprised. "To the potluck?"

"I mean, you're here, might as well get the full experience. Food, music, awkward small-town dancing. It's kind of a rite of passage around here."

"I'll have to check my schedule. I'm very busy, you know." She giggles.

"Ah, yes, extremely full. Packed with romance novels and raccoon adventures." I chuckle.

She shoots me a playful, pointed look. "Hey, I'll have you know both are highly demanding hobbies."

"Oh, no doubt. Very demanding."

She pauses. "Should I bring a dish to pass? Would you like help setting up?"

"Sure." A grin tugs at my lips. "Do you even know how to cook, City Girl?"

Her eyes widen in mock horror. "Yes, thank you very much. I'll have you know I'm a very good cook. Why don't you come over tomorrow night and I'll make you dinner to prove it."

I raise a brow, playing along. "Is this a challenge?"

"It's a promise." For a second, there's something real in her voice, something a little braver than before.

"Alright then." I nod. "Tomorrow night. I'll bring dessert. Just in case."

She laughs and nudges me with her elbow playfully. "Shut up. Is five o'clock, okay?"

"Five's perfect. I'll come hungry and skeptical."

She gives me a mock glare, but I catch the smile tugging at the corners of her mouth.

"I better go." She takes a small step back. "I really do have a few things to do today, and no, not read a romance book, smart ass." She laughs. "Thank you for the tour. I had a good time."

I chuckle. "Sure. I'll just assume it's raccoon-related business, then."

She laughs again, turning slightly. "See you tomorrow, Country Boy."

"Five o'clock," I call after her, still smiling at the nickname. Then, with a little more hope than I mean to let show, I add, "I'll walk you back."

She glances over her shoulder, smiling. "Okay."

11

Prep for Seduction

Kinsley

I kind of thought he would offer to walk me back. When he did, I was relieved that our day wasn't over just yet. Now, walking beside him, down the same path I came up earlier, I feel a little sad to be going. We don't say much, but the silence isn't awkward. It's peaceful.

I had a really good time today. But more than that, I had a great time with him. Maybe it's all in my head, but I can't shake the feeling that he's holding something back. Like every time our arms brush or I catch his eyes lingering just a second too long, there's something there. I wish he wouldn't fight it. But maybe he doesn't know how I feel. Maybe he's holding back because he thinks I'm the one who isn't sure. It's on me now, to say it, to make the first move.

When he pulled me from behind his back earlier and our bodies were suddenly so close, I don't think he realized what that did to me. I would've let him kiss me right then. I would've let him do anything. In that moment, I was putty in his hands, and part of me still is.

"I need to know," he says, his hands shoved in his pockets, eyes scanning mine. "Last night at dinner, did you know I was going to be there?"

85

The question catches me off guard. I didn't think he would bring it up. "No." I shake my head. "Judy didn't mention anything."

He nods slowly, like he's not surprised, "That's what I thought." He starts, then stops himself. He lets out a quiet breath. "I guess I owe you an apology."

"For what?" But I think I know the answer.

"For being...distant...weird at dinner. I didn't handle it well." He kicks at a loose pebble on the path, his shoulders tense. "I didn't expect to see you. I'm going to be honest with you, I was trying to avoid you." He cringes as he stares at the ground.

"Why?"

With our last words hanging in the air between us, we step off the path behind Judy's cabin, mine coming into view.

I ask again, quieter this time. "Why?"

He doesn't answer right away. The silence stretches, thick with everything he's not saying.

We reach my door when he finally speaks. "Because I knew if I saw you again, I'd crack." His voice is low. "I'd lose control."

I stop at my front door and turn to face him. With all the courage I can muster, I say, "Lose control, Miles. I'm not fragile, I won't break."

The words leave my mouth before I can second-guess them, and my heart pounds. Saying it aloud, peeling back the armor, making it clear I'm all in. But I mean every word.

He freezes. I see the battle in his eyes, the careful control he's held onto slipping away. His jaw tightens. Then he steps forward suddenly, his hand is at the back of my neck, firm, forcing me to look up into his eyes. My chest presses against his, my body arching toward him instinctively, craving what only he can give. He leans down, his mouth inches from mine, his breath warm against my lips.

"I need you to understand what you're asking for, Kinsley."
His voice is rough.

"I do," I whisper, breathless. "You."

That's all it takes. His mouth crashes onto mine, and it's not gentle. It's heat and hunger, something that's been caged too long. My hands fist his shirt, gripping onto him like a lifeline. His hand knots tighter in my hair, angling my head just the way he wants it. His lips devour mine like he's starved for the taste of me. I moan into him, and he deepens the kiss, his tongue sliding against mine with a dominance that makes my knees weaken. He presses me back until my shoulders hit the door, his hips locking against mine, anchoring me there like I belong under him. I can feel the full weight of his desire now. He pulls back abruptly breaking the kiss. I'm lost when his lips tear from mine, and he takes a step back.

"Miles?" I whisper, confusion lacing my voice as I catch my breath. My body still hums with the shock of his touch.

He stares at me for a second, then gives me that crooked smirk. "I don't think you're ready, Kinsley."

Before I can answer, he reaches out, brushing his thumb slowly over my lower lip sending fresh shivers down my spine.

"I'll see you tomorrow." And just like that, he's gone. Leaving me pressed against the door, breathless, and aching in ways I didn't know were possible.

I step into my cabin, half-shocked, my legs barely working. I've never been kissed like that. Never wanted someone so badly it felt like a need. Inside, the cabin is quiet, except for the sound of my rapid heartbeat. I lean back against the door and close my eyes, trying to catch my breath, trying to make sense of what just happened. Does he really think I'm not ready? Or is he playing a game. I think it's the latter. Well, Miles, I can play your game. I'll show you just how ready I am!

Pulling my phone from my pocket, I dial Naya.

She answers on the second ring. "Hey, girl."

"Hey. You got plans today?"

"Nope, why?"

"Perfect." I'm already heading for my closet. "I need a few new outfits, a couple of strong drinks and I have a story to tell." My heart is still thudding from the kiss, my whole body buzzing. "I need to look so good tonight that Miles forgets how to breathe. You in?"

There's a pause, then her grin practically echoes through the line. "Oh, I am so in."

"When can you be ready?"

"Girl, I'm ready now. I'll meet you at the bakery. We can ride together. See you in twenty."

I pull up and Naya's leaning against her car. I slide into the passenger seat of her Jeep and let her take the wheel, mostly because I have no idea where we're going.

As we head toward a boutique in a neighboring town, I tell her everything. The kiss. The way Miles pulled back. The way he dominated me. By the time I finish, Naya lets out a whistle.

"Girl. That man is teasing you. Building it up until you explode right in his hands." She shakes her head with a smirk. "You're right. You need killer outfits, make him choke on his own restraint."

I laugh, but it's laced with something else. Determination. "That's the plan."

The boutique smells like vanilla. Soft classical music plays through the speakers, and sunlight filters in through wide windows, catching on rows of silky dresses, curve-hugging jeans and strappy tank tops.

Naya claps her hands as we step inside. "Let the games begin."

"Operation: Take Down Miles." I laugh as I head straight for a rack of dresses.

I remember what he said to me, "Make sure to wear pants, I can't be held responsible if you don't." On a mission, I let my fingers skim over the fabrics, lace, satin, cotton that would cling just enough.

"Try this," Naya says, tossing a black wrap dress at me. "And this," she adds, grabbing a blood-red halter that looks borderline dangerous. "Also, we're not leaving without trying this one on. That's non-negotiable."

I giggle and follow Naya to the dressing room, my arms overflowing with possibilities. Inside the small space, I slip into the red dress first. It's short with a low neckline, accentuating all my curves. Enough to make a man forget how to breath.

When I step out, Naya's jaw drops. "Kinsley," she breathes. "He is absolutely going to lose his damn mind when he sees you in that."

I spin once, checking myself out in the mirror. "I love it. I'm definitely getting it." I pause, cocking my head. "But I don't think it's right for dinner at my place."

Naya grins, unbothered. "True but we'll find something that says, 'I'm sweet, but I bite' for dinner tonight."

Slipping back into the fitting room, I try on five more dresses, some too tight, some too flashy, some just not it. But then I pull on the last one, and everything shifts.

It's a deep wine-colored dress with off-the-shoulder sleeves, fitted through the waist, and flowing gently to mid-thigh. Soft, feminine, but not shy. I smooth my hands down the sides, take a breath, then step out.

Naya gasps. "Girl, that's the one!" She walks a circle around me. "This dress screams I'm the whole damn meal and the fine wine that comes with it."

I grin at my reflection, feeling powerful and soft all at once. *Check mate, Miles,* I think to myself. Grabbing the perfect brown leather three-inch heels, my outfit is complete.

Naya and I spend another thirty minutes shopping, weaving through racks like women on a mission. By the time we head back to town, the sun is starting to set.

We roll into The Fireside Lounge. The lounge is dimly lit with warm wood paneling. The low hum of conversation and clinking glasses fills the room. A live band plays as people dance on a small dance floor surrounded by tables.

We grab a booth near the back, and a server walks over with menus we barely glance at.

"Two burgers, fries, and whiskey and colas, please," I tell her. "Heavy on the whiskey."

She laughs and walks off, and Naya raises a brow. "Now this is how you prep for war. In heels, whiskey and a good friend to gas you up."

I clink my glass against hers when the drinks arrive. "To good dresses and bad decisions."

I devour my burger in record time. We sit there for a couple of hours, sipping our drinks slowly, plotting my next move.

Naya drops me off at my car with a wicked grin and one last reminder. "You better call me tonight after Miles leaves…IF he leaves." She points a finger at me, giggling.

I laugh, shaking my head. "You'll be the first to know. Promise." I wave goodbye, still smiling, and drive back to the cabin, going over my dirty little plan.

When I reach my door. I freeze. Resting against the door is a bundle of wildflowers tied with twine. My heart skips a beat. I scoop them up, balancing them awkwardly with the four bags of clothes hanging from my arms. Once inside, I drop everything onto the couch and unfold the note. It's from Miles.

City Girl,

Thanks for today. I had a great time.

On my walk back I saw these

and thought of you.

See you tomorrow.

Country Boy

I nearly melt into a puddle right there on the floor. The flowers, the note, the way he called me City Girl. It's not grand or flashy. It's simple. Thoughtful. The fact that he thought of me at all. I carry the flowers into the kitchen and drop them into a vase I found under the sink. I lean against the counter, my stomach fluttering in a way I haven't felt in a long time. I can still feel him. His hands on me. His mouth on mine. Shaking the thought, not wanting to obsess over him, I busy myself putting away my new clothes and getting ready for bed. But it doesn't matter. I still fall asleep to the memory of his kiss.

***

The morning light wakes me early, rays of light slipping through the cabin windows. I stretch, still feeling the lingering warmth from yesterday, and shuffle into the kitchen. While the coffee brews, I wander over to the wildflowers Miles left me. I take a slow breath, letting their sweetness fill me, and smile to myself.

Back at the stove, I whip up some French toast, the warm scent of cinnamon and vanilla filling the cabin. I eat at the island, still in my sleep shirt. As I scroll through my phone, I decide it's a good morning to share. I snap a few pictures of the wildflowers on the counter, then add the ones I took of the lake and the farm. A quiet kind of joy settles in as I post them to social media. Then I text my mom letting her know I'm fine and having a good time.

Grabbing my cup of coffee, I head outside and settle into the lounge chair facing the farm. The sun bathes my skin, its warmth sinking into me as I take a slow sip. I glance out toward the lake and spot Miles sprinting back and forth, clearly chasing something. It takes me a second, but then I see it… a cat, darting across the grass with ridiculous speed. I laugh as it easily outruns him and climbs up a nearby tree, leaving Miles staring up helplessly. Still smiling, I pick up my phone and text him.

Me: Do you need emergency services? Fire, medical, police?

I watch from my chair as he pulls out his phone, reads the message and turns to look my way. A moment later, my phone buzzes.

Miles: Haha smart ass. Are you stalking me? It was only one kiss.

I laugh out loud, nearly spilling my coffee.

Me: Don't flatter yourself, it wasn't that good.

A total lie. Just thinking about that kiss sends a pulse of heat through me. I reach up and brush my fingers across my lips, remembering the way his mouth claimed mine.

Miles: That's not what your body was saying.

Ignoring the fact that he's right, I fire back.

Me: Bold words for a man who got shown up by a cat.

I hit send with a smirk, already picturing the look on his face.

Miles: Don't worry, I always catch what I chase.

Heat rolls up my neck when I read his text.

Me: Catch me if you can, Country Boy. See you tonight.

"Except, I'm not running," I say to myself out loud.

Miles: Challenge accepted. See you tonight, City Girl.

I sip my coffee and watch as he pulls his shirt over his head, climbs the tree with ease, clearly putting on a show. Shaking my head with a smile, I walk inside.

While tidying up the cabin and getting ready for tonight, my phone buzzes on the counter. I glance at the screen. It's Ben. For a second, I consider letting it go to voicemail. I'm sure he saw my post this morning.

"Hello?" I'm already hoping he doesn't ruin my good mood.

"Hey." He pauses and waits for me to carry the conversation, as always.

"What do you need, Ben?"

"I saw your post this morning. I thought you said there wasn't anyone else?"

I let out a sigh, sharp and tired. "I already told you, I'm not seeing anyone. And even if I were, it's none of your business."

"I saw the picture of the flowers, and I just got worried I was losing you." That voice. That whiny, guilt-tripping tone. God, what did I ever see in him?

"Ben, you lost me nine months ago. I spent too long making excuses, holding onto something that wasn't real anymore. You need to let it go." My thumb hovers for a second. "I'm blocking your number. Bye." I hang up and press block before I can think twice. Then I set my phone down and get back to cleaning, my mood bruised but not broken.

When Miles gets here, I want to look hot. Not cute. I want time for the full, everything shower. I crank up my cooking playlist early and head for the bathroom, already feeling the heat of anticipation stir beneath my skin.

12

Wet Skin, Reckless Hands

Miles

The sun's hanging low by the time I get Rocket back to the stable. He's worn down after hours of grazing. I rub him down slowly, working the curry comb in wide circles across his side, but my mind's not on the task, It's on her, and that damn kiss.

When she looked up at me with those eyes and told me to lose control. Told me she wasn't fragile. She wanted me. My restraint was gone. Her lips on mine, her body pressed close, the way her breath hitched when I pulled her tighter. The way her fingers twisted in my shirt like she didn't want to let go. I didn't want to let go either. Still don't. But I had to.

I step out of the stall and lean against the stable wall, staring out at the pasture. There's a knot in my chest I can't work loose. I want her...God, I want her. But wanting her isn't the problem. It's what comes after. The fear of letting her in just to watch her leave. Of giving myself over to something I already know has an expiration date. That's what's tearing me up. But I will keep my composure from here on out because once we cross that line there's no going back, and I know she'll return to Seattle.

I finish up at the stable and I drive five minutes into town, windows down, dust still clinging to my jeans. I park outside the Cranberry Ridge Grocery. I smile remembering the night we played the game and head straight for the chocolate ice cream. Her favorite. I toss it in my basket and head home. Not wasting time. Hoping no one stops to talk.

Back at the house, I tuck the carton into the freezer. For a second, I just stand there, hand on the door, wondering if it's a good idea to see her again. But I already know the answer. I can't stay away. So there's no point pretending I can.

I head for the shower. Stripping out of my dusty clothes, I turn the water hot and let it run over me, washing away the sweat and the weight of the day. My hands brace against the tile, head bowed, water beating across my back.

I kill the water and step out, dragging a towel across my face, down my body. Steam covers the mirror. I head to the bedroom and pull open the closet. My usual stained, worn jeans and T-shirt doesn't feel like enough tonight. I pause, then reach for the navy button-down, a crisp white T-shirt and a pair of faded jeans. I roll the sleeves up to my elbows and leave it open. It doesn't look like I tried too hard, but it's better than looking like I just came in from mucking stalls.

I run my hands through my hair leaving a messy look. I step into my clean brown leather boots, pat my pocket to make sure I've got my keys and phone, then head to the kitchen. I grab the ice cream from the freezer door. As I walk to my truck, clouds are rolling in, low. It looks like it might rain tonight.

Once I get to the cabins I step out, ice cream in hand. I walk the path to her cabin, gravel crunching under my boots. From here, I can already hear music drifting out through the open windows. I'm not nervous, not exactly. But there's a pull in my chest, a hesitation, a feeling I haven't let myself have in a long time. I'm looking forward to tonight more than I want to admit. I square my shoulders and knock on the door.

When the door swings open, whatever words I had planned disappear. My eyes widen, taking her in. She's wearing a dress. On purpose. Soft fabric, bare shoulders, legs… God, her legs. She's not just answering the door. She's making a statement. Testing me. And she knows exactly what she's doing. And damn if it doesn't work. My chest tightens, not just from want, but from knowing she chose this moment, this look, just for me. *Shit.*

I meet her eyes again, trying to keep my voice steady. "You always wear dresses for dinner?" I ask, even though I already know the answer.

She smirks. "Only if I want to." She waves me inside.

I step in, and the warm scent of lemon pepper baked salmon and roasted potatoes hits me right away. The island's set with two plates with the wildflowers I gave her sitting in the middle.

I toe off my boots at the door and follow her into the kitchen.

"Need help with anything?"

She turns just as I hold out the ice cream. Her eyes light up when she sees the label. "Chocolate?" She grins. "You remembered." She takes it from my hands, and her fingers brush mine, just for a second, but long enough to feel it. The contact is small, almost nothing, but it buzzes through me like live bees. For a moment, all I can think about is how badly I want more.

"It's almost done. Thanks for this. And the flowers." She nods toward the island.

I lean back against the counter, arms crossed, one ankle hooked over the other, just watching her move. The sway of her hips, the way her dress clings when she reaches for a dish. I want to drag her into me. I want to forget about control. But I don't. Not yet.

I watch as she turns, stepping in close, really close, and my eyes don't leave her for a second. She reaches around me for the potholder, her arm brushing my chest, her body just shy of touching mine. *Oh, you little tease.* I know exactly what she's doing. She's playing a game. But I like it. So, I say nothing. I stay right where I

96

am, arms still crossed, letting her feel the heat rolling off me. Letting her know I noticed, without saying a word. If she wants to play, I'll play. But when I make my move, she won't be teasing anymore.

"Would you like wine or beer?" She opens the fridge without looking back.

"A beer would be great," My voice a little deeper than I intend.

She grabs two and a bowl of salad, then turns and hands me both bottles, making sure to brush my hand again. Deliberate. Just enough to notice. She places the salad on the island while I twist the caps off the beers. I hand her one, her fingers grazing mine again. I take a drink from mine, eyes still on her. She takes a sip of hers too, then glances at me with a smile that says she knows exactly what she's doing.

She sets dinner on the island, and we both take our seats side by side. No need for distance, not tonight. "Dinner looks amazing." I glance over the spread she's laid out. "You enjoy cooking?"

"Yes." Her smile softens. "I just don't have much time back home. My schedule's tight." Sadness flickers in her eyes for just a moment. She passes the dishes one by one, and we both fill our plates.

I take my first bite, and my eyes widen. "Wow! I was wrong, City Girl. This is damn good."

She smiles, casually shrugging one shoulder. "I know."

"You'll have to teach me how. I can't cook. I can grill, though."

We eat and talk, and somewhere in the middle of my second helping, she asks what meals I can cook. When I rattle off the short list, scrambled eggs, pancakes, tacos and anything that can go on a grill, she laughs.

"Remind me not to let you near my kitchen unsupervised," she teases, taking a sip of her beer.

"No promises." I smirk, stealing another roasted potato.

She starts telling me about her mom, how they used to cook together when she was a kid. How her mom always had music playing in the background, dancing around the kitchen like it was part of the recipe. "That's why the playlist." She gestures toward the speaker in the corner. "It just feels right. Makes the kitchen feel like home."

I nod, chewing slowly, watching her as she talks. There's a softness in her face when she speaks about her mom. A warmth that makes me want to know every piece of her past, not just the ones she's comfortable with sharing. We sit like that for a while. No pressure. No rush. Just two people learning each other, one story, one smile at a time.

When we finish dinner, I help clear the island and load the dishwasher. She hums along to the music still playing in the background. When I dry my hands on a towel, she's already at the fridge grabbing us another round. She holds a bottle out to me, eyebrow raised. I take it. "Thanks." I pop the cap and take a sip. "That was seriously good. Might've been the best meal I've had in a while."

She grins and bumps her shoulder into mine. "That's just because your usual diet sounds like a twelve-year-old left unsupervised."

I chuckle, leaning back against the counter. "You want to take a walk?"

She gives me a half-smile. "Sure."

We slip on our shoes and head for the patio door. Outside, it's dark, cool air brushing against our skin, the breeze soft but steady. Clouds stretch across the sky, hiding the stars, the kind that tells you rain is coming.

We walk side by side toward the lake. "I think it's going to rain in a little while." I glance at the sky. "Might want to stay close to the cabin."

She doesn't argue, just shifts her gaze toward the dock, and we both turn that way. As we reach the dock, the breeze picks up, carrying the scent of rain and lake water. The wood creaks under our steps, worn by weather and time. She walks ahead of me just a bit, hips swaying like she knows I'm watching. Because I am.

"I don't mind getting a little wet," she says over her shoulder, voice light but loaded.

My brow arches before I can stop it. "Careful, City Girl. You say things like that, you're gonna give me the wrong idea."

She stops at the edge of the dock and turns toward me, that same half-smirk playing on her lips. "Who says it's the wrong idea?"

I take a step closer, slow and measured. "You keep pushing like that, I'm not gonna be the one getting wet." I watch her closely, feeling the tension pull tight between us. My ability to stop is slipping with every second she holds my gaze.

Her breath hitches just enough for me to notice, but she recovers quickly, tilting her chin up in challenge. "Maybe that's what I'm hoping for."

My hands flex at my sides. Every instinct in me wants to grab her. Pull her in. Taste that smart mouth again and remind her exactly who she's messing with. But I don't. Not yet. I just smile, low and dangerous. "Keep testing me, Kinsley. See where it gets you."

Just as she takes a bold step forward, challenging me, the sky cracks open and sheets of cold rain drench us in seconds. We both freeze for half a second, then bolt.

I'm faster, but I reach back and grab her hand, pulling her along as we sprint up the path, laughing like idiots. By the time we reach the cabin, we're soaked to the bone, breathless and dripping. She fumbles with the door, laughing harder when it sticks. I nudge it open with my shoulder, and we tumble inside, water pooling beneath our feet.

"I'll grab towels." Her hair is plastered to her cheeks, eyes sparkling.

She disappears down the hall and comes back with two big towels, tossing one to me as she starts patting herself down. But the moment I look at her, really look, I go still. Water trails down her neck, over her chest disappearing at the rim of her dress. Her skin's flushed from the run, hair clinging to her face in wild strands, and somehow, she's never looked more goddamn sexy. I pull off my button-down shirt, even my T-shirt is soaked. She steps close and reaches out with her towel, brushing it gently over my shoulder. It's a soft touch, innocent enough. But it undoes me.

I grab her hand, and she goes still, just for a second. But it's enough. Enough to feel her pulse jump beneath my fingers. Enough to see the flicker in her eyes, the shift from playful to hungry. She wants this as badly as I do. Not just the kiss. All of it. The closeness, the risk, the heat. I realize, this isn't a game to her anymore. It's a choice. I step in, close enough to feel the heat radiating off her damp skin. Water drips from her hair, trailing along her collarbone, and my eyes follow it down before dragging back up to hers.

"You've been testing me all night." My voice is low, rough with everything I've been holding back. She doesn't deny it. Just stares up at me, lips parted, breath quickening. I don't wait for another signal. I close the distance and crash my mouth onto hers. Dropping her towel, she grips my soaked T-shirt. It's heat and want and every bit of restraint I've been choking down since the second she opened the damn door in that dress.

13

Guided by His Hands

Kinsley

Pressed against the wall, Miles' kiss is hungry but controlled. His body molds to mine, heat rolling off him in waves. I arch into him, needing more, my nipples tight and achy against the solid wall of his chest, the friction shooting a shiver down my spine. It's not just need...it's unraveling. And I don't want him to stop.

His mouth leaves mine slowly, his breath warm and uneven against my lips. He searches my eyes, as if asking a question. I slide my hand up, threading my fingers into the back of his neck, gripping hard. My silent answer is clear. I want more. He snakes an arm around my waist and lifts me effortlessly, the towel still in his hand. His mouth finds mine again, hot, demanding. Our tongues tangle in a kiss that steals the breath from my lungs, and I moan into him, the sound raw and needy.

His grip is tight as he walks us to the kitchen island, every step making me more aware of the press of his hardness between my thighs, the strength in his arms, the way I want him like I've never wanted anyone before.

He lowers me slowly onto the counter, his movements deliberate, as if savoring the feel of me in his arms. When our mouths part, he steps back, eyes heavy with restraint. My thighs clench involuntarily, craving the heat of him again. His gaze drags over me like he's trying to memorize every inch, every curve.

I lick my lips, breath catching, and watch as he struggles to steady himself. With the towel still gripped in his hand, he lifts it to my jaw, tracing just beneath it, catching the lingering drops of rain sliding from my soaked hair. I inhale sharply, not from the chill, but from the fire building between us. His eyes don't leave mine, even as the towel trails lower, just brushing the top of my nearly bare chest. I reach up, fingers brushing his as he guides the cloth down. The moment our skin meets, he growls low in his throat, a sound full of warning and want.

The towel slips from his fingers, grabbing my wrist, holding me still. His jaw tightens, the muscle ticking as he battles the pull between restraint and desire. His fingers curl tighter around my wrist, anchoring me, grounding himself. His eyes blaze into mine, dark and unflinching, searching for any flicker of hesitation.

"Is this what you want, Kinsley?" A primal edge cuts through his voice.

My breath shutters. "Yes," I whisper, my voice thick with need.

He releases my wrist, and in the next breath, his hands are on my thighs, gripping them hard. He parts them with a rough urgency, pushing them open until I'm spread wide on the counter. My dress rides up with the motion, bunching around my waist, revealing the thin scrap of black lace that barely covers me.

His eyes lower, and a dark sound escapes him. "Fuck." He groans, licking his lips.

He grabs my wrist again, commanding, and brings my hand to my lips. His eyes lock on mine, burning with hunger and challenge.

"Show me what you want me to touch," he murmurs, voice low. The words send a jolt straight through me. Heat rushes under

102

my skin, flooding every inch of me. It's so erotic, so raw. My heartbeat pounds in my ears. I can already feel the pulse of release building low in my belly, just from his voice, his confidence, the way he watches me.

When I start to move, he stops me, gently pulling my hand back to my mouth.

"Slow, baby." His voice is low and coaxing. "Let me show you."

With his hand wrapped around mine, he guides my fingers over my lips, down my chin, tracing each movement like it's sacred. His eyes never leave my hand, and mine never leave his eyes. Slowly, he slides my hand down the column of my neck, heat blooming wherever we touch. When we reach my chest, he presses my hand harder over one aching nipple, the friction making me gasp. My head tips back, a soft moan escaping my lips. He groans, eyes heavy as he moves our joined hands along the curve of my breast, then down, slow, torturous, across my ribs, my stomach, until we hover just above the center of my spread legs.

"Miles," I whisper again, desperate, trembling, not wanting him to stop.

He steps in, only leaving a sliver of space between us. My hand hovers just above my parted thighs, shaking with the effort not to move. He leans down, his mouth hovering over mine, breath brushing my lips.

"What do you need, Kinsley?" His voice is hard, like steel.

"You." I pant breathlessly, the word falling from my lips like a confession. His mouth crashes into mine, fierce and claiming, and he guides my hand lower, over the burning heat of my swollen center. A loud moan rips free into our kiss, and he growls in satisfaction, breaking away just enough to speak.

"When you come," he says, voice rough and full of command, "I want you thinking of me."

The words hit me like a jolt, hot and raw and claiming. My breath catches, my body tightening with the need to obey. He wants that power over me, and God help me, I want to give it to him. Every inch of me aches with the weight of his words. Then, just like that, he steps back, leaving my hand trembling between my thighs. He drags his fingers slowly down my inner thigh, a final tease that makes my whole body shudder.

"I'll see you tomorrow. Thanks for dinner." He smirks, his voice cool but his eyes still burning. He turns, walking out the front door like he didn't just set me on fire.

Absolutely shocked, I just stare at the door. He walked out. He actually walked out, leaving me a sopping mess on the damn kitchen counter. My legs are shaky as I slide down, heart still pounding and lips still tingling. *What the hell just happened?* I felt him. I felt his hardness. I know he wanted me.

Flustered, I stomp into the bedroom, yanking off my damp clothes and tossing them in a heap. I towel off the rest of the rain, then throw on the warmest, most unsexy pajamas I brought, just out of spite.

Back in the kitchen, I scoop myself the biggest bowl of ice cream I can manage and plop onto the couch with a dramatic huff. Muttering in frustration, I take a bite, glaring at the door like it personally offended me. "Unbelievable." I totally need advice. Still reeling, I grab my phone and text Naya.

Me: You free? I need to talk. Like now.

Ten seconds later, my phone rings.

"Hey. Explain why your night is over so soon."

I groan. "It's a long story. And I'm leaving out some of the steamier parts."

"Mm-hmm. I don't need all the R-rated details. Just tell me what he did."

So, I do. The kissing, the heat, the kitchen counter, and the part where he just walked out. Leaving me a trembling mess with a bowl of ice cream and questions.

He was supposed to be the one begging. Ripping my clothes off. Not leaving me half-wrecked and overthinking every breath I took around him.

Naya's voice drips with amusement. "Girl, can't you see what he's doing? He's edging you. Working you up until he finally takes you all the way. It's fucking hot."

I groan, flopping deeper into the couch. "It's not funny."

She actually laughs. "Oh, but it kind of is. You're all worked up, and he's out there somewhere being a smug little tease."

"How long does he plan on edging me?" I snap, digging into the ice cream like it's going to soothe anything. "I'm not sure I can take much more of this."

"Well, either he's building up to the best sex of your life, or he's a sadist with incredible self-control. Either way, you're the one who lit the match." I can practically hear her smirking through the phone.

I sigh. "I guess I did. The touching. The leaning into him. The damn dress."

"Exactly," she says, like she's been waiting for me to admit it. "You lit the match, now light his fire."

"What?"

"Turn it back on him. Edge him back. Make him the one squirming. Make him regret not taking you right there on that counter. Make him beg for it."

A wicked little thrill flutters in my chest. The thought of turning the tables isn't just tempting, it's exhilarating. Powerful. I've spent so long reacting to him, pulled under by every glance and touch. But this? This is me taking the lead. And I'm ready.

I pause, imagining the look on Miles' face if I flipped the script. Heat coils low in my belly again, but this time it's paired with a wicked little spark.

"You're evil."

"I prefer 'strategic.' You want control back? Take it. Trust me, men like him, dominant and cocky, they lose it when you start playing their game better than they do."

I pause, a slow smile tugging at my lips. "You're right. I started this, now I'm going to finish it."

"That's my girl!"

I groan. "But let's be honest, the man's got more restraint than I do, so I'll definitely have to up my game."

"Then do it. You've got all the power, babe." Her voice is full of confidence, like she's already picturing the victory. Like she trusts, without a doubt, in my ability to seduce a man into losing every ounce of willpower he has.

I nod, mostly to convince myself. "You're right. I can do this. I hold the power." But even as I say it, my stomach flips. Miles is good. Really good. He's not some easily flustered guy who crumbles. He's patient. Controlled. Worst of all, he already knows I want him.

"Thanks for your advice." I let out a sigh. "I owe you one."

"Yep. But don't worry you can pay me back with all the details." Naya laughs. "Now go get some sleep. Tomorrow's the big game, and you've got a farmer to conquer."

I hang up the phone and rinse out my bowl, the weight of the conversation still humming in my chest. After locking the doors, I head to bed, but sleep eludes me.

I can still feel his lips on mine, the way his body pressed against me like he belonged there. His voice echoes in my head. "When you come, I want you thinking of me." The memory of him guiding my hand down my body burns hotter with each heartbeat. I peel off my oversized pajamas, letting the cool air kiss my bare skin, and slip beneath the covers. My body still aches, still hums for a touch that isn't there. But I know what I need.

My fingers slide down my body taking the same path Miles guided me earlier, and it feels like more than touch, like it's his hands on me, guiding every move. My breath comes faster, not just from need, but from the memory of him. The way he looked at me like I was his. My hand slips beneath the band of my panties, grazing over my soaked, swollen bud. A soft moan slips past my lips as I begin to circle, slow and deliberate, just like he would. My back arches, breath catching, and when the release crashes through me, I cry out his name like a prayer I can't hold back. Exhausted, I fall into a dreamless sleep.

***

I blink awake slowly, stretching beneath the covers, sore in the best way from the tension and release of last night. For a moment, I lie still, eyes on the ceiling, the memory of his voice still thick in my head. "When you come, I want you thinking of me." I did. God, I did. And now? I'm more hooked than ever.

I roll out of bed, padding into the kitchen in my underwear and a loose tank top, flipping on the coffee maker. As it gurgles to life, I stare out the window, my mind already spinning. Today, I'm taking the reins. He has no idea who he's messing with. He better be ready. I'm done being the only one squirming.

While I wait for my coffee, I step back into the bedroom and grab a pair of shorts. The morning light pours in as I draw back the curtains in the living room. I grab a bowl of fruit, settle onto the couch and start scrolling through my phone. Just as I'm standing to clear my cup and bowl, I catch movement out of the corner of my eye. I freeze. It's Miles.

He walks by the window, a board slung over one shoulder, and my breath catches. My heart jumps a beat, not just because he looks ridiculously hot in work mode, but because this might be my chance. I want to rattle him, get under his skin the way he's been getting under mine. He's heading toward the dock, boots crunching on the dirt path, sleeves pushed up, jaw set like he's got a job to do.

This is it. Time to shine. I rush to the window and peek out. He's focused, completely unaware. Perfect. I sprint to the shower and make it the fastest one of my life. When I'm out, I throw my hair into a messy bun, dab on just enough makeup and head straight for the dresser. I rummage until I find the bikini I brought. The tiny one. The one I almost didn't pack. I grab my phone and a book and step out the patio door.

14

Harder Than a Two-by-Four

Miles

Leaving her cabin tonight is one of the hardest damn things I've ever done. It took every ounce of self-control not to stay. Not to give in. No matter how badly I want her. I step out into the rain, soaked again, but I barely feel it. My body's on fire, and every muscle is strung tight. My jeans cling uncomfortably to my hard dick, and the throbbing pressure makes every step to my truck agonizing.

I grip the steering wheel harder than necessary as I pull away, jaw tight, trying to focus on my driving and not the way her lips felt on mine. The way she moaned when I guided her hand. The look in her eyes when her hand slid down between her legs.

God, the taste of her mouth is still on my tongue. And I left her there, trembling and breathless, on the damn counter. I groan, shifting in my seat, trying to relieve the pressure in my jeans to no avail. I don't regret walking away, but I'm hanging by a thread.

Pulling into my driveway, I'm still thinking about how badly I wanted to bend her over that counter and make her forget her own name. I climb out of the truck, tugging at my jeans, trying to adjust myself. The ache is unbearable, but honestly, I've got no one to blame but myself. I could've given her what she wanted. Happily.

Hell, I still want to. I'm teetering on the edge of full-on blue balls. This game we're playing, it's actually kind of fun.

When I step into the house, Miss Dashworth is waiting at the door. She makes a break for it, but I block her path and slam the door shut. "Not tonight, you little monster," I mutter, toeing off my boots. "No way I could catch you right now."

I head into the kitchen, grab a glass and fill it with cold water. I down the whole thing in one go, trying to chase away the heat still burning under my skin. I head upstairs, peeling off my wet clothes and tossing them in the hamper. I turn the shower on hot, step in and let the water pour over me. Steam rises around me, but it's not enough. My cock is still rock hard, heavy and aching. Just thinking about her soaked, breathless, legs spread wide for me. I wrap my fist around my cock, remembering the soft moan that slipped from her lips when I pressed her hand down over her own pebbled nipple. I start stroking, slow at first, dragging out the pleasure like I'm savoring every second of her. Her voice, her body, the way she said "You" like I was the only thing in the world she wanted. My pace quickens. I imagine her doing the same thing right now, fingers sliding over her soaked pussy, whispering my name. The pressure builds low and fast, heat curling tight in my stomach. My body tenses, and I groan her name as I come hard, ropes of release spilling over my hand and washing away under the spray. It doesn't ease the ache. If anything, it makes me want her more.

Slightly relieved, I cut the water and step out of the shower, the steam still clinging to the air. I towel off, the heat finally starting to fade from my skin. I throw on a clean pair of boxers and head straight to bed, the exhaustion finally catching up with the tension I've been carrying all damn night. But even as I sink into the mattress, muscles loose and warm, her face is still the last thing I see when I close my eyes.

**

I wake the next morning with her still on my mind, still wanting to be near her. Getting dressed, I head downstairs, scramble up some eggs and start the coffee pot. I eat standing in the kitchen, as usual, no point dirtying the table.

Tonight, the guys are coming over for beers and a bonfire, but all I can think about is seeing Kinsley again. I know I won't make it through the day without getting a glimpse of her, So I head out to the barn, grabbing a few boards and my toolbox. The dock near her cabin needs repair, it's a good excuse. I load everything into the truck and drive around the lake. I don't know what time she usually wakes up, but most mornings I've seen her out on the patio with a cup of coffee.

I park and step out, grabbing my supplies and heading toward the dock. I spot Judy stepping out of her cabin, arms crossed with an amused smile tugging at her lips.

"Oh hi, honey. How was your night? I saw you leaving Kinsley's place last night."

I pause mid-step. I actually wanted to talk to Judy, and now's as good a time as any. "Hey, you got a minute? I wanted to talk to you about something."

Her expression softens with interest. "Sure, why don't you come inside?" she says, gesturing toward her cabin. I set down the boards and toolbox, wiping my hands on my jeans, and follow her in.

She pours us both a cup of coffee, and we settle at the table. She gives me that smile, the one that says she's ready for gossip.

Her eyes twinkle. "So, what did you want to talk about?"

I take a slow sip of my coffee, then level her with a look. "I want to know what you've been up to."

Her smile widens. "Me?" she says with fake innocence.

"Don't play innocent, Judy. I know you've been meddling."

She gasps dramatically, hand to her chest. "Meddling? I would never."

111

I arch a brow, and she snorts into her mug.

"Fine." She laughs mischievously. "Maybe I nudged a few things. But you're a stubborn one, Miles. Someone had to."

I narrow my eyes, trying not to smile. "Judy, I want to know everything you've done. Don't leave anything out." My voice has a little edge, just enough to make my point, but not so much that it cuts. She's still my aunt. And above all else, she gets my respect, even if she's clearly lost her damn mind.

She sighs dramatically, like confessing her crimes is some great burden. "Okay, fine. When Kinsley called to book the cabin, I was going to say no since the season was over. But I put her on hold and maybe looked her up online."

I arch a brow. "You searched her?"

She waves a hand. "Of course I did. And when I didn't find anything bad, no mugshots, and saw how pretty she was, I offered her a discount to stay the full month. Said it was an 'off-season special.'"

I blink at her. "You bribed her to stay longer?"

She admits it, clearly pleased with herself. "Yes, I had a plan. When she got here, I might've let a little air out of her tire."

I stare. "Judy, you didn't?"

"Just a little!" she insists. "Enough that I hoped you'd have to go rescue her. I even watched from my porch to see if you'd leave, but you never did. Old Man Floyd ruined everything."

"Judy, she could've been hurt." The thought of that disturbs me. "What were you thinking?"

She rolls her eyes, unfazed. "Don't be silly, Miles. I drew her a map, sent her the long way around so she'd avoid traffic and any deep ditches. And…" She pauses, sipping her coffee with a smug little smile. "I wrote your phone number on the back. Just in case."

I stare at her, somewhere between impressed and horrified. "So, you sabotaged her tire and played matchmaker?" I try to sound annoyed but fail. Deep down, I'm torn between disbelief and gratitude. Because as ridiculous as her schemes are, part of me knows I wouldn't have made a move without her shove.

She shrugs like it's the most logical thing in the world. "I nudged fate. That's all. And judging by the way you looked leaving her cabin last night, I'd say it's working."

I sigh, exasperated. "What else have you done?"

Judy doesn't even pretend to feel guilty. She brightens like she's been waiting to confess. "Well," she begins, stirring her coffee like it's casual chit-chat, "when you didn't leave to help her with the tire, I called and sent you to the store. Thought maybe you'd run into each other there."

I stare at her. "Seriously?"

She nods, completely unapologetic. "And I may have, purposefully, baked an extra pie. Just so you'd have a reason to meet her."

I rub the back of my neck, irritated and a little impressed. "So basically, you've been engineering this whole thing behind the scenes?"

Judy shrugs. "You're welcome."

"Is there more?" I lean back in my chair, bracing myself.

Judy lifts her mug, eyes dancing. "Only that I invited you both to dinner. Had her bring your favorite cookies and didn't tell either of you."

I shake my head, biting back a laugh. Honestly, I want to tell her I'm a little disappointed. But the truth is, Judy's been the best damn wingman ever. So instead, I just sigh. "No more meddling. Just let whatever happens, happen. Got it?"

113

She grins, entirely unbothered. "Got it." She's clearly lying, and we both know it.

I stand and kiss Judy on the forehead. Before stepping out the door, I glance back one more time and point a finger at her. "No more meddling." She waves me off, eyes twinkling with mischief as she sips her coffee.

Grabbing my things, I head down to the dock, hoping to catch a glimpse of Kinsley. But when I walk past her cabin, she's nowhere in sight. I get straight to work, peeling up the old boards. Still, I keep glancing toward her place like a damn fool.

That's when I see her, laying out in the sun, face up, wearing the world's smallest bikini. Confidence radiates off her like heat from the deck, and it hits me low and hard. She knows exactly what she's doing. Smirking, I shake my head. *Oh, she's good... But I'm better.*

I stand and pull off my T-shirt, muscles stretching just a little more than necessary, and get to work on the dock. I keep her in my peripheral vision, trying to stay focused, but then she stands and turns around. She bends, slow and deliberate to set her book down, giving me a perfect view of her ass. I'm no longer pretending not to look.

When she turns and saunters toward me, hips swaying, I catch myself biting my bottom lip. She stops right in front of me. "It's a beautiful day for a swim. Is the dock safe to use?"

You little temptress. I stand to meet her gaze, giving her a slow once-over that I don't bother hiding.

"It is now." I nod. "But tell me, City Girl, do you even know how to swim?"

She arches a brow, smirk deepening. "Please." She steps just a little closer. "I swim better than most people walk."

Then she leans in, her voice smooth. "Question is, can you keep up, Country Boy?"

I let out a low laugh, shaking my head as she walks backwards to the lake.

"Oh, I can keep up." I peel off my boots, tossing them aside. Her eyes are still on me, so I take my time unbuttoning my jeans and sliding them down, revealing my boxers, not that I care. I'm not wearing wet jeans two days in a row. "Question is, what happens when I catch you?" I ask when my jeans hit the ground.

She glances over her shoulder, one brow raised, eyes sparkling. "Guess you'll just have to find out." Then she dives in, smooth as a damn otter, leaving nothing but ripples and a challenge in her wake. I don't even hesitate. I'm right behind her.

She surfaces ahead of me, laughing as she kicks off and puts distance between us. "Oh, it's like that?" I call out, grinning as I start after her.

"Try to keep up, Country Boy!" Her voice echoes off the water. I chase her, cutting through the lake with long strokes. She's fast, faster than I expected but she keeps glancing back, making sure I'm still behind her. Tempting me. Twice I nearly catch her, fingertips brushing her ankle, but she kicks away, laughing so hard she nearly swallows water.

"You keep running…" I close the distance between us. "And I'm gonna think you're scared."

"Of you?" she calls over her shoulder. "Never."

That's when I pick up my pace. One last push, and I lunge forward, grabbing her around the waist. She squeals and tries to wriggle free, but I've got her now, pulled up tight against me, both of us breathless and laughing.

"Told you I'd catch you," I murmur near her ear.

She turns, lips so close I can taste the grin on her face. "Took you long enough."

"The chase is the best part." My voice drops, half referring to the swim, half to last night's teasing.

She wraps her arms around my neck, pressing her body flush against mine. Her hardened nipples brush my chest, sending a spark straight through me. There's no way she doesn't feel how hard I am pressed firmly against her thighs beneath the water. Her eyes flick to mine, and for a moment, neither of us move. The playful energy lingers, but under it something heavier, hotter.

She shifts slightly, just enough to feel all of me, and leans in until her lips graze my jaw. "So, what happens now that you've caught me?" she whispers, wrapping her legs around my waist.

My jaw tightens the second I feel her heat through the thin fabric between us, pressed right against the hard length of me. "Kinsley." My voice is filled with a warning.

I'm one second, one breath, one slip away from pushing her bottoms aside and sliding into her right here in the lake. She just smirks, head tilted with shameless confidence, and slowly grinds her hips against me, letting the warm, slick heat of her pussy drag across the full length of my throbbing cock. Every muscle in my body locks up.

She leans in, lips brushing my ear. "Still think the chase is the best part?"

Hell no. Not when she's this close. Not when I can still feel the heat of her against me. But before I can say it, she's already gone.

Without warning, she drops her legs from around my waist and slips from my grasp, diving beneath the surface. By the time I blink, she's already swimming away. I'm left floating there, hard as hell, stunned and thoroughly impressed.

15

Seduction. Shock. Shelter.

Kinsley

I swim to shore with a grin tugging at my lips, satisfaction humming through me. I'm proud of myself for gaining the upper hand. He's strong, steady and ridiculously hot, but right now, he's the one left stunned in the water. Exactly where I want him.

While I've still got the lead, I move fast. No time to lose. I briskly walk to the cabin, water dripping down my skin as I grab two towels. Then I turn on my heel and head back to the dock, heart pounding with adrenaline and maybe just a little heat. Okay…a lot of heat.

Feeling how hard he was surprised me. Realizing how big he is, that makes my breath catch, equal parts thrill and nerves. It wasn't just physical; it was the rush of knowing how real this is becoming. I almost gasped when I slid up him, but I kept it together. There's no mistake, he wanted me. I know damn well he'll need a minute in that water before he can walk up this dock looking halfway composed.

I reach the dock, towels in hand, and settle onto the warm wood, legs stretched out, pretending not to look. He's still in the water, floating for a moment, arms spread, head tilted back like he's trying to soak in the sky or chase away the heat I left buzzing through him.

Then he starts swimming toward shore, slow and steady, like he's got all the time in the world. But I don't miss the tension in his jaw. I bite my lip, pleased with myself, trying to suppress a giggling fit. By the time he pulls himself up onto the dock, water streaming off his body, boxers clinging to every inch of muscle, I've got my best innocent face locked in.

I offer him a towel like I didn't just swim circles around him, physically and otherwise. "Thought you might need this."

He takes the towel with a slight nod, then drops down beside me like nothing happened. No heavy breathing, no lingering looks, just stretches out on the dock, arms behind his head, eyes closed like he's settling in for a damn nap. Like I didn't just grind against him in the water. Like he's not still hard under that towel. Maybe it didn't affect him like I thought it did.

My fingers twitch. I want to poke him. Or kiss him. Or demand he admit I got to him. He finally opens one eye and looks at me. "Something on your mind, City Girl?" Cocky. Smug. And far too composed. *Damn it.*

I roll onto my side to face him, brushing damp hair off my cheek. This time, I don't smirk. Don't tease. "How do you do that?" I'm quieter now, a little more serious. His brow lifts, but he doesn't play dumb. He knows exactly what I mean.

"How do you stay so calm? Like I didn't just…" I trail off, frustrated by how much he's gotten under my skin, and how badly I want him to stay there. He doesn't answer right away. Just watches me for a beat, eyes darker now.

His voice is low and steady. "I'm anything but calm, Kinsley. But I like control." The way he says it, it's not a warning. It's a confession. He rolls onto his side, mirroring me, propped on one elbow. His eyes search mine, not playful now, but quiet. Intent. Like he's asking a question without saying a word.

118

Just as I'm about to say something, I catch movement over his shoulder. My eyes lock on it. A bear, nose lifted like it caught our scent. I go rigid. The words die in my throat. Miles' eyes narrow instantly. He reads my face, doesn't even look before reacting. In one smooth motion, he grabs me and rolls us both off the dock. We hit the water hard, the cold shocking the air from my lungs as we sink beneath the surface. Everything goes muffled. Weightless. Then we break the surface again, gasping. He pulls me close, scanning the shoreline, voice low and urgent in my ear.

"Don't move. Just float. Let's see what it does."

We float slowly, away from the dock, keeping our movements small and quiet. The bear sniffs around, its massive frame shifting along the edge of the lake. It doesn't seem to be in a hurry, just curious. But we don't take any chances. When we finally drift far enough to feel a sliver of safety, I realize I'm shaking. Not just a little. My body trembles uncontrollably, cold water clinging to my skin, adrenaline burning out fast. My teeth chatter, sharp and loud in the silence between us. Miles notices at once. He pulls me in close, arms strong around me.

"I've got you." His voice is calm, steady.

I risk a glance back toward the dock. The bear is there. Its massive paws press down on the same place we were stretched out. My body shudders again, this time not from the cold. What if I hadn't seen it? What if I'd been one second slower? What if Miles hadn't reacted so fast? The weight of it hits me all at once, how close we came.

"Miles," I whisper, my voice trembling now for a different reason.

"I know, baby," he says quietly, like he can feel the thoughts racing through me. His arms tighten around me in the water. "But you did. You saw it."

I close my eyes and press my forehead to his shoulder, breathing in the scent of lake water and woodsmoke clinging to his skin. I relax, knowing Miles won't let anything happen to me, but I'm still a little scared and still shaking.

That's when I hear it. "Miles! Kinsley!" Judy's panic cuts through the air.

I lift my head just in time to see her charging toward the dock in a frenzy, shotgun in hand, arms stretched wide like she's ready to take on the entire wilderness. She's barefoot, hair flying, and wearing a garden smock. The bear, startled by the noise and the sight of her barreling forward like a one-woman army, freezes for half a second, then turns and bolts, crashing back into the woods.

Even though the danger's gone, even though Judy's still yelling and pacing the dock like she's looking for a second round, Miles shifts his grip, adjusting me gently in his arms. His voice is calm but firm. "Let's get you out of here."

We swim back to shore, Miles not letting me go. With strong strokes, he pulls us through the water until we reach the shore. Completely focused.

He lifts me just enough to get my feet under me and guides me through the shallows, never letting go, never rushing. As soon as we're on solid ground, he wraps the towel around my shoulders and pulls me close.

"Oh, sweetheart, are you okay?" Judy rushes to us the moment we reach the shore, shotgun still in hand. She cups my face gently, her palms warm despite everything. "You scared the life out of me."

Miles steps in, his voice rooted. "I'm going to take her in, get her dried off." He looks at Judy with real gratitude. "Thank you."

Judy nods, eyes soft but still sharp. "Go on, I'll bring your things up to the cabin and leave 'em by the door."

Miles gives her a small nod, then shifts his arm more securely around me. "Come on, City Girl." He gently guides me toward the cabin. "Let's get you warm."

I'm freezing from the cold water and adrenaline dump. My teeth are chattering, and goosebumps line my skin. I don't argue. I just lean into his warmth and let him lead me. Once we step inside the cabin, the warmth hits us like a gentle wall, but it's not enough. I'm still shivering, soaked to the bone. "I'm so cold."

Miles doesn't hesitate. He lifts me, one arm beneath my knees, the other around my back, and carries me through the hallway like I weigh nothing. He pushes open the bathroom door with his shoulder, then leans in and twists the shower knob with one hand, turning the water on high. Steam begins to rise instantly, fogging the glass. He tests it with his fingers, then looks down at me, his voice low. "You'll warm up quick." He steps in, with me still in his arms. The water cascades over us both, hot and steamy, washing away lake water, cold, fear. He just holds me there. Solid. Quiet. Unmoving. Until I find my words.

I rest my head on his shoulder. "Thank you." He presses a soft kiss to the top of my head. I close my eyes, breathing him in. I tilt my face up, my eyes searching his.

"Are you okay?" My tone soft, worried by how quiet he's gone.

"Yes," he says simply, brushing a wet strand of hair from my face.

I slide out of his arms, the warmth of the water quickly replaced by the chill in the air and look up into his eyes. Then I step closer, rising up on my toes, and press a gentle kiss to his lips. It's not deep. It's not rushed. Just full of quiet meaning. Then I step out of the shower without a word. Behind me, I hear the water shut off. I reach for the towels, hands steady now, grabbing one for him and one for me.

We dry off in silence, still wrapped in the quiet aftermath of everything. I slip from the bathroom and pad to the door, opening it just enough to find his clothes folded neatly on a chair outside, exactly where Judy said she'd leave them.

I bring them in and set them down nearby, and Miles disappears back into the bathroom to change. I head to my bedroom, choosing a soft pair of leggings, tugging on a worn sweatshirt, running my fingers through my damp hair as I glance in the mirror.

When I step back into the living room, he's already there, fully dressed, boots on, and waiting. His eyes meet mine across the room. He's distant and reluctant.

"Would you like something to drink?" I walk into the kitchen and flip the coffee pot on. Normally I don't drink coffee this late in the day, but right now I just need something warm in my hands.

Miles steps into the kitchen behind me. "No. I need to check on the animals, and I've got a few things to get done. Thanks for asking."

I nod without turning around, staring at the coffee slowly dripping into the pot. But then I hear his footsteps, closer this time. Before I can say a word, he steps in behind me and gently turns me around to face him. His hands come up, cupping my face and kisses me with relief. When he finally pulls back, he lingers close.

"I'll see you around," he says quietly, his breath warm on my lips. He takes a small step back, his hands drifting from my face to my arms, giving me one last grounding touch before releasing me.

He reaches for the door, hesitates with his hand on the knob and glances over his shoulder. "Judy'll be by to check on you." His eyes hold mine for just a second longer. Then, he walks out into the late afternoon.

I grab my coffee and sit on the couch, pulling a throw blanket over me. I turn on the TV, needing something, anything, to distract me. I wish he could've stayed. I really don't want to be alone. Karma's a bitch. And she hits hard. I tried to seduce him, make him beg, and what did I get? A fucking bear. One second I was riding a high, feeling sexy and in charge, and the next, I was frozen in fear. That shift, was so fast, so jarring. Yeah, I won't be pissing karma off again. Besides, I kinda like him in control.

When I saw the bear, I froze like a scared little kid. I feel stupid. I didn't do anything. But Miles, he was fast. He didn't even look over his shoulder. He just knew by the look on my face. When my body wouldn't stop shaking, he took control, like he always does. He carried me to the shower not out of want. To make it better. And he did. Just holding me worked. But he went above that, washing the cold from my body, the fear from my bones. That's when I felt the shift in his mood like he was worried, maybe even upset, but I don't know why.

Suddenly, there's a knock at the door, startling me back to reality. It's Judy. Happy for the company, I open the door and step aside.

"Come in." My voice comes out quieter than usual.

Judy steps inside without hesitation, her eyes scanning me like a mother hen taking inventory. She sets a small bag down by the door. "How are you feeling?"

"I'm still a little cold, is all," I lie. The truth is, I just don't want to be alone. But Judy sees right through me.

"I thought we could play a few card games. Might help lighten the mood."

"That sounds perfect." We play for a couple of hours. She beats me every single time, and I start to suspect she might be a card shark in disguise. By the time we finish, I'm feeling much better.

"Would you like to stay for dinner?"

"That would be lovely," she practically sings, already halfway to the door. "I'll run to my cabin and grab the cake I baked this morning for dessert. I'll be right back!"

Her excitement makes me chuckle. As the door closes behind her, I head to the kitchen and start dinner. I decide to keep it simple. Tacos. It makes me think of Miles and his short, laughable list of cooking abilities.

Judy returns a few minutes later, a carrot cake in hand and a big smile on her face. She helps in the kitchen, chopping lettuce and tomatoes while I brown the ground beef. We make tacos and eat on the couch, plates in our laps, just enjoying each other's company. No big conversations. No pressure. Just the comfort of not being alone.

After we finish eating, Judy glances over at me. "Feel like taking a walk?"

I hesitate but then nod. "Sure, why not." We stop by her cabin on the way out, and she grabs a lantern. An actual lantern, with a handle and flickering light and everything. It's the most country shit I've ever seen. But I roll with it. I let her lead the way. As soon as we step onto the path behind her cabin, I know exactly where we're going. Miles' house. My heart thuds with every step.

16

Swing First, Talk Later

Miles

When I step out the door of her cabin, I'm angry with myself for getting too close. I see Judy sitting in a rocking chair just outside her cabin. As I approach, she lifts her head, a small smile on her face.

"Is everything okay now?"

I try to subdue the anger simmering inside me, anger mostly aimed at myself. My jaw clenches before I manage to speak. "Everything's fine. I won't be back to check on her. You'll need to do that."

I start to walk away, but Judy sets her book down and calls after me. "What happened? Why are you so upset?"

"Nothing happened. I just, I can't do this." I gesture sharply between myself and Kinsley's cabin.

Judy rises to her feet, her tone gentle but firm. "Miles, no one was hurt. Don't do something you'll regret."

I suck in a breath, irritation flaring. "Stop meddling, Judy."

She takes a patient breath, crosses her arms but doesn't push further. "I'm going to let you have your moment, but sooner or later, you're going to have to face her."

I don't say anything else. Just turn and walk. Each step away from Judy feels heavier than the last. By the time I reach my truck, my hands are fists and my chest feels too damn tight.

I slam the door harder than I mean to and start the engine, gravel spitting under the tires as I pull away. The silence in the cab doesn't help. It just gives my thoughts more room to yell at me.

I'm mad at Judy for pushing. Mad at Kinsley for showing up and messing with my head. But mostly, I'm pissed at myself for being weak. For letting my guard down. For letting her in.

"Stupid." I grip the wheel tighter. "Should've known better."

She's got this way of getting under my skin, twisting me up inside with that damn smile and all that fire in her. I tried to keep my distance. I tried. But I couldn't stop myself, and now look at me, acting like some heart-struck fool in a truck full of regret.

Yeah, she wasn't hurt. I know that. But if I hadn't acted in time, if something had happened... that's the part that scares me most. I've got feelings for her. Deep ones. Ones I didn't see coming and sure as hell didn't ask for, and now they're tangled up in everything. I can't shut them off.

I won't go through what my mom did, waiting day after day, never knowing if my dad was coming home from the woods. Watching her wear that fear like a second skin. I can't live like that. I won't sit around praying someone I care about makes it home. I won't live with that kind of fear, not ever. I've got a farm to think about. A life I've built with my own two hands. I can't let some woman, no matter how strong or stubborn or beautiful, come in and shake it all loose. Even if every part of me already feels like it's unraveling.

Pulling into my driveway, I kill the engine and slam the door hard enough to rattle the windows. I head straight for the barn, grab the axe without a second thought and make my way to the woodpile behind the house. If I can't quiet my head, I'll exhaust my body.

I swing. Over and over. Each log splitting under the weight of my anger, my frustration, my goddamn feelings. Sweat pours down my face and soaks through my shirt until I yank it off, tossing it to the ground. My chest heaves, breath coming fast, but I don't stop. Not yet. Muscles burning, hands raw around the handle, I keep going, because stopping means thinking.

I'm mid-swing when I hear a voice behind me. "Damn, you planning to chop wood for the whole county?" It's Reed.

I drop the axe and lean forward, hands braced on my knees, panting hard. I don't answer right away. He waits a second, then adds, "Judy called." *Of course she did.*

I shake my head and grab the axe again, ready to take another swing, ready to split something wide open just so I don't have to feel what's crawling under my skin. But Reed steps forward, and grabs the handle before I can bring it down.

"Reed, let go of the fucking axe," I spit, eyes locked on his.

He doesn't flinch. "Not until you stop acting like a damn psycho."

My grip tightens, jaw set. We're locked in a silent standoff, both too stubborn to back down. The tension stretches thick between us, me vibrating with frustration, him standing there like a damn wall I can't swing through.

"Talk to me, Miles. Or swing and take my damn hand off. Your call."

I huff and drop the axe. It lands with a dull thud in the dirt. I won't hurt him. We might've thrown punches as kids but not now. Still, I'm damn close. I don't meet his eyes. Instead, I stare out past the tree, toward the lake, toward her cabin.

"What did Judy tell you?" My voice is tight.

Reed doesn't answer right away. I hear him shift beside me, crossing his arms. "That you pushed Kinsley away. That you're pissed. That you're scared."

That last part lands like a punch to the gut. "I'm not fucking scared," I snap, but the words sound weak even to me.

Reed lets the silence hang, like he's giving me space to admit what we both know what's true.

"What do you want me to say, Reed?" I bark, finally turning toward him. "That I like her? Fine. I like her. A lot. And she's gonna leave and today she could've been hurt." The words rip out of me like a confession I didn't mean to make.

"I knew it the second I met her. She's not staying. This place? This life? It's not hers. And I got involved anyway." I drag a hand through my hair. "So yeah, I'm fucking stupid, alright?" I shoot him a look, daring him to argue. To agree. To say anything at all. Reed doesn't flinch.

"If that's how you really feel, then send her packing. Make her leave now. Do yourself a favor and shut the door before it gets any harder." He steps closer, not angry, just honest. "But if you do, you're gonna regret it. Probably forever." He lets that sink in, eyes locked on mine. "So, ask yourself, Miles, are you really willing to risk that? To walk away from the possibility that she's the one? Just because you're scared?"

I run my hands through my hair, fingers tugging at the roots, then lean my head back and close my eyes. All the fear, the frustration, the longing, it's all still there, buzzing under my skin like static. But when I speak, it's quiet. Final. "No."

Reed doesn't say anything, just stands there, letting the answer settle between us. I open my eyes and look out toward the lake again. Toward her.

Reed claps a hand on my shoulder. "Come on, let's grill up some burgers before the guys get here."

He starts walking toward the house, and after a second, I follow. "Tell me how this whole thing even started between you two."

I let out a tired breath, half laugh, half sigh. While the grill heats up, and the sun dips low behind the trees, I tell him everything. Well, almost everything. Reed leans against the porch post, sipping a beer, while I flip burgers and unload the mess that's been building in my mind for days. I tell him about the grocery store, the surprise pie, the long walk back from the trail. I tell him how she challenges me, makes me laugh, drives me absolutely insane in the best and worst ways. I leave out the part about the kitchen counter. Some things are better left unsaid.

By the time Dylan and Luke pull up, I've said more than I thought I would. Reed doesn't say much, just listens, nods, tosses in the occasional grunt of understanding like only a brother can. And somehow, I feel a little less wrecked.

Dylan bounds up the steps like he owns the place, a twelve-pack of beer tucked under one arm and a crooked grin on his face. "Judy called me," he announces, like it's the most normal damn thing in the world.

I groan and glance at Reed. "Of course she did."

"She said you're being a stubborn ass and might need backup," Dylan sets the beer on the table, pulling one out like he's settling in for a show.

"Fantastic," I mutter, flipping a burger with more force than necessary.

"Hey, I'm just here for the drama and the food," Dylan says, popping the cap and taking a long drink. "Preferably in that order."

Reed chuckles, and for the first time all day, I let myself crack a small smile. Just for a second. Then Luke rolls in with beer and a bag of chips with a look that says he knows something, too. Great. Now it's a damn intervention.

We light the bonfire once the sun disappears behind the forest. I definitely have enough wood to burn. Hell, I probably chopped enough to last the next twenty bonfires. The flames crackle and pop, sparks rising into the night as we settle around it with full plates and cold beers. It doesn't take long before we're poking fun at each other, laughing like a bunch of overgrown adolescents with too much history and not enough maturity to let anything slide.

Dylan starts in on the time Reed fell off the tractor trying to impress a girl. Reed fires back with a story about Dylan crying after getting chased by a goose when he was eight. Luke manages to throw in a one-liner that sends beer spewing from Dylan's nose. We laugh so hard my stomach hurts. For a little while, I forget about everything else, about the cabin across the lake, about the ache sitting just beneath my ribs. Tonight, I let it go. Just for a little while.

A soft glow flickers through the trees, heading toward us from the path. My chest tightens the second I recognize it. A lantern. Judy's the only person I know who still insists on using a damn lantern, like it's 1905. I shake my head, half-expecting her to show up with one of her cryptic sayings or a fresh pie. But when they step into the firelight, it's not just Judy. Kinsley's with her. Suddenly the fire feels hotter, and my whole body tenses like it's been hit with a live wire. Kinsley doesn't know I had a battle with myself today and as far as I'm concerned, she never will. At least not yet. Maybe someday I'll tell her how close I came to walking away and how damn hard it was not to.

Before I can say a word, Dylan bolts upright, nearly tripping over his chair in a rush and steps in front of her, extending a hand. "Hi, I'm Dylan. Unattached. Emotionally stable. Good with my hands."

Reed slides in next to him. "And I cook. Just sayin.' Farm-raised and single."

Luke doesn't even try to hide his grin. "Careful now, boys. Miles might finally explode."

I step forward, slow and sharp. "Touch her and I'll bury you both behind the barn." I know what they're doing. They're purposely trying to make me jealous.

The guys back off just a step, cracking up. Reed claps me on the back. "Relax, just making sure you're still breathing."

I shoot them a glare. "You two ever shut up?"

"Not when we're this entertained," Dylan says, flopping back into his chair.

I glance at Kinsley, who's clearly enjoying the show. Despite everything, I can feel a smile tug at the corner of my mouth.

Once the banter settles and Kinsley steps back beside Judy, the guys shift their attention like a pack of golden retrievers spotting their favorite person.

"Well, look who finally brought class to the party," Reed jokes, stepping up to give Judy a kiss on the cheek.

"About time," Dylan chimes in, wrapping her in a quick hug. "We were out here roughin' it."

Luke, not one to be outdone, swoops in with exaggerated charm. "Miss Judy, you look radiant tonight. That lantern glow suits you."

Judy laughs, clearly eating it up. "Y'all are full of it but keep talkin'."

She basks in their attention, smiling like a queen holding court. She's been the heart of this place for a while, and we all know it. We might give her hell sometimes, but when she walks in, everything shifts just a little warmer.

"I brought Kinsley. Figured it was time she met all of you."

Dylan, unable to help himself turn on the charm. "Ladies, allow me to be a gentleman for once." He makes a dramatic show of grabbing two chairs from the porch and dragging them over to the fire. Then he looks directly at me, smirking, and says to Kinsley,

"You can sit next to me. I promise I only flirt when I'm sober, which means you've got about fifteen minutes."

Luke snorts. Reed nearly chokes on his beer. I narrow my eyes at him, slow and warning. "Dylan."

"What?" he says innocently, plopping into his own chair. "She deserves options."

"If you keep running your mouth, you're gonna be sittin' on the ground holding your nose." I snatch the chair right out of his hand, give him a playful punch to the arm, and set it down next to mine, right where I want her. Kinsley hides a smile, but her eyes say everything.

Judy slides her chair right in the middle of us like it's a throne and we're her court jesters. Which, honestly, we probably are. I head over to the cooler and grab a couple of beers, handing one to each of them. They both accept without hesitation, and the shenanigans start back up.

But this time, everyone's involved. Kinsley's throwing jabs like she's known us her whole life, Judy holding her own and firing back twice as hard, the guys competing over who can tell the most ridiculous story from our childhood.

After a while, Judy stands up, brushing off her jeans with a small sigh. "Alright, boys. I've had my fill of your nonsense for one night."

Luke steps in before she can say more. "Come on, I'll drive you back."

She gives him a pat on the cheek. "You're a good man, Luke." Then she throws a wink at the rest of us. "Try not to burn anything down while I'm gone."

They walk around the house, and a few minutes later, Luke's truck rumbles away. Reed and Dylan are another story. They've had more beers than they should've, and it shows.

He grins, not even trying to hide it. "No, you don't."

"You're walking me, but don't get cocky about it." He's already won, and we both know it, but I'll be damned if I hand him a victory lap, too.

He chuckles, then, without a word, reaches down and grabs my hand. I blink, surprised. His grip is warm, steady, fingers lacing with mine like it's the most natural thing in the world. So naturally, I pounce on the opportunity. I lift our joined hands between us, arching a brow. "Wait, are you secretly the one that's too chicken to walk this path alone?"

His expression shifts slightly, so fast I almost miss it. Just a flicker. A tightening of his jaw. Then his eyes lock on mine, sharp and unreadable. For a second, I forget how to breathe.

"Is that what you think?" His voice is low, quiet in a way that doesn't match the smirk from earlier.

I meant it as a joke. I meant to keep it light. But the way he's looking at me now, he's not hiding behind humor anymore. It makes my heart kick hard against my ribs. I try to recover, try to stay in control. "I don't know," I say, forcing a shrug. "You're the one initiating handholding on a spooky path."

Quickly, he spins me toward him before I even register what's happening. My breath catches, adrenaline flooding through me like a crashing wave. Suddenly I'm chest to chest with him, one hand on my throat the other on my waist, he squeezes lightly, his mouth inches from mine. The flashlight drops slightly in my grip, casting a beam across the trees.

"Are you scared now?" His tone dark, almost a dare.

I should say no. I want to say no. But there's no air left in my lungs, and the way he's looking at me, strips me bare.

"Yes," I whisper, So quiet I'm not sure I even said it out loud. Not because I'm scared of him, but because at this moment I'm so turned on, I have to squeeze my thighs together to stop the ache.

His mouth tilts into the faintest smile. "You should be." He growls.

"I'm not scared of you," I breathe, needing him to know. "I'm scared of what this feels like."

I reach out and grip his chest, fingers curling into his shirt, nails digging in just enough to ground myself. His heartbeat thunders beneath my palm, steady and strong, like he's holding it all in by sheer force.

"What are you scared of?" I ask, barely above a whisper.

His jaw clenches. His whole body tightens, like he didn't expect the question, or like he's been holding back the answer too long. He leans in, slow and deliberate, his nose brushing mine, breath warm against my mouth. My eyes flutter shut, the contact so achingly tender I could cry from the weight of it.

"Only one thing scares me." His voice is strained, ragged with truth. "I'm scared of what I'd do if something happened to you."

The words hit me like a punch straight to the gut. My eyes fly open in shock, No one's ever said that to me before. Not with their hands on me like I'm something breakable and worth protecting.

Then he shakes his head, slowly pulling back. His hands leave my body, and I feel the loss instantly. But he doesn't let me go completely, his fingers curl back around mine, grounding both of us.

We walk in silence. The tension between us builds with every step, thick and tight like it's clinging to our skin. By the time we reach my cabin, it's a miracle I'm still standing.

I turn to face him, heart hammering. "Do you want to come in?"

He doesn't answer. He just drops my hand, steps forward and cups my face.

"I want to." His voice is raw against the quiet. "God, Kinsley, I want to."

Then he kisses me. It's toe-curling, like he's telling me all the things he can't say with words. When he finally breaks the kiss, breath ragged, his forehead rests against mine. "That's why I can't."

My heart clenches, but I nod, trying to find air. "Then kiss me like that again tomorrow."

He takes a slow step back, the weight of the moment still thick between us. Then, of course, he smirks. "Do you plan on wearing that bikini again tomorrow?" he asks, voice casual, like he didn't just kiss the life out of me. "If so, what time? I want to make sure I don't miss the show."

I stare at him, stunned for half a second. Then I narrow my eyes. "If I do," I say sweetly, "I'll call Dylan." The second the words leave my mouth, I see it. That flicker in his expression. The smirk falters, jaw tightens, and just like that, he's lit up.

His eyes darken as he steps forward again. "Don't."

I raise a brow, playing it cool even though my heart's thudding like crazy. "Don't what?"

He stops just inches from me, voice low and dangerous now. "Don't play with me, Kinsley."

I tilt my head, fighting a smile. "Why not? You started it."

His jaw clenches, and for a second I think he's going to kiss me again. Harder this time. Rougher. But instead, he steps back, running a hand through his hair like he's trying to shake me off.

"You're impossible," he mutters, like he's half exasperated, half turned on, backing away before he does something reckless.

"You like it," I tease, grinning as I head inside.

He throws a look over his shoulder, smirk back in full force. "Yeah, and that's the problem. Good night, Kinsley."

"Good night, Miles." With that, he walks off into the night, hands in his pockets like he's not leaving me completely unraveled on my own damn porch.

As I walk into the cabin, I let a long exhale. "What a day." The words slip out under my breath. I head straight to the bathroom, take a quick shower and slip into a tank top and shorts. With a glass of wine in hand, I curl up on the couch, finally letting myself process everything that happened tonight.

Meeting his brother and friends was a lot. But in the best way. Reed, his brother, looks so much like Miles it's a little unsettling. He's little taller, maybe. I know he's a firefighter, and he's got tattoos down his arm. There's a quiet intensity about him, like he's the one everyone leans on when things go sideways.

Luke wasn't what I expected at all. Dressed down, relaxed, but I can tell he's a businessman. Dark brown hair, around the same height as Miles. He's kind of a mystery, smooth, a little playful, but guarded in a way that makes you wonder what he's hiding.

Dylan is tanned, tattooed and built like someone who works hard for a living. With that dark blonde hair and easy laugh, he feels like the type who's always got a project going. I heard Miles say he owns a construction company. Makes sense. They're all good-looking men, ridiculously so. But Miles? He's the one. In my eyes, there's no comparison.

All of them have this closeness, the kind you don't fake. The kind that comes from growing up together, going through real shit, and coming out the other side stronger. It reminded me of Raelynn and me, how we know each other without needing words.

Then there's Judy. God, she was so happy tonight being with them all. It was heartwarming, the way they love her, how natural it is between them. And I get it now. I really do. She's everything, sharp and warm and a little bit wild. I had such a good time with her today.

The wine warms me as I sink deeper into the cushions, thinking about everything Miles just said. That he's scared of

Reed tries to stand, wobbles, and points toward the house. "I call the big guest room."

"You always call the big guest room," Dylan grumbles, stumbling after him.

"Because I'm faster, smarter and better looking."

"Keep telling yourself that." They vanish inside, trading insults and bumping into furniture.

Kinsley and I are the only ones left. I feel like the group took some kind of silent cue from Judy. The quiet between us now feels loaded, like something's about to shift.

17

A Dare in the Dark

Kinsley

We sit in a pocket of quiet, the guys long gone, the fire dying down to glowing embers. The stars are brilliant tonight, clear and bold in the inky sky, and for a second, it all feels too peaceful to speak. But silence with Miles is tricky. It's not awkward. It's not uncomfortable. It's just, full. Like there's a whole conversation happening in the quiet, and I'm the only one not fluent in it.

I glance over at him. "So, your friends are a trip."

Miles snorts softly. "That's one word for them."

"I mean, Dylan practically proposed. Reed offered me food and his entire dating résumé. And Luke just gave me this look like he already knows everything about me."

"They're as subtle as sledgehammers," he says, smiling into his beer. "But they're good guys."

"You seem different tonight." I keep it light, just testing the waters. "More relaxed."

He shrugs one shoulder. "Hard not to be with them around. They don't let me stew for long."

I file that away. Stew? So maybe there was something under the surface earlier. Maybe I wasn't the only one feeling off. "You don't seem like someone who stews."

He glances at me then, that steady gaze of his pinning me in place. "I don't. Usually."

Something about the way he says that makes my stomach flip, but he doesn't elaborate, and I don't push. I'm not sure I'm ready to know what's behind that shift.

"I'm glad I came tonight."

Miles doesn't answer right away, but when he does, it's quiet. "Me too."

Just two words. But somehow, they say enough.

I stand slowly, brushing my hands off on my leggings. I force a small smile. "I better head back." The second the words leave my mouth, my chest tightens. I don't want to go. Not really. But I also don't want to drag him away from his night with the guys.

From inside the house, I can still hear laughter, then something crashing against the wall, followed by what sounds like Reed cursing and Dylan laughing so hard he can barely breathe. Definitely still awake. Definitely still drunk.

"I should let you get back to them." I tip my head toward the house. "Sounds like they need adult supervision."

Miles doesn't move at first. Just watches me, his face unreadable in the firelight. Then he slowly stands. "I'll walk you back," he offers, already stepping toward me.

"No, really," I cut in quickly, holding up a hand. "It's fine. Be with your friends. I think I can manage."

He doesn't stop walking. Even after I try to wave him off, even after I pretend I've got this covered, he keeps coming until he's standing right in front of me. Close enough that I can smell the fire on his skin. Close enough that I forget to breathe. He reaches out,

135

slow, lifting my chin with two fingers, tilting my face up until I have no choice but to look him in the eyes.

"Kinsley, we both know you're scared of the dark."

I swallow hard, my pride fraying at the edges. "It's not that bad."

One brow lifts. His lips twitch into a smirk that cuts straight through me. "In that case, go ahead. I'll see you tomorrow."

He takes a half-step back, cocky as hell, like he's calling my bluff, and the worst part is, he's right. I know it. He knows it. My mouth opens, but nothing comes out. Because I'm bluffing, and we both know damn well I don't want to walk down the path alone. Not after today. Not with my nerves still shot and the dark feeling thicker than usual. But the stubborn part of me pulls out my phone and turns on its flashlight. I can only see one foot in front of me, making it even harder to see past its shitty beam.

The part that hates being read like a book wants to turn around just to prove a point. So, I lift my chin. "Fine." I turn and take one step toward the path. Then another.

My hand is shaking, gripping my phone so hard I could snap it. I tell myself it's fine, that I'm fine, but the shadows feel heavier tonight, pressing in like they know I'm bluffing. Great. I get to the edge of the path, and suddenly the shadows feel alive. A low rustle to my left makes my heart flutter.

I stop. I don't turn around. Not yet. But I hear him behind me, still standing there. Waiting. Smirking, probably. My fingers tighten even more.

"You're enjoying this way too much," I mutter, not looking back.

"Little bit," he calls, voice warm with amusement. "I do like being right."

I finally spin around and stalk back toward him. "I hate you."

He grins, not even trying to hide it. "No, you don't."

"You're walking me, but don't get cocky about it." He's already won, and we both know it, but I'll be damned if I hand him a victory lap, too.

He chuckles, then, without a word, reaches down and grabs my hand. I blink, surprised. His grip is warm, steady, fingers lacing with mine like it's the most natural thing in the world. So naturally, I pounce on the opportunity. I lift our joined hands between us, arching a brow. "Wait, are you secretly the one that's too chicken to walk this path alone?"

His expression shifts slightly, so fast I almost miss it. Just a flicker. A tightening of his jaw. Then his eyes lock on mine, sharp and unreadable. For a second, I forget how to breathe.

"Is that what you think?" His voice is low, quiet in a way that doesn't match the smirk from earlier.

I meant it as a joke. I meant to keep it light. But the way he's looking at me now, he's not hiding behind humor anymore. It makes my heart kick hard against my ribs. I try to recover, try to stay in control. "I don't know," I say, forcing a shrug. "You're the one initiating handholding on a spooky path."

Quickly, he spins me toward him before I even register what's happening. My breath catches, adrenaline flooding through me like a crashing wave. Suddenly I'm chest to chest with him, one hand on my throat the other on my waist, he squeezes lightly, his mouth inches from mine. The flashlight drops slightly in my grip, casting a beam across the trees.

"Are you scared now?" His tone dark, almost a dare.

I should say no. I want to say no. But there's no air left in my lungs, and the way he's looking at me, strips me bare.

"Yes," I whisper, So quiet I'm not sure I even said it out loud. Not because I'm scared of him, but because at this moment I'm so turned on, I have to squeeze my thighs together to stop the ache.

His mouth tilts into the faintest smile. "You should be." He growls.

"I'm not scared of you," I breathe, needing him to know. "I'm scared of what this feels like."

I reach out and grip his chest, fingers curling into his shirt, nails digging in just enough to ground myself. His heartbeat thunders beneath my palm, steady and strong, like he's holding it all in by sheer force.

"What are you scared of?" I ask, barely above a whisper.

His jaw clenches. His whole body tightens, like he didn't expect the question, or like he's been holding back the answer too long. He leans in, slow and deliberate, his nose brushing mine, breath warm against my mouth. My eyes flutter shut, the contact so achingly tender I could cry from the weight of it.

"Only one thing scares me." His voice is strained, ragged with truth. "I'm scared of what I'd do if something happened to you."

The words hit me like a punch straight to the gut. My eyes fly open in shock, No one's ever said that to me before. Not with their hands on me like I'm something breakable and worth protecting.

Then he shakes his head, slowly pulling back. His hands leave my body, and I feel the loss instantly. But he doesn't let me go completely, his fingers curl back around mine, grounding both of us.

We walk in silence. The tension between us builds with every step, thick and tight like it's clinging to our skin. By the time we reach my cabin, it's a miracle I'm still standing.

I turn to face him, heart hammering. "Do you want to come in?"

He doesn't answer. He just drops my hand, steps forward and cups my face.

138

"I want to." His voice is raw against the quiet. "God, Kinsley, I want to."

Then he kisses me. It's toe-curling, like he's telling me all the things he can't say with words. When he finally breaks the kiss, breath ragged, his forehead rests against mine. "That's why I can't."

My heart clenches, but I nod, trying to find air. "Then kiss me like that again tomorrow."

He takes a slow step back, the weight of the moment still thick between us. Then, of course, he smirks. "Do you plan on wearing that bikini again tomorrow?" he asks, voice casual, like he didn't just kiss the life out of me. "If so, what time? I want to make sure I don't miss the show."

I stare at him, stunned for half a second. Then I narrow my eyes. "If I do," I say sweetly, "I'll call Dylan." The second the words leave my mouth, I see it. That flicker in his expression. The smirk falters, jaw tightens, and just like that, he's lit up.

His eyes darken as he steps forward again. "Don't."

I raise a brow, playing it cool even though my heart's thudding like crazy. "Don't what?"

He stops just inches from me, voice low and dangerous now. "Don't play with me, Kinsley."

I tilt my head, fighting a smile. "Why not? You started it."

His jaw clenches, and for a second I think he's going to kiss me again. Harder this time. Rougher. But instead, he steps back, running a hand through his hair like he's trying to shake me off.

"You're impossible," he mutters, like he's half exasperated, half turned on, backing away before he does something reckless.

"You like it," I tease, grinning as I head inside.

He throws a look over his shoulder, smirk back in full force. "Yeah, and that's the problem. Good night, Kinsley."

"Good night, Miles." With that, he walks off into the night, hands in his pockets like he's not leaving me completely unraveled on my own damn porch.

As I walk into the cabin, I let a long exhale. "What a day." The words slip out under my breath. I head straight to the bathroom, take a quick shower and slip into a tank top and shorts. With a glass of wine in hand, I curl up on the couch, finally letting myself process everything that happened tonight.

Meeting his brother and friends was a lot. But in the best way. Reed, his brother, looks so much like Miles it's a little unsettling. He's little taller, maybe. I know he's a firefighter, and he's got tattoos down his arm. There's a quiet intensity about him, like he's the one everyone leans on when things go sideways.

Luke wasn't what I expected at all. Dressed down, relaxed, but I can tell he's a businessman. Dark brown hair, around the same height as Miles. He's kind of a mystery, smooth, a little playful, but guarded in a way that makes you wonder what he's hiding.

Dylan is tanned, tattooed and built like someone who works hard for a living. With that dark blonde hair and easy laugh, he feels like the type who's always got a project going. I heard Miles say he owns a construction company. Makes sense. They're all good-looking men, ridiculously so. But Miles? He's the one. In my eyes, there's no comparison.

All of them have this closeness, the kind you don't fake. The kind that comes from growing up together, going through real shit, and coming out the other side stronger. It reminded me of Raelynn and me, how we know each other without needing words.

Then there's Judy. God, she was so happy tonight being with them all. It was heartwarming, the way they love her, how natural it is between them. And I get it now. I really do. She's everything, sharp and warm and a little bit wild. I had such a good time with her today.

The wine warms me as I sink deeper into the cushions, thinking about everything Miles just said. That he's scared of

something happening to me. I didn't see that coming. He's always so steady, so composed, like nothing could ever rattle him. But that was raw. Real. It caught me completely off guard.

If I'm being honest with myself, I don't think I've ever had someone care like that before. Not with that kind of weight behind it. I like him. I really like him.

It's crazy. My past boyfriends, flings, none of them ever made me feel like this. Like I'm coming apart and grounding all at once. Like I'm seen. Protected. Wanted. After tonight, after those words, I know he feels it, too. Whatever this is between us, it's real. And I want to see where it goes.

I finish the last sip of wine, the glass now warm from my hands, and set it gently on the coffee table. The cabin is still, the only sound the soft hum of crickets outside and the faint ticking of the clock on the wall. I let out a slow breath, my thoughts still tangled in Miles' words, when he said he couldn't come in but he wanted to.

I push off the couch, my body heavy with the kind of exhaustion that sinks into your bones and head to the bedroom. Flicking off the lights as I pass, the bathroom nightlight casts a soft glow down the hall. Once under the covers, I lie still, staring at the ceiling. Then I close my eyes and let the quiet take me.

18

Mine All Day

Miles

The house is still quiet except for the muffled sounds of the guys gathering their things, getting ready to head out. There's laughter, the slam of a car door and the familiar banter that usually makes me smile. But today, I've got other things on my mind. I want to spend time with Kinsley. Just the two of us. No bear attacks, no unexpected guests, no damn interruptions. So, I call her while my coffee brews.

"Good morning, City Girl."

"Good morning." Her voice is thick with sleep, followed by a soft yawn that makes me smile.

"Got any big plans for today?"

"You just happen to catch me on my day off." She chuckles. "Why?"

"Well," I say, trying to sound casual. "I thought we could spend the day together."

There's a pause. Just long enough for doubt to creep in.

"I'd like that."

I clear my throat, trying to pull it together. "When can you be ready?"

I can practically hear the smile in her voice. "I'll need at least an hour."

"An hour?" I'm a little shocked. "Why so long?"

"Unless you want me to wear my tank top and booty shorts out." She giggles teasingly.

My brain short-circuits. Damn it. Now that image is stuck in my head, and definitely not helping me act like a gentleman.

"If we actually want to leave your cabin, I'm gonna need you to get dressed." I can feel the tension in my jaw just thinking about it.

She laughs. "I'll see you in an hour, Country Boy."

I hang up, grinning like an idiot. Damn, I'm in trouble and I like it.

I head upstairs to shower, already thinking about what to wear when my phone buzzes again. Her name lights up the screen.

"Kinsley?" I answer, surprised. "Miss me already?"

"What should I wear?" She sounds playful but just a little unsure.

Something about that hint of uncertainty makes my chest tighten. She always seems so confident, it hits different when she lets her guard down with me. "I don't know where we're going."

I laugh. "Casual. Anything but booty shorts."

"Damn! That was my first choice. Fine, casual it is. See you soon." She giggles.

We hang up again, and I head straight for the shower. I'm in and out in five minutes, towel slung around my neck as I make my way to the closet. I pull out a pair of distressed jeans, a fitted black T-shirt and my black boots. Simple. I get dressed and head downstairs with forty-five minutes to kill.

Why does it take women so long? Shaking my head, I grab a cup of coffee and sit at the table, eyes drifting to the clock. It doesn't seem to be moving.

I arrive ten minutes early and knock on her door.

"Come in!" she shouts from somewhere inside. I step in and close the door behind me. A second later, her head pops out of the bedroom doorway.

"I'm almost ready, just a few more minutes!"

"Casual, City Girl," I call out with a grin.

She steps out a minute later, smirking. My breath hitches like I just took a punch to the gut.

"This IS casual. If you'd said formal, I would've needed two more hours."

I open my mouth to fire something back, but nothing comes out. My heart kicks hard as I take her in.

She's wearing a long-sleeve, fitted shirt tucked into a tan, mid-thigh mini skirt. Black boots hug her legs just over the knee. Her hair's down, flowing halfway down her back. Big hoop earrings catch the light. Her lips are painted the softest pink, and her makeup makes those green eyes of hers impossible to look away from.

I stare. Way too long. And I know it because she raises an eyebrow at me.

"Wow, you look..." my eyes take her in slowly before I finish, "beautiful."

"Thank you," she whispers, a blush rising in her cheeks.

I reach for her hand. "Did you eat breakfast?"

"No," She rolls her eyes. "Someone was rushing me."

"Okay, first stop, food."

"The first stop?" she repeats, eyeing me curiously.

"Yeah, you're mine all day."

I watch as she suppresses a smile.

I lead her to the truck and open her door like a proper gentleman. She doesn't say anything, but the way her eyes soften tells me she noticed. I close the door gently behind her and circle around to my side.

Our first stop is the Sweet Spot bakery for coffee and donuts. I remember her telling Judy she really liked Naya. So, I thought it would be nice to visit her. When we pull into the parking lot, Kinsley lights up.

"Naya and donuts?" she squeaks, clearly excited.

I laugh. "You said you really like Naya. Thought it'd be nice to have breakfast with your friend."

She doesn't respond right away, just reaches out, squeezes my hand, then practically jumps out of the truck.

I laugh again, watching her take off toward the front door, then quickly follow behind her.

We step inside. A little bell rings, and Naya steps out from the back. Her smile widens the second she sees Kinsley. Then her eyes shift to me. She blinks, surprised, then looks back to Kinsley with raised brows and a silent question in her expression. She pulls off her apron as she rounds the counter. The two of them hug tightly. Naya leans in, whispering something I can't hear.

But Kinsley answers out loud. "Miles and I are spending the day together."

Naya's eyes flick back to me, then to Kinsley again, smiling now, but with that look only women seem to know how to give each other. The kind that says, "Oh, really?" And yeah, I'm pretty sure I

145

just became the topic of girl's night. Part of me is amused. The other part? A little proud.

Naya steps back behind the counter. "Well, what can I get you guys?"

Kinsley and I both step up. I go with a cinnamon twist, she picks a frosted chocolate, and we both get coffee. As I pay, I glance at Naya. "Would you like to join us?"

"Sure," she smiles. "Let me grab a coffee. I'll be right out."

We find a small table near the window, and a minute later Naya joins us.

"So," she starts, looking between us with a grin, "what do you guys have planned today?"

Kinsley beats me to it. "I don't know all the details. Miles just told me to dress casual and be ready."

Naya raises a brow. "So, it's a surprise."

Kinsley nods, taking a sip of her coffee. "Apparently, I'm his all day."

I lean back a little, arm resting behind her chair. "You sound real upset about it."

She doesn't look at me. "I'm reserving judgment until after the donuts."

That pulls a quiet laugh out of both of us.

"I like this." Naya gives Kinsley a look I can't quite read, but I know it means something.

Kinsley just rolls her eyes and bites into her donut.

I don't say much. I just sit back, sip my coffee and watch her. The way she smiles and laughs with her friend. We talk a few more minutes before the bell above the door rings and a customer walks in. We say our goodbyes, Kinsley hugs Naya and then we're back in the truck. On to the next stop.

I take a turn off the main road. "Detour?" she asks, raising a brow.

"Just thought I'd show you a few places."

As we drive, I point out the old church where Reed broke his arm trying a skateboard trick to impress a group of girls, the pasture Luke and I used to sneak into and pretend to be cowboys and tried to ride goats.

Each memory gets a laugh out of her, and damn if it doesn't make me want to keep going just to hear it again.

"You were wild."

I shoot back, flashing her a smirk. "Still am."

By the time we pull back onto the main road, her laughter's still echoing in my head.

We pull into the driveway of The Second Chapter bookstore.

"I thought we could look for horror books together," I tease.

"Only if they have killer raccoons in them." She chuckles.

I glance over at her. "Actually, I thought we could look for a couple of cookbooks, and you could teach me how to cook."

Kinsley claps her hands together, eyes lighting up. "I can't wait to see this." She pokes fun at me. "We should probably start with something simple, like grilled cheese."

I shoot her a look. "Wow. Low expectations right out the gate?"

She shrugs, all fake innocence. "Just trying to set you up for success, Country Boy."

I laugh. "Oh, it's going to be a train wreck."

"I can't wait," she says, smiling at the thought.

We step inside, the familiar scent of old books wrapping around us. I wave to Mrs. Sara behind the front counter. She's wearing her usual sixties-inspired outfit, complete with bold prints and big jewelry.

"Hello, Miles!" she calls out.

Kinsley doesn't waste a second. She's already heading straight for the cookbook section like she's on a mission. When I catch up, she's got a book in her hands and is flipping through it with intent.

I lean over her shoulder to see what she's reading, catching the faint scent of her shampoo, something warm and a little sweet. She points to a recipe for beef stroganoff. "This might be an option," she says, tapping her finger on the page. She hands me the book and grabs another, flipping through it just as quickly. I can't help but watch her. The way she's so focused, so serious, it's kind of adorable.

She taps her chin thoughtfully. "Maybe this one." I laugh as she grabs three more books and repeats the process.

She grins but doesn't look up. "Don't laugh. This is serious. I won't have my student failing."

After an hour, we narrow it down to two books, Easy Recipes and Cooking for Beginners. I look at the covers, then glance at her, deadpan. "I'm a little offended. What kind of message are we sending here?"

She shrugs, completely unbothered. "That we're being realistic."

She grabs both books anyway, clearly not trusting me with the decision, and heads to the counter. Damn, she's cute. I follow her up, step in close and lean down just enough to speak low in her ear.

"So, teacher, how strict is your grading policy?"

She glances at me with a smirk. "That depends. Do you plan on setting off the smoke alarm or burning water?"

I grin. "Maybe both." She laughs, handing the books to Mrs. Sara, and I swear that sound does something to me.

"Lucky for you." She nudges my side. "I grade on effort." I drop the cash on the counter and slide an arm casually around her waist.

"Then I'm getting an A."

"Okay, Mr. I Can Make Scrambled Eggs," she snorts as we step out the door.

"I'll have you know," I say, holding it open for her, "my eggs are fantastic. That alone should earn me a gold star."

She slides into the seat, flashing that cocky little smile. "We'll see what kind of mess you leave on the counter this time."

I bite my lip, instantly flashing back to the night I left her on that same counter, breathless, and alone. Shaking my head, I shut her door and make my way around.

Sliding into the driver's seat, I glance over, voice low and even. "Next time I use the counter, I'll make sure I finish the job."

She freezes for half a second, just long enough to know I got to her, then slowly turns to face me, one brow arched like she's already loading her shot.

"Well, for the record," she says, voice like silk, "next time you leave a mess on the counter..." she leans in, eyes locked on mine, "there'll be no dessert for you."

Then she leans back, completely smug, flipping open the cookbook. I can still feel the heat of her hand under mine, remember the way I guided her hand across her body. Then left her there, wanting more.

I glance over, jaw tight. "That's cruel."

She doesn't even look up. "Actions have consequences, Country Boy."

I laugh, shaking my head as we pull into the parking lot of the local ice cream parlor.

Kinsley glances up, excited. "Ice cream?"

"Yep. The dessert I'm actually allowed to have."

She squints at me, amused. "You're skipping out of your consequence."

I lean over, grinning. "I prefer the term negotiating. Besides, what kind of monster skips dessert?"

Her smile cracks. "You did! But fine. I'm picking the flavors."

"Deal," I say, hopping out and heading around to open her door.

As she steps down, she tosses over her shoulder, "And I get to taste yours first."

"You can have a taste. But don't get handsy with my cone, City Girl."

She laughs. "Can't make any promises." She orders classic chocolate for herself and a black cherry for me. Something I've never tried. Two cones later, we step out into the warm afternoon.

"Let's walk to the next stop," I say, nodding down the sidewalk.

She raises an eyebrow. "There's a next stop?"

I grin. "Told you, you're mine all day." She blushes, her gaze dropping to the sidewalk as a small smile tugs at her lips.

We walk another block in comfortable silence, ice cream cones slowly disappearing. When we stop, she looks up to find us standing in front of a narrow brick building with a faded green sign that reads, Allen Antiques.

I open the door and gesture her in. The moment she steps inside, her eyes light up. The place is full of soft golden light and overflowing with old treasures, glass cases filled with vintage jewelry and worn leather books. A weathered grandfather clock ticks in the corner. But it's the wind chimes that catch her first. Dozens of them, hanging near the center of the room, some made from crystal, others from seashells or repurposed bits of metal. They move gently in the draft from the ceiling fan, letting out soft, uneven melodies that fill the air.

"Oh, wow," Kinsley breathes, spinning slowly, taking it all in. "This place is incredible." Her eyes are wide as they flit from a hand-carved rocking horse to a stack of vintage postcards bound with twine. I don't say anything. I just watch her because this is exactly why I brought her here. She drifts toward the wind chimes, brushing her fingers over them.

From the back of the shop, the owner steps into view. She looks up, spots him, then glances my way with a smile. "Floyd?"

"Yep. Floyd Allen." AKA Old Man Floyd.

He reaches us, cranky as ever, but there's the faintest shift in his expression when he sees Kinsley.

"Miles," he says, gruffly. I chuckle. That's about as friendly as it gets.

Then his eyes land on her. "Kinsley."

She smiles warmly. "Hey, Floyd. It's good to see you."

He looks between us. "Didn't peg you for his type."

She laughs, and I raise a brow.

Floyd doesn't smile, but there's a flicker of amusement in his eyes before he mutters, "Don't break anything," and disappears into the back.

Kinsley chuckles as he walks away, shaking her head. "He's great."

151

"Great is generous," I say, but I'm smiling, too.

We spend the next two hours wandering through the relics, talking about simpler times and laughing over odd finds.

From typewriters to creepy-looking dolls, everything in the shop pulls her in. Kinsley takes her time with every little thing, like she's uncovering some secret joy in each corner. And watching her do it? That might be the best part of all.

When we finally make it to the counter, she's holding a wind chime made from old silverware and a crystal vase for her mom. Floyd rings us up without looking our way. "You got the potluck managed?"

I try not to roll my eyes. "Yes, it's all handled."

He grunts like he doesn't believe me, then turns to Kinsley. "Keep an eye on this one." He shoots me another pointed look. I see it, his seldom seen playful side. Subtle. Dry. He must really like her. Not that I blame him.

19

Hot Guys, Heavy Tables

Kinsley

Walking out the door of the antique shop, I lift the bag in my hand and smile up at him. "Thank you for this," I say softly. "And for today."

"You're welcome." He slips his hand in mine. "Are you hungry? I thought we could end the day with dinner."

"Dinner sounds perfect."

We walk back to the truck. When we reach the passenger side, Miles opens the door and I slide in. He leans down, kisses me, then whispers against my lips, "I've wanted to do that all day." Before I can respond, he closes the door, leaving me wanting more.

He climbs in and starts the truck, and we drive across town. When we pull into the lot of The Fireside Lounge, I recognize it at once. It's where Naya took me.

He hops out and opens my door. As I step down, I reach for his hand. When our fingers graze, he looks down, because I reached for him first. Then he lets them intertwine with his.

Inside, we're greeted by the host. She smiles brightly. "Table for two?"

Miles nods. "Yes. Somewhere in the back, please."

She guides us through the cozy, dim space, and we slide into a booth across from each other. A few moments later, our server appears with menus. "What can I get you to drink?"

We both order a beer, giving ourselves a moment to look over the menu.

Miles glances up from his menu. "What sounds good to you?"

I lower mine just enough to meet his eyes. "What I want isn't on the menu."

His jaw ticks. Eyes darken. That slow, simmering heat flashes between us like a lit match on dry grass. "Careful, Kinsley." His voice is filled with feral warning. "I'm trying to be a gentleman."

My breath catches. For a second, all I can do is stare. The way he's looking at me right now, like he's two seconds from laying me across the table, makes my skin buzz.

My mouth opens, then shuts again, fast. Smart. Because one wrong word, and I know he'll make good on whatever he's holding back. God help me, I'll let him.

He chuckles at my silence, slow and smug.

I roll my eyes, mostly to keep from squirming in my seat. I flip my menu open again. "What's good here?"

He leans back, still watching me with that knowing look. "Everything's good, but the steak's my favorite." I nod, pretending to focus on the options, even though my pulse is still racing. Anything to keep from crawling across the table.

The server returns, and we both order the steak. Once she's gone, I take another sip of my beer and finally ask, "Why did you want to spend the day with me?"

He sets his beer down and looks me in the eye. "I wanted to take you on a real date. With the potluck just two days away, things are about to get busy. Reed and Luke will be here, and it's gonna get hectic fast."

He pauses, like he's choosing his words carefully. "I just thought, we might not have much time once all that starts. And if we do, it won't be alone."

"I'm glad you asked me."

Our food arrives, giving us a natural break in the conversation. We eat, talking about preparations and all the chaos and festivities the potluck will bring, and that's when it hits me. I know exactly what I want to make for the potluck. I'll need Naya's help, but it's perfect. And I'm keeping it a secret, for now.

As we leave the restaurant and climb back into the truck, I can feel the day winding down. And honestly, I don't want it to.

"I had a really good time today," I say, glancing over at him. "Thank you."

He keeps his eyes on the road, but I catch the small smile pulling at his lips before he glances my way. "Me too, baby."

It's not the first time he's called me that, but just like the other times, it hits me low and warm. My stomach does a little flip.

When we pull into the driveway, the sun has dipped below the trees. Rounding the truck, he opens my door without a word. We walk slowly toward my cabin. Neither one of us wanting the day to end. The air is quiet, the kind of calm that only comes at the end of a good day. I don't want to break it.

Reaching the door, I turn to face him. He brushes a strand of hair from my face, eyes soft, smile just barely there.

"Thank you," I whisper. "Would you like to come in?"

"Yes." He gently presses a kiss to my lips. The kind that doesn't rush, the kind that lingers. When he pulls back, his forehead rests against mine for a beat.

"But I won't. Good night, City Girl."

I smile. "Good night, Miles."

As I step inside, my mind is already replaying today. I know I'll be thinking about him long after my head hits the pillow.

***

The next morning, I wake early and wander into the kitchen, still smiling. I whip up some scrambled eggs, wondering if Miles is doing the same across the lake. I eat at the island, sipping coffee, feeling pretty good about the day ahead. Then my phone rings. Raelynn.

I answer quickly, excited to tell her everything. "Hello?"

"Hey." I hear it instantly, something's wrong.

I sit up straighter. "What's wrong?"

She sighs, and I can tell she's about to cry. "It's Jacob. We haven't gotten along for months. I tried, Kins. I really did. He agreed to go to counseling and then didn't show up. He said he was busy and would make the next one, but..." she trails off with a sniffle. "I don't believe him. I think it's over."

"Oh, Raelynn, I'm so sorry. What an asshole."

I stand, already scanning my mind for what I can do. "What do you need me to do? Say the word. Do you want me to come home?"

"No! Absolutely not. Maybe you can call into the office sometime this week and start the paperwork? For a divorce." Her voice shakes a little, but there's strength underneath it.

"You're sure this is what you want?" I ask gently. "Because whatever you decide, I'll back you up."

156

"Yes." She sounds more certain now. "I don't want to live like this anymore."

I reach over, grabbing my laptop. "We'll get it started today. I just need to ask you a couple questions."

"Okay."

"How fast do you want this done?"

"As soon as possible."

"All right. We've got two options. One, you leave all joint items to him, take your personal effects and your car, and we ask for half the assets. That's the fastest route. Or we can do a full split down the middle. That'll take about six months." There's silence on the other end as she thinks.

"I don't want anything. He can have it. I just want out."

I nod, even though she can't see me. "Okay. I'll have the paperwork sent to your email. Fill out all the background information, joint and personal. List every asset so the judge can see you're being generous. Once it's back, I'll review it and have Mel file it the next day."

"Thank you," she says, her voice soft but full of relief. "Seriously, Kinsley. Thank you."

"Always. Whatever you need. You'll get an email within the hour. We'll take it one step at a time, okay?"

"Okay," she breathes. "I love you."

"I love you, too."

There's a pause, one of those quiet, heavy ones that come after big decisions.

"Talk soon?"

"Of course, and if you need me call day or night."

157

The call ends, and I set the phone down gently on the counter. I stare at it for a moment, taking a deep breath. Then I open my laptop and get to work.

Once I finish drafting the initial paperwork, I grab my phone and text Mel.

Kinsley: Hey, heads up. I'm helping Raelynn file. I'll be sending over the packet soon. Can you be ready to file with the courthouse the same day?

Her reply comes back almost instantly.

Mel: Absolutely. I'll check my inbox every thirty minutes. Just say the word.

I exhale, shoulders relaxing just a little. It's not an easy thing Raelynn's doing, but I'll make damn sure it goes as smoothly as possible.

Closing my laptop, knowing I've done all I can for today, I grab my coffee and step out into the late afternoon sun. The warmth feels good, grounding. I settle into one of the patio chairs and let my eyes drift toward the field across the way. From here, I can see a couple of large white tents already standing, and two more in the process of going up. Preparations for the potluck are well underway.

That's when Judy appears, seemingly out of nowhere. "Kinsley, good morning!"

I nearly launch myself out of the chair, clutching my chest. "Judy! You scared the shit out of me."

She laughs, unbothered. "Sorry, honey. Didn't mean to sneak up on you." She pauses, smiling wide. "I came to ask if you'd be interested in being a judge for the chili contest. You're not from around here, so no one can accuse us of rigging it."

I grin. "I'd love to."

"Perfect!" She claps her hands together, delighted. "Now, my next question, any chance you want to help with decorations today?"

"I would, actually," I say, already standing. "Let me run in and get cleaned up. I'll meet you over there."

"Take your time, sweetheart," she says, already turning toward her car. "You're gonna have fun with this."

I head inside to get dressed, keeping it simple since I know I'll be working. Yoga pants and a fitted crop top. Hair up in a ponytail, a little mascara, some lip balm. Done. I grab my keys and phone, step outside and take the path around the lake, parking near Miles' truck. The second I step out, I pause to take in the view. The setup's already halfway there, tents up, chairs stacked, decorations in piles, but there's still a lot left to do.

I spot Judy near one of the tents and make my way over. I shove my phone and keys in my pocket. "Put me to work. What do you need?"

She pats my shoulder with a grin. "Let's get the boxes out of my car first. Then I'll show you where everything goes."

Eight boxes later, we're knee-deep in streamers and balloons. I start hanging decorations while Judy directs traffic like a small-town general, calling out names and giving orders with her signature cheer.

As I'm tying off a balloon, my eyes catch movement across the lawn. Miles and Reed, each carrying two massive tables like they weigh nothing. I pause mid-knot. Hot! That's the only word for it. They're both all muscle and purpose, sleeves rolled up, forearms flexing, focused and sweaty in the best possible way. I'm not the only one who notices either. Two women under a nearby tent actually stop what they're doing, staring open-mouthed. I quickly shut mine. No need to look as desperate as I feel. Still, damn.

I'm crouched next to one of the boxes, pulling out more streamers when that prickling feeling hits the back of my neck.

159

Someone's watching me. I glance over my shoulder, and sure enough, Miles is leaning against a tent pole, hands in his pockets, that signature smirk already on his face.

He takes his time walking over, all calm confidence and barely concealed mischief. When he reaches me, he doesn't say anything at first, just leans in and lands a playful smack on my ass.

"I like these pants," he says, low and way too satisfied with himself.

I stand up slowly, eyebrow raised, trying not to smile. "Do you, now?" Before I can say anything else, he suddenly drops his keys at my feet.

"Oops," he says, all faux innocence. "Do you mind?"

I cross my arms, trying to act unimpressed. "Seriously?"

He just grins, eyes locked on mine. "I figured you owed me after the bikini incident."

I roll my eyes, but I bend down anyway, very slowly, making sure he gets exactly the view he was hoping for.

When I hand him the keys, he takes them with a wink. "See? Teamwork."

"More like shenanigans," I mutter, but I'm grinning now, too.

He leans in, presses a quick kiss to the top of my head, then steps back. "I better go. I've got about twenty more tables to unload."

"Sure." I glance over his shoulder. "But before you go, you should know you have an audience."

He pauses. "What?"

I point behind him toward the tent where two women are definitely not being subtle about staring. "Those two have been watching since the second you and Reed showed up carrying tables. Might want to give 'em a little show."

Miles glances back, smirking. When he looks over at them, they quickly pretend to be busy. "Maybe I'll bring Luke into it. Really give 'em something to talk about."

I shake my head, laughing. "You're all shameless."

He winks. "Only for you, City Girl." Then he turns and walks off, leaving me smiling like a complete idiot in a pile of half-inflated balloons.

I open the next box and start pulling out more decorations when I hear a loud whistle. I glance up and nearly choke. Miles, Reed and Luke are walking across the field, with two tables each, shirtless, like they just stepped out of a calendar shoot. And just to really drive it home, they're glistening. Water slicking down chests, abs, arms, like someone hosed them off backstage.

I laugh. Not a polite giggle, a real, full-out laugh. There is no way that sweat is real. Miles hadn't had a single drop on him five minutes ago. They totally did this on purpose. As they pass, Miles shoots me a quick glance. He's trying not to smile, biting his lip like he knows exactly what kind of chaos they're causing.

Judy walks up beside me, hands on her hips, eyes on them, too. "Those boys." She shakes her head. "Always up to something."

"Yeah," I grin. "And they know exactly what they're doing."

She chuckles, nudging me with her elbow. "And don't pretend you're not enjoying the view."

I don't even try to deny it. Because, honestly, it's the best damn distraction I've had all day. "Oh, I'm definitely enjoying it."

The next few hours fly by as I move from tent to tent, unpacking boxes, hanging decorations and dodging more than a few flying streamers. Judy left about an hour ago to pick up pizza and beers for everyone, promising to return with enough food to feed a small army.

I'm halfway up a ladder, arms stretched to tie the last streamer, when I feel a strong hand wrap around my waist. Before I can react, I'm gently pulled back down. My feet hit the ground, and I know it's Miles before I even turn. He keeps his hand at my waist, steadying me as I spin to face him.

"Pizza's here," he says softly, reaching up to tuck a loose piece of hair behind my ear.

"Thanks for the heroic rescue," I tease, tilting my head.

"Can't have you falling before the main event."

"Which one? Judging chili or watching you flex?"

He shrugs like it's a toss-up. "I'm good at multitasking."

I snort as he takes my hand and pulls me toward the food tables. Reed's already inhaling a slice like it's a competitive sport, and Luke's guarding the pepperoni like it's state treasure.

Miles hands me a slice. "Careful. It's hot."

"So are you," I deadpan, "but I still manage."

He pauses, eyes flicking to mine, impressed, then he laughs shaking his head. "You're a menace."

"And yet, here you are."

He leans in just enough to whisper, "Yeah, here I am."

Everyone piles around a couple of empty tables, plates full of pizza and cups of beer in hand. The mood is relaxed, filled with easy laughter and the kind of teasing that only happens when people are comfortable.

Reed, never passing up an opportunity, eyes me over his slice with a crooked grin. "You want Miles to blow on your pizza, too, or just cut it into little bites for you?"

I raise an eyebrow, not missing a beat. "Depends. You need someone to hold your hand next time you lift a table, or are you finally ready for big boy furniture?"

The group bursts into laughter, even Luke nearly chokes on his beer. Reed lets out a low whistle, grinning as he shakes his head.

"Well, damn," he says, glancing at Miles. "You've got your hands full with this one."

Miles leans back in his chair, smirking as he takes a sip of his drink. "Don't I know it."

The way he says it, half proud, half amused, sends a little jolt though me. I look over at him and catch the flicker of something warm in his eyes before he turns back to his plate like it's nothing.

20

Control Is a Lie I Tell Myself

Miles

Everyone starts packing up, calling it a night until tomorrow, when we'll finish the rest. Laughter fades into the hum of car engines and the soft rustle of tents in the evening breeze.

I glance around, looking for Kinsley. She's under one of the tents, still working through a box like the day isn't winding down around her. Of course she is. I head over just as Reed and Luke holler their goodbyes from across the lawn.

"See ya!" Luke calls.

"Don't stay out too late," Reed adds with a smirk.

I wave them off. Kinsley does too, and just like that, we're the last two standing. Finally. I reach for her hand and tug her gently toward me. My voice dips, thick with heat. "We're alone now."

Her eyes flick up to mine, playful and knowing. "I see that." She steps in close enough that I can feel the heat coming off her skin. "What should we do?"

I tilt my head, eyes dropping to her mouth for a second before finding her eyes again. "Well," I murmur, "we could finish unpacking."

She arches a brow. "That doesn't sound like fun."

"Good," I say, stepping into her, closing the space between us. "Because that's not what I was thinking."

Her breath catches as I slide my hands around her waist and pull her tight. I dip my head, brushing my lips over hers before I kiss her deeper. Her hands fist in my shirt, tugging me closer.

The kiss turns deep and hungry. Her back hits one of the tent poles, my hand sliding up under the hem of her shirt, fingertips grazing warm skin. She makes a soft sound that shoots straight through me. My other hand tangles in her hair as her fingers roam my chest, exploring.

I spin her around by her hips, facing her away from me, pressing her back against my chest. I flex my hips, letting her feel how hard she makes me. She moans softly, the sound curling around my spine. I brush her hair to one side, leaning in to kiss and suck just beneath her ear. Her skin's warm, smooth, and she tilts her head back, resting it against my chest like an invitation.

My mouth trails a slow path from her ear to her collarbone, biting, sucking, and tasting every sweet inch. She trembles slightly, and my hand glides across her stomach under her crop top, slowly rolling over her hip. When I reach the waistband of her yoga pants, I slide my fingers just under, letting them rest there, teasing the edge, lingering.

She presses her back into me, and I grit my teeth when her round ass pushes up against my cock. She tilts her head, giving me more. I bite my lip to keep myself from ripping down her pants and fucking her over a table.

My hand on her stomach tightens slightly, sliding a bit lower, not rushing, just enough to make her gasp again. Her fingers come up to grip my forearm, not to stop me, but to hold on.

"I've been thinking about this all day," I murmur into her skin, voice rough.

She turns her head slightly, eyes meeting mine over her shoulder, dark and dazed. "Then stop thinking," she whispers.

I groan low in my throat, voice thick with restraint. "Wrap your arms around my neck, and if you move them, I stop. Do you understand?"

Her breath catches with anticipation, and she whimpers. "Yes."

She slowly trails her hands up, fingers tracing the lines of my arms and chest. When she locks her hands behind my neck and tilts her head, I kiss her. My tongue brushes her bottom lip, and when she opens for me, our tongues dance. Her body pressed tight to mine.

I slowly trace my hand down under the band of her lace panties and pause. Her body arches into my hand, begging for more. I reach up with my other hand and slide it under her lace bra, cupping her plump breast. I can't help but groan into her lips when my fingers roll over her pebbled nipple. She lets out a broken sound, head falling back against my chest. I pull her hardened nipple as I inch my fingers down further and pause again.

I break the kiss, and her eyes lock on mine. "Did you touch yourself?" I ask through my clenched jaw, though my voice wavers just enough to give me away. I don't just want to hear her say it, I want to know she was thinking about me.

"Yes," she pants, begging for more. "Miles."

"What did you think about, Kinsley?" I move my hand down a little further. She freezes and inhales a deep breath, her body vibrating with need.

"Say it, baby, and I'll give you what you need."

Breathing heavy, she whispers, "You."

I slide my finger between her folds, finding her swollen, wet nub. Her body starts shuddering. She grinds into my hand, chasing her buildup. Her head falls back against my chest, and her arms start to loosen from behind my neck. I pull my fingers off her wet, aching center. Her hips buck forward, searching for my touch.

"Arms, Kinsley." I demand. She tightens her arms firmly around my neck. I slide my fingers through her wetness and resume slow, steady circles over her clit.

"You're so wet for me," I growl. Her body tenses, and I know she's about to come. I press down harder, circling her juices over my fingers. I tug at her nipple, sending pleasure building through her until her legs start to shake.

"Don't let go," I whisper into her neck.

"Miles," she cries out, moaning as she starts to come apart. Her body arches further when I start moving faster, adding more pressure.

"Oh my God!" she screams as her orgasm rips through her body. I don't slow down, dragging her release out until her body starts to relax. When she falls limp, I pull my hands out. My whole body is tight, aching, because watching her come undone in my hands, hearing her lose herself like that, has me so hard it hurts. She turns to face me, her cheeks pink, eyes burning. I bend to kiss her, and she wraps her hands around my neck.

"Is that what you needed?" I ask between her lips.

Still trying to catch her breath, she whispers, "Yes. What do you need?" she asks, eager to keep going.

I break the kiss, cupping her face before I answer. "Just this, baby."

She furrows her brow, clearly questioning me.

"I told you." I brush a quick kiss against her lips. "I need you to understand what you're asking for first."

Her eyes search mine, but she doesn't push. Not yet. She slowly rests her cheek against my chest, catching her breath. I hold her until her breathing evens out.

"Come on, I'll walk you to your car." I slip my hand in hers.

"I'm a little confused," she admits.

I'm confused, too, because if I take her all the way, if I really let go, she'll be mine. In every way that counts. Until she's not.

"I know, baby. But I promise I'll tell you when it's time," I say, hovering over her lips.

I kiss her softly. She reaches up and touches my face, her fingers warm against my skin.

When she pulls away, she meets my eyes. "I trust you, Miles."

Those four words hit like a jolt, I slip my hand into hers and walk her to her car. Neither of us say much, but it's not uncomfortable, just quiet.

At her door, she turns to face me. I kiss her slow, lingering. Pulling away, I murmur, "See you tomorrow."

She smiles. "Good night, Miles." I step back, hands in my pockets, and watch her drive away.

Not wanting to rub my dick raw because I've fisted my cock almost every day, I decide to take a walk near the lake. Everything from the past couple of days floods my mind. This girl is breaking me in ways no one else ever has. And as much as I've tried to fight it, nothing I do can stop the pull I feel toward her.

I watch as her car pulls into the driveway. It's too dark to see her walking, but I know she made it when the lights flick on in her cabin. Only then do I finally head inside.

***

I wake the next morning already wondering when I'll see her again. I head to the kitchen and pour a cup of coffee just as Reed walks in. He doesn't say anything, just grabs a mug, fills it and settles beside me. We stand there quietly, both of us sipping, neither one much of a morning person.

After a while, Reed looks over at me, his expression serious. "You've got it bad for her, huh?"

I let out a slow breath. "Yeah, I think I might. She's pretty damn perfect."

He nods once, like he already knew. "She leaves in a couple weeks," I add, quieter now. That part stings more than I want to admit.

Reed grunts, then glances at me over his mug. "Have you told her?"

I shake my head slowly. "No. And I won't, not in so many words. I won't make her choose me over the life she has in Seattle."

Reed sets his mug down with a quiet clink. "You're not making her do anything, Miles. You're just being honest." He pauses, watching me. "She's a grown woman. Let her decide what's worth staying for."

I swallow thickly, pretending like I didn't just flinch inside. Because deep down, I know he's right, and that scares the hell out of me.

I take another sip of coffee, then set the mug down and turn away. "Let's get to work." I brush past his advice like I didn't hear it. Reed doesn't push. He just follows, quiet, but I know he's still thinking about it.

As we step outside, a couple of rental trucks pull into the drive. Reed and I jump in to help unload stage pieces, the dance floor and lighting equipment. We spend the next few hours working with the vendors, setting up for the live band. But I keep glancing over my shoulder. She's not here.

I spot Judy moving through the chaos, pointing people in the right direction, but still, no Kinsley. My stomach tightens. Maybe I pushed her too far last night. Maybe I read things wrong. But no, if I had, she would've said something.

I hold on to that thought, forcing myself to stay focused. Distracted or not, we manage to get almost everything done.

It's nearly dinner, so Reed and I fire up the grill, tossing on burgers and sausages while Judy makes quick work of the side dishes. Before long, everyone gathers around, laughing, drinking beers, filling their plates. Everyone but her.

I try to stay present, but my eyes keep drifting toward the driveway, the path. Her car isn't at the cabins. There's no sign of Kinsley. I haven't heard from her all day. Should I call? Is she okay?

I barely touch my food. Judy notices. She leans in, voice soft. "What's wrong? You not feeling well?"

"I'm fine," I lie, pushing my plate away. "Just not that hungry." She pats my shoulder gently, gives me a look like she knows better, then moves on to mingle with the rest of the group.

I sit alone on the porch, watching everyone laugh and talk, plates in their hands, beers cracked open. But I don't join in. My eyes stay on the road. Then I see it, a car turning down the drive. I squint, trying to make it out. When I recognize the rental, my heart kicks hard. Kinsley.

Before she's even parked, I'm on my feet. By the time she steps out and shuts the door, I'm already there, crossing the gravel in long strides. I don't say a word. I just wrap her in my arms, pick her up off the ground and kiss her, right there, in front of everyone, because I don't care who sees.

I set her down, but I don't step back. Her eyes meet mine. "I'm glad you're here," I say quietly.

She touches her lips, grinning. "Did you miss me, Miles?"

"Depends. Are we talking 'miss you like crazy' or 'miss you like peace and quiet'?"

She laughs, nudging my chest. "Such a pain."

"But you still showed up," I tease.

She leans in just a little. "Maybe I missed you, too."

The words hit like a rush of heat. I've been carrying that tension in my shoulders all damn day, and just hearing her say that, like she means it, knocks the wind out of me in the best way.

I tilt my head. "Maybe?"

She shrugs, playfully. "Don't get a big head about it, Country Boy."

Too late.

21

The Birds Are Not Okay

Kinsley

I woke up late this morning, later than I meant to. Probably because I was up half the night thinking about Miles. About his hands, his mouth, what he said. I swear my heart hasn't slowed down since.

Still half-asleep, I reach for my phone and blink at the screen. One missed call from Mel. *Shit.*

I slip out of bed, dragging the blanket with me around my shoulders and head to the kitchen. The floor's cold under my bare feet, but I'm already dialing her back as I start the coffee.

"Hello, Ms. Brighton," Mel answers. with her classic customer service voice.

"Hello, Mel." I don't bother correcting the formal use of my name for what feels like the hundredth time. At this point, it's part of our routine.

"Is everything okay?" I rub a hand over my face as the coffee machine hums to life.

"I hate bothering you on your vacation," she says with a huff, clearly frustrated. "But we've exhausted all options in Mrs. Perry's case."

That gets my attention fast. "Okay, what's going on?" The concern creeps in quickly.

Mel continues to explain, voice clipped. "Mr. Perry emptied one of their joint accounts and is now threatening Mrs. Perry and her pet birds, of all things. She's furious. Said she doesn't want another associate handling it. She wants you personally." I press my fingers to my temple.

"The court date's already set. It's Tuesday."

I blink. "That's three days from now."

"Yep."

I quickly open my laptop, heart sinking. "Mel, what time is the court hearing?" I'm already dreading the answer. Worried I'll have to leave tomorrow right in the middle of the potluck.

"Family court, 9:00 a.m. sharp. Downtown."

I close my eyes and exhale, already working through the timing in my head. It's tight but doable. If I leave early enough on Monday, I can have a meeting that day, make the hearing on Tuesday and still be here for the potluck.

"I can make this work," I say, more to myself than to Mel. "I'll be at the hearing."

"This is what I need from you." I'm already clicking through tabs on my laptop. "Book me two round-trip tickets for as early as you can Monday morning. Have a car pick us up when we land. Let Mrs. Perry know to meet me at the courthouse thirty minutes early."

"Two tickets?" Mel asks cautiously.

"Yes," I say, without offering more. "I'll send the passenger details shortly."

173

"So, you're planning on returning to your vacation after?" Her tone shifts into something more curious. "And you're bringing someone with you?"

I laugh at the surprise in her voice. I can practically hear the gears turning.

"You met someone, didn't you?" she asks, trying, and failing, not to squeal.

"Maybe." I grin into the phone.

"Oh my God, you totally did!" she blurts, full-on giddy now.

I hush her quickly. "Shh! Just in case he can't go, make one of the tickets refundable."

"Fine, fine." She buzzes with delight. "But you did meet someone."

I sigh, smiling to myself. "Yeah, I did. But it's not a thing yet. Not really."

"Well," she says, smugly, "you don't invite not-a-things to court hearings and fly them across state. Just saying."

I laugh. "Oh, shut up. I'll send you his info if he can make it. Thanks for all your help."

"Mm-hmm," she hums, clearly not buying my attempt at downplaying it. "Can't wait to meet this mystery man."

I shake my head, still smiling. "I'll see you in a couple days."

Before I can hang up, she adds: "I also thought you should know, Ben has been calling the office lately."

"That's because I blocked him. Call the phone company and have them block his number at the office. Then go ahead and block all emails as well, and thanks for letting me know."

"You got it. See you in two days."

174

Now that I'm running super late, I rush to get dressed, grab my keys and head straight for the Sweet Spot Bakery. Naya agreed to teach me how to make her famous mint chocolate chip cookies, my secret contribution for the potluck.

The second I step through the door, the warm, sweet smell of sugar and vanilla wraps around me. Naya looks up from behind the counter, already grinning.

"You're late."

"I know, I know," I say, breathless. "But I come bearing enthusiasm and a deep desire to not burn your kitchen down."

She laughs and waves me in. "Come on, let's get baking. You've got a reputation to earn."

She walks me through the recipe several times, patient as ever, even though I keep messing it up in increasingly creative ways. The first batch spreads too thin. The second batch? Somehow salty. Don't ask.

"You sure you passed chemistry?"

I narrow my eyes at the mixing bowl. "Barely," I mutter. "But I aced creative disasters."

But finally, after several hours, a lot of flour and one near meltdown later, I get it right. The last batch comes out golden, soft in the middle, with the perfect balance of mint and chocolate. I hold up a cookie triumphantly.

"Look at you," Naya croons, mock wiping a tear. "My little cookie monster's all grown up."

I laugh, ridiculously proud. "These better blow some minds at the potluck."

"They will." She bumps my shoulder. "You earned it."

With my double batch of cookies in hand, Naya and I hug tightly before I thank her again and promise to see her tomorrow. I leave the bakery feeling lighter, and maybe a little proud.

175

My next stop is Cranberry Ridge Grocery, where I gather everything I need for the pasta salad I plan to bring to the potluck, too. By the time I'm done, the sun is already low in the sky, well past dinnertime.

I swing by a ridiculously greasy fast-food place, grab a burger and head straight to the cabin to drop everything off. I don't even bother unpacking. I'm only there for a few minutes before I'm back in the car, already on my way to Miles' house.

I haven't seen him or talked to him all day, and the weight of that is starting to get heavy. Especially after last night. I drive over, nervous and hopeful, practically ghosting him and suddenly desperate to see him.

The moment I step out of the car, I don't even get the door fully closed before I'm wrapped in Miles' arms. Relief and longing slam into me at once, my whole body melting into his. He lifts me off the ground, his lips finding mine in a kiss that's firm and full of relief. I needed this just as much as he did. Maybe more.

With brief hellos and "I missed you" banter done, he takes my hand and gently guides me away from the crowd. Past the tents, past the murmured chatter and clinking bottles, until we reach the back porch. Hidden from the rest of the world.

We take a seat next to each other, the soft creak of the porch swing blending beneath us. Miles leans forward, elbows on his knees, then runs a hand through his hair like he's working up to something.

"What's going on?" I ask gently, watching the way he exhales before finally meeting my eyes.

"When I didn't see you today, I thought maybe I crossed a line last night." He searches my face, eyes scanning for something; regret, hesitation, anything.

But I shake my head slowly. "You didn't cross any line I didn't let you." I say it with more calm than I feel, but inside, my heart is beating out of rhythm. Because yeah, I let him, and I want more.

His jaw flexes slightly, like he's still not convinced.

"I'm sorry I didn't reach out today." I scoot a little closer so our knees touch. "Believe it or not, I was extremely busy. I even had to eat crappy fast food for dinner. That's how bad it was."

That gets a tiny laugh out of him. "Now that's a real tragedy."

"It is," I say with mock seriousness. "I may never recover."

He finally leans back, the tension in his shoulders easing just enough for me to feel it.

"But I do want to tell you something." I take a deep steadying breath, and glance out at the lake before turning back to him. "I have to return to Seattle the day after the potluck. A court hearing came up that I wasn't expecting."

Miles doesn't speak right away. His jaw ticks, but his eyes stay locked on mine, waiting for me to continue.

"It's not a long trip," I add quickly. "Just one day. I'll be back the next night."

He nods slowly, unreadable. "You're flying out alone?"

I hesitate, then shake my head. "No. I was hoping you'd come with me. I already booked two tickets, one refundable, just in case."

His brow lifts slightly, surprise flickering across his face. "You want me to go with you?"

"I do," I say nervously. "But no pressure. I just thought I'd ask."

Miles leans back in his seat, processing everything. Then, finally, he speaks. "Yeah. I'll go."

Relief floods through me, unexpected and overwhelming. "Really?"

He nods. "If you're asking, then I'm going." A small smile tugs at his mouth. "You already booked my ticket. Would be rude to waste it."

I laugh, heart a little lighter. "Well, I did hedge my bets with the refundable option."

His eyes warm, and he lifts my hand to his lips, pressing a soft kiss to my knuckles. "I'm still not backing out."

We sit side by side as I go over the details. I tell him we'll be driving two hours to Spokane for the flight, leaving early Monday morning and flying back the following evening.

Miles listens closely, nodding. "Sounds like a plan." He's already pulling out his phone. I watch as he types up a quick email to Mel using the address I gave him and sends over everything she'll need for the flight.

When he's done, he slides the phone back into his pocket and glances at me. "Anything else I need to know before I officially become your courtroom arm candy?"

"You'll need to look devastatingly handsome and pretend you find legal talk fascinating."

He raises a brow. "Pretend? I was going to bring a notebook and everything."

I snort. "Great. Just don't raise your hand during the hearing."

He leans in, eyes twinkling. "Only if I need clarification on courtroom flirting protocol."

I shake my head, laughing. "You're impossible."

"Impossibly charming," he says with a grin, clearly pleased with himself.

"More like dangerously distracting," I mutter, sipping my water to hide my smile.

I stand, brushing my hands on my jeans. "Let's go say hello to everyone and see what you guys managed to accomplish today."

Miles stands with me. "Only if you promise not to be too impressed."

I roll my eyes playfully. "I can only stay a few more minutes. Then I've got a bulk-sized pasta salad to make for tomorrow."

He grins. "Nothing says romance like chopped peppers and elbow macaroni."

"Exactly."

I greet everyone with a smile, stopping for quick conversations here and there. Laughter, easy chatter. There's a warmth to it all that reminds me just how special this place is. Eventually, Miles joins me, leading me over to show off the progress.

"Stage, dance floor… not bad, huh?" He points with pride in his voice.

I nod, impressed. "You guys got a lot done."

He walks me over to the tent we'd stood under last night, that same familiar smirk on his face. "This one's my favorite stop at this year's potluck."

I roll my eyes and swat his arm. "Oh my God." I can already feel the blush creeping up my neck.

He leans in, mouth brushing close to my ear. "You said that last night, too." He pulls back, smug grin in full force, and yeah, the blush makes it all the way to my face.

He walks me to my car, opening the door. I turn to face him, not quite ready to say goodnight.

"I'll be back first thing in the morning. I told Judy I'd help with the last-minute decorating."

179

He nods, then leans in and presses a kiss to the top of my head. "I'll most likely be up. The bounce houses still need to be set up. That's the only thing left, other than a few odds and ends."

I smile, heart light. "Then I'll see you in the morning."

"See you then," he says with a soft kiss goodbye.

I enter my cabin and head straight for the kitchen, rolling up my sleeves as I start the first batch of pasta salad. I turn on my playlist, something upbeat to keep me going, and pour myself a whiskey. Today's been long, and the hum of music and the burn of the drink help take the edge off.

After two hours and two glasses later, the pasta salad is finally done. I click the lid onto the oversized bowl, shuffle things around in the fridge to make space and cram it in. Done and ready for tomorrow.

Afterward, I grab a quick shower, letting the steam melt away what's left of the day. Then I crawl into bed, exhausted but content. For the first time this whole vacation, I set my alarm. I want to be ready for whatever tomorrow brings.

22

Men vs. Hens

Miles

I'm up before sunrise, the house quiet except for the low hum of the fan. For a second, I just sit on the edge of my bed, rubbing the back of my neck and staring out the window.

All I can think about is her. Not seeing her yesterday messed with me more than I want to admit. Every time I looked around and didn't find her, by the tents, in the crowd, even over by Judy, I felt it. That absence. Like something was missing I didn't know I'd started counting on. When her car finally rolled up the drive and I saw her step out, my whole damn chest exhaled. *Yeah. I've got it bad.*

I thought I had a pretty solid handle on how I felt about her. But yesterday made it clear. I'm not just interested. I'm already invested. All the way. And it scares the hell out of me.

It's around six in the morning when I hear Reed walk in the door. I get ready and head downstairs. I find Reed already in the kitchen, coffee in hand. I grunt a lazy greeting and pour myself a cup. He grunts back. Typical. We finish our first cups in silence, like most mornings he's here.

I clear my throat. "Can you cover the farm for me tomorrow and Tuesday?"

He eyes me over his mug. "Yeah, why?"

"I'm going with Kinsley to Seattle for a court hearing she has to be at."

That gets his attention. His brow lifts, curious. "Overnight? Are you two fucking?"

A punch to the arm stops anything else he was going to add. "No, jackass."

He smirks, rubbing his arm like I actually hurt him. "Yeah, right. Everyone saw you kiss her yesterday."

"It was just a kiss," I lie, the words leaving a little too fast. We've definitely done more than kiss.

"Okay," he says slowly, the disbelief clear in his voice.

I just shake my head and sip my coffee, pretending like this conversation never happened. I hear the rumble of a truck pulling down the driveway and set my cup in the sink. Reed does the same behind me. "The bounce houses are here," I say, slipping on my boots.

When I step outside, I spot Judy and Kinsley near one of the tents, chopping vegetables and arranging them in trays. I head down the stairs and make my way over.

"Good morning, ladies." I lean in and kiss Judy on the cheek.

She smiles down at her cutting board, looking smug as hell. When I kiss the top of Kinsley's head, I glance back, and Judy's giving me that told-you-so look.

I shoot Kinsley a quick wink and head over to the truck where Reed is giving directions to the driver. We help unload the bounce houses and the heavy blowers that come with them. It takes the better part of two hours to get everything staked down and fully inflated. I chose a pink and purple castle for the girls and a pirate ship for the boys, both towering, bright and impossible to miss.

Reed steps back, hands on his hips, then pats me on the back. "These were a good idea."

"Thanks." I look over our handiwork. "They'll be a hit with the kids."

Seeing it all come together like this feels pretty damn good. Judy and Kinsley approach, eyes wide with excitement.

"Wow, Miles, these are perfect," Judy says.

"We should test them out!" Kinsley claps her hands.

"Go ahead." I gesture toward the pirate ship.

She laughs and practically runs for it, slipping her shoes off as she goes. Judy chuckles and heads back to the food prep while Reed disappears to feed Rocket before everyone arrives.

I make my way over to the entrance, watching Kinsley bounce around like a kid on a sugar high. She stops, catches my eye and grins.

"From in here, no one can see us."

I raise a brow, kick off my boots and climb in. The second I reach her, I scoop her up and toss her gently onto the inflated floor. She rolls over, laughing so hard her eyes start to water. I jump and land on my back beside her, sending her flying a little from the bounce. When she lands, she ends up tucked against my side. I turn, cupping her face in my hand and kiss her.

"Thanks for helping with everything."

"You're welcome," she breathes, still smiling.

I start to sit up, but she grabs my arm and pulls me back down. Now I'm hovering over her. Her eyes burn into mine, and I know I need to get the fuck out of this bounce house before I do something reckless. Because right now, she looks absolutely

183

beautiful. Cheeks flushed, lips soft and pink, hair fanned out around her head and the heat radiating off her is making it impossible to think straight. My pulse pounds, and for a second, I wonder if she can feel how close I am to losing control. Her chest rises and falls, and my gaze trails lower.

Through clenched teeth, I lean in and tell her just that. "I need to get out of this bounce house before I use the bounce to my advantage." I push down on either side of her body, bouncing her up and down under me, showing her what I mean. I bend and kiss her again. We both roll to our feet and slide out of the bounce house, slightly winded and grinning like idiots.

As I help her down the last step, she smiles up at me. "Well, that could've been the best use of a bounce house in history."

I chuckle. "Pretty sure they'd have to rewrite the safety manual."

She laughs, brushing a hand through her hair. "Next time, maybe let me take my earrings off first."

"Next time," I echo, eyeing her with a grin, "I'm bringing a timer. I feel like we had at least thirty more minutes of questionable decisions in there."

She winks. "You bring the timer; I'll bring the poor judgment."

"Deal," I say, already thinking about how hard it's going to be to keep my hands off her the rest of the day. We slip on our shoes, still smiling, and go our separate ways.

The moment she disappears around the corner, I run a hand through my hair and exhale, trying to get my head straight. Thirty more minutes? Hell, five would've done me in. My pulse still hasn't slowed, and my hands are twitching like they miss the feel of her already.

I spot Reed near the chicken coop. When he sees me coming, he chuckles like he knows exactly what just happened.

"You're SO fucking her."

"Just helping test the safety features," I reply dryly, grabbing the feed bucket.

He huffs a laugh. "Right. Does the safety check involve rolling around on top of her or was that a bonus feature?"

I give him a look, but it's pointless. I'm not even trying to hide it anymore. "She's different."

"Yeah, I figured that out the second you almost sprinted across the lawn yesterday to kiss her in front of everyone."

I don't answer right away because he's not wrong. And for once, I don't care who saw. Changing the subject, I nod toward the chickens pecking at the ground. "You ready for the hard part?"

Reed follows my gaze, eyes narrowing. Our next task: wrangle these little monsters into the barn coop so the kids don't mess with them.

"This is gonna be chaos. The second I grab one, the rest are gonna take off like rockets."

"We need to plan this out," Reed agrees, eyeing the biggest hen like it's a personal challenge.

I sigh. "Step one: let's try not to look like complete fools in front of everyone."

Reed shakes his head, resigned. "Yeah, we're in trouble."

I chuckle, knowing he's right. "On my count, grab two. Then we'll only have to chase down the last two."

"Got it," he says, cracking his neck like he's about to enter the ring.

"One…two…three."

I lunge and snag two hens, one under each arm. Reed, on the other hand, looks like he's in a full-on wrestling match with the biggest one.

"What the fuck!" he shouts, stumbling. "This bitch is feisty!"

"You got this!" I laugh, hauling my two toward the barn.

He follows behind, still muttering curses, one squawking chicken flapping wildly in his grip.

Ten minutes later, Reed and I are bent over, out of breath, sweating and still two damn chickens short. Judy walks up, laughing like she's been watching the whole debacle.

"I could watch this all day," she teases, "but we've got things to do. Let me show you how it's done."

She grabs the feed bucket, gives it a few shakes and starts walking like she's got all the time in the world. The last two chickens peek out from their hiding spot, heads tilting. Judy keeps walking, shaking the bucket, not saying a word. Like magic, those little monsters fall in line behind her like she's the damn Chicken Whisperer. Reed and I just stand there, staring in disbelief.

"Did that seriously just work?" he mutters.

I shake my head. "Don't question it. Just accept that we've been outsmarted by an old woman and a couple of chickens."

I pat Reed on the back in silent acceptance of our defeat, and we make our way over to the stack of chairs that still need to be placed around the tables. The band pulls in and starts their sound check, music playing at a low volume as we work.

I glance over and catch sight of Kinsley. She's busy making signs for the chili contest and jotting down the rules for the bounce houses. Her hips sway slightly to the music, her laughter rising easily at something Judy says beside her. My guess is Judy just told her about our chicken adventure. She looks so damn happy. Comfortable. Like she truly belongs here.

When I finish with the last of the chairs, I make my way over to her. She doesn't see me coming until my arms wrap around her waist and I lean in to peek over her shoulder. Of course, her penmanship is perfect. Is there anything about this woman that isn't?

"Looks good."

She turns to face me, eyes sparkling. "Me or the sign?"

"Definitely you. But the sign's not bad either."

"I aim to impress." She tilts her head slightly, clearly enjoying herself.

"You don't have to try."

The air between us tightens. She grins and steps back, just as Judy walks up beside us.

Kinsley clears her throat, brushing her hands off. "I'm almost done here, just a few more finishing touches. Then I need to get cleaned up and grab the pasta salad. I'll be back after that."

I nod, my hands still resting loosely at my sides. "Okay. I'll see you later. I still have a few things to finish up."

She smiles, holding my gaze, before turning back around to finish her handiwork.

I head back toward the barn just as Reed steps up beside me, glancing around.

"What's left?"

"Nothing I can't finish on my own," I say, wiping my hands on a towel. "Go in and get cleaned up."

"Okay. It won't take me long." He heads into the house, leaving me to finish up.

In the barn, I grab a few extension cords and start running them out to the chili cook off tent, knowing there'll be an abundance of crockpots and heating plates that'll need to be plugged in. Tangled up in cords, I pause when I hear fast footsteps. Judy barrels into the barn, out of breath, eyes wide. One look at her face and I know something's wrong. I drop the cord and stand upright, my muscles tightening as I move toward her. "Judy, what is it?"

She tries to speak, panting, clutching her chest. "There's a man," she manages, voice strained. "Kinsley…" she squeaks, still trying to catch her breath. My blood runs cold. My heart jolts, adrenaline spiking through me so fast it makes my hands shake. I don't wait for more. I'm already moving.

23

Unwelcome

Kinsley

Judy and I are just finishing the last two signs when I feel a pair of arms wrap around my waist from behind. Smiling, I turn, ready to tease Miles for being back so soon. Only it's not Miles. My whole body stiffens, heart thudding as I look up.

"Ben?" The name flies from my lips, sharp and cold. My breath catches, stomach plummeting as my brain scrambles to process the sight of him. A split second of fear pulses through me before it burns away. I yank myself out of his grip, fury already building. "What the hell are you doing here?"

"I came to talk to you," he says, eyes wide with faux sincerity.

"I don't want to talk. That's why I blocked you," I snap, voice rising. From the corner of my eye, I see Judy slowly backing away, sensing the tension.

"How did you even find me?" I demand, half yelling now.

Ben shifts uncomfortably but doesn't back down. "You posted pictures. Your location was on them."

I silently curse myself. Stupid mistake. A flood of anger surges through me, hot, shaking, violent. How dare he track me down like some kind of animal?

"We are never getting back together. Ever!" I'm barely able to hold myself still. "I meant what I said."

That's when his face changes, soft and pleading giving way to something uglier. Dread flickering through me as I register the shift. The heat in his eyes, the curl of his lips, something dark unfurls in the pit of my stomach.

"Oh, I get it," he sneers. "You're fucking someone else now, right? That's why you're acting like a goddamn whore."

My mouth falls open in shock. Never once has he spoken to me like that. My fists clench on instinct, the urge to hit something strong.

"Leave. Now." I turn to walk away, my eyes sting, tears threatening to fall. Not from sadness, but from anger. But I don't get far.

Ben grabs my arm, yanking me back. Before I can react, his hand clamps under my chin, forcing me to look at him.

"You're going to talk to me!" he yells. "I came all this way."

I wrench my head free from his grip, heart racing as panic fights rage in my chest. "I said no!" My voice cracks as I step back, breath coming fast.

He blinks, suddenly trying to reel it in. "I'm sorry. I shouldn't have said that," he mutters, like those words can undo what just happened. "But you ARE going to talk to me."

His fingers tighten around my arm, not painfully, but firm enough to make it clear he isn't letting go.

"No, I'm not!" I yank against his hold. "You don't get to show up here and demand anything from me."

His jaw clenches. "Kinsley, don't do this. We need to talk. You owe me that much."

I stare at him, my pulse pounding. "I owe you nothing. You made damn sure of that showing up here."

He steps in closer, his grip still firm, and suddenly his voice dips lower, rougher. "So this is about him, isn't it? That farmer I saw walking away from you. Are you playing house with him? You fucking him now?"

Shock burns through me. "Let go!" My voice trembles with fury. "Right now!"

"You've changed," he spits. "This isn't who you are."

"No," I cut in, my voice rising. "This is exactly who I am. You're not going to tell me otherwise."

His fingers tighten again, just a little too much, and that flicker of fear mixes with the anger already boiling in my blood. Then I hear it. Heavy, deliberate footsteps behind me. A beat later, a voice slices through the air, calm but dangerous.

"If I were you," Miles says, voice low and laced with steel, "I'd get your fucking hands off her before you lose the ability to use them."

Ben stiffens, eyes snapping up. Still, he doesn't let go. Even with Miles standing just feet away, eyes locked, voice sharp as a blade, Ben still holds on.

Miles steps inches from his face, his movement tight, like a storm gathering force, on the edge of breaking. He grabs the front of Ben's shirt in one tight fist, jerking him back with enough force to finally make him release me. I stumble a half step, but before I can fall, Miles' other hand is already on me, steadying.

"Behind me," he commands.

I don't argue. I move, sliding behind him, one hand resting on his arm. He's tense; every muscle drawn tight like a wire ready to snap.

"Don't hurt him," I say softly, not for Ben's sake, but for his. I don't want this to be something he regrets.

Miles glances back at me, just enough to register the touch, the plea. Then his attention shifts back to Ben. He shoves him hard, just one solid push that sends Ben stumbling a few feet back.

"You need to leave," Miles grits out. "Right fucking now. Before I stop asking."

Ben's eyes dart between the two of us, me standing just behind Miles, and Miles standing like a wall between us. For a second, I think he might lunge again. But he doesn't.

He swears under his breath, spits something bitter I can't even make out and turns away. I don't let go of Miles's arm until Ben gets to his car, slams the door and drives out of sight.

I take a deep breath, trying to steady myself. Miles turns to look at me, and all the anger I was holding onto slips away. One single tear escapes, sliding down my cheek before I can stop it. I blink hard and take another shaky breath.

His eyes catch the tear. I see the shift and his entire body goes rigid. His jaw clenches, his fists curl, he spins around, scanning for Ben. Rage burns off him in waves. Because I cried. Because Ben made me cry. But Ben's already gone.

When Miles turns back to me, that fire still in his eyes, I don't wait. I throw myself into his arms. He catches me instantly, holding me tight like he needs it as much as I do. His hand presses to the back of my head, the other around my waist, grounding me, easing the tremble in my limbs as I curl into him.

We just stand there, locked together, holding on. Breathing each other in. Letting the worst of it pass. After another minute, Judy walks up quietly and places her hand on my shoulder.

"Born ready." I slip the badge on and grab my scorecard.

I dig in, spoon by spoon, bowl by bowl, bracing myself for heat, flavor, and the very real possibility of crying in public.

By the time I finish, my mouth is on fire, I can't feel my tongue and snot threatens to run out of my nose. I blink hard, trying not to ruin my makeup as the heat creeps all the way to my ears.

Judy returns just as I start fanning my face with the scorecards like my life depends on it. "How's it going?" She laughs.

"Oh my God!" I gasp, chugging the last of my water. "You could've warned me!"

Still laughing, she holds out a napkin. "Where's the fun in that?"

"I'm pretty sure I lost hearing in my left ear about twenty minutes ago," I mutter, wiping at my face carefully.

"You survived the gauntlet," she says with a wink. "That means you're officially one of us."

I shake my head, still panting. "Oh, good. Since it's official, I'm never doing that again. Find some other sucker from the city next year." I laugh as I grab another water.

Judy chuckles and pats my back. "We'll have a winner once the other judges finish." She nods toward the blue ribbon.

"Yep." I slip off my name badge. "I'm going to find Naya." I wave over my shoulder as I head out into the crowd.

I walk through the crowd, taking in the full sweep of the festivities; laughter, music and the smell of home-cooked food. I feel the warmth of this place wrap around. The contrast is jarring, but it's also comforting. People laughing, plates piled high with food, kids lining up for the bounce houses, couples on the dance floor. It's warm, lively and exactly what a small-town potluck should be.

I spot Naya seated with her family at a nearby table. She looks up, and the moment she sees me, her face lights up. She stands quickly and meets me halfway, her grin as wide as ever.

"Girl, that dress!" She gives me a once-over and wags her eyebrows.

I laugh, feeling a blush rise to my cheeks. "Thanks. You look fantastic, too." And I mean it. She's rocking a burnt orange romper cinched at the waist with a brown leather belt that shows off her figure.

We take a seat next to her family, and Naya starts introducing me to her mom and dad, each of them warm and welcoming in that effortlessly small-town way. We chat for a while, sipping drinks and laughing.

Then a good song comes on, upbeat. Naya claps her hands together. "Oh yes! I love this song. Come on." Before I can respond, she's grabbing my hand and dragging me toward the dance floor.

"Wait, I'm not warmed up!" I protest, laughing as I stumble after her.

"You don't need a warmup," she calls over her shoulder. "You need rhythm and confidence. You've got both, now move!"

We stumble onto the dance floor, laughing as we mix into the crowd. Naya grabs my hands and spins me. For a few minutes, it's just the music, the laughter, and the feeling of being free. We dance like idiots, and it's exactly what I needed.

"Are you okay, sweetheart?"

I pull back from Miles, just enough to turn toward her, and fall into her embrace. Her arms wrap around me like safety itself.

"How did you know I was in trouble?"

She touches my cheek, eyes soft. "I saw it in your eyes, sweet girl."

"Thank you." I squeeze her hand for a second longer before I turn back to Miles.

Without hesitation, I step right back into his arms, needing more of him, needing a little longer to let my heartbeat calm and the world make sense again.

Judy pats Miles' shoulder as she steps away. "I'm glad you didn't kill him," she mutters, then walks off without looking back, knowing exactly what would've happened if Ben had stayed a second longer.

Miles lets out a slow breath, his arms still tight around me, one hand moving gently up and down my back.

I take one more deep breath, then pull back and straighten up, lifting my chin with as much dignity as I can manage. "Okay. I need to get cleaned up. I have a chili contest to judge."

Miles doesn't let go of me right away. His eyes search mine, brows pulling together. "You're not going back to the cabin alone."

I blink. "Miles, I'm fine."

He shakes his head, jaw tense. "You just had a man grab you and call you things that…" He breaks off, visibly reining it in. "I know you can handle yourself, but I won't risk you being alone right now."

"Miles," I start again, softer this time, but he cuts me off with a look.

193

"Judy will go with you," he says firmly. "She's probably already loading a gun in her purse anyway."

As if on cue, Judy appears around the corner, hands on her hips like she's been summoned by name. "I heard my name. What's going on?"

Miles looks at her, dead serious. "Can you walk Kinsley to the cabin?"

Judy narrows her eyes slightly, scanning my face, then nods once. "Of course."

"She's not going alone."

Judy pats his chest. "Relax. If I can scare a bear away, I can handle this."

I touch Miles' arm gently. "I'll be okay. I promise."

His eyes meet mine, hesitation written all over him, but he finally nods.

"I'll see you back here soon," I say, stepping away with Judy.

"You'd better," he replies, still watching me like I might disappear.

Judy and I start toward the cabins, her muttering something under her breath about "city boys with no sense." We walk side by side down the path in silence. She doesn't ask for details. We just let the peace of the walk settle between us, the soft crunch of gravel the only sound.

By the time we reach my cabin, the tightness in my chest has eased. "I've got it from here," I say gently, offering her a small smile. "Thank you again, Judy."

She gives me a look, one that says she's not entirely convinced. "I'll be nearby." She points to her cabin.

Once she turns and heads back to her own cabin, I step inside. The door closes behind me with a soft thud, and I immediately scan

194

the space. Everything is just as I left it. Still, I lock the door behind me and lean against it for a breath, letting the tension release from my shoulders.

A shower helps, hot water washing away the rest of my nerves. I blow-dry my hair straight. Once my hair is done, I slip into the navy-blue maxi dress with thin spaghetti straps and a delicate fall-colored floral print that flows with each step. Today, I go a little heavier on the makeup than I normally would on vacation, bolder eyeliner, a swipe of plum gloss. I'm about to meet a lot of new people, and I want to look my best. When I check the time on my phone, my eyes widen. The potluck starts in ten minutes. "Shit."

I slip on my sandals, grab the massive bowl of pasta salad and the tray of mint chocolate chip cookies, balancing both against my hip as I head for the door. I manage to lock it behind me without dropping anything.

I briskly walk to my car, arms full, when Judy steps out of her cabin like she'd been waiting for me. She's changed into a deep burgundy dress with short sleeves that flows all the way to the ground.

"Wow," I say, pausing. "You look beautiful, Judy. Got a hot date waiting for you?"

She waves a hand at me, laughing. "Oh, please. I don't have time for men. But you… you're going to knock his socks off in that." She wags her finger at me.

"Thanks." My cheeks warm.

"You ready?" I adjust my grip on the pasta salad. My arms are definitely feeling the weight of it now.

"Yes. lead the way."

We both climb into our cars and head toward the biggest event of the fall.

When I pull into the driveway, I park beside the house, surprised by how many people are already here. Cars line the road, and voices carry across the lawn, mixing with the soft hum of music in the background. As I step out of the car, Reed is already making his way down the steps.

"You need a hand with that?" he calls out.

"Sure, thank you." I pop open the back door and lift out the pasta salad. I pass it to him carefully, then grab the tray of cookies.

He glances down at them. "Mint chocolate chip?"

"Yes. Do you like them too?"

He snorts. "Hell no. Miles is the only one I know who actually likes those things."

I laugh. "Yeah, I don't get it. They taste like toothpaste."

Reed chuckles. "You're not wrong."

We walk together, weaving through the crowd toward the food tent. The air is thick with the smell of chili and grilled meat. I set the tray of cookies down on the dessert table while Reed places the pasta salad among the other sides and mains.

"Thanks again," I say, giving him a grateful smile.

"No problem."

I head straight for the chili contest tent and immediately stop in my tracks. I'm absolutely blown away by how many different kinds there are, some bubbling in crockpots, others simmering in cast iron pots, each one labeled with a number and a name like Firehouse Five Alarm or Mama June's Sweet Heat.

Judy spots me and waves from the judges' table. "We made it just in time!" she calls, grinning.

I smile and walk over, picking up the little laminated badge she made with Judge Kinsley written in sparkly letters. Of course, she added glitter.

"Ready?"

"Born ready." I slip the badge on and grab my scorecard.

I dig in, spoon by spoon, bowl by bowl, bracing myself for heat, flavor, and the very real possibility of crying in public.

By the time I finish, my mouth is on fire, I can't feel my tongue and snot threatens to run out of my nose. I blink hard, trying not to ruin my makeup as the heat creeps all the way to my ears.

Judy returns just as I start fanning my face with the scorecards like my life depends on it. "How's it going?" She laughs.

"Oh my God!" I gasp, chugging the last of my water. "You could've warned me!"

Still laughing, she holds out a napkin. "Where's the fun in that?"

"I'm pretty sure I lost hearing in my left ear about twenty minutes ago," I mutter, wiping at my face carefully.

"You survived the gauntlet," she says with a wink. "That means you're officially one of us."

I shake my head, still panting. "Oh, good. Since it's official, I'm never doing that again. Find some other sucker from the city next year." I laugh as I grab another water.

Judy chuckles and pats my back. "We'll have a winner once the other judges finish." She nods toward the blue ribbon.

"Yep." I slip off my name badge. "I'm going to find Naya." I wave over my shoulder as I head out into the crowd.

I walk through the crowd, taking in the full sweep of the festivities; laughter, music and the smell of home-cooked food. I feel the warmth of this place wrap around. The contrast is jarring, but it's also comforting. People laughing, plates piled high with food, kids lining up for the bounce houses, couples on the dance floor. It's warm, lively and exactly what a small-town potluck should be.

I spot Naya seated with her family at a nearby table. She looks up, and the moment she sees me, her face lights up. She stands quickly and meets me halfway, her grin as wide as ever.

"Girl, that dress!" She gives me a once-over and wags her eyebrows.

I laugh, feeling a blush rise to my cheeks. "Thanks. You look fantastic, too." And I mean it. She's rocking a burnt orange romper cinched at the waist with a brown leather belt that shows off her figure.

We take a seat next to her family, and Naya starts introducing me to her mom and dad, each of them warm and welcoming in that effortlessly small-town way. We chat for a while, sipping drinks and laughing.

Then a good song comes on, upbeat. Naya claps her hands together. "Oh yes! I love this song. Come on." Before I can respond, she's grabbing my hand and dragging me toward the dance floor.

"Wait, I'm not warmed up!" I protest, laughing as I stumble after her.

"You don't need a warmup," she calls over her shoulder. "You need rhythm and confidence. You've got both, now move!"

We stumble onto the dance floor, laughing as we mix into the crowd. Naya grabs my hands and spins me. For a few minutes, it's just the music, the laughter, and the feeling of being free. We dance like idiots, and it's exactly what I needed.

24

She Danced Anyway

Miles

I stand just to the left of the dance floor, leaning against a tent pole, beer in hand, eyes fixed on her. Kinsley dancing with Naya. God, she looks so goddamn good. Laughing, spinning like the earlier storm never touched her. She looks free, hair straight, flowing behind her when she spins. As much as I want to walk over there, pull her into my arms and hold her close, I won't. Not yet. She's with her friend, smiling wide, and after the shitstorm she dealt with earlier, she deserves this moment. So, I wait.

My mind keeps pulling me backward. Back to that moment, seeing her frozen under another man's hands. The same prick she'd blocked, tried to avoid. There he was, gripping her arm like he owned her, saying things I should've broken his jaw for.

I'd never seen her look like that before. It was a mix of anger and fear. Then that goddamn tear rolled down her cheek. Something in me snapped. If Ben hadn't walked off, I don't know how far I would've gone.

Even after he left, I didn't let myself relax. I watched her, jaw aching from how hard I was clenching it. Judy was calm, and I know Judy wouldn't hesitate to protect, not just Kinsley, but anyone. She walked Kinsley back to her cabin, and I stood there, making sure they made it all the way inside. Only then did I breathe.

I needed a minute after that. To wash the sweat and adrenaline off. I asked Reed to keep an eye out for her, told him not to let her out of his sight until she was back in the middle of everything. He didn't question it. Just nodded and stayed alert like I knew he would. Later, he came to find me. "She's judging chili," he said, smirking, knowing Kinsley was about to be set on fire. That's when I filled him in on what happened.

Now, here I am, cleaned up, calmer and waiting. Because she's dancing now. Laughing again. And that's all I want for her. Happiness. To feel safe.

After what Ben said, how he looked at her, like she was his to claim, I'm still burning. But not with rage. Not anymore. Because she's mine. Maybe not forever. I'm not foolish enough to believe that. But for as long as she's here, she's mine.

I tried to stay away at first. Told myself it was the smart thing. Then I gave in. Slowly. Cautiously. I convinced myself I had time. That taking it slow would keep me from getting in too deep. But I'm already there. Now, I'm done waiting. Done pretending I don't want all of her. As soon as this crowd clears and we're alone, I'm taking what's mine.

When the music stops and she steps off the dance floor, laughing, she spots me. Her smile fades just a little when she catches the burn in my eyes. She leans over, says something to Naya with a quick pat to her shoulder, then starts walking my way.

I push off the tent pole, drop my beer bottle in a recycling bin, my eyes never leaving her, and meet her halfway. As soon as she's close enough, I cup her face, bring her closer. "You look beautiful," I whisper into her lips and kiss her, deep, possessive, with everything I've been holding back since the first day she got here.

I claim her right there in front of everyone, and I don't care that the whole fucking town sees. When we pull apart, her eyes stay locked with mine.

"I missed you, too," she says, a soft smile playing on her lips.

I clench my jaw, trying not to drag her off somewhere private. I take a steadying breath before I speak.

"I more than missed you. I need…" I cut myself off before I say too much. But she knows. I can see it in her eyes. Her breath hitches as she steps in closer, rises on her toes and presses a kiss to my cheek.

"Okay," she whispers, then eases back.

Fuck. That didn't help calm me. If anything, it made it worse. "Kinsley," I say, low and quiet, a warning, a plea. A silent "be careful." Because I'm already barely holding on.

She nods, understanding exactly what I'm NOT saying, then takes a slow step back, her smile softening.

"Let's walk around and mingle." Her hand reaches for mine, fingers brushing first. I don't hesitate. I slide my hand into hers.

We weave through the crowd together, her fingers laced with mine, her smile genuine. People greet us as we pass, some familiar, others not, but Kinsley handles them all like she's been doing this for years. She laughs, shakes hands, compliments casseroles she definitely didn't try. I watch her, amused and impressed.

We stop near one of the long tables where Luke, Reed and Dylan are posted up with beers in hand, talking shit like it's a sport.

"Well, if it ain't the queen of chili," Dylan says, tipping his bottle toward Kinsley.

She groans. "Please, don't remind me. I still can't smell anything."

Reed laughs loud, clapping her on the back. "That's how you know you did it right."

"You did it last year, didn't you?" she asks, narrowing her eyes.

"Sure did. Took me two full days to recover. Thought I was having an allergic reaction to flavor."

"I drank five bottles of water," she says, holding up fingers for proof. "I had to blink away tears so I wouldn't ruin my makeup."

"You looked like you'd seen battle when I walked by earlier." I stifle a laugh.

"Don't act like it wasn't yours and Judy's idea for me to get involved." She elbows me gently. "You all could've warned me. Where was the chili support group?"

"We were busy placing bets on how long you'd last," Luke deadpans.

"Who won?"

Dylan grins. "Judy. Said you'd make it all the way through, but you'd cuss us out after."

She raises her beer. "Smart woman."

"Next year, I'm getting you a bib and a fire extinguisher," Reed says.

"Next year, I'm picking the judges." Kinsley points at me. "And you, sir, are first on the list."

They all laugh, and the teasing keeps going, easy and light. The kind of back-and-forth that means you've been accepted. Kinsley leans into it effortlessly charming, quick witted and confident in all the best ways. I just stand there, watching her hold her own like she's been part of this circle for years.

The speakers crackle, and Judy's voice rings out from the small stage near the dance floor. "All right, folks! It's that time. We have our official chili contest winner!"

The crowd starts to gather, cheers rising in anticipation. Kinsley groans playfully and hides her face against my shoulder. "If she calls me up there, I swear I'm running."

I laugh, slipping my arm around her waist. "Relax, she's just announcing the winner. No speeches needed."

Judy's got a blue ribbon in one hand and a microphone in the other. "This year's winner, by unanimous judge approval, is Bob Holland!" Everyone cheers, and I notice others who had chili in the contest congratulating Bob.

The music picks up again, something fun and upbeat, and people start drifting back toward the dance floor. Couples sway in pairs, kids dart around chasing each other.

Kinsley tugs my hand. "Come on. I want to see the bounce houses in action."

We walk toward the field where they're set up. The pirate ship and castle are lit up under string lights, packed with giggling, screaming kids bouncing like their lives depend on it.

"Look at them, totally fearless."

"They're wild animals," I reply, watching one kid launch himself across the entire castle.

She laughs, leaning her head on my shoulder for a second before straightening again. "Have you eaten yet?"

"I was waiting on you."

She grins. "After the chili, you might have to wait until tomorrow. Let's get you some food." She pulls at my arm.

We make our way over to the food tents, still buzzing. As we approach, I immediately notice a tray of mint chocolate chip cookies at the end of the dessert table.

I nudge Kinsley gently with my elbow. "Are those what I think they are?"

She tries to play it cool, but her smile gives her away. "Maybe."

I raise a brow, already reaching for one. "You made these?"

"Mm-hmm," she hums, watching me bite into it. "With a lot of help from Naya."

I glance over at her, mid-chew. "You baked with Naya?"

"Oh yeah." She crosses her arms like it's a story worth telling. "She walked me through the recipe three times. I still managed to mess up the first two batches. One came out like paper-thin pancakes, the second was accidentally salty."

I laugh, licking a smear of chocolate off my thumb. "Sounds about right."

"But the last batch?" she says proudly, lifting her chin. "Perfect. Naya even said so. Might've cried a little. Not me, her. Probably."

I chuckle, shaking my head. "Well, for the record, they're amazing. Best thing I've had all day."

She nudges my side. "They're definitely better than the chili."

"Infinitely better." I reach in and grab another one. "That chili nearly killed you."

"Oh, I remember. My tongue still hasn't recovered." She points to the water bottle tucked under her arm. "I've been clinging to this like it's life support."

I take another bite, watching her out of the corner of my eye. "So, you baked cookies for me and risked your life for the honor of judging chili?"

She lifts a brow. "What can I say? I'm committed."

"Damn right you are." I lean in, brushing a kiss to her cheek. "And just so we're clear, this cookie just solidified your place in the town."

"Oh good." She smirks. "All it took was almost poisoning myself and bribing the locals with sugar."

"Welcome to small-town politics," I tease.

We eat... well, I eat, and Kinsley picks at the blandest food she can find, like she's afraid of setting her mouth on fire again. Then we head toward the cooler where the guys are now congregating.

The sun's starting to dip behind the trees, casting everything in a golden wash. Laughter rolls across the field, only a few kids still bouncing, and the music from the speakers hums low and easy.

Reed lifts his beer when he sees us coming. "She lives!" He laughs.

"Barely," Kinsley deadpans, earning a round of chuckles from the group.

Judy walks up behind us, her voice warm but serious. "I was just filling the boys in on what happened earlier."

I glance at Kinsley to make sure she's okay with it, and she gives a small nod.

"Son of a bitch," Dylan mutters, shaking his head. "You handled it better than I would've, Miles."

Reeds jaw ticks. "Touch someone like that in front of me, and they're not walking away."

"I might have thrown a punch or two," Luke adds, voice low. "But you handled it. Didn't make a scene. That matters."

I shrug, taking a sip of my drink. "Didn't feel calm at the time."

Kinsley's hand brushes mine again, and I glance down just as our fingers lace together. Her eyes meet mine, quiet gratitude behind them.

They all keep talking, voices easing back into normal, the topic shifting to something lighter, but I quietly step back.

"I'll be right back," I murmur, giving Kinsley's hand a squeeze.

She glances at me, curious but trusting. I head off through the thinning crowd, weaving around tables until I find the band gathered by the small stage, packing up a few cables.

"Hey!" I draw the lead guy's attention. "How much for a few slow songs before you call it for the night?"

He eyes me for a second, then grins. "For you? Just a couple of beers."

I hand him a folded bill anyway. "Appreciate it."

By the time I make it back to Kinsley, the first notes are already floating through the air. A few couples naturally drift toward the open space in front of the stage.

I step in close, lean down to her ear. "Dance with me?"

She smiles before I even finish the question, reaching for my open hand. "Yes."

We start walking toward the dance floor, moving slow as the music plays on. Before we get there, a familiar voice stops us in our tracks.

"Good job not messing up the potluck." I turn to find Old Man Floyd standing there, arms crossed, expression as dry as ever, but his tone carries something suspiciously close to approval.

My brows lift. "Thanks," I say, surprised. That's probably the nicest thing he's ever said to me.

Floyd tips his chin at Kinsley. "You clean up nice, young lady."

She grins. "Thank you, Floyd."

He huffs, pats me on the shoulder and mutters, "Night, kid," before turning and heading out. For a second, I just stand there, surprised by how much that simple gesture means coming from him.

We both watch him go, a little stunned.

Kinsley blinks up at me. "Did that just happen?"

"I think it did," I say, still half in disbelief. "Might need to mark the calendar."

She laughs. The sound alone is enough to pull me back to the moment.

The music swells gently as we step onto the edge of the dance floor. Couples already sway around us, arms looped, heads tucked close. I turn to her, holding out my hand again.

"Ready?"

"Yes." She steps into me. Her body presses against mine, soft curves aligning with every part of me that's already way too aware of her.

I rest my hand low on her back, just above dangerous territory. She tilts her head up, her eyes locking with mine, full of heat and something darker, something hungry.

"You keep looking at me like that…" Breath warm against her skin. "You're gonna make me forget we're not alone."

Her fingers brush lightly against the back of my neck. "Who says I'm not trying to?"

My hand tightens on her waist. "Kinsley," I warn, voice low.

"Miles," she mimics, soft and sultry. Then her teeth graze her bottom lip, and fuck me if that isn't the end of my restraint.

I shift my hand slightly lower, fingers brushing the top curve of her ass. "One more second of this, and I'm dragging you behind that tent."

Her breath catches. She doesn't move. Doesn't pull away.

207

"Do it," she whispers, teasing, but her voice is just as wrecked as mine.

God, I want to. Right here, right now. But I don't. Instead, I pull her tighter, our bodies flush, hips barely swaying to the rhythm now. The crowd has thinned to just a few scattered couples, the music softer, the air heavier. Judy and the guys wave their goodbyes from across the lawn. We barely notice.

Another slow song starts, and we don't let go. She rests her head against my chest for a beat, and I press a kiss into her hair, breathing her in like I'm trying to calm something wild in me.

But there's no calming it. Not tonight, not after everything that's happened. Her ex putting his hands on what's mine. The way she bounced back from a morning that should've wrecked her. The way she fits so damn easily with my friends, with my family, like she's always belonged here. I want her. Not just tonight. I want her for as long as she's here. I won't ask her to choose. I won't be the reason she gives up the life she built in Seattle. But until she leaves, she's mine. Here, with her body against mine like this and the way her fingers keep brushing just beneath the collar of my shirt. I know she feels it, too.

The music fades out, the last notes lingering in the air as we step off the dance floor. Neither of us says much, just fingers intertwined, hearts still pounding. We find an empty table, still a little breathless, letting the quiet settle between us as the band starts breaking down their gear. A few murmured voices carry through the night, but mostly, it's stillness.

"They were good." Kinsley nods toward the musicians as they begin loading up.

"You think everyone had a good time?"

She leans back in her seat, her smile soft. "Definitely. It felt like something people will talk about next year."

I watch as the last of the amps get packed away. "You were a big part of that."

She nudges my foot under the table, grinning. "I just judged chili and tied some streamers."

"You handled more than that."

Her eyes meet mine, warm and steady. "So did you."

We fall quiet again, watching as the band's van pulls away, headlights disappearing into the night. For the first time all day, we're truly alone.

"I should probably get going," she says, thumbing over her shoulder toward her car.

I lean in, resting my forearms on my knees, eyes locked on hers. "Is that what you want?"

She mirrors my posture, her tone soft but steady. "You know what I want," she says, her gaze never leaving mine. "The question is, what are you willing to take?"

That line sits between us, heavy and sharp, charged with everything we haven't said out loud. I feel it in that place where logic used to live. My jaw ticks as I study her, searching for hesitation, but there isn't any. Just a flicker of defiance in her eyes, the kind that dares me to stop pretending I'm not already all in.

25

Every Inch of Want

Kinsley

I've felt the shift in him all day, the way his restraint frayed little by little. The kiss. The dance. The way he looked at me after Ben left. Possessive need ran through him. I want to see what happens when I push just a little more.

So, I lean back in my chair, eyes never leaving his. I can feel the weight of his gaze on me, hungry and slow. Then I rise to my feet, slipping off my sandals one by one and letting them fall to the grass. He doesn't move. Just leans back in his chair, lounging with an easy confidence, watching me like he's already unwrapping me in his head. Relaxed. Confident. Too confident. Perfect.

I flash him a wicked grin. Then, without warning, I hike my dress to my knees and take off, barefoot and laughing, bolting straight for the castle bounce house. Behind me, I hear the scrape of his chair and a low curse that makes me laugh harder.

I know he could've caught me; he had every chance. But he didn't. He let me go, dress hitched in my fists, bare feet pounding the grass as I sprinted like a maniac toward the castle bounce house.

Now I'm inside, the thick air pressing in around me, my heart racing. Not from the running, but from the look in his eyes as he leans one arm against the inflated wall, the other buried in his pocket, just watching.

I jump, just a little at first. The floor gives, soft and buoyant beneath my feet. My dress lifts around me, floating like something out of a dream. His eyes track every movement. Not blinking. Not smiling. Just consuming. I stop and face him, tension coiling in the space between us.

Reaching up slowly, I pull one spaghetti strap over my shoulder. Then the other. His eyes flicker, just barely, the heat in them intensifies. He pushes off the wall, stepping into the center opening like he's being pulled by a string. I wrap my arms over my chest, keeping the dress from falling, trembling, from nerves, adrenaline, desire.

His voice is low and impossibly hot. "Drop your arms."

I pause because I want him to feel this moment. Then I let one arm fall. His jaw ticks. I drop the other. The dress slips down, a soft whisper of fabric pooling at my feet.

Standing there, in my white strapless bra and matching thong, bare legs, bare shoulders, I'm suddenly struck by how vulnerable I feel. Nothing stands between us now but the fragile thread of his restraint, and even that's starting to unravel.

His eyes darken, his body tightens, but he doesn't move. Neither do I.

I thought teasing him would be a good idea. Something fun. A little sexy power play to mess with his head, get even for all the ways he's turned me inside out. But now I'm standing here, bare shoulders, nearly naked, dress around my ankles, and suddenly it's not a game anymore.

God, the way he looks at me, it's the kind of gaze that should make me want to hide, but instead it sends a slow, aching pull low in my belly. It's hot. It's possessive. But it's reverent too, like he wants to worship every inch of me. Knowing I bring that out in him, it does something to me. It's power. But it's also terrifying. I swallow, pulse wild.

"I didn't think you'd just, stare."

His lips part, just barely. He blinks once, slowly, like he's dragging himself out of whatever storm I just stirred up inside him. Still holding my gaze, he reaches down and toes off his boots, calm, unhurried. My breath catches. Next, his hands go to the back of his neck. He grabs the collar of his shirt and pulls it over his head in one smooth motion, tossing it aside. Suddenly, I forget how to breathe.

His chest is broad, every inch of him cut and sun-kissed. His abs ripple with every breath, his body shaped by years of work and sweat. His arms flex as he moves, thick and powerful, veins trailing like roadmaps I want to trace. And that V, sharp and low, disappearing beneath his jeans, makes my knees go a little weak.

His voice is low and rough, like gravel over silk. "You need to know, Kinsley, there's a line. And you're standing on the edge of it."

"What happens if I step over it?"

"If you step over, baby," his voice dips into something dark and primal. "I'm not letting you go until you know exactly who you belong to."

I take a step forward, slow and deliberate, out of my fallen dress. His jaw ticks. His eyes, dark, fixed, don't stray from mine.

He urges me through clinched teeth. "Turn around."

Without hesitation, I do. My back faces him now, the thin strap of my thong hugging my hips, my breath shallow as the air brushes cool over my heated skin. There's a beat of silence, thick and heavy. Then I hear it, the sharp inhale, the low curse under his breath.

His voice gets rougher, deeper. "Take off your bra."

My hands twitch at my sides, heart pounding like a drum inside my chest. He still hasn't touched me. But he doesn't need to. Because I'm already burning. With my back still to him, I reach around slowly, fingers fumbling just a little as I find the clasp. I undo it, one hook at a time, then the bra slips down the front of my body, letting it hit the floor. I look over my shoulder, needing to see him.

His eyes are locked on me, storm dark and heavy with heat. "Fucking gorgeous."

I turn my head forward again, breath shallow, skin prickling. There's a flutter of uncertainty flowing through my mind. Standing there, nearly bare in front of him, it's the most exposed I've ever felt. Maybe that's why he's letting it stretch like this. Because he knows.

The floor shifts again under my bare feet, and I know he's stepped in behind me. I can feel the heat of him at my back, even though he's still not touching me. My heart thunders against my ribs, every inch of me wired and waiting.

"Miles," I whisper, soft like a plea. The anticipation is a living thing now, coiled tight in my stomach.

He doesn't answer with words. Instead, I feel his hand gather my hair and sweep it forward over my shoulder. Then his mouth is on me, hot, deliberate kisses trailing from the nape of my neck down to the curve of my shoulder. His lips are warm, and the contrast makes me shiver. My whole body shudders, breath catching, nipples hard and aching in the cool air. His touch is slow, methodical. Like he wants me trembling.

He lets my hair fall, and his palm slides down the center of my spine, warm and steady, until it reaches the small of my back. There, he pauses. Then his other hand moves, skimming up the back of my thigh, over the swell of my ass, until both hands settle at my hips. He hooks his thumbs in the waistband of my thong.

"Breathe, baby." His lips brush the shell of my ear.

213

I exhale shakily, the sound embarrassingly loud in the quiet air. He lowers them inch by inch, his fingers grazing my skin, until the fabric slips past my knees and pools at my feet. I step out of them, still facing away, heart hammering.

His hands return, slow and reverent, squeezing the curve of my ass before gliding forward to rest low on my belly. He presses his mouth just beneath my ear again, his voice like gravel.

"Turn around and face me."

I do. Slowly. The moment our eyes meet, something inside me snaps. The hunger in his gaze, the restraint in every line of his body, it wrecks me. I'm standing there, completely bare, while he's still in his jeans, shirtless, muscles tensed and jaw tight. I want to pull him into me. I take one step toward him. He doesn't move. Just watches.

I reach for the button on his jeans, desperate to feel him, but he catches my wrists, stopping me. "Don't rush this, baby. I want you to feel every second."

My thighs press together instinctively. The ache is a steady throb now, need crawling across my skin like fire. I want him so badly I feel like I might explode.

He lets go of my wrists and brings his hands to my face, thumbs brushing my cheeks. His kiss is slow this time, deep, consuming, his tongue teasing mine until I'm moaning into his mouth.

When he breaks the kiss, he doesn't rush. He lets his mouth travel down again, tracing my collarbone, biting the soft skin at the base of my throat. His teeth graze lightly, and I gasp. His hands slide over my sides, across my ribs, just brushing the curve of my breast, cupping it until his mouth reaches my nipple. He flattens his tongue, slowly tasting me. He bites down softly, sucking further into his mouth.

"Please. I need more… all of it."

214

He hums like he's considering it, and something about the way his eyes darken makes my whole body tense with anticipation. A fresh wave of heat rushes through me. Then he steps back slightly and drops to his knees in front of me. "Let me see how wet you are."

My eyes widen. He kisses my hip, sucking and biting lower, until his mouth is on my center. My head falls back instantly, lips parting as a moan slips free. His tongue moves slowly at first, soft, almost lazy, like he's savoring me. The sensation is so good I can barely think. Every lick is measured, purposeful, sending sparks up my spine.

I try to move my hips, desperate for more, but his hands pin them in place with firm, unrelenting strength.

"Take it," he says against me, the vibration of his voice sending another ripple through my core. "You taste so good, baby."

I whimper, nodding frantically, because I can't form words. My hands tangle in his hair, nails scraping his scalp as I arch into him. Still, he drags it out. He's methodical. Cruel in the best way. I'm unraveling inch by inch, breath short, body trembling.

"Please, Miles, I can't."

"You can," he growls. "Come on my tongue."

His tongue circles, presses, licks deep. He reaches up and slides two fingers inside me, stretching me, curling into the perfect spot, and it hits me, sharp and sudden. I cry out, shaking as I come against his mouth, vision going white at the edges as I scream out his name and praise God at the same time. "Miles, oh my God!" He doesn't stop, stretching out my orgasm until my legs start to give in.

When he rises, I'm breathless, quivering, still pulsing with aftershocks. He kisses me again, messy, full of heat, the taste of my arousal on his tongue.

He pulls back only far enough to speak. "Do you want more?"

I kiss him hard, whispering against his mouth. "Yes."

He smiles, wicked and warm. "Not out here."

Before I can argue, he throws me over his shoulder, swats my ass. I let out a surprised laugh. He's already moving, striding out of the bounce house with purpose. I cling to him, giddy and breathless. He stops and sets me on the cold ground. He grabs his shirt and slides it over my head, pulling my hair out of the collar. Then, without warning, I'm thrown back over his shoulder again.

He carries me across the yard and up the steps to his house. The door creaks open, then closes with a soft thud behind us. We don't stop. Up the stairs, two, three at a time. At the top, he finally sets me down, just outside his bedroom door.

"I've never been in here," I whisper, catching my breath.

"Baby, you're not going back to that cabin tonight." He pushes the door open.

We step inside, and then his mouth is back on mine, hungry now, all his restraint burning off as he backs me toward the bed. Then he stops. He looks at me for a long beat, then reaches forward and slowly pulls his shirt off my body, baring me again. But this time, it feels different. Intentional.

He kneels in front of me again, hands sliding up my thighs. "I'm not done with you," he says, eyes locked on mine. "Not until you're shaking again."

His fingers brush between my thighs, and I gasp, already sensitive. "You feel that? That's mine. Every drop of it."

He rises, chest to chest with me now, hands exploring every curve with reverent slowness. He palms my breasts, rolls my nipples between his fingers.

I arch into him, whimpering. "Every time you gasp, every shiver, mine."

I nod, breathless, aching. "Miles, please."

216

He hushes me with a kiss, slow and deep, while one hand trails down again, slipping between my legs, circling gently.

I'm shaking already, from the inside out. "Good girl. Now lay back."

I do as he says, heart thudding as I lower myself onto the bed, the sheets cool against my overheated skin. He watches me, standing at the edge, his chest rising and falling like he's holding back a storm.

Then his fingers go to the button of his jeans. I can't look away. He undoes it slowly, eyes locked on mine, then pushes them down his hips and steps out, leaving only his black boxer briefs stretched tight across his hard cock. My breath catches. He's big. Hard. And so damn hot.

"Miles," I whisper.

His mouth curves into something feral. "You still want more?"

"Yes… God, yes."

He leans over me, planting one hand beside my head while the other brushes the inside of my thigh. He touches me like I'm breakable, but his voice is anything but gentle.

"Then you're gonna take it, slow, deep, every damn inch."

A shudder rips through me. His fingers trail through my slick heat, circling, teasing, never quite enough. I arch into his touch, desperate, aching, but he's patient. Too patient. He takes his time, driving me right to the edge again.

"I love how responsive you are," he murmurs, voice like a drug. "One touch and you fall apart."

"I can take it," I pant, back arching. "Please."

He growls low in his throat, then finally slides his boxers down. My eyes drop instinctively. Holy hell. He's beautiful. Thick and hard, the head already slick, and he catches me looking.

217

"Don't get shy now, City Girl." He leans over me, dragging the length of his body against mine.

He reaches between us, guiding himself to my entrance, just nudging. "Look at me." His voice is low and demanding.

The second our eyes lock, he pushes in, slow, steady, letting me feel every inch of him. I gasp, clawing at his shoulders, overwhelmed with the stretch, the pressure, the pleasure curling deep in my belly.

He groans above me. "Fuck, you're so tight."

I wrap my legs around his waist, anchoring him to me. "Don't stop."

"Not a chance," he growls.

Then he starts to move. Long, deep thrusts that steal my breath and unravel every coherent thought I've ever had. His mouth is on mine again, then my neck, my breasts, everywhere. His rhythm is slow, controlled, but I can feel the tension building in him with every thrust. And in me.

I'm coming apart, moaning his name, hands gripping him like he's the only solid thing in the world. He picks up speed just enough to push me closer, his hand sliding between us again, rubbing tight circles over my swollen clit.

"Let go for me," he rasps against my mouth. "Come, Kinsley. Now."

I do. With a cry that rips through me. My whole body shakes as I come, and he follows with a groan, hips bucking once, twice, before he stills, emptying himself buried deep inside me. The only sound is our breath, tangled and gasping.

We lie tangled together, my head resting on his chest, his hand splayed wide across my back like he's staking a claim. His skin is still warm, damp from the heat we made, and I can feel the steady thud of his heart against my cheek. Neither of us speaks at first. The room is quiet except for the slowing rhythm of our breathing and the distant hum of night crickets outside the open window.

Then I feel it. The shift. His chest rises with a deeper breath, and his fingers grip ever so slightly on my spine. When he speaks, his voice is low, firm. The same voice that gave me orders in the bounce house. The one that makes my pulse skip.

"You're mine."

I blink, slowly lifting my head to look at him. He's staring at the ceiling, jaw tight, expression unreadable. But something about the way he said it lingers in the space between us, heavy and real. I feel it settle inside me, deeper than any touch, any kiss. It's not just possession. It's something else. A claim laced with emotion he's too careful to say out loud. When his eyes drop to mine, they burn with certainty.

"Until you leave," he adds, his voice unwavering.

I swallow, heart thudding.

"I don't want anyone else touching you. Looking at you like they've got a chance." His voice deepens, threading with possessiveness. "Because they don't. Not here. Not while I still have time with you."

I don't speak. I can't.

He lifts a hand and cups my cheek, his thumb brushing softly under my eye. "I know what this is. I know you have a life back in Seattle, and I'm not gonna ask you to give that up. But I need you to know something, Kinsley." His fingers flex slightly. "While you're here. Every second. Every night. Every part of you is mine."

I breathe out shakily, the heat in his gaze undoing me all over again. He leans in, brushing his lips over mine. Not hard. Not rushed. Just a kiss filled with promise. With something deeper than either of us has said out loud. And then he pulls back, eyes still locked on mine.

"You got that, City Girl?"

"Yeah," I whisper. "I got it." But I already know the truth. Part of me won't belong in Seattle anymore. Because some pieces of me are already his.

26

The Shirt. The Skirt. The Shift.

Miles

She's out cold, curled up against me, one leg thrown over mine like she's holding me in place. I lie here for a while, just staring at the ceiling. My arms are around her bare back, her skin warm under my hand. I can still feel the way her body moved under mine. Still hear the way she said my name. That's the kind of thing a man doesn't forget.

She shifts in her sleep, nose brushing my skin, and I tighten my hold just a little. Yeah, she's mine until she leaves.

I wake up to rain outside the window. Kinsley's still asleep, tangled up in my sheets, one hand tucked under her cheek, peaceful, with Miss Dashworth curled at her feet. I don't move right away. Just lie there a minute, watching her breathe, trying to memorize the way she looks. Maybe hold on to the feeling that this might last. Even though I know it won't. She has a whole life in Seattle; an apartment, a career, a courtroom waiting for her. This...whatever this is between us, it's real. But it's borrowed time. That thought makes me hold my breath a little longer, like I can stretch the moment if I just stay still enough.

She stirs a little but doesn't wake. I roll out of bed, careful not to wake her, and grab a pair of sweats from my closet. I head downstairs. I start the coffee and crack a few eggs, frying them up in the cast iron while the skillet heats for pancakes. Nothing fancy, just enough to give us a good start before we head out. Not to mention, it's the only thing I know how to cook. It's only one night in Seattle for that court hearing, but I know it's going to be a long day. So, I figure I'll do what I can and make her breakfast. Get her to the airport. Then I get to watch her in action and see her life, the life she'll go back to. The one I've never seen. The one I'm not sure has a place for someone like me. Yeah, that thought hits harder than I want to admit. Part of me wonders if I'll fit in her world at all, or if this thing between us only works out here, where things are simpler. Where it's just her and me. But tomorrow we'll come right back here. Until her vacation's over, I want every minute of her time spent with me.

I hear her moving around upstairs. A minute later, she walks into the kitchen, hair in a messy bun, wearing my shirt. Damn, it looks good on her.

She pauses when she sees the plates. "You made pancakes?"

"And eggs." I pull out her chair. "Didn't want you starving before we hit the road."

She sits, takes a bite, then looks up. "These are actually good."

"You sound surprised."

"I expected toast." She laughs.

"You expected wrong, baby."

She grins, sips her coffee. "My clothes are still in the bounce house, aren't they?"

"Yep."

She groans. "I am NOT walking out there like this. In daylight. With witnesses."

"You want me to grab them?" I ask between bites.

"If you don't, I'll deny everything. Pretend I blacked out."

I laugh. "You were strutting around in my shirt. Kind of hard to miss."

"Maybe I should own it. Walk right out there, head held high." She points her fork at me. "In your shirt and bare assed."

"The shirt looks better on you anyway." I give her a slow once over. "But bare assed? Not happening. That view's only for me."

I tug on my boots by the door and glance over my shoulder. "What time do we need to head out?"

She's still at the table, fork in hand. "Seven."

"You want me to drive?"

She lifts her coffee cup, gives me a look like I should already know the answer. "I hate driving."

Figures. I crack a smile and open the door. "I'll grab your clothes. Try not to miss me."

She just rolls her eyes, but I catch the hint of a grin as I step outside.

It doesn't take long to cross the yard and scoop up the dress and bits of lace she left behind in the bounce house. The sun's up now, rain falling in a light mist, but her clothes are safe inside. If anyone's awake, they're getting one hell of a show. I gather it all and head back inside.

She's standing when I walk in, reaching for the bundle in my hands. I pass it over without a word, but she leans in, presses a quick kiss to my mouth.

"Meet me at the cabin in thirty minutes?" She's already pulling my shirt over her head, dressing right there in the living room like I'm not even standing two feet away. Of course, I stand and watch.

She slides the dress up her legs, adjusts the straps and smooths her hair up into that messy bun I'm quickly getting addicted to.

I walk over, cup her jaw and kiss her hard enough to steal her breath. "If you do that again, we won't make it to Seattle."

She giggles, eyes lighting up, and presses one more kiss to the corner of my mouth before slipping past me, barefoot, like she didn't just wreck me all over again.

"Thirty minutes," she calls over her shoulder.

"Twenty," I call back, chuckling, because I know it's definitely thirty.

I take a quick shower, letting the hot water clear my head. I'm still wound tight from last night, wanting more, and her stripping in the living room didn't help. By the time I'm out and dressed, I toss a few things into a duffel bag: change of clothes, toothbrush, the basics. I'm not packing for a vacation. Just a day. Still, part of me wishes it were longer.

Before heading out, I shoot Reed a quick call.

"Don't forget the rental crews are showing up this afternoon," I remind him.

"I got it. You headed out?"

"Yeah, just about to pick her up."

His tone's heavier than usual. "Good luck, man." I don't say anything back, just end the call and head out.

I climb into the truck and take the familiar path toward her cabin. When I pull in, Judy's already outside, arms crossed, a knowing smile tugging at her mouth.

She nods toward Kinsley's cabin. "She's just grabbing her bag."

"You here to see her off or interrogate me?"

"Both," she says with a wink.

She studies my face for a second, like she's waiting for me to spill the gossip. Then she nods, pats my shoulder and heads back toward her place without another word.

The front door opens, and there she is…bag in hand, messy bun still in place, but now dressed in soft joggers and a fitted tee. Comfortable. Natural. Still completely distracting.

I take her bag and place it in the back with mine, then open the passenger door. She hops in, tucks her legs up under her and makes herself comfortable without hesitation. It makes me smile, knowing she trusts me enough to relax like this.

The roads are quiet; it's still early. We talk about a little of everything, favorite movies, awkward school stories, the time Reed got kicked by a goat, but eventually, the conversation circles back to Judy. Her meddling. Her big, not-so-subtle push that brought Kinsley into my life. I figure it's time she hears it from me.

I glance over at her. She's watching the trees pass by, window cracked slightly, the breeze tugging at the few strands of hair that slipped from her bun. "I should probably tell you." My fingers drum on the steering wheel. "How we actually met."

She turns her head, one brow lifting. "What do you mean? You helped me at the store?"

"Because Judy sent me." I shoot her a sideways glance. "She called me and said she needed a few things for dinner, which she didn't. Gave me a list, hoping I would run into you."

Her lips part slightly, surprise flickering across her face. "She set that up?"

I nod. "There's more." I take a deep breath and tell her how she got the cabin for a month and the internet search. The flat tire. The map going the long way to town, avoiding deep ditches and traffic.

"Wait, are you telling me I've been driving the long way to town this whole time? How long does it normally take?" She leans forward to get a better look at me. I can't help my smile.

"Five minutes." I laugh outright at her expression, shaking my head at just how far Judy went to orchestrate this whole thing. The woman really left nothing to chance.

Kinsley leans back, laughing softly, shaking her head. "That woman's relentless."

"Yep. Full-blown matchmaking scheme."

There's a pause, then she nudges my arm lightly. "So technically, I should be thanking her."

"Technically," I say, eyes still on the road, "but don't tell her that. I'll never hear the end of it."

We keep talking and laughing about Judy's matchmaking shenanigans all the way to the airport in Spokane. By the time we pull into the terminal, my face actually hurts from smiling.

We both hop out, and I grab our bags from the back, slinging them over one shoulder. Kinsley pulls out her phone, already scanning for the check-in info. We make it through TSA quicker than expected, no body searches, no weird questions, no delays. It's smooth. Almost suspiciously smooth.

We board with thirty minutes to spare and find our seats toward the back. As soon as we settle, Kinsley crosses her legs and slips her arm through mine, resting her head on my shoulder as the plane taxis down the runway. The moment we lift off, she exhales like she's readying herself for her unexpected day in the office and courtroom.

It's a short flight, barely above an hour, and when we land, we move fast through the gate. Kinsley spots the driver right away, standing near baggage claim with a sign that reads: Ms. Brighton and Guest.

The guy nods politely, takes our bags without a word and leads us outside where a black town car waits at the curb. We slide into the back seat together, her knee brushing mine as the doors close, and the city starts to move past our windows.

The driver pulls up in front of her apartment building and idles at the curb.

"I'll be right back." Kinsley grabs both our bags before I can even offer to help. I watch her disappear through the front entrance, then lean back and scroll through my phone while she's inside, answering a few texts and checking in with Reed.

A few minutes later, the door opens, and I look up and forget how to breathe. She steps out looking like a goddamn problem. That black pencil skirt hugs her curves like it was sewn onto her body, the slit in the back teasing just enough to mess with my head. The white button-down is tucked in clean, top three buttons undone just enough to hint at everything underneath. Sleeves rolled up, sharp and effortless. Three-inch black heels click against the sidewalk like some kind of warning. Her hair's pulled into a sleek, tight bun. Gold hoops. Bold red lips. A little more eye makeup than usual, smoky. She looks like power. Like sin dressed in business casual. And for a second, I forget how to think. It's not just lust, it's awe. Like watching a lightning storm roll over the mountains, dangerous and impossible to look away from. She's not just walking into her world, she's owning it. And I'm standing here on the edge, wondering how the hell I got lucky enough to be next to her at all.

I'm out of the car before I can think twice, stepping up to her as she reaches the curb. My hand lifts to her chin, tilting her face up to mine, and I press a soft kiss to her mouth, barely there, careful not to mess up that red lipstick or end up wearing it.

"Fuck, baby. You look sexy as hell."

227

"Thank you." She brushes a faint kiss to my lips before stepping past me. I hold the car door open, and once she's inside, I slide in next to her.

As the door shuts and the driver pulls away, I lean in close, my voice just for her. "I can't wait to pull that skirt up later."

She lets out a quiet groan, head tilting toward mine, her mouth near my ear as she whispers, "That's why I wore it."

My jaw tightens. I settle back in my seat, smirking. This day just got a hell of a lot longer.

We pull up in front of a clean brick building, tall windows reflecting the morning sun. The sign over the glass double doors reads: Brighton Family Law Firm.

The second the car stops, Kinsley shifts. She opens the door and steps out with that quiet confidence she wears so damn well. But before we reach the doors, she pauses. Inhales deep. Shoulders back. Then she turns and gives me a quick wink before facing forward again, her expression smoothing into something sharp and polished. Boss mode. And somehow, it makes her look even hotter.

She pushes open the door and walks in like she owns the place, because she does. The place is clean, sleek, all glass and steel with soft touches that scream expensive and smart. Just like her.

A woman at the front desk stands the second she sees Kinsley. Mel, I think. She rushes over, arms open.

"Look at you!" She pulls Kinsley into a hug before glancing at me. Then her eyes widen.

Mel leans in close and whispers something that makes Kinsley laugh. Then Kinsley says loud enough for me to hear, "I'll talk with you after I get settled in." She looks back at me, cheeks a little pink. I have the feeling they're talking about me.

She turns to me, her hand brushing lightly against mine as she introduces us. "Miles, this is Mel. Mel, this is Miles."

Mel's polite, friendly, and definitely still giving me the once-over.

"Nice to meet you." She hands Kinsley a file. "Raelynn's paperwork. Mrs. Perry's file is already on your desk."

"Perfect," Kinsley replies, slipping into that boss voice so naturally it actually gives me goosebumps. She was born for this.

We start walking, and I place my hand on the small of her back, a silent gesture. As we step through the large wooden door into her private office, I take it all in. Framed degrees, a few soft personal touches, and a heavy desk that looks like it could outlast a nuclear war. It fits her. Classy. Clean. Unshakable.

She sets the file on her desk, already flipping it open. I move closer, not because I need to, but because I want to. She looks up. I don't say anything. I just stare at her for a beat, the way her bun is pulled tight, how that skirt hugs her hips, how she commands the room without saying a damn word.

"You're dangerous in this setting."

She lifts a brow. "Why's that?"

I don't answer, just step in, hook a finger under her chin, and kiss her, deep and slow. No words. Just everything I'm feeling, pressed into her mouth. When I pull back, her eyes are still on mine, a little dazed. Yeah. She felt it.

She leans back in her chair next to mine, lips tugging into a half smile. "You gonna keep staring at me like that, or are you planning to behave while I work?"

I lift a brow. "Are we here so you can work, or are we skipping straight to fucking on your desk?"

Her jaw drops, just for a second, before that grin curves even wider. "You're impossible," she mutters, standing and walking around her desk and powering up her computer.

I watch her settle in, graceful and all business now, like I didn't just say something that would've gotten me slapped in any other office. I lean back in the chair across from her, scrolling through my phone, though my eyes keep drifting.

She's focused, typing fast, flipping through folders, pulling thick law books from her shelf. Every now and then, she glances up at me. I don't say a word. I don't want to pull her out of that zone. Just watching her work is something else. Sharp. Confident. The exact reason I won't ask her to give this up. Even if a part of me wants to. Wants her back in my bed, in my world, where things are slower and less cutthroat. But this? This is who she is. And I won't be the one to take it from her, no matter how much it costs me to watch her slip back into a life I might never belong to.

After a couple of hours, she stands, stretches slightly, then steps out to talk with Mel and grab something from the printer. I glance at the door once she's gone. Yeah. Dangerous doesn't even begin to cover her.

She steps back into the office, cheeks flushed, lips pressed together like she's trying not to smile. I stand, meeting her halfway. I reach up and brush my thumb over the soft curve of her cheek. "Why are you blushing?"

She laughs, eyes sparkling. "Because Mel cornered me for details about you."

My brow lifts. "And?"

"I gave her the PG-13 version," she says, biting her bottom lip.

I grin, stepping a little closer. "You sure about that? Because your face says you were thinking about the X-rated one."

She lets out a soft laugh, glancing toward the wooden door. "I'm not about to have her walk in and catch me thinking about you naked."

I lean in, lips close to her ear. "Too late, sweetheart."

Her breath hitches, just enough to make me smirk, before she gently pushes me back toward my chair with a quiet, amused, "Sit down, Country Boy. I've got work to finish."

I sit. But the smile doesn't leave my face.

27

Commando

Kinsley

While I work, flipping between Mrs. Perry's file and Raelynn's paperwork, I do my best to stay focused. But it's nearly impossible with him sitting across from me like that. Relaxed. Legs stretched out, ankles crossed. That same damn smirk playing on his annoyingly hot face.

He hasn't said a word in over an hour, but he doesn't have to. The way he looks at me when he thinks I'm not paying attention, it's a kind of distraction all its own.

I peek up again because I can't help it, and sure enough, he catches me. Doesn't move. Just arches a brow like he knows exactly what he's doing to me. I shake my head and glance down at the screen, biting back a smile.

I send another round of papers to the printer, and not even two minutes later, I hear the door creak open. Mel steps in, a stack of documents in hand and a knowing gleam in her eyes.

"Your print job." She sets them on the corner of my desk. Then gives me a look that clearly says we're going to talk about him more later before slipping right back out.

I sigh and glance at the time. Just past noon.

I look up at Miles. "Hungry?"

"Starving."

The way he says it makes it really hard to tell if he's talking about food or not. Either way, it's definitely time for a break.

I shut down my computer, stack the papers neatly on my desk and glance over at Miles. "We're meeting Raelynn for lunch at Downtown Café."

He stands, stretching long and slow, and my eyes, traitors that they are, rake over him from head to toe. When he looks back at me, I quickly shift my gaze, pretending to check the time.

We step out of my office and into the lobby. Mel's on the phone, headset snug against one ear, typing as she talks. She places her caller on hold the second she sees us.

"We'll be back in a couple of hours." I pause at her desk. "Can you have the conference room ready for Miles when we return? I'd like to give Mrs. Perry some privacy." Mel nods, already making a note. "And please be in attendance for the meeting. Maybe between the two of us, we can keep her on task and not let this drag out until midnight."

Mel laughs, flipping her pen between her fingers. "My schedule's already clear, boss. See you soon."

Miles and I exchange a glance before heading for the door, his hand brushing the small of my back again.

The moment we turn the corner, putting the office out of sight, Miles grabs my hand and spins me into his chest. His palm finds the back of my neck, and then his mouth is on mine, firm, unapologetic, right in the middle of the sidewalk. Someone mutters as they brush past us. Another person makes a sound of complaint. I don't care. I reach up and wrap my arms around his neck, holding him there, letting myself sink into the kiss like I've been waiting for it all morning. Because I have.

233

I'd be lying if I said I hadn't been thinking about this exact moment ever since he said we could skip the work and get straight to fucking on my desk. I almost locked the door and told him to take me. Almost. But the walls at the firm aren't exactly soundproof, and Mel's desk is one wall away. So, I behaved.

Right now, though, I'm not thinking about being professional. I'm thinking about how his lips feel, how his hand tightens just slightly on my neck, how kissing him here, out in the open, feels like I'm claiming him.

Breaking the kiss, we fall into step side by side, walking hand in hand the five blocks to the café.

I took a longer lunch break today so we could enjoy it, no rush.

"Have you ever been to Seattle?" I ask as we cross a quiet intersection.

"A few times. Never stayed long."

We fall into an easy silence after that, comfortable. Natural. But my mind drifts anyway. I think about last night. About the way he touched me. The words he whispered. The way he pulled me apart so slowly, like I was something to savor. I've never felt like that in a man's arms, never felt so wrecked and safe all at once. Body and soul. And that's what scares me. Because when I leave, I know my heart will break. I already feel the cracks forming. But still, I wouldn't trade this for anything. Whatever happens next, he's worth it. This is worth it.

I glance over at him, and as if he can sense the shift in me, he looks down, his eyes locking onto mine. He stops, gently brings my hand to his mouth and presses a soft kiss to my knuckles.

I search his face. "Thanks for coming with me."

He holds my gaze. "I told you, baby. Until you leave, every moment is mine." *God.*

We keep walking, and I notice heads turn. A few women glance his way, some not even bothering to hide it. Of course they look. He's tall, broad, effortless with that rolled-sleeve confidence and those unreadable eyes. He looks like the kind of man who knows exactly what he wants and how to get it.

We reach Downtown Café a few minutes later, my favorite little spot tucked between a bookstore and a florist. It's quaint, always smells like cinnamon and espresso, and the windows are open wide to let in the early afternoon breeze.

Miles holds the door for me, his hand brushing the small of my back as I step inside. The little bell overhead jingles, and a few people glance up from their tables. I spot Raelynn right away, already seated at a table in the back, waving at us with a tired smile.

I lean toward Miles as we walk. "Prepare yourself. She's been through a lot lately."

He scans the place as we move through it. "I can handle it."

Of course he can. He looks like the kind of man who could handle a wildfire with just that calm, quiet energy he carries around. As we approach the table, Raelynn stands, and I immediately pull her into a hug.

"You look good."

"You look like you just stepped off the cover of a fashion magazine." She pulls back, glancing at Miles. Her eyebrows arch slightly. "And, hello."

"Raelynn, this is Miles," I say. "Miles, Raelynn."

They shake hands, and I can already tell Raelynn's going to corner me later for details.

We sit, and Miles pulls out my chair like a damn gentleman, then takes the seat beside me.

The server comes by, and we order two sandwiches, a salad and iced coffees. Raelynn talks a little about Jacob and the impending divorce, how she's doing and what comes next. Miles listens without interrupting, his arm casually resting on the back of my chair like he belongs here. Like we belong together. I can't lie, sitting between them, I feel strangely settled. Like my two worlds, Seattle and Cranberry Ridge aren't so separate after all.

After we eat, Miles excuses himself, something about giving us space. He squeezes my shoulder before he leaves, and I watch him walk away, trying not to let it show how much I already miss him the second he's gone. Raelynn wastes no time.

She leans in across the table, eyes wide. "Okay, spill it. All of it. Don't hold out on me."

I laugh, but it's soft. A little nervous. "It's a lot."

"So?" she says, grinning. "I'm getting divorced. I can handle 'a lot.'"

I glance down at my cup, take a deep breath and start from the beginning. I leave out the heavier stuff, no need to bring Ben into this, but I give her the real story. The slow build. The tension. And then last night, it all snapped into something undeniable, something so real it scares me. When I'm done, her jaw drops.

"Holy shit, Kins. That's…wow… And hot… Also, wow."

I smile faintly. "Yeah."

She watches me for a moment, then asks, quieter this time, "How do you feel about coming back here in under two weeks?"

"Honestly?" I stare out the window for a moment. "It makes me a little sad. Sadder than I thought it would. Like I've barely had time to catch my breath, and now I'm counting down the days until it's gone."

Raelynn doesn't interrupt. She just lets me talk.

"But I'm also, grateful. Grateful I got to feel something this good. Even if it doesn't last. Even if it's just for right now."

She reaches across the table, squeezes my hand. "You're allowed to want more. To hope for more."

"I know," I say, but my voice wavers. Because wanting more? That's the crazy part.

Miles returns a few minutes later, balancing a small plate of fresh baked cookies and a tall cup of iced coffee. He sets them on the table in front of me with a grin that's way too proud of himself.

"You were gone for cookies?"

"Not just any cookies." He reaches over to slide the coffee closer to me. "A refill, since someone drained hers before lunch."

Before I can say thank you, he leans down and kisses the top of my head, casually. Maybe it is now? Still, I feel my cheeks flush.

Raelynn raises a brow, grinning. "Well, if that isn't the most disgustingly sweet thing I've ever seen."

Miles just shrugs and takes a seat beside me, stealing one of the cookies off the plate and popping a bite into his mouth. He's relaxed again, legs stretched out, arm resting across back of my chair again. Close but not possessive. The warmth of him next to me anchors something deep inside.

I look at Raelynn, who's already helping herself to a cookie. "You've got good taste."

"Yeah. I really do."

I wipe my hands on a napkin and turn a little more toward Raelynn. "Your paperwork's done. I'll file it first thing tomorrow. Jacob will be served by someone from my office within the week."

She nods slowly, absorbing it.

"You should be ready for the fallout," I add gently. "This is usually when spouses start getting emotional or unpredictable. The moment it's real, that's when it hits."

"I know." Her voice is steady. "But I've already been hinting at it. Dropping little signs so it's not a total shock. I think deep down, he knows it's coming."

I reach across the table and squeeze her hand. "Good. Just keep your phone close. If he reacts badly, anything at all, I want to know."

She nods again. "Thanks, Kins. Really. I don't know what I'd do without you."

I scoff. "Probably still waiting for him to go to therapy."

She snorts. "Don't remind me."

We all stand to leave, walking out of the café together. Raelynn pulls me into a tight hug before heading in the opposite direction. "Call me soon."

"I will. I promise."

As soon as we start walking, I reach for Miles' hand without thinking. He threads his fingers through mine like it's second nature. We move down the sidewalk in sync, the afternoon breeze cooling the sun on our skin.

"So, do you think he'll be that upset when he gets served?"

I glance at him, catching the concern in his eyes. "Jacob's always been hot-headed," I say quietly. "I asked her once, after a really bad fight, if he ever put his hands on her. She swore he didn't."

Miles watches me closely. "But you don't believe her?"

I sigh, looking down at the sidewalk. "I want to. I really do. And I've never seen any marks. But something in the way she talks about him, the way she tenses up sometimes, I just don't know."

He stops walking, tugging me gently to a halt. I look up.

"She'll be okay. She seems strong. And smart. Like someone who knows how to protect herself."

I nod, but the worry's still there, clinging to the edges of my thoughts. We walk in silence for a while, comfortable and quiet. Miles senses my mind drifting, and after a moment, he shifts gears.

"So, tell me. What exactly did you two talk about while I was gone? I saw your face when I came back. Hers, too. What did I miss?"

I smirk, pretending to think about it. "Oh, just the usual girl talk; life, work, how insanely hot you are in bed."

He chokes a little on his laugh. "That came up, huh?"

I glance sideways at him, all faux innocence. "I might've mentioned that someone kept me up for hours."

His eyes darken a shade, that slow building fire lighting up behind them. "You say that like it's a bad thing."

"Oh, it was exhausting," I tease, dragging the word out, my voice lower now. "In the best kind of way."

He leans in, voice rough. "I'll take that as a challenge."

I lift a brow. "So, it wasn't your best?"

He stops walking, turning fully to face me. "You want better?"

I close the distance, lips brushing just under his jaw. "I want more."

His jaw tightens, his hands flex at his sides and I swear he fights the urge to grab me right there on the sidewalk.

"I swear to God, Kinsley," he mutters, half a growl.

I grin up at him. "What? Can't handle the truth?"

He shakes his head, smirking. "You're trouble."

I start walking again, swaying my hips just a little extra. "You've got no idea."

He falls into step beside me, that heat simmering between us, stretching tight and electric.

"I'm starting to think we should've taken your desk for a test drive after all."

I hum, smiling to myself. "Don't tempt me. My office walls are thin."

He leans in close, voice a whisper at my ear. "Good. Let them hear."

Just as we step into the office lobby, I compose my expression and shift back into professional mode. Mel glances up from her screen and gives me a nod.

"Mrs. Perry will be here in twenty minutes."

"Perfect, thank you."

Then, with the audacity only Miles could get away with, he bends down and murmurs, "In twenty minutes, I could make you come twice on that desk."

I blink. Hard. But I don't stop walking, don't look at him, don't even breathe differently. Only the slight twitch of my jaw betrays the jolt that runs through me. Mel doesn't notice. Thank God.

Once the office door clicks shut behind us, I spin on my heel and swat at him, whisper-shouting, "I cannot believe you said that in front of Mel."

He catches my wrist, smirking. In one smooth move, he spins me and bends me over my desk. My palms hit the surface, and his hips press firmly against mine from behind, letting me feel how hard he is. My breath whooshes out of me in a shocked gasp.

His mouth is at my ear, dark and dangerous. "You really want to test how soundproof these walls are?"

I can't speak. My heart is thundering, my body instantly lit. He steps back, slow and smug, like he didn't just detonate something inside me.

I push myself upright, fix my blouse and smooth a hand over my skirt, heart racing. Then I walk, calm, composed, right over to him where he's dropped into the chair like he owns the room.

I step between his spread legs and lean in, just enough that only he can hear me.

"Too bad you didn't lift my skirt," I whisper, voice like silk. "You would've seen I'm not wearing any panties."

His jaw tenses. I watch the fire light in his eyes as he exhales slowly, dragging his tongue over his bottom lip like he's tasting the thought. Before he can say a word, I turn and walk away, taking my seat behind the desk with a grin tugging at the corners of my mouth. His control might be ironclad but not with me. Not today. He shifts in his seat, clearly trying to regain some composure, when there's a knock at the door.

"Come in," I say smoothly, just as Miles huffs and mutters under his breath, shifting in his seat to hide the bulge in his pants. "Fuck, Kinsley."

Mel pops her head in, eyes flicking between the two of us like she knows she just walked into something.

"Mrs. Perry's here early."

I straighten in my seat, all business again. "Okay, I'll show Miles to the conference room. Go ahead and bring her in."

Mel nods and disappears down the hallway. I rise from my chair and glance at Miles, who's still watching me like I've got a bomb ticking under my skin. I smooth my skirt again, pointedly, and motion toward the door.

"This way, Mr. Control."

He stands slowly, eyes still dark, and follows me out. The air between us hums, but I don't look back.

We step into the conference room, and the moment the door clicks shut, Miles moves. He pins me gently but firmly against it, his mouth crashing into mine. The kiss is hot, deep, completely undoing me. A soft moan escapes as his hand slides up my leg, stopping just before he reaches between my thighs.

"Mrs. Perry is waiting." He licks his lips and steps away, dropping into one of the leather chairs, looking far too satisfied with himself.

I blink, still catching my breath, frustration blooming hot in my chest. I smooth my skirt, check my hair, then glance back at him with a slow, dangerous smile. *Shit.*

His grin is pure sin. I open the door and walk out like nothing happened, composed, professional, but still burning.

For the next two hours, Mel and I tag-team a strategy with Mrs. Perry. The table fills with paperwork: forms to put a legal hold on their joint accounts, a formal request for a restraining order and documented proof of the money he's already drained. Mrs. Perry pulls out photos of the damage he caused to her car, each image another nail in the coffin of any defense he might try to muster. We move fast, efficiently. Mel knows what to ask, I know what to file, and Mrs. Perry, bless her, keeps it together better than most. It's messy, but she's done playing nice. And now, she has backup. When we're finally done, we all rise. Mel walks Mrs. Perry out, offering soft reassurances and a timeline for the next steps.

I take a deep breath, roll my shoulders, and head straight for the conference room. Time to check on the man who very nearly wrecked my professionalism earlier, and who's been waiting ever since.

28

Mess Maker

Miles

Kinsley opens the door with a soft smile, but I can see it, she's tired. Not just in her eyes, but the way her shoulders sit a little lower than usual. Still, she says, "Let's go home. I've got a car waiting." And damn if that doesn't sound good.

I stand, grabbing my jacket, and follow her back to her office. She moves on autopilot, shutting down her computer, gathering two thick files, sliding them into her bag. I don't say anything, just lean against the door and watch her. Every movement is efficient and practiced. She's still in boss mode, but I can tell it's running on fumes.

She tucks her chair in, gives the room a final glance, then turns to me. "Ready?"

"Yeah." I step in line beside her.

It's just before four when we make it to the lobby. She stops at Mel's desk, thanks her for all the help today and reminds her to meet her at the courthouse at eight sharp. Mel promises she'll be there with coffee and backup.

I give Mel a small wave, and she gives me a knowing look, one that says she's figured out a little more than Kinsley probably intended.

We step out into the early evening rush, the city alive with movement. Kinsley doesn't pause, just leads the way into a waiting black car parked at the curb. The door closes behind us, and for the first time all day, she leans back and lets herself exhale. I reach over, grab her hand and link our fingers together.

"It's been a long day, baby." I lean in to kiss her shoulder.

She turns her head, eyes soft as they meet mine. "Yes, it has," she says, and then adds with a small sigh, "but I still have a few more things to do with the case. I just figured I could do them at home."

I nod, already pulling out my phone. "What do you want for dinner? I'll order us something while you work."

She smiles, the kind that tells me she's grateful, tired, but grateful. "That sounds perfect."

"Anything you're craving?"

She rests her head back again and hums. "Surprise me."

I kiss the top of her head and start scrolling. "You got it."

I order Thai food online while we're still in the car, sending it straight to her apartment.

When we pull up, she leads the way, unlocking the door and stepping inside. I follow and stop just past the threshold, taking it in. Boxes. Stacked neatly in corners. Unopened. The place is clean, but it doesn't feel lived in.

She sets her bag down. "Come on, I'll show you around."

She walks me through the kitchen, her small home office tucked into a nook, points out the bathroom, and finally her bedroom. More boxes.

I nod toward the unopened boxes piled in the corner. "How long have you lived here?"

She sighs, a little embarrassed. "Almost a year."

I raise a brow. "A year?"

She shrugs. "I haven't had time to unpack. I pick at it on days I get home early. Or weekends when I don't already have plans."

I don't say anything right away. Just walk over to the window and glance out at the city view. It's pretty, in a cold sort of way; glass, steel and traffic below. I turn back to her. She's standing there in her own home like she doesn't belong in it. Like she's just passing through. And maybe she is.

I think about today, how she handled one emotionally wrecked client and Raelynn's upcoming divorce, kept her cool in court prep, juggled paperwork like it was breathing. She's sharp, fast and brilliant. But all of it looks heavy. And if today was just one day, I can only imagine what a normal week looks like for her. She deserves more than boxes and burnout.

I walk over and cup her jaw, thumb brushing her cheek. "You're doing good, City Girl."

Her eyes soften just before I kiss her, slow, warm, just enough to tell her I see her.

Then the doorbell rings. She pulls back with a grin. "That's dinner."

I watch as she walks to the door, barefoot, still wearing that damn skirt. She looked so sexy today. I had a hard time keeping my hands to myself. I almost lost my cool in the conference room.

She opens the door, and the delivery guy's eyes widen the second he sees her. *Great*. He grins a little too wide, standing there like he forgot he's supposed to hand her the bag.

His eyes rake over her, bold as hell. "You, uh, need help with anything else?"

I step out from around the corner, crossing my arms and level him with a look. "No. She doesn't."

He jumps, thrusts the bag into her hands and practically sprints back to the elevator.

She closes the door, laughing. "Miles."

I raise a brow. "What?"

"That poor guy."

I chuckle. "He was about to offer to tuck your napkin in for you."

She laughs again, shaking her head as she heads to the kitchen.

We eat at the small table, the food's good. She tells me about her life here. The long hours. The weight of the cases she takes on. The nights she comes home and forgets to eat. The weekends she sometimes works through because, in her words, "If I don't fight for them, who will?" But I see it. In her voice. Her face. She smiles when she talks about her work, but there's a hollowness behind it, like she's convincing herself. She's content but not happy. Not really.

There's pride in what she's built. Respect for the people she helps. But there's also loneliness in the spaces she doesn't talk about. In the unopened boxes stacked in corners. In the way she moves through her own apartment like it belongs to someone else.

I push a little, just curious. "You ever think about leaving?"

She chews slowly, sets her chopsticks down. "Sometimes. When it's quiet and I let myself imagine something different."

"And?"

She looks up at me, that same softness flickering in her eyes. "And then it's Monday."

I nod. I get it.

We finish dinner quietly, the kind of comfortable silence that comes when there's nothing left to prove. After we clean up the kitchen, she grabs her files, and I settle on the couch, flipping through the channels. But I'm not watching the TV. I'm watching her.

She reads while pacing, barefoot, ink pen in hand. Every few steps she stops, scribbles something, then chews on the cap while she thinks. Her blouse is a little wrinkled from the day, sleeves still rolled up. Her hair's down now, a messy wave falling over one shoulder.

She's in her element, focused, sharp, and I should probably leave her be. But damn, she was hot today. Not just in the skirt and heels, though yeah, that didn't hurt. It was the way she moved, commanded the room.

My fingers twitch. My whole body's on edge from just watching her work. I want to pull her into my lap, kiss her, run my hand over her body. But I wait. My pulse hums. Because I know what's coming when she finally sets those files down.

When she finally stops pacing, pen still in hand, she looks at me and smiles. "I think I'm done for the night."

I sit up straighter. She walks over to the table, slips the pen into her bag and presses the file closed with both hands. Her eyes lift to meet mine.

She rounds the couch, stopping right in front of me. I tilt my head back to look at her, hands already reaching, already hungry. "Come here."

She steps closer, and I trail my palms under the back of her skirt until I hit the curve of her ass. Her skin is warm smooth, and bare. My thumbs press in, pulling her closer as the fabric rides up her legs.

She watches me for a beat, lips parted just slightly, then lifts her hands to the buttons of her blouse. Each pop of fabric is a test. My composure. My patience. My sanity.

She parts the sides of the blouse, revealing a soft pink lace bra, barely there and doing nothing to hide how hard her nipples are. My jaw clenches, breath catching in my throat. I don't look away. Can't. She's not wearing panties. I already know that. But now, standing above me like this, unwrapping herself like a gift, it's fucking hot. My fingers dig into her hips. She's doing this on purpose. She wants control. And as much as every muscle in me is begging to flip the script, throw her down, and take it...take her...I don't.

I let her have it. Because watching her, knowing what she wants, what she's asking for without saying a word. I sit back slightly, letting my hands slide down just a bit, but I don't move to take over. Not yet. I'll give her this moment. But she has no idea how far I'll take it once she gives me the green light.

She lowers herself slowly to her knees in front of me, never breaking eye contact, and fuck if that doesn't make it hard to stay still.

I lean forward, one hand sliding around the back of her neck, holding her gently but firmly in place. Her skin is hot beneath my palm, pulse fluttering just under my thumb.

I kiss her, slow, deep. Her lips part for me without hesitation, and the moment my tongue brushes hers, a soft sound slips from her mouth, shooting straight through me.

My other hand trails from the nape of her neck down the curve of her spine, taking my time. Her skin shivers beneath my touch. Then I reach around, fingers working at the clasp of her bra. She doesn't move. Doesn't flinch.

The second it gives, I slide the straps from her shoulders, letting the lace fall between us onto the floor. She's bare now, kneeling, breathing hard, and so fucking beautiful I can't think straight.

I sit back slightly to take her in, my thumbs stroking slowly across her collarbones. Her nipples are peaked, chest rising and falling fast, eyes locked on mine.

She gently pushes me back, and I let her, settling against the couch. My hands rest on the armrests, my body coiled tight beneath the surface. I watch every move she makes. She knows exactly what she's doing to me.

Her hands slide up my legs, over my thighs, light enough to tease but firm enough to drive me insane. When her palm grazes over my hardness, a growl builds low in my throat. She presses her hand there, tracing the length of me through my jeans, and I swear to God it takes everything I have not to lose it. She reaches for my belt. I grab her wrist. Her eyes snap to mine, wide.

My gaze doesn't waver. I hold her there, my voice low, rough. "You keep touching me like that, baby, and I'm not going to be able to let you lead anymore."

The corner of her mouth lifts, just a hint of a smile, like that's exactly what she wanted.

"Shh, baby just let me touch you."

Her calling me baby has my body fighting for control. *Fuck.* My whole body jerks forward slightly. I stop myself from grabbing her. I loosen my grip, let her hand continue. She slides my jeans down just enough, and I lift my hips so she can strip them lower. My dick strains hard against the thin barrier of my boxers. Her eyes drop to it. She licks her lips.

When she peels them down and I spring free, she draws in a slow breath, like she's savoring the moment. And then she leans forward.

"Kinsley," I growl. Her eyes flick up, startled.

I lean forward, one hand at her jaw, the other gripping the back of her neck. "You're good at teasing," I murmur, thumb brushing her cheek. "If you put those pretty little lips on my cock, you'll swallow the mess you make."

Her breath hitches, pupils wide, small smile growing on her face. "I'm counting on it." I lean back releasing my grip.

Her lips part as she leans in, eyes locked on mine the whole damn time like she's daring me to stop her. I don't. Her breath fans across the head of my cock, warm and teasing. She presses a kiss to the tip, just a kiss. My hands fist at my sides. She does it again.

Then her tongue flicks out, a light drag over the most sensitive part of me. My hips jerk forward, instinct taking over, but I bite it back. Barely.

"Jesus, Kinsley." I growl. She smiles, slow and smug, then slides her mouth over me, inch by inch. The heat, the pressure, the way her lips seal tight, it's goddamn perfect. I reach down and brush the hair from her face, watching every move, because I need to see it. Need to see her like this.

"Look at me," I order, voice tight.

She glances up, eyes glassy and dark, and that one look almost undoes me. I exhale hard, jaw sharp, so tight I feel it in my neck.

"You're gonna kill me." I settle one hand on the back of her head, not pushing, just holding. Anchoring. She hums around me, and the vibration sends fire up my spine.

Her mouth works me slow at first, torturous, her tongue circling, teasing, taking me in deeper. I brace a hand on the couch behind me. "Just like that. Fuck, baby, you feel so good."

Her fingers curl around the base of me, matching the rhythm of her mouth, and every muscle in my body goes tight. I shake my head once, jaw locked. She sucks harder, her hand tightens. I feel it building low in my spine. My head falls back, my hips flex. I quickly lean forward gripping the back of her head, fingers wrapping in her hair. I thrust forward once holding her head still. I come, filling her mouth as I groan her name. She hums her approval. As the last of my seed shoots out, I pull my cock from her mouth with a pop.

"Swallow it," I growl. She does, not breaking eye contact. When she slips her tongue out licking a pearl of come off her lip, I'm instantly ready for more.

My voice is rough from everything she just did to me. "Stand up, baby."

She rises slowly, eyes not leaving mine. I run my hands up her legs dragging her skirt up around her waist. She straddles me without hesitation, one knee on each side of my thighs. Her hands press into my shoulders, steadying herself.

Her body is soft heat against mine, and I swear I can feel every breath she takes. I grip her hips, guiding her over the head of my cock. I slam her down until we're flush. She cries out, head falling back. I drag my tongue down her neck to her chest, taking her hard nipple between my lips. My hands tighten involuntarily. I thought I had strong. But the moment she moves, slow and purposeful, I feel it snap. *God help me.*

She rocks her hips, and I groan, deep, raw, pulled straight from my gut. She sets the pace at first, teasing me with every roll of her body. I feel everything, every shift, every squeeze, every sound she makes. She's driving me out of my mind.

I press my mouth to her throat, breathing her in, tasting her sweet skin. My hands travel up her spine, fingers digging into her back like I need to anchor myself to keep from losing it completely.

She moans softly, moving faster now, and I feel her fingers grip my shoulders like she's barely hanging on. Her lips find mine again, messy and hungry. *That's it. Control gone.*

I shift, wrapping an arm tight around her waist and pressing my other hand to the small of her back. I drive into her harder now, setting the rhythm, my mouth finding hers between ragged breaths.

She cries out again, as I continue thrusting hard inside her. Her pleasure, her surrender, it's more than I can handle. I growl into her neck, voice shaking. "You feel that? That's what you do to me."

251

She nods, breathless, barely coherent. Her nails scrape down my back. It builds, fast, hot, relentless. Our rhythm turns frantic, bodies slick, breath tangling between kisses. Her head falls back, and I watch her, memorize her.

When she finally shatters around me, her body clenching around my dick, she cries out. And I lose it. Everything inside me goes tight, white-hot. I hold her close as I fall with her, both of us shaking, wrecked and breathless as our orgasms rip though us.

She's still in my lap, breath slowing, skin flushed. And for a second, I don't move. I just hold her, stunned by how deep this runs. This isn't just sex. It's her letting go. It's me holding on. I press a soft kiss to her shoulder, then her mouth. She melts into me with a sound that hits deep.

I lift her in my arms. "Shower."

She nods, trusting, and wraps herself around me. I carry her to the bathroom, turn on the water and step into the steam-filled space. She moves under the water first, letting it cascade down her body. I join her, pulling her gently against me.

We don't talk. We just touch. My hands run soap along her shoulders, her back, her hips. Slow, soothing strokes. She turns, does the same for me. Her fingers on my skin are soft, careful.

"This okay?"

"More than okay."

We rinse, sharing quiet kisses in the mist. When the water cools, I shut it off and wrap her in a towel, then myself.

I climb in bed beside her, pulling her close. Her head rests on my shoulder, fingers tracing my skin.

"Sleep," I murmur. "Big day tomorrow."

Her breathing slows. And for once, the only thing I want is already in my arms.

29

Power in Pumps

Kinsley

Miles' body is pressed against my back, his arm still wrapped around me like he has no intention of letting go. For a few quiet minutes, we don't move, just breathe together. It's a strange kind of peace, but I hold onto it, because I know what today holds. Normally I'm not nervous. But knowing he will be here watching has me anxious. I want him to see me at my best. Like I need to prove something, but I don't, not with him. But I can't help feeling this way.

Eventually, we move. Quiet. Focused. I slip into the fitted black suit. Pairing it with a deep red blouse and matching red heels, that mean business. I run a flat iron through my hair until it's sleek and straight, then swipe on a bold red lip and enough eye makeup to make my eyes pop. When I step out of the bedroom, Miles is already dressed, white button-down, navy slacks, brown shoes, belt to match. The top two buttons of his shirt are undone, casually sexy in that infuriating way he does without even trying.

He looks up at me, one brow ticking. "You trying to distract the judge?"

253

"Only if you think I can."

The car is waiting outside, just like the driver promised. But first, we stop for coffee and croissants from a corner café. It's routine for most people, but for us, it's something new, something that feels a little like normal in the middle of all this chaos.

We sip our drinks in the back seat, our thighs touching, fingers brushing now and then, but we don't say much. There's a low hum of tension between us, not the heated kind we usually fall into, but something steadier. Present.

When the car pulls up to the courthouse, I glance over at him. He meets my eyes and nods once. He's with me. And I feel it in my bones. We step out together, side by side, and I square my shoulders as we head up the steps.

Miles finds a seat nearby while I meet Mel just inside the courthouse lobby. The air is crisp with nerves and early morning tension. We move to a quiet corner where I hand her my notes from last night.

She scans them quickly, nodding with approval as we talk through my approach. "We've got a complication. Mr. Perry's attorney is trying to argue that the funds he withdrew were his personal earnings, saying he had every right to take them."

I clench my jaw but keep my expression neutral. "Then we prove otherwise. We have the joint account statements. The deposits. The patterns. If we're lucky, a judge who gives a damn."

About twenty minutes later, Mrs. Perry arrives, looking nervous but determined. We all gather briefly near the front lobby and go over everything one last time; what we're asking for, what we expect to be challenged on and how we'll respond. She listens intently, nods, even manages a small smile when I squeeze her hand.

Once everything is clear, I step away and scan the hallway for Miles. He stands as soon as I approach. Without thinking, I lift onto my toes and kiss him softly, grounding myself in that small, steady moment of calm.

"It's time."

He nods. No words, just quiet support. We follow Mel and Mrs. Perry into the courtroom. Miles finds a seat toward the back, and I glance over my shoulder once before stepping forward and taking my place at the counsel table.

The courtroom settles into a hush as the judge enters. I rise smoothly, professional mask in place, and greet the court with practiced ease.

Then Mr. Perry's attorney opens his mouth, and the temperature in the room seems to spike. He launches into a carefully crafted argument. His tone is overly confident, claiming that the funds Mr. Perry withdrew were paid to him prior to their marriage, deposited into the joint account for convenience. He insists there was never intent to share those funds.

I listen, waiting, watching the judge's face, taking mental notes. When he finally pauses, I rise. "Your Honor, the funds in question were not segregated. They were deposited into a joint account and used for mutual expenses including rent, utilities and credit card payments." I hold up the exhibit folder. "We have six months of statements here. Each deposit and withdrawal show a pattern of shared financial use. Mr. Perry cannot now claim singular ownership simply because he regrets the consequences."

The judge leans forward, flipping through the documents as I walk him through the highlights. "We are requesting an immediate freeze on the joint accounts to prevent further depletion, and a temporary restraining order given the photographic evidence of vehicle damage and a documented pattern of intimidation."

Mr. Perry's attorney cuts in. "Objection, Your Honor. There is no proof Mr. Perry was responsible for the damage."

I pivot. "We have sworn testimony, timestamps and a surveillance photo of Mr. Perry at the property within an hour of the incident. The estimate for damages is included in Exhibit B." The judge gestures for the file, flipping to the photos. "Furthermore, the sum of eighty thousand dollars was withdrawn in three separate transactions, all within forty-eight hours of the separation filing. These funds were used for personal purchases, including hotel stays and a new television, per transaction details. We ask that these funds be ordered returned."

Mr. Perry's attorney throws in another rebuttal, questioning the timeline, and even attempting to diminish Mrs. Perry's credibility.

"Counselor," the judge warns him, "keep it relevant."

I don't sit. I step forward. "Your Honor, Mrs. Perry is not on trial. She is here to protect her livelihood and personal safety. We are not speculating. We have proof."

The judge folds his hands. "You don't waste time, Ms. Brighton."

"No, Your Honor," I reply, calm and direct. "Neither does Mr. Perry when draining accounts and keying cars."

The judge flips through court documents, frowning. "Emergency financial order granted. Joint accounts frozen. Mr. Perry is ordered to return the withdrawn funds within ten business days. Temporary restraining order approved for ninety days pending full hearing. Repair costs will be included in preliminary restitution."

I exhale slowly and sit. Behind me, I hear Mel whisper something soothing to Mrs. Perry, who looks like she might cry. But it's relief this time.

We gather our things, and as I walk out of that courtroom, I feel it. Not just pride. Not just victory. I feel like myself. And I know Miles saw the whole damn thing.

I glance at the clock on the lobby wall and realize the hearing ran longer than I'd expected. We need to get moving if we're going to make our flight.

As we step out into the hallway, Mrs. Perry wraps me in a tight hug, her voice thick with gratitude. "Thank you, Kinsley. For everything."

I hug her back. "You're welcome. We'll be in touch before the final hearing."

She pulls Mel into a hug next, and I take the opportunity to hand Mel Raelynn's file. "Can you take this down to the clerk's office and have the paperwork drawn up? I want Jacob served next week."

Mel nods, tucking the file under her arm. "You got it. And Kinsley, nice work in there."

"Thank you for all your help today." We hug and say our goodbyes with the promise to call her later, before she hurries down the hall.

I turn and spot Miles waiting on a nearby bench. When I approach, he pulls me into his arms without hesitation. He presses a kiss to my temple. "Jesus. You were a badass in there."

His words settle something inside me. After a quick kiss, we hurry outside to the waiting car. We still have to grab our bags from the apartment, and if we don't move fast, we're going to miss our flight back to Spokane.

We hurry into the apartment, both of us moving on autopilot. There's no time to change, so we just grab our bags. Miles grabs the trash on the way out while I close the blinds and make sure the place is locked up tight behind us.

The driver gets us to the airport with ten minutes to spare before boarding. I press my head back against the seat for a second, finally letting the courtroom adrenaline fade. The shift is subtle, but I feel it, like I'm peeling off the armor, piece by piece now that I'm just Kinsley again. Not the attorney. Just me. With him. We hustle through TSA, thankfully no delays, and make our way to the gate just as the boarding group is called.

We step onto the plane, find our seats in the middle and finally sit down, for the first time all day.

As soon as we settle into our seats, Miles turns toward me with a crooked grin, nudging my knee with his. "You know, watching you in court today? Kind of terrifying. In a hot way."

"Terrifying?"

"Oh yeah. I was sitting there thinking, 'Damn, I better never piss her off.'"

I arch a brow. "You better not. Unless you're into punishment. In which case, be my guest."

He chuckles. "You didn't even blink when that guy tried to talk over you. I almost laughed right there in court. The way you stared him down? Savage. I thought you were gonna throw your heels at him."

I lean back. "I considered it. But I like these heels."

He grins, and just like that, the tension from the day starts to ease.

When the plane lands, we gather our bags and head to the parking lot. As soon as we climb into his truck, Miles reaches over and laces his fingers through mine. I hold on for a while, but the exhaustion creeps in fast, and somewhere along the drive, I doze off.

I wake to his hand brushing my cheek. "Baby. We're back."

It's after dinner by the time we get back; Miles must have ordered pizza while he drove. By the time we step through the front door, the delivery driver's pulling into the driveway.

"Perfect timing." He tosses me a wink as he heads to the door.

"Thank God," I say, flopping onto one of the kitchen stools. "I was about five seconds away from chewing on the seatbelt."

Miles laughs, already grabbing two plates. "I'd offer you my arm, but I don't think I could recover from the teeth marks."

I roll my eyes and grab a slice as soon as he sets the box down. And then another. And another.

"Are you on your third slice?" he asks, raising a brow halfway through his first.

"I blacked out. Don't judge me." I take a swig of my beer and let out a satisfied sigh. "You think courtroom me is terrifying? Try me when I'm hangry."

Miles chuckles, shaking his head as he reaches for another slice. "Noted. Feed the lawyer or face the consequences."

"Exactly."

There's a knock on the door just as I'm licking sauce off my thumb.

"Miles?" Judy's voice calls.

"In here," he answers, setting down his plate.

Judy strolls in smiling, a brown paper bag tucked in her arms. "I'm so glad you two are back. I baked you a welcome-back apple pie."

My eyes practically light up, and Miles chuckles as he catches my expression.

"She brought pie," I say, whispering like it's a sacred offering.

Judy laughs and sets the bag on the counter, pulling out a perfectly golden pie that smells like cinnamon and heaven. "It's still warm. Thought you might need something sweet after that trip."

"How'd court go?" She looks between us like she already knows we won but wants to hear the details anyway.

Miles leans back against the counter, arms folded. "She was a shark. Tore that poor bastard's attorney apart. It was beautiful."

Judy's eyes sparkle as she turns to me. "I knew it. I knew you had fire in you."

I shrug, trying to play it off, but my grin gives me away. "Let's just say Mr. Perry won't be draining any more accounts."

She claps her hands. "Well, that calls for an extra slice then."

Miles grabs plates again, handing Judy one. "She already ate three slices of pizza. I might have to roll her to bed."

"Worth it," I mumble around a bite of crust.

Judy hugs us both before leaving, the smell of pie still lingering in the air. I help clean up the dishes, rinsing plates and humming to myself while Miles dries them. When we're done, I dry my hands and glance at him over my shoulder with a grin forming.

"Thanks for dinner," I say sweetly, walking around the counter and thumbing over my shoulder toward the door. "I better be going."

His brows pinch, but I don't wait. I start toward the door like I'm really leaving.

The second my fingers touch the knob, I let out a squeal as Miles grabs me from behind, lifts me off the floor and spins me around. I'm laughing and gasping at the same time as he gently tosses me onto the couch. I land with a bounce, and before I can move, he crawls up over me, caging me in with his arms on either side of my head, his grin smug and downright sinful.

"Baby," he murmurs, nose brushing mine, "I told you. You're stuck with me until you leave."

I roll my eyes dramatically. "Fine. But I'm billing you for room and board."

He laughs low in his throat. "That's fair. I'll pay in orgasms."

I pretend to think about it, tapping my finger to my chin. "Hmm, in that case, I'd like to extend my stay."

His smirk deepens. "Good. Because you're not going anywhere for now." He plants a loud kiss on my forehead and rolls off me, stretching as he stands. Without a word, he heads upstairs. A minute later, he returns, holding a worn T-shirt that smells like him.

I stand slowly, locking eyes with him as I begin to undress, first sliding off my jacket and pants, then unbuttoning my blouse, revealing my red lace bra and matching panties. His gaze sharpens, hungry and unblinking.

Still holding his stare, I reach behind my back and unclasp my bra, letting it fall to the floor. Then, without breaking eye contact, I pull his T-shirt over my head.

"Catch me, then." I grin wickedly and bolt for the backdoor.

Behind me, I hear him laugh followed by a muttered curse. I make it nearly to the back door before I hear him gaining on me. This time, I'm ready. Just before he reaches me, I spin around and dodge into the dining room, darting around the table.

"I thought you were faster than that," I tease, breathless.

He grins, eyes dark with heat. "Keep talking, baby."

We circle each other like it's a game, step for step, until I think I've got enough space to make another run for it. But I don't get far.

With a laugh, he lunges and catches me, strong arms wrapping around my waist. I squeal as he lifts me off the ground. I wrap my legs around his waist and my arms around his neck. Still breathless, I lean in and bite his bottom lip, playful and taunting.

"Now that you've caught me," I whisper, "what are you going to do?"

He growls against my mouth, voice low. "I'm going to take you upstairs, lay you out on that bed and eat you so slow and deep you forget your own name." His mouth trails to my jaw, hot and wet. "And when you're begging for more, I'll flip you over and fuck you from behind until your legs don't work and my name is the only word you can say."

I shudder in his arms, my laugh dissolving into a moan. "Then what are you waiting for?"

He carries me upstairs like he's done before, confident, sure, hungry. What follows isn't quick or rushed. It's hours of surrender. Hands, sweat and gasps. Growled commands in the dark. He touches every inch of me like it's his. Takes me in every position like he's making a claim. And I let him, because I want it just as much. Maybe more. We go until our bodies are spent and our skin is slick and flushed. Eventually, we fall asleep, the blankets a mess around us.

30

Captain Kinsley

Miles

Kinsley's already up. I sit up, run a hand down my face, still tasting sleep and everything we were last night. For a minute, I just sit there, letting the quiet wrap around me. The room smells like her, sweet and sharp, like the lavender lotion she uses.

I pull on a pair of jeans and a T-shirt, barefoot as I head downstairs. She's not in the kitchen. But then I hear it, the soft creak of the porch swing. I walk toward the screen door and stop.

She's there, knees pulled up to her chest, coffee cup cradled in her hands, hair still a little messy from sleep. She's staring out over the lake like she's trying to memorize it. The way the morning light catches her profile nearly knocks the breath out of me. She looks peaceful. Goddamn, she's beautiful like this. Unaware of how much she's settled herself right into the middle of my life. But it's more than that. I think about yesterday. About the way she stood in that courtroom, sharp, fierce, composed. The way her voice never shook even when she was going for blood. She's good at what she does. Damn good. Her clients are lucky to have her.

I hate that the clock's ticking. That every morning like this is one less before she leaves. I rub the back of my neck, sighing quietly, trying to shake the weight pressing into my chest. Then I step out onto the porch and sit down beside her.

"Hi," she says softly, not looking at me right away. There's something in her voice, something wistful.

"Hi. What's wrong?"

She exhales, eyes on the lake. "I'm going to miss this place." She turns to look at me. "I'll miss you."

Her words hit me hard. I want her to stay. I want her to choose this. Choose me. But that has to be her decision. I won't push her. "Me too," I say quietly.

We sit in silence for a while, the kind that's full of everything neither of us is saying.

Then I glance at her. "Do you want to stay at the house with me? Until you leave?"

She looks over, sadness in her eyes. "You think that's a good idea?"

I huff a soft laugh. "No. Probably not. But I want it anyway."

She hesitates for half a second before nodding. "Me too."

I lean in and kiss her, slow and soft. She drops her knees and turns toward me fully, like she's all in, for now. When we part, I stand and offer my hand. "Come on. Let's go get your stuff. I've got plans for us."

She smiles, taking my hand as she rises. "You're always up to something."

I grin, giving her fingers a playful squeeze. "Damn right I am."

I toss her a pair of my gym shorts, grinning as she holds them up with a look of pure disbelief. "They're huge."

I laugh. "You're five-foot-nothing. What did you expect?"

She narrows her eyes playfully as we walk out the front door. "Five-two, thank you very much."

"Sure," I tease, starting the truck. "Maybe if we count the bun on top of your head."

She huffs, but there's a smile tugging at her lips as she climbs in beside me, the gym shorts cinched tight and still threatening to fall off her hips.

"They should come with a warning label for short people," she mutters, adjusting the waistband again. "Or maybe just say: 'Contents may vanish entirely inside garment.'"

I glance over as I pull onto the path. "Warning: May cause inappropriate thoughts when worn by ridiculously short, sexy women?"

She gives me a look. "You're impossible."

"Yet you've agreed to stay with me," I say, tossing her a wink. "What does that say about you?"

She smirks, pulling the waistband tighter as the shorts threaten to slide again. "That I clearly have a thing for hot farmers who cause trouble."

I chuckle, eyes on the road but grinning. "And here I thought you were the responsible one."

She glances my way. "Oh, I am. But even responsible girls have their weaknesses."

"And I'm yours?"

She doesn't answer right away. Just looks out the window, her fingers tightening slightly around the waistband of my oversized shorts. There's something in her expression, quiet, a little distant. Like her thoughts are pulling her somewhere I can't quite reach.

"Yeah," she finally says, voice soft. "You are."

I see it, the shift in her. The way she's fighting something inside, maybe trying to hold on to the moment while already bracing for the end. I don't push. Not yet. I just nod, keeping one hand on the wheel.

She turns her head back to me, a flicker of a smile lifting one corner of her mouth. "So, what's the plan today?" She's lighter now, like she's trying to shake off whatever just settled over her.

"I was thinking." I glance over at her with a grin. "Today's a good day for me to teach you how to use a canoe." Her eyebrows lift, intrigued. "And then tonight, you can teach me how to cook. We'll hit the store for ingredients, maybe stop and see Naya for dessert. What do you think?"

Her smile spreads wide, lighting up her whole face. "That actually sounds fantastic."

I stop the truck in the driveway, gravel crunching beneath the tires. "Alright, let's grab your things."

We make quick work of it, moving through the cabin together, folding clothes, packing up the last of her stuff. She moves fast, efficient, like she's done this a hundred times.

Still, I glance at the growing stack of bags by the door and shake my head. "I can't believe how much stuff you brought. How did you even get all this in that little car?"

She laughs, hoisting one of the bags onto her shoulder. "Like a jigsaw puzzle. And now I have even more to take back."

I nudge one of the bags with my boot. "What the hell did you pack? It looks like you brought your whole closet."

"Well, I needed options. Cute clothes, comfy clothes, emergency heels."

"Heels? You're in the middle of nowhere," I tease. "What, just in case you had to strut through a cornfield?"

She shrugs, unbothered. "What can I say? I like to be prepared."

I hold up a full-on winter coat with a look of pure disbelief. "Prepared for what? A freak snowstorm in September?"

She snatches it from me with a smirk. "Climate change is real, Miles. I didn't survive Seattle weather by trusting forecasts."

I chuckle. "If it snows here this week, I'll eat your emergency heels."

She grins wide. "Deal. And I'll make sure you wash 'em down with a pumpkin spice latte."

I groan. "God help me."

As we load the truck, Judy steps out of her cabin, arms crossed and a smug look stretching across her face.

"What are you two up to?" she calls out, voice full of knowing mischief.

I walk over, meeting her halfway as Kinsley wrangles one last bag into the back seat. I lean in and kiss Judy on the cheek. "Kinsley's going to stay with me at the house."

Judy's smile widens like she just won a bet. She leans in, eyes sparkling. "I knew she'd be good for you."

I place a hand gently on her shoulder, grounding us both. "She's still going home," I remind her, quieter.

Judy's gaze flicks past me to Kinsley, who's standing by the truck, brushing her hair out of her face in the breeze.

"For now." Then she pats my chest, gives a little wave to Kinsley over my shoulder and heads back inside without another word. Judy meant well. She tried, really damn hard, to make this happen. Even if it was nosy and wrong in about six different ways.

After driving back and hauling all her bags upstairs, I help her tuck her things into the empty closet in my room. She changes into her own pair of shorts and a soft T-shirt while I head down to the kitchen and make us a couple of sandwiches.

We settle on the couch, plates in our laps, flipping through the cookbooks we got from the bookstore.

I tap a page. "What about this one?"

Kinsley tilts her head, considering the recipe for chicken teriyaki. "That should work." She pulls out her phone and snaps a picture of the ingredients for our shopping trip later.

Just as she lowers the phone, Miss Dashworth leaps onto the back of the couch like a feline ninja. Kinsley yelps and nearly tumbles onto the floor, catching herself with one hand on my leg. Her eyes dart to the source of the ambush.

"Oh my god," she says, pressing a hand to her chest. "She scared the shit out of me." Miss Dashworth meows like she's sorry and rubs against Kinsley's leg.

Kinsley softens instantly. "You're a good girl," she coos, reaching up to pet her like they didn't just have a jump-scare moment. "Just, maybe lead with a 'hello' next time."

I chuckle. "She likes you. That's rare."

Kinsley shrugs, smiling. "Smart cat."

"Come on, City Girl. Time to teach you how to canoe." I toss her a grin as we walk out the back door and down toward the lake.

I untie the canoe and hold it steady while Kinsley steps in on the far side, careful and focused like she's navigating a minefield. Once she's seated, I step in behind her and push us off with one smooth motion. The canoe glides out onto the lake, the water calm and glassy beneath us.

I dip my paddle into the water. "Alright, here's how you go straight, and here's how you turn." I demonstrate slowly, keeping us in the center of the lake. Then I stop paddling and lift the oar for her to see. "Grip it like this."

Kinsley studies my hands like she's prepping for a final exam.

I chuckle. "Babe, it's not rocket science."

She rolls her eyes, laughing. "Shut up. I just want to get it right."

When her hands mimic mine, I nod. "Perfect. Now, your turn. Paddle us back to the dock."

She starts strong. I'll give her that. But things go south fast.

We veer left, then harder left, until we're slowly spinning in the middle of the lake like a lazy carnival ride.

"Try switching sides when we start to turn too much," I offer, grinning. "You're driving this like a drunk person."

"I got it," she huffs, determined, sweat starting to bead at her temple.

I laugh and hold my hands up in surrender. "Okay, okay. It's all you."

She paddles with fierce determination. And we spin in three full circles.

Now I'm laughing so hard I nearly tip us over. "You're doing amazing, sweetie," I manage through breathless laughter.

"What the hell am I doing wrong?" She laughs with me, clearly trying to keep a straight face and failing.

I finally pull myself together. "Alright, watch me again." I guide the paddle through a few clean strokes. "Like this."

She watches, nods, then gives it another go, mimicking each move with intense focus.

"Look at you," I say as the canoe finally starts drifting in a semi-straight line. "Captain Kinsley: Master of the Lake."

She snorts. "Don't jinx it, Country Boy."

We finally start inching closer to the dock, slow and a little crooked, but it's progress.

Kinsley exhales like she just finished a marathon. "That was the most humbling thing I've done in years."

I grin behind her. "What, learning from me?"

She twists enough to glare over her shoulder. "You're lucky I'm holding a paddle."

I laugh, and she almost smiles too, until the canoe bumps the dock with a soft thud.

"Boom. Nailed it." I reach to grab the edge and steady us. I hop out first and hold the canoe steady again as she climbs out.

"You're never letting me live that down, are you?"

"Not a chance."

She swats at my shoulder with her paddle, which only makes me grin harder.

"You did good, though." I lean in and brush a kiss against her cheek. "You didn't tip us, you didn't cry, and I only feared for my life twice. That's a win in my book."

She narrows her eyes. "Next time, we're doing yoga on paddleboards."

"Oh hell no."

We pull the canoe up onto the bank and flip it over to dry. As we head back toward the house, her hand finds mine. I squeeze gently, glancing at her out of the corner of my eye. Her cheeks are flushed from the sun and the laughing, hair windblown and tangled from the lake breeze.

"Hungry?"

She nods. "Starving after that workout."

"Perfect," I tug her a little closer. "Let's hit the store. We've got a date with teriyaki chicken."

The grocery store trip is quick, shockingly efficient, considering I've got Kinsley beside me sneaking things like chocolate-covered almonds and fancy cheese into the basket when she thinks I'm not looking.

"You planning to seduce me with snacks?" I raise a brow as she drops yet another item in.

She shrugs, not the least bit guilty. "Never take me shopping when I'm hungry."

I lean closer. "Noted. But for the record, you don't need snacks to seduce me."

Her grin is wicked as she pushes the cart toward the checkout. "I know."

We bag everything and head out, the sun starting its slow dip behind the trees. On the way back, we stop by Naya's bakery. The scent hits us before we even open the door, warm sugar and cinnamon.

Naya lights up when she sees us walk in. "Well, look who finally made it back from the city."

Kinsley rushes forward and hugs her. "Court ran long, but it's done. And it went really well."

"I've got fresh snickerdoodles cooling," Naya says, heading toward the counter. "And that lemon tart you like."

Kinsley's eyes go wide. "You didn't."

"I did. For you. One night only." Naya grins, then lowers her voice. "You gonna tell me everything later?"

Kinsley nods. "Promise."

We don't stay long, just enough time to grab dessert, trade a few jokes and promise to come by later in the week. When we climb back into the truck, Kinsley already digging into the tart with her fingers, her eyes fluttering closed as she takes the first bite. "Holy

271

hell," she murmurs around a mouthful, cheeks flushed with delight. "This is better than sex. Almost."

I glance over at her, tart crumbs on her shirt and zero concern on her face. She doesn't care what she looks like around me. And damn if that isn't the cutest thing I've ever seen.

31

Counting Down from Nine

Kinsley

The ride back is quiet in the best way, comfortable, easy. Miles has one hand on the wheel, the other resting on the console between us, fingers occasionally brushing mine like he just needs to feel I'm still there.

I glance over at him, the way his jaw ticks slightly when he's focused, the way the late sun filters through the window and lights him up like some kind of slow-burn fantasy. And somehow, he's mine, at least for now. It feels impossible and electric, like holding onto something wild and warm that could vanish if I blink too long. My heart aches with it.

The trees thicken as we hit the familiar turnoff toward his place…our place…I guess, for the next nine days. I should feel weird about that. But I don't. I feel settled. And that scares the hell out of me.

I've been wrestling with these feelings all day, trying to push them aside, trying to just enjoy what time we have left. But they're still here. Still growing. I like him. Really like him. And the more time I spend with Miles, the more I know leaving is going to hurt. Part of me wants to run before I fall any harder, before it's too late.

But I also know that if I go now, not all of me will make it back to Seattle. Something will stay here with him, in this house, under this sky.

So, I take a breath and push the panic down, just for now. I can deal with the hard part later. Right now, I just want to be with him. Still, I need someone to talk to, someone who knows me well enough to call me on my shit. Tomorrow, I'll call Raelynn. I need her voice, her honesty, her ability to see through me even when I can't.

Back at the house, I carry the tart while Miles grabs everything else, groceries, the bag of extras I snuck in, and a cocky grin like this is all part of some grand adventure. Which, I guess, it kind of is.

Once inside, I set the tart on the counter and roll up my sleeves. The moment the cookbook hits the counter, I slide straight into teaching mode. I flip to the recipe, smooth the page flat and scan the ingredients while Miles unloads behind me.

"I'll need the large skillet, cutting board, a mixing bowl and that measuring cup." I point without looking. He moves around the kitchen with ease, pulling out pans and tools. I don't know my way around his kitchen yet, but I will. I'm already filing away where the knives are, how his cabinets creak and which drawer has the bent measuring spoons.

We lay everything out neatly, prepping our workspace like we're about to perform surgery instead of making dinner. I glance over at him, already watching me like he's waiting for his first command.

I bite my bottom lip. "Maybe we should've started with boxed mac and cheese."

He raises a brow, already grinning. "Wow, smart-ass."

I wink. "You like it."

He laughs, stepping behind me, hands brushing my waist as he reaches for a spoon. "You're lucky I do."

Just then, music fills the room out of nowhere. I turn and see him holding his phone and a small Bluetooth speaker, a smug smile on his face.

"Did you make a kitchen playlist?" I ask, surprised he remembered.

"It's part of the recipe." He repeats my own words back to me from the first few days here.

It's things like this. Not grand gestures or anything worth a lot of money, just sweet, thoughtful moments that make my heart swell. *This is who he is. And how the hell am I supposed to survive leaving him? But I have to. Right? Everything I've built is in Seattle.*

I shake my thoughts away before they can settle, crossing the room to him. I rise onto my toes, and he wraps an arm around my waist, steadying me as I cup his face and kiss him softly.

I walk him through the steps, start with the sauce, don't overcrowd the pan, and for the love of everything holy, measure the soy sauce before dumping it in. He listens, mostly. But about five minutes in, he's stirring too fast, flinging drops of sauce across the counter.

"Hey!" I swat at him with a dish towel. "Are you cooking or finger painting?"

He holds the spoon up in defense, smirking. "This is my process."

"Your process is messy."

"You're messy," he throws back, stepping in a little closer. My cheeks warm instantly, heart skipping as he leans in with that teasing smile. I roll my eyes to play it cool, but it doesn't fool either of us.

I try to stay focused, I really do, but it's hard when he's leaning in like that, voice low and teasing, that damn shirt of his hugging his arms just right.

I slide the cutting board toward him. "Chop the garlic."

He squints at it. "That's not garlic. That's tiny onions."

I blink. "Are you serious right now?"

"Half serious."

He makes a mess of the garlic, half of it ends up stuck to his fingers, the rest somewhere under the cutting board. I sigh dramatically, reach over to help, and our hands brush. He catches my fingers, brings them to his mouth and kisses my knuckles.

"Best cooking class I've ever taken."

My heart skips, but I shake it off. "Flattery won't save dinner." But it turns out, we don't need saving. Because somehow, despite the chaos, the flirting, the back-and-forth, our teriyaki chicken looks good. It smells even better.

I slide a bite onto a plate and hand him a fork. He tastes it, brows lifting.

"Well?" I ask, arms crossed.

He nods, impressed. "I'd burn my tongue for this."

I laugh. "Next time we try something harder."

He smirks. "I thought this was the foreplay."

I roll my eyes but lean in, brushing a kiss to his cheek. "Let's eat, Country Boy. Dessert's still waiting."

We sit at the kitchen island with our plates piled high. I watch Miles take another bite, chew, then glance at me over the rim of his fork.

"I don't want to brag, but I might be a natural."

I snort. "You spilled soy sauce on the ceiling."

"And yet," he gestures at his plate, "this is damn good."

"Miracles do happen."

We eat side by side. The conversation is easy; light teasing, comments about the food and plans for tomorrow. It feels so domestic, so natural, I almost forget this isn't permanent. Almost.

When we're done, I clear the plates while Miles grabs forks and the tart box from the counter.

He lifts the lid, eyes widening. "You ate this much on the way home?"

I lick my lips and shrug, feigning innocence. "I was sampling. Quality control."

He cuts a slice and slides it toward me with a slow shake of his head. "You're lucky you're cute."

I take the fork and flash him a grin. "I know."

We clean up together, his hand brushing mine occasionally, his smile easy and warm. The rain taps softly at the windows, steady and soothing, and once the kitchen's clean, we settle into the couch. He tosses a blanket over both our legs and finds some movie neither of us really cares about. I tuck myself into his side, his arm around me, my head on his chest. The steady rhythm of the rain, the soft flicker of the screen and the rise and fall of his breathing lull me into a warm haze.

***

I wake up warm, cocooned in blankets, the room dim with early morning light filtering through the rain-streaked windows. For a second, I forget where I am, until I roll over and see him beside me, still asleep, mouth slightly parted, one arm slung across my side like even in sleep he doesn't want to let me go.

I blink, and it all comes back in pieces. The couch. The movie. The steady rain. And the way his arms wrapped around me as he carried me upstairs. I slip out of bed as quietly as I can, careful not to disturb him. He doesn't stir. Just shifts a little.

Padding downstairs, I make my way to the kitchen. The house is quiet except for the hum of the fridge and the soft tap of rain on the windows. Miss Dashworth rubs against my legs as I start the coffee, the familiar scent filling the room almost instantly. I pour a mug, wrap both hands around it and step out onto the back porch.

The rain is steady, light but constant, rippling across the lake in soft concentric circles. The trees sway gently, leaves dripping. Everything feels still. Like time paused just for a moment. Like it's giving me space to breathe. I breathe him in, too. The thought of Miles. Of how easy it's become to exist in this place. With him. And how hard it's going to be to walk away from it all.

I sip my coffee and try to shake it off. But the ache's already there. Eventually, I turn back inside, setting the mug down with quiet determination. I'm not ready to think about the end. Not today.

I move to the fridge, pulling out eggs, cheese, bread and butter. The skillet sizzles to life, the smell of butter melting filling the quiet kitchen. I'm mid-scramble when I feel arms wrap around my waist from behind. I jump slightly, then smile as Miles presses a kiss to the top of my head, his body warm against my back.

I glance at him over my shoulder. "You want some coffee?"

"Yes, please." His voice is thick with sleep, followed by a long yawn.

I laugh softly, pulling away just enough to pour him a mug and slide it across the island. "Not a morning person?"

"Not at all." He rubs a hand over his face as he takes a grateful sip. "But this helps."

When breakfast is ready, I plate everything and join him at the island. We eat side by side, the rain still whispering against the windows. It's simple; eggs, toast and coffee.

He nudges my foot gently under the counter, eyes still a little sleepy, but his grin is unmistakable. "I could get used to this." *So could I.* But I don't say it out loud.

278

We finish eating, still lingering over the last sips of coffee when Miles' phone buzzes on the counter. He glances at the screen, swipes to answer and leans back in his stool.

"Hey," he says casually, then after a pause, "Yeah, sounds good. See you then."

He ends the call and sets the phone down. "Reed's coming by this afternoon to go fishing. You want to join us?"

I hesitate, then shrug, a little sheepish. "I've never been fishing before."

His jaw drops like I just told him I've never had water before. "Never? Oh, City Girl, you've been missing out."

I laugh, cheeks warming. "I guess I was too busy dodging traffic."

"You're about to get an education." He stands and stretches. "And maybe a little dirt under your nails."

"Oh great," I mutter, but I'm already smiling.

He helps me clean up, stacking dishes and wiping down the counter beside me. When we're done, he leans in, his hands braced on either side of the island and brushes a kiss close to my lips. "Thanks for breakfast. I need to feed the animals."

"Okay, I'm going to take a shower."

He groans softly, eyes dropping to my mouth, then lower. "I'd rather be in the shower with you than out there freezing my ass off with the animals."

Knowing exactly how to buy myself a little time to call Raelynn, I grin. "How about you feed the animals, and I'll wait naked in the bathroom for you to finish?"

He mock runs toward the door like I just issued a life-or-death challenge, grabbing his jacket off the hook. "Don't start without me," he calls, flashing a grin over his shoulder.

I laugh, shaking my head as the door swings closed behind him. I wait for a beat before grabbing my phone from the counter. I tap Raelynn's name and hold the phone to my ear, pacing lightly across the kitchen floor.

She answers on the second ring. "Hey, girl. How's farmland?"

I smile. "Rainy. And kind of amazing."

There's a pause on her end. "Uh-oh. You've got that tone."

"I don't even know how to explain it. I just, I really like him. More than I planned to. And the thought of leaving?" I sigh.

Raelynn doesn't hesitate. "Then don't leave with regrets."

"I don't know what that means."

"It means," she says firmly, "do whatever makes you happy. Even if it's messy. Even if it's temporary. Just don't hold back and pretend it didn't mean something."

I lean against the counter, rubbing my face. "What about my life in Seattle? I can't just walk away from everything."

"You're not stuck. You're just scared. And that's okay. But don't let fear be the thing that decides what you do next."

I blink fast, eyes stinging. "Damn it, Rae. Why do you always do this?"

"Because I know you. And I want you to be happy, but I can't tell you what to do, babe."

"Thanks. I love your face."

"I love your face, too."

I hang up and set the phone down, still unsure what to do.

I peek out the window and see Miles walking toward the house, his jacket damp from the rain. He's done feeding the animals. I bolt upstairs to the bathroom, stripping as fast as I can, my pulse buzzing with anticipation. A few seconds later, I hear heavy boots thudding up the stairs.

The bathroom door swings open with a bang, and there he is, grinning like he just hit the jackpot. "What'd I miss?" His eyes sweep over me.

I can't help but laugh, catching the look on his face, like he's prepared to throw dirt on me if I've already showered without him.

We never even make it to the water. First, we test the limits of the vanity, knocking everything to the floor in the process. When we finally shower, it's not exactly quick or clean, but we both emerge flushed and grinning, toweling off with a kind of contented energy that's getting harder to ignore.

Back in the bedroom, we pull on jeans and long sleeves. The rain's stopped, the sun pushing through the clouds just enough to cast a warm haze over the lake. Reed should be here any minute.

As if on cue, we're heading downstairs just as the familiar sound of tires crunching gravel echoes through the open window. By the time we make it outside, Reed is stepping out of his truck, ball cap low and grin already in place.

"Well, well," he drawls, eyeing us both. "Look who finally made it out of the bedroom."

Miles shoots him a look. "Careful, or I'll make you bait your own damn hook."

Reed chuckles, unfazed. "Please. Like I haven't been carrying your fishing game for years."

I bite my lip, holding back a smile as I fall in beside Miles. "Should I be worried I'm walking into a competition?"

Reed grins at me. "Nah, you'll be fine. I'm the only one with something to prove. Miles here just wants to impress you."

Miles smirks. "I already did that this morning."

Reed lets out a bark of laughter while I elbow Miles in the ribs, cheeks burning. "You two are ridiculous."

"Let's catch some fish," Reed says.

"She's never been fishing before, and if it's anything like her canoeing, we're in trouble," Miles says, grinning.

"What? I'm a natural." I gasp with mock offense.

Reed laughs. "You're going to have to tell me that story."

Miles presses a kiss to the top of my head, as he walks toward the barn. "I'll get the poles. You two bond over my suffering."

Reed shakes his head, grinning. "You're trying to conquer the lake. I can't wait to hear this."

"Just so you know, I got us back to the dock."

From inside the barn his voice is thick with amusement. "Eventually."

32

Hooked

Miles

The skies finally clear, and a few rays of sun peek through as we make our way down the grassy slope toward the dock. Kinsley walks between Reed and me, carrying her pole like it's a loaded weapon. And honestly, with her? It might as well be.

I cast first, showing her the basics. Reed follows. Kinsley watches carefully, nodding like she's about to defuse a bomb instead of tossing a line in the water.

"All right, your turn." I step back to give her space.

She grips the pole, tongue caught between her teeth in concentration. "Okay, I got this." Famous last words. Her first cast doesn't go far; it plunks straight into the water about four feet in front of her. There's something so damn cute about how serious she gets, like catching a fish is life or death.

Reed snorts. "Hey, you'll catch all the baby fish that hang by the shore."

"Just warming up," she says, resetting.

The second cast goes farther, right over the dock railing.

The third? That's the one that snags Reed.

"Shit!" he yelps, stumbling back as the hook catches the fabric of his sleeve.

Kinsley gasps, dropping the pole. "Oh my god! Did I…are you…did I get skin?!"

Reed rubs his arm dramatically. "I didn't sign a waiver, you know."

"Oh, hush. You'll live." Kinsley crosses her arms, pouting just enough to make me grin.

Despite the chaos, we eventually settle in. Kinsley even manages a halfway decent cast and cheers like she just won the Super Bowl. The rest of the afternoon is mostly quiet, lines in the water, the occasional ripple across the lake.

My dad used to say, "You know what you think about when you're fishing? Fishing." Most of the time, that's true. But not today. Today, I'm thinking about her. About how easy this all feels. About how much I like her. How much I want her to stay. But if her life in Seattle is what makes her happy, if that's where she belongs, then I won't ask her to change that. I'll let her go. Even if it's the exact opposite of what I want. Because whatever this thing between us is becoming, it can't be a leash. It has to be a choice. And that choice has to be hers.

A sudden squeal pulls me out of my thoughts. "I got one!" Kinsley yells, eyes wide with pure panic and excitement.

I chuckle, already reeling in my own line. "Relax, babe. Just keep reeling and lift your pole."

She fumbles to follow instructions, arms flailing, eyes darting toward me like I'm the only thing between her and certain doom. "What do I do?!"

Reed and I are both laughing now. "You're doing it." I grab the net. "Just don't let go."

"My arms are burning! Is it a shark or something?!"

"Nope," Reed says through a grin. "Probably a bass."

She wrestles the line like she's reeling in Moby Dick, and when the fish finally breaks the surface, I scoop it up with the net, biggest catch of the day.

Kinsley drops the pole and jumps up and down like a kid who just won the state fair. "I did it!"

I shit you not, she does it three more times. Each one a bass, all between seventeen and twenty inches. Meanwhile, Reed and I spend hours catching a bunch of panfish barely worth measuring. I take pictures of her holding up each fish, wearing the same grossed out face.

As we pack up at the end of the day, Reed shakes his head and mutters. "We've been outfished by a rookie."

I grin, glancing toward Kinsley, still glowing from her victory. "Beginner's luck." But I'm proud of her.

Reed and I clean the fish, prepping them for dinner while Kinsley hovers nearby, pretending not to make faces every time we gut one. Judy shows up just as we're finishing up, carrying a big bowl of potato salad and a smile.

We grill the fish out back, and when everything's ready, we all gather around the table, plates full, laughter louder than the frogs croaking near the lake.

Stories fly around like they always do. Reed reenacts Kinsley's panicked battle with her first catch, complete with flailing arms and shrieks. Judy nearly chokes from laughing so hard. Kinsley rolls her eyes but can't stop smiling. The food's good, the company's better.

Eventually, Reed stands, stretches and offers to drive Judy home. We say our goodbyes with full bellies, and then it's just the two of us, the house quiet again.

Kinsley leans against the counter, rubbing her eyes with the back of her hand. "I had a really good time today," she says around a yawn. "Thank you."

"Me too, babe." I step closer. "Come on, let's get to bed. I've got even better plans for tomorrow."

Her brow lifts slightly, playful. "Better than outfishing you?"

I grin. "Way better."

***

I wake up with Kinsley wrapped around me.

"Good morning."

She smiles sleepily, voice raspy. "Good morning."

We make our way downstairs. I stand at the counter, waiting for the coffee pot to finish sputtering to life. Kinsley opens the fridge, scanning the shelves before peeking at me over her shoulder.

"What do you want for breakfast?"

I shake my head. "Let's keep it light. We're hitting the farmer's market, and we'll be sampling food all day."

She shuts the fridge and rubs her hands together with excitement. "Tell me more."

I chuckle. "Baked goods, fresh produce, flowers, furniture…hell, they've got everything. You'll love it."

Her eyes light up, and I cross the kitchen to grab us both mugs.

"And after that, we'll come back here, get cleaned up and head out for drinks at Fireside Lounge."

She grins, wrapping her fingers around her mug. "That sounds perfect."

What she doesn't know is that I've arranged for everyone to be at the Fireside Lounge later, sort of a quiet goodbye party. Mostly because I want her to myself for the last seven days she's here. No distractions. Just us.

"I'll make us peanut butter toast." She skips off to the pantry.

I smile, watching her go. It's ridiculous how easy it is to make her happy, how light the house feels when she's in it. We eat our toast and sip our coffee on the couch while I check the weather on my phone. I glance over at her. "Looks like it's going to rain off and on today."

Her shoulders dip slightly. "Does that mean we can't go?"

"Not at all." I nudge her knee with mine. "Most of the farmer's market is under big tents. We'll be fine."

Just like that, she's smiling again. "When should we leave?" She stands to clear our plates.

"That depends, how long will it take you to get ready?"

An hour, I think to myself.

She taps her chin like she's seriously considering it. "I need an hour."

I laugh. "Okay then, we leave in an hour."

She bolts up the stairs like she's on a mission, and two minutes later I hear the shower kick on. As much as I want to follow her, I keep my ass planted on the couch. If I go up there, she's definitely going to need more than an hour. Exactly one hour later, she comes down the stairs, and it's worth the wait. She's wearing jeans, a fitted black top that hugs every curve and a jean jacket. Casual. Effortless. Sexy as hell.

***

We park in the grass along the edge of the farmer's market, and the moment Kinsley steps out of the truck, I know this is going to be a good day. She spins in a slow circle, taking it all in, rows of

287

colorful tents, families milling about, the smell of grilled corn and something sweet in the air.

"This is way more than I expected," she says, wide-eyed.

"Told you. It's practically a religion around here."

I watch her light up over jars of jam, hand cut soap and beeswax candles shaped like pumpkins. She samples everything she can get her hands; on honey sticks, fruit leather, even pickle-flavored popcorn. I swear she's making friends with half the vendors as we go.

"You planning to eat everything before we get to the good stuff?" I ask, watching her lick jam off her thumb.

"Don't test me," she fires back playfully, wiping her hands on a napkin. "I'm conducting important market research."

God, she's beautiful when she's like this, unfiltered, a little messy, completely herself.

We stop at the stand with the blackberry jam, and her whole face lights up. She turns to me with that look, like I just pulled off some grand romantic gesture when all I did was drive her here.

She drops the jar into the basket next to the strawberry incense and some kind of handmade lotion I'm pretty sure smells like a meadow in spring. I don't ask questions. I just swipe my card and nod when the vendor throws in a free honey stick with a wink in Kinsley's direction.

By the time we leave, my arms are full of bags, jars clinking, paper sacks rustling, one bag threatening to rip from the weight of all her "essentials."

Meanwhile, she's skipping ahead, chewing on a stick of beef jerky like she didn't just shop like she's prepping for the end of days.

I shake my head, grinning as I follow her to the truck. "You gonna offer me a bite or just flaunt it all the way home?"

She glances over her shoulder, eyes sparkling. "You laughed at me for buying it."

"I laughed at you for buying six kinds," I correct.

"And now you want in." She tears off a piece and holds it just out of reach. "Admit I was right."

I raise a brow, stepping closer. "You were right."

She pops the jerky into my mouth with a satisfied smile. "Damn right I was."

I load the bags into the truck while she climbs in, already fiddling with the radio and humming under her breath. When I slide into the driver's seat, she turns to me with that smile, the one that's becoming a problem.

We ride in a comfortable silence, the kind that doesn't need filling. The radio hums low between us, some easy, familiar tune drifting through the speakers. I glance over and catch her mouthing the words, tapping her fingers against her thigh in rhythm. She doesn't know I'm watching, her guard's down, her smile small but real.

God, this is what I want. Just this. Her singing along to the radio while we drive back with a truck full of unnecessary jam and overpriced incense.

We pull into the driveway. She hops out first, bags rustling as we unload the last of our market haul. Inside, we put everything away in an easy rhythm.

"I'm gonna go change." She kisses my cheek, then heads upstairs.

An hour later, I'm in a fresh button-down and dark jeans, adjusting my cuffs when I hear the creak of the stairs. I turn, and time stops. She's wearing a red mini dress, sleek, fitted, with a plunging neckline that makes my mouth drop open. Her hair falls in soft waves over her shoulders, and the heels she's wearing do something dangerous to my ability to think straight.

"Jesus." I breathe.

Her smile is smug. "Too much?"

I shake my head slowly, taking her in from head to toe. "No. I mean, how am I supposed to take you out in public looking like that and not start a fight?"

She arches a brow, amused. "So dramatic."

"You have no idea." I step closer, sliding a hand around her waist. "You realize I'm gonna spend all night pretending I'm not imagining what's under this dress."

She leans up on her toes, lips brushing my jaw. "Then stop pretending."

I groan softly, burying my face in her neck, trying to hold on to some kind of restraint. "You're making it real hard to leave this house."

"That was the idea." She winks, pulling back just enough to turn toward the door. "Come on, Country Boy. If I have to wear heels, you have to show me off."

"Deal," I say, opening the door for her with one last glance. "But I'm warning you now, after dinner and drinks, I'm cashing in."

The truck ride is quiet and short. My hand rests on her thigh. I catch her smiling to herself, when we pull into the Fireside Lounge. I kill the engine and walk around to her side. She's already waiting, that red dress hugging her in all the right ways. I open the door, and she steps out slowly, a knowing glint in her eyes. I offer my arm. She takes it. As we reach the entrance, I stop with my hand on the door.

She looks up. "What?"

I lean in close, lips brushing her ear. "If you keep looking at me like that, we're not making it to dessert."

Her smile deepens. "Then you better open the door fast." I do, and we walk in together, arm in arm.

33

Whiskey and Warnings

Kinsley

A young woman greets us at the host stand with a bright smile. Before I can say a word, Miles steps in. "We're in the back near the dance floor."

I expect her to check a list or ask for a name, but instead, she says, "You must be Miles. Right this way."

My brow furrows. "What's going on?" I glance up at him. There's no way she should've known we were coming. I didn't know until this morning.

He just reaches for my hand, that soft smile playing on his lips, and we follow behind the host.

When we round the corner, I stop in my tracks. Everyone is here. Reed, Luke, Dylan, Judy, Naya, even Floyd is leaning against the bar. My heart swells and breaks all at once.

I look up at Miles, wide-eyed. He leans down and whispers, "I wanted you to have time with everyone before you go. Thought tonight would be a good night for it, so we could have the last week to ourselves."

My heart aches when I think of every late-night talk, every unexpected laugh, every quiet look across a crowded room. These people feel like home in a way I didn't know I needed. And Miles, he's the one I'll never be ready to let go of. I'm going to miss all of them. But him…him most of all. I blink fast, waving a hand in front of my eyes to stop the tears before they fall.

Miles puts his arm around me reassuringly. "Come on, let's have some fun tonight."

I take a shaky breath, nodding, and by the time we cross the room, my smile is back in place. They greet me with hugs, cheers, teasing. Naya is the last one to pull me into her arms. I hold her tight, then whisper, voice thick with emotion. "I don't want to leave."

Naya squeezes me tighter. "I know." Her voice catches with a sniffle. Then she steps back, wiping under her eyes.

"Let's eat shitty food and get so drunk we forget how to be sad."

I laugh through the lump in my throat. "I'm in."

I mean it. With how heavy my heart feels right now, all I want is for the ache to stop. Just for a night. Just long enough to breathe. So tonight, I'm going all in.

Miles orders wings, pizza and a big salad for all of us. It's set up buffet-style across two high-top tables with a stack of plates, easy for everyone to grab what they want whenever they feel like it.

I don't feel much like eating, though. Instead, I flag down the server and order a round for the table, on me, with extra shots for Naya and myself. The glasses arrive just as Judy steps forward, holding hers high.

"To good friends." She toasts eyes sweeping over the group, then landing on me. "And even better memories."

We all raise our glasses. I sip my drink and turn to Naya. We both smile, that silent understanding passing between us, and throw back our first shot in perfect sync. The burn hits, but it only makes us laugh harder.

The whole table erupts with laughter and chatter. Jokes fly across the table like ping-pong balls, fast, ridiculous and fueled by each new drink. Stories get louder, wilder, more unbelievable with every refill, and nobody's keeping score. Naya and I keep drinks in our hands, clinking glasses and swaying a little to the music humming in the background.

After a while, Floyd rises from his seat, brushing crumbs from his shirt like he's got someplace real important to be, classic Floyd. He makes his rounds, saying his typical short goodbyes, until he stops in front of me.

"Well, Kinsley." His voice is gruff but kind. "It was nice meeting you. Hope one day I'll see you again."

I wrap my arms around him without hesitation. "I'm going to miss you. And I'm sure one day, I'll be back."

He pats my back twice, a little awkward, a little endearing. "You better be. Don't let these fools corrupt you too much." And with a wink, he's gone.

I'm left standing there with a full heart and an empty glass, doing my best not to fall apart.

Miles and Reed must've heard the whole goodbye. Both of them are standing a few feet away, eyes wide, clearly stunned by how sweet Floyd just was. I wave them off with a laugh and head straight for the nearest server, ordering another drink like I'm on a mission. And maybe I am. Objective: No Sadness Tonight.

A few minutes later, Judy gives me a warm hug and promises to see me again before I leave. "Don't disappear without saying goodbye," she warns with a mock glare.

"I wouldn't dare." I hug her tightly. Then she's gone, too, and the ache creeps in again, until Dylan stands up, lifting his beer like he's making a declaration.

"Well," he says, loud enough to get everyone's attention, "now that we don't have to be respectful anymore…"

Reed groans. "Oh hell, here we go."

"Let's turn this thing up a notch!" Dylan declares with a wicked grin, grabbing a tray of shot glasses. Just like that, the energy shifts. The goodbye haze lifts, the music gets louder, and the real party kicks off.

The night takes off like a freight train, loud music, laughter echoing off the walls and drinks flowing like a river. We party like fools, the whole group letting loose in a way only small-town folks, and one tipsy city girl, can.

Miles sticks to a couple of beers, always the steady one, the anchor in the middle of all the chaos. A night like this…messy, loud and spinning fast…I find myself clinging to that steadiness like a life raft. Meanwhile, Naya and I are well past tipsy, buzzed and bubbly and absolutely thriving.

We dance like no one's watching, even though everyone definitely is. I pull Miles onto the dance floor, dragging him through a clumsy spin before planting a kiss on his cheek and skipping off with Naya again. He just shakes his head, smiling.

Later, we migrate to the pool tables. I watch Miles line up a shot, all calm precision and quiet focus. I lean over the table, way too close, pretending to examine his aim while giving him a full view down my dress.

He groans under his breath. "You play dirty."

I grin. "I'm just trying to learn."

"You're trying to kill me."

"Semantics."

Naya cackles from behind me, nearly spilling her drink. We're a mess. A beautiful, chaotic mess. Then we head to the bar for yet another drink. That's when two guys we've never seen before sidle up, clearly drunk and thinking they're smoother than they are.

"Wanna dance?" one of them slurs, flashing what might be a charming smile if we hadn't just watched him spill half a beer on his own shoes.

Before either of us can respond, Reed materializes like a bodyguard out of nowhere.

"Find someone else," he says flatly, stepping between us and the two strangers. "Move along."

The guys look like they're about to argue until they catch the warning look in Reed's eyes. They mumble something and back off, just as Miles starts making his way over from the pool tables.

Naya and I clutch each other, giggling like we're fifteen. "We were totally going to say yes, but Reed spoiled all the fun," I tease as Miles walks up, fully aware I'm lighting the fuse on a firecracker and pretending it's harmless.

His eyes darken instantly. He steps in close, way close. His arm slips around my waist, pulling me flush against him until I'm not sure if it's the alcohol or his nearness making me dizzy.

His lips brush just beneath my jaw, voice low and possessive. "Say yes to anyone other than me and I'll make damn sure you can't walk straight for a week."

A shiver rolls down my spine, heat pulsing low in my belly as the possessiveness in his voice wraps around me. I can't even form a comeback. I just stand there, wrecked and wanting.

Heat floods my face. My mouth goes dry. I'm blushing, full-on red-faced, and he knows it.

Smirking like the devil he is, Miles presses a quick kiss to my jaw, then strolls off like nothing happened, clapping Reed on the back as he passes.

Reed raises a brow. "What the hell did he just say to you?"

I can't even speak. I just shake my head and fan myself with my hand, grinning like an idiot.

Naya howls. "Oh, girl! You're so done for!"

"I know." I rub my hands together with a devilish smile. "I can't wait!"

Reed shakes his head and rolls his eyes dramatically. "I'm getting a beer. That's enough trauma for one day."

We all grab our drinks from the bar. Naya and I are already flushed and breathless from laughing too hard. She clinks her glass against mine. "One more?"

I down the shot and nod, feeling bold, a little wild. "Hell yes."

We both kick off our heels, giggling like maniacs as we stumble barefoot toward the dance floor. We've drank just enough to feel untouchable. The music's thumping, and we can't resist.

We dance harder, spinning, swaying, tossing our hair and shouting along to the lyrics like it's our last night on earth. My feet slap against the hardwood, my heart thumps in rhythm with the bass. Everything else…Miles, the goodbye looming, the ache in my heart…gets drowned out in the sound, sweat and lights.

Naya grabs my hand, spinning me in a circle, and we laugh until our sides hurt. I glance up through the haze and see Miles at the edge of the room, arms crossed, watching me with that look again, the one that sets fire to every inch of my skin. But I don't stop. I dance harder. For me. For him. For this night that I don't want to end.

Naya and I are both completely wasted, slurring our words, hanging on each other for balance, and laughing so hard it hurts. I think I've laughed more tonight than I have in months. Maybe years.

Miles walks up, his hands tucked in his pockets, brow raised but mouth fighting a smile. "You ready to go, babe?"

I shoot him a blurry-eyed grin, swaying slightly. "Nope."

Naya giggles beside me, nearly dropping her drink as we prop ourselves up on barstools. "Yeah, we're not ready." She points somewhere vaguely in his direction.

She squints. I squint too. "I think I see two of him."

"Yeah, me too."

Miles steps closer and gently wraps an arm around my waist, steadying me before I can slide off the stool. "Yeah, I think you're more than ready," he murmurs, amusement tugging at the corner of his mouth.

"But we were dancing," I protest, poking his chest with a finger that misses slightly.

"I know," he says, soft and patient, "and you looked good doing it. But I think it's time to call it a night before one of you ends up passing out on the dance floor."

"Pfft." I wave him off, nearly toppling again. "I'm fiiiiine."

He catches me easily, cradling me against him. "That's exactly what every drunk girl says before she tries to pet the bouncer's beard."

Naya snorts. "Did that one time."

"I rest my case." Miles shoots Reed a look over my head, and just like that, our night is coming to an end.

Naya had already arranged a ride, so she sends a quick text to her dad. A few minutes later, he pulls up at the curb. Of course, it takes all three guys to help her to the car. She's giggling, clinging to Miles, and dramatically declaring she's "completely fine." Just before she climbs in, we hug tightly, swaying on our feet. We don't say goodbye, because we both know this isn't the end of anything for us. I turn to the guys, one by one, exchanging hugs and promises.

"You better come back," Dylan says with a wink.

"Seriously," Luke adds, pointing at me.

"I will." My voice is thick with emotion.

As the last of them filters out, I take a deep breath and spin on my heels to face Miles.

"Okay, Hotstuff," I slur, a lazy grin pulling at my lips. "Let's get out of here so I can thank you properly for tonight."

He kisses the top of my head, his voice low and warm against my skin. "How about we see how you feel when we get back."

I narrow my eyes, gripping his arm for balance. I smirk up at him, tilting my head just slightly as I lean in closer. "Are you doubting my ability to fuck just because I'm a little drunk?"

His smile deepens as he leans in. "No, sweetheart, I just don't want you passing out before the good part."

I laugh, swaying into him. "Not a chance."

He wraps an arm around my waist, steadying me as we walk to his truck. "We'll see."

He helps me into the truck, my shoes resting on my lap. When he leans in to buckle me, his touch is gentle, careful, like I'm something precious. The door clicks shut, and I watch him move around the front of the truck, with broad shoulders, that easy stride I know so well now.

When he slides in beside me, his hand finds my thigh, warm and grounding. We pull away from the curb, the town lights blurring into streaks outside the window. I watch the night roll by in a sleepy haze, the cool glass against my cheek, his thumb tracing slow circles on my leg. That's the last thing I remember.

34

Roses and Restraint

Miles

I park the truck near the house, glancing over at Kinsley, completely out cold, mouth slightly parted, her head still resting against the window. I chuckle softly, shaking my head. She's going to feel this in the morning.

I slip out, round the truck, and open her door as quietly as I can. She barely stirs when I unbuckle her.

"Come on, baby." I lift her gently in my arms. She murmurs something that sounds suspiciously like 'Hotstuff' but doesn't open her eyes.

Inside, I carry her up the stairs, laying her down carefully on the bed. I pull the blanket up over her, brushing her hair away from her face. She sighs softly and curls onto her side.

Downstairs, I feed Miss Dashworth, who meows like she hasn't eaten in years, then turn off the lights and lock up. The house settles into quiet, and rain starts tapping softly at the windows.

Back upstairs, I change into gym shorts and crawl into bed beside her. She doesn't move, just instinctively shifts closer, like her body knows mine. I wrap an arm around her, tucking her into my side. She's home. Even if it's only for now.

She shifts in her sleep, pressing her face against my neck with a soft sigh. My arm tightens around her automatically, like holding her closer might somehow slow down time. Might make the next seven days stretch out longer than they really are.

I stare up at the ceiling, the soft rise and fall of her breath grounding me, but my mind is anything but quiet. *I don't want her to leave.*

It hits me full force, like it has a hundred times before, only sharper now. More real. Every little moment, her dancing barefoot in the kitchen, cursing at fishhooks, making my old house feel like something more than just mine, it all rushes through my head. She's only been here a few weeks, but it already feels like everything's been re-written around her. And the truth is, I'm scared. What terrifies me is not knowing if she feels even a fraction of the same. Because I've never asked. Never opened that door.

What if this is just a fling for her? A break from the city? A sweet escape with the country boy before she goes back to her real life in Seattle? I rub my hand over my face, jaw tight. Part of me wants to ask her to stay. Hell, I nearly did the other night. It was on the tip of my tongue. "Stay with me build something here." But I bit it back, because asking would feel like pressure. Like a demand. Like tying her down when she hasn't said she wants to be tied to anything. If she only said yes to spare my feelings, I couldn't live with that. She deserves to choose. To really choose. But what if she doesn't? What if she walks out of here in seven days and never looks back?

I glance down at her. She looks peaceful, wrapped in my sheets, curled into my chest like she's been doing since the potluck. God, I want her to stay. But I won't ask. Not yet. Maybe not at all. Because if she's going to stay, I need it to be because she wants to. Not because I begged her to. Not because I asked her to change her life for me. Because she looked around at this life and saw something worth staying for.

I'm halfway through my second cup of coffee when I hear her footsteps on the stairs, slow, dragging, like her body's trying to figure out how to function again.

I glance toward the living room just as she appears, one hand gripping the railing, the other cradling her head like it might fall off if she lets go. Her hair's a wild mess, eyes squinting like the light's burning into her brain. She's now dressed in the softest, warmest-looking pajamas I've ever seen, flannel pants and one of my sweatshirts hanging off one shoulder. She looks miserable, and somehow, impossibly adorable. It hits me with a rush of tenderness, the kind that makes you want to laugh and wrap someone up in a blanket at the same time.

I fight a grin as I sip my coffee. "Morning, sunshine."

She glares at me like my voice might be the final straw. "Why are you so loud?"

"I barely said anything."

She shuffles into the kitchen like she's crossing a desert. "Coffee?"

"Already made." I slide a mug her way, watching her grip it like it's the only thing keeping her level. She takes a sip, exhales like she just took a hit of morphine.

"You're a good man, Miles." She winces. "I think I might be dying."

"You're not dying." I reach for the aspirin bottle on the counter and toss it to her. "You're just hungover. Bad."

She frowns. "Everything hurts. My brain's too big for my skull. I think my feet are swollen."

I chuckle. "That's what happens when you and Naya start trying to outdrink the whole bar."

301

She groans and rests her forehead against the cabinet. "Never again."

"Sure."

"I mean it."

"Okay, babe."

She lifts her head just enough to give me a narrow-eyed look. "Stop being cute and helpful. It's making me suspicious."

I step behind her, gently rubbing her back. "How about some greasy eggs and toast? Or do we need to start with dry toast and prayers?"

She groans again, this time less dramatic. "Both. Maybe toast first, and a hug. But like a gentle one. I'm fragile."

I wrap my arms around her loosely, kissing the top of her head. "I got you, Fragile."

"How about we take it easy today? Watch some trash TV, cook dinner together. You tell me what you want, and after chores, I'll brave the store." I raise a brow. "Or you wanna hit the bar again? Really lean into that hangover?"

She groans, rubbing her temples. "You're evil."

I chuckle. "So, dinner in?"

She narrows her eyes playfully. "Only if you promise not to judge me when I pick something carb loaded."

"No promises. But I'll get it anyway."

She turns to face me, eyes soft but serious. "Thank you. For last night. For this morning. For everything."

I reach out, brushing my fingers down her arm. "You don't have to thank me."

She opens her mouth, then hesitates, like she's about to say something else.

"I…" Her eyes flick away for a second, then back to mine. "Thank you. Again."

I study her for a beat, curious, but I don't press. Instead, I just squeeze her hand and offer a small smile. "Anytime."

"I'm gonna shower," she murmurs, fingers brushing through her messy hair. "Maybe that'll help this hangover."

"Alright, text me what you want from the store."

Just as I step onto the porch, I reach back and swat her ass. She squeals, giggling behind me, and I grin like an idiot as I pull the door closed.

I'm halfway down the steps when my phone dings. I glance down and there it is, her grocery list. It has all the ingredients for baked mac and cheese, a bag of potato chips and chocolate ice cream. Followed by a kissy face emoji.

I huff a laugh, shaking my head as I head toward the stable. "Comfort food and kisses," I mutter. "Girl knows exactly how to get what she wants."

I pocket my phone and head toward the stable, boots crunching against the damp gravel. The morning air is crisp, clouds still hanging low after last night's rain. Rocket sticks his head over the stall door the second he hears me coming, ears flicking forward like he's been waiting.

I pour his feed, watching as he digs in, tail flicking contentedly. I lean against the stall door, arms folded. *Damn it, I want her to stay.* I want mornings like this to be the norm. I want her laughter in this barn, her clothes in my closet. I want more than a few weeks and a goodbye.

But I can't ask. Someone asked me once to give this up, and I couldn't. How could I expect her to? I run a hand over Rocket's neck. "She makes it real hard not to hope, doesn't she, boy?"

I close up the stable and make quick work of feeding the chickens. Then I hop in my truck, and five minutes later, I'm pulling into the grocery store parking lot. As I reach the entrance, a familiar figure steps in front of me. Naya.

She squints at me through oversized sunglasses, her coffee clutched like it's the only thing keeping her steady. "Is Kinsley alive? Because I think I died twice this morning."

"She's alive. Barely. Looked like a hungover kitten when she came down, hair all over the place, eyes half shut."

Naya groans dramatically. "Ugh, tell her not to look in any mirrors. I saw my reflection this morning and nearly filed a missing persons report for my dignity."

I chuckle, stepping around a cart some guy abandoned halfway down the sidewalk. "You two were a mess last night."

"You're welcome." She flips her sunglasses up to glare at me. "We were trying to give you one last memory of us in our prime."

"Oh, it's burned into my brain. Especially the part where you both tried to order drinks in a language that doesn't exist."

"That was drunk Spanish," she replies with a shrug. "Very exclusive."

I shake my head, still grinning. "Kinsley sent me on a mission. Baked mac and cheese, potato chips and chocolate ice cream."

Naya nods in solemn approval. "She's got her priorities straight. Alright, I'll let you get to it. Tell her I love her. And also tell her I expect a formal apology for the number of shots she encouraged."

I give her a mock salute. "Will do. You going to survive the rest of the day?"

She starts walking backwards toward her car. "I'm not making any promises. If you see a body in the parking lot later, mind your business."

I laugh again and shake my head, pushing through the doors of the store. I gather everything on her list; cheese, pasta, chips, ice cream. On a whim, I grab a bouquet of roses from the floral section. Figured she earned them. Hell, she earns them every damn day.

I check out, load the bags into the truck and make the short drive home. Once inside, I carry everything in and place the bags on the counter. The roses go straight into a vase in the center of the island.

I head upstairs and find her standing in front of the mirror blow-drying her hair. She's wearing one of my T-shirts and a pair of sleep shorts, bare feet tapping lightly against the floor. She flips off the dryer just as I step into the room.

Her eyes meet mine in the mirror, and a smile tugs at her lips. "Hey," she says, voice soft.

"Hey yourself." I lean against the doorframe, watching her like a man with no business looking at her this long and this hard. "You clean up alright."

She laughs, setting the dryer down. "You get everything?"

"Yup." I step further into the room. "Enough cheese to clog an artery."

Her face lights up, and I swear, that smile could knock the wind out of me.

Just then, her phone buzzes on the nightstand. She picks it up, reads the message and snorts.

"It's Naya," she says, grinning. "She said, and I quote, 'I think I died twice this morning. Tell Miles my soul is still somewhere on the bar floor.'"

I chuckle. "Ran into her at the store. She looked like she'd been hit by a truck."

Kinsley lets out a full laugh, rubbing her forehead. "That makes two of us. I thought I was going to have to crawl to the shower."

"Glad you didn't. I would have had to carry you again, and that would've turned into something only one of us has the energy for."

She grins at me over her shoulder. "You saying you wouldn't have enjoyed it?"

I raise a brow. "Oh, I'd enjoy it. Just wouldn't be gentle about it."

Her eyes spark, and she bites her lip like she's holding back another laugh. "You're terrible."

"You like it."

She doesn't deny it. Just shakes her head with a soft smile and heads for the door. "Come on, let's have some ice cream."

When we hit the kitchen, her eyes land on the roses. She stops. "Miles."

"They're just flowers," I say quickly, not wanting to make it too heavy. "But they made me think of you."

She walks over slowly, fingertips brushing the petals. "They're beautiful."

"You are." I watch her lean over to smell the roses.

She turns, eyes soft, shining just a little more than they were before. "You keep saying things like that, and I might never leave," she murmurs.

My throat tightens, but I just smile and reach for a bag. *Maybe I should keep saying them.*

35

Thunder in My Chest

Kinsley

We sit on the couch, legs tangled, flipping through the endless loop of TV channels with a heaping bowl of chocolate ice cream between us and an open bag of potato chips on the coffee table. I scoop another bite, salty and sweet mixing perfectly on my tongue. Now that I have some food in my system, I feel a little better.

I glance at the vase on the island, the roses he picked up without saying a word. It's not just the flowers. It's everything. The way he carried me in after I passed out in the truck. The way he covered me up last night. The way he teases me just enough to make me laugh but still looks at me like I'm something worth holding onto. He didn't make a big deal about it. He just took care of me. Like he's done since the moment we met in the grocery store. And that scares the hell out of me because I'm starting to realize that it's not just the vacation anymore.

We spend the entire afternoon doing nothing. With food in my stomach and Miles next to me, the hangover fog finally starts to lift. My head stops pounding, and I feel like myself again. Eventually, I peel myself off the couch and go upstairs to change; sweatpants, an old T-shirt and a quick braid down my back. I come back down feeling human again.

"I think it's time we make that dinner." I step into the kitchen barefoot, already reaching for the fridge door. Miles joins me, stretching lazily, as I start pulling out ingredients; cheese, milk, butter and pasta. But before we even get the cutting board out, both our phones go off at the same time, shrill and jarring.

My heart leaps into my throat. "What the hell was that?"

Miles grabs his phone, eyes scanning. "Severe thunderstorm warning. Winds up to sixty miles per hour. Hail. Tornado watch."

I blink, staring at him. "That sounds pretty bad. What should we do?"

Miles is already halfway to the back door, peering out toward the lake. The sky's turning fast, charcoal gray, low and intense.

"Looks like we've got about an hour or two before it hits."

Then he turns to me. "I need to double-check the barn. Secure everything that's loose. Make sure the animals are safe. Give me your keys, I'll park your car in the barn."

I nod, already moving. "I'll help."

Miles stops me with a look and a small shake of his head. "No, baby. Stay inside. No need for both of us to get soaked." His eyes flick over me with a teasing grin. "At least not until after dinner."

Heat rushes to my cheeks, and I lean up to kiss him. "Okay. I'll finish making dinner." I trail my fingers down his abs. "Then I can properly thank you for last night."

He leans in, his voice low, close to my ear. "Just how do you plan on doing that?"

I brush my lips across his, barely touching, and whisper, "Maybe I'll get on my knees." I slip my keys into his pocket with a quick wink.

As I turn away and head back toward the kitchen, swaying my hips just a little, because if he's going to brave a storm, I might as well give him something to think about. I turn to catch one last look at him smiling before he disappears out the back door. I don't bother turning on a playlist; I want to be able to hear if and when the storm hits.

I boil the pasta and start the cheese sauce, stirring slowly as the kitchen fills with the comforting scent of garlic and melted cheddar. Once it's all in the oven, I set the timer for forty-five minutes.

I wander into the living room and peek out the rain-speckled window. Miles is out there in the drizzle, gathering up the chickens and ushering them into the barn coop. His shirt is clinging to his back, hair damp from the rain, but he moves with this calm certainty that makes my heart twist.

I really like him. Maybe more than like. And I only have six days left. I do miss my firm. I miss my parents. But the thought of leaving here, of leaving him, I think that's going to be harder than I imagined.

I turn back to the counter and grab my phone. My thumb hovers for a second before I tap "Mom." She picks up on the second ring.

"Hello, honey," she says warmly, and I hear my dad shout in the background, "Is that Kins?"

"Yes, it's Kins!" she hollers back, and I can't help but chuckle.

"Hi, Mom. How are you guys?"

"Oh, you know. Living the retired dream. Your dad's picked up golf, and I joined a book club with the ladies from church."

"That's great!" I'm genuinely happy they've found hobbies that don't revolve around me.

"How's your vacation? Don't you leave in a week?"

I sigh. "Six days."

There's a pause. "What's wrong?"

She knows me too well. "I could use your advice," I admit. "But you've gotta promise not to freak out."

"I'm listening."

So, I tell her. The clean version, of course, about Miles, the lake, the town, the people. I tell her about the cooking, the porch mornings, the canoe debacle, the fishing trip. She doesn't interrupt, just listens, like she always has. When I finish, there's a long silence on the other end.

"What is it you're asking me, Kinsley?"

I swallow hard. "What should I do? I really like him, Mom."

"You want me to give it to you straight?"

"Yeah," I say, heart thudding. "Of course."

There's a pause. A long one. Then Mom speaks, her voice calm but firm. "Kinsley, you've only known this man for a month."

I open my mouth to argue, the words already forming, how he makes me laugh, how safe I feel with him, how rare it all is. But I stop myself. Because I know she's not trying to hurt me. And maybe, just maybe, she's right. Still, it doesn't stop the ache from blooming in my chest. But she keeps going.

"What about your life in Seattle? Your career? The firm you've built practically from the ground up? Everything you've worked so hard for. You can't seriously be thinking about throwing all of that away for a man you just met."

Her words hit like cold water, but she's not wrong. She's not being cruel, just honest.

"I can hear it in your voice; you have feelings for him. Real ones. But, sweetheart, are those feelings strong enough to last when the excitement of this little escape fades and you're standing there realizing you gave up everything you've worked for?" She sighs softly, and I can picture her now, probably sitting at the kitchen table, fingers curled around a mug of tea, concern etched across her face.

"I know, Mom, but I really like him. And I think he feels the same."

"You think?" she echoes. "Has he asked you to stay? Has he told you he loves you?"

I hesitate. "Well, no, but…"

"And have you asked him if he wants you to stay? Told him how you feel?"

"No," I admit, the word slipping out quietly.

There's a gentle sigh on the other end of the line. Not judgmental, just concern. "Kinsley, I'm not trying to be harsh. I know how strong you are, how smart you are. And I can tell this isn't just a fling to you. But you're making life-size decisions based on maybes and feelings you've both tiptoed around. That's not love. That's potential. And potential only works if both people show up for it, fully."

I lean against the counter, staring blankly out the window as Miles disappears into the barn. Her words sting, but not because they're mean. Because they're true.

He hasn't asked me to stay. I haven't asked him how he feels. Not directly. Sure, his actions tell me he likes me, likes me a lot. But love? Commitment? A real future?

"You're right, Mom. Thanks for setting me straight." My voice is soft, but I mean it. "I love you."

"I love you, too, sweetie. I'll see you in six days."

We hang up, and I set my phone down, staring out the kitchen window. Miles is out by the barn, moving something under the awning. He looks up just in time to catch me watching and gives me a little wave.

It makes me smile, how effortless it all feels with him. But my mom's words linger. How does he feel about me? He's never said anything about me staying. He hasn't told me he loves me. And I haven't told him how I feel either.

Maybe that's the conversation we need to have. Soon. Maybe even tonight.

A sharp beep pulls me from my thoughts. The timer for the oven.

I open the door and pull out the dish. The baked mac and cheese is golden and bubbling, crispy at the edges, exactly how it should be. I set it on the counter and exhale, the weight of uncertainty still lingering. But at least dinner's perfect.

I shake off my thoughts. Tonight isn't the night for pressure or confessions. I just want to enjoy dinner with him.

I walk to the front door and swing it open to call for Miles, but before I can say a word, Miss Dashworth darts between my feet and bolts out onto the wraparound porch.

"Hey!" I gasp, reaching for her, but she's already gone, fast for such a fluffy furball.

She tears down the side of the porch, her gray tail flicking like she knows exactly what kind of chaos she's causing. She squeezes between the railings and, God help me, jumps off the porch.

"No, no, no," I mutter, rushing after her.

I fly down the back steps barefoot, hitting the wet grass at a run. The drizzle has picked up, soaking my hair and clothes in seconds. I scan the yard and spot her trotting along the edge like this is all one big game. I slow down, trying not to spook her.

"Here, kitty, kitty," I call softly, crouching low, voice all sweet and squeaky. She turns her head and watches me.

"Miss Dashworth!" I groan, picking up speed, slipping in the slick grass before catching myself. My feet are getting tender; pine needles, wet leaves and uneven earth stabbing with every step. But I don't stop.

I can't lose her. I can't lose his cat. How the hell would he ever forgive me? She races farther, heading toward the edge of the forest. My heart shutters. "No, no, please don't." She disappears between the trees. I stop at the forest, chest heaving. Everything in me says don't go in. But there she is, barely visible, sitting at the base of a tree, her back to me like this is just another day in her evil little cat life.

This is my shot. One shot. I take a deep breath and run after her, dodging branches and slipping on wet pine needles. The forest floor is a mess of undergrowth, soggy moss and hidden roots. My feet scream, but I ignore it. All I can think is: *Don't let her get away. Don't let him down.*

The forest is darker than I expected, cooler too. The moment I pass under the thick canopy, the rain lessens, muffled by the leaves, but the ground is soaked. Each step squishes or slips. My T-shirt clings to my skin, and goosebumps ripple down my arms as I push deeper, eyes scanning for that gray blur.

"Miss Dashworth!" I call again, voice breathless now, heart pounding like I've been sprinting for miles.

I spot her up ahead, weaving between two trees like she's just out for a leisurely stroll. I stumble over a root and catch myself on a low branch, cursing under my breath.

She glances back at me. "Oh, don't you dare," I whisper, half pleading, half furious. "Just stop." But she doesn't. She picks up speed, tail flicking high.

I chase her around trees, over logs, through thorny brush that scratches my ankles. My breath starts to hitch. I'm soaked, barefoot, lost, and now I can't see the house anymore. Still, I don't stop. I keep her in sight, but she's always just far enough away to make it hell.

Finally, I have to pause. My lungs burn. I double over, hands on my knees, panting hard. Miss Dashworth pauses too, crouched by a mossy stump. I stand up slowly, keeping my eyes on her. I don't want to spook her again, not when I'm this deep in.

"Okay, I get it. You're fast. You win." She doesn't move. I inch closer, not chasing, just approaching. But the second I reach for her, she bolts again. My stomach twists.

"Dammit," I snap, the panic surging now. I'm too far from the house. I don't know how long I've been running. I'm cold. I'm soaked. And I'm alone. But I can't give up. I push forward again, branches whipping my face, feet slamming the ground. My heart thuds, every part of me screaming to stop, but I won't, not without her. She dashes through a tight patch of trees, and I follow, nearly losing her, until she finally makes a mistake.

She stops beneath a downed log, hesitating. I pounce. I fall to my knees in the mud, arms wrapping tight around her middle before she can bolt again.

"Got you," I breathe, heart hammering, tears mixing with the rain. "You little brat, I got you."

She squirms once, then settles in my arms like she meant for this to happen the whole time. I sit back against the log, clutching her close, shaking all over. My hair's dripping. My feet are torn. My legs are covered in dirt and scratches. But I don't care. I got her.

I let myself breathe, just for a minute, sitting there in the forest muck with her squirming against my arms. Then I rise to my feet, legs trembling, and start retracing my steps the way I think I came. The trees all look the same now, and the path I made feels like it's already vanished behind me.

That's when the wind starts to howl. It comes in sharp, angry gusts, slamming through the trees and kicking up leaves and forest debris in every direction. Miss Dashworth burrows her head into my chest, letting out a tiny, frightened mewl that squeezes my heart. I tighten my grip on her, trying to shield her from the storm.

The rain, already steady, turns to sheets. Heavy, drenching. Even through the thick canopy above, it soaks me instantly. I can barely see the sky, it's gone a murky shade of gray-blue, almost as dark as dusk, and it's barely past dinner.

"Okay, it's okay," I whisper, more to myself than to her. I tuck her under my shirt, against my bare skin, hoping the warmth and closeness will keep her calm. She presses against me, trembling, claws gently kneading my skin but not digging in.

I keep walking, but the forest's turned against me. Branches sway violently. Tree limbs creak and groan. Lightning flashes somewhere in the distance, followed by a long, rolling boom of thunder. My stomach twists. I have to get out of here. But right now, I need shelter.

I spot a dense pine tree with thick, low-hanging branches, almost like a natural canopy. It's not much, but it's something. I hurry toward it, crouching low, careful not to jostle the cat. Dropping to my hands and knees, I crawl beneath it, the ground soft and needled beneath me. It's cramped, but at least the branches block the worst of the wind and rain. I curl my body around her, shielding her as best I can, wiping water from my face and trying not to cry.

"Just ride it out. Just a little while. We'll be okay."

But deep down, panic claws at me. Because I don't know if Miles knows I'm out here. I don't know if he even knows I left the house. And I have no idea how to get back.

The rain starts to lighten, at first. But then I hear a new sound, soft but distinct, a tick against the pine needles. Then another. Tiny pieces of ice begin to fall from the sky like warning shots. Hail.

Miss Dashworth squirms under my shirt, sensing the shift. I grip her tighter. At first, the pieces are small, like frozen peas bouncing off the forest floor. But then they start getting bigger. Much bigger. A golf ball–sized chunk crashes through the branches above me, slamming into the dirt inches from my hand. I flinch.

Then another hits the ground beside my knee, hard enough to send pine needles flying. And then one hits me. Square in the back.

I suck in a sharp breath, the pain immediate and deep. And then another strikes. And another. I curl tighter, throwing my arms over the cat, trying to shield her with my body. The hail pelts me relentlessly, each one like a hammer to my spine and shoulders. I cry out once, twice, as one hits the back of my neck, another my thigh. The sound is deafening, the hail ricocheting off tree limbs, the forest floor and me. I can't tell if I'm shaking from the cold, the fear or the pain.

Lightning forks across the sky, close…too close, turning the forest into a momentary black-and-white photograph. The thunder follows immediately, a violent crack that vibrates through my bones. I squeeze my eyes shut, swallowing a sob.

Miss Dashworth stays tucked beneath my shirt, pressed to my body, trusting me even as I'm falling apart. The whole storm is over me now. And there's nothing to do but wait and pray it passes. I cling to the hope that Miles will realize I'm not inside. That he'll come for me. But for now, I stay still on my hands and knees, shaking, hurting, and whispering.

"Please, just let this end."

As the hail fades to heavy rain, I crawl out from beneath the tree, body aching and soaked to the bone. Every movement is stiff and cold, but I have to keep going. Miss Dashworth is still tucked under my shirt, trembling but safe.

I stand on unsteady legs, wind lashing my face, hair whipping wildly. The shadows between the trees make it hard to see, but I convince myself I know the way back.

A branch snaps back and smacks me hard across the face. I hit the ground with a cry, touch my cheek, and find blood. I force myself up, squinting into the gloom. Everything looks the same; trees, moss, stumps. Still, I press on.

My bare feet slip on wet roots and sharp rocks. I'm shivering, teeth chattering, clutching the cat to my chest. Time blurs. I try to remember, did I turn left at that log? Wasn't that tree behind me? Panic rises, sharp and fast, but I swallow it. Just keep walking. Nothing looks familiar. Not the twisted tree. Not the moss-covered boulder. Not the slope ahead. I turn in a slow circle, heart racing. I don't know the way back. I'm lost. Does he know I'm gone? Will he come for me? *Please, Miles. Please find me.*

36

No Service

Miles

Through the window, I catch a glimpse of her watching me, and I shoot her a small wave. I've got maybe thirty minutes before the worst of the storm hits.

I pull the chicken feed under the awning and jog to the dock. The wind's already kicking up, the lake choppy. I secure the canoe to the dock posts, then head for the truck and drive around to the far side of the lake to do the same with the other one. By the time I'm back, the sky's darker, heavier.

I park the truck in the barn, yank her keys from my pocket and squeeze into her car. My knees press into the dash, chest nearly touching the wheel. I chuckle. "How the hell does she even fit in here and still manage to drive? It's like piloting a teacup with tires." I get it tucked safely next to my truck. Back in the barn, I toss some feed into the coop to keep the chickens busy through the worst of the storm, then lock everything up. The wind's howling now, bending the trees around the property.

At the stable, I open the gate, just in case things get really bad. Horses are smarter than we are sometimes, they'll know when to seek shelter. I linger for a moment, resting a hand on Rocket's neck, grounding myself in the calm before it all hits.

Just as I'm about to step out of the stable, the wind picks up, howling as sheets of rain dump from the sky. I stop in the doorway, watching the downpour. My stomach growls, and all I can think about is Kinsley's mac and cheese. I bet it's a thousand times better than the boxed stuff. The rain lightens for a second, and I make a break for it.

The second my boots hit the porch, hail starts to fall, first pea-sized, then suddenly, golf balls. I watch it bounce off the ground, hammer the roof and splash across the lake's surface. Thunder cracks loud enough to rattle the windows. I wince, hoping nothing breaks.

Just as I'm about to head inside, I catch a trash can tumbling across the lawn, spinning wildly in the wind. I slip my boots back on and wait until the hail softens into a steady downpour, then dash off the porch. I grab the can and drag it back, shoving it into the corner of the porch. I kick my boots off again and step inside, soaked and cold.

The smell hits me instantly; creamy, rich, warm. Mac and cheese. My mouth waters. "I'm gonna get changed before dinner!" I call out, heading upstairs. No answer.

I grab a towel, dry off quick and change into joggers and a T-shirt before padding back down the stairs. The mac and cheese is cooling on the stove when I step into the kitchen. I glance around, half-expecting her to catch me in the act as I sneak a bite. But it's already room temperature. I grab a spoon and take a bite. *Yep, way better than boxed.*

Still chewing, I wander into the living room, expecting to find her curled up on the couch. But it's empty. Maybe she went upstairs. I head up and check the bedroom, nothing. Bathroom, empty. I call out her name, a little louder this time. No answer. Frowning, I check the spare rooms. Still nothing.

I head back downstairs, now moving faster. Living room, kitchen again, dining room. The other bathroom. Even the laundry room and the basement. No sign of her.

As I cross the house to the front porch, I shove the door open, and the wind nearly knocks me back. Lightning tears through the sky like a warning. She's not here. I swing the door wider, wind slamming into me, and lightning cracks across the sky in a jagged web. The storm's rolling in fast, too fast. I circle the porch, scanning the yard, calling her name over the wind. Still nothing.

Panic prickles at the back of my neck as I step back inside, heart thudding. I pull out my phone and call her. It rings once, twice, and then I hear it. From the kitchen. I follow the sound and see it lit up on the counter. Her phone. Still here. My stomach drops.

Maybe she went outside to help me, maybe she got caught in the storm and is waiting it out in the barn or stable. That has to be it.

I take the stairs two at a time, grabbing my keys from the pocket of my soaked jeans. I bolt back down and out the front door, slipping my wet shoes on as I go. Rain slams against my face as I sprint to the barn. I fumble with the lock, finally yank the door open and step inside, soaked to the bone again.

"Kinsley?" I call out, voice echoing through the dark space. Nothing. I turn and run for the stable, hope clinging to my ribs. *Please be here.* But Rocket is the only one inside, standing quietly, tail flicking. No Kinsley. *Shit.*

I jog back to the barn and climb into my truck, heart pounding. I take the long path toward the cabins, hoping, praying she's walking, maybe just trying to get back.

The wipers fight to keep up with the sheets of rain. Visibility is crap, and every bend in the trail has me squinting through the downpour. Suddenly, I slam the brakes. A massive tree branch lies across the road. "Come on," I grit, throwing the truck into park.

I leap out, wind nearly tearing the door from my hand. I run to the front and haul the heavy branch to the side, slipping in the mud, then jump back in and keep going.

When I pull into the driveway near the cabins, I don't bother shutting the door. I check each one, knocking hard, calling her name. Nothing. I run to Judy's place and pound on the door.

She opens it, eyes wide. "Miles? What are you doing out in this. Come inside, you're soaked!"

I step in, breath ragged, wiping rain from my face. "Have you seen Kinsley?"

Her expression shifts to worry. "No, why? What's wrong?"

"I was outside securing everything before the storm. When I got back, she wasn't there. I searched the house, the barn, the stable, and I called her phone. It's still in the kitchen."

Judy, always the optimist, pats my shoulder. "I'm sure she's around here somewhere. She's smart. She wouldn't go outside in this weather."

I take a breath and nod, trying to believe that. "You're right. Maybe I just missed her."

I kiss Judy's cheek and hurry back out into the storm. The wind and rain are still pounding, thunder echoing across the lake. I drive slower this time, searching the road like I expect her to suddenly appear. When I pull up to the house, I don't bother parking in the barn. I stop right next to the porch, jump out and rush inside.

I check every room again, this time more carefully. Nothing. Back in the kitchen I stop, glancing around. And then it hits me, Miss Dashworth. I haven't seen the damn cat. I grab the food container and shake it, pouring some into her bowl. Normally, she'd come running. She doesn't. *Shit.*

I drop the container on the counter and bolt for the porch, running the full wrap-around. No sign of Kinsley. No cat. Nothing. I stop near the back door, heart racing, scanning the lawn. A flash of lightning lights up the tree line, and that's when it clicks.

If the cat got out and Kinsley chased her, I would've seen her in the front yard. Or the side. She had to have gone out the back. *Fucking cat!*

I spin around and sprint inside, grabbing the flashlight from the drawer and bursting out the back door. The rain is relentless, blinding, soaking through everything as I run across the lawn, slipping in the grass.

I reach the edge of the forest, yelling her name. Thunder cracks overhead. Nothing. I step into the trees, raising the flashlight, scanning every inch of forest my beam can reach. "KINSLEY!" I shout. "KINSLEY!"

The ground is a mess of wet leaves and mud, and every step is a struggle, but I don't stop. I won't. She's out here somewhere. I'm not going back without her.

I push deeper into the woods, the flashlight beam cutting through sheets of rain and tangled branches. The storm hasn't let up, it's only gotten worse. Thunder cracks so loud it shakes the ground beneath my boots, and the wind roars through the trees, bending their trunks and tearing leaves from the branches.

"KINSLEY!" I yell again, voice straining over the howl of the wind. "WHERE ARE YOU?"

The beam of light jumps with every step, sweeping over twisted roots, slick moss and broken branches. I scan everything; shadows between tree trunks, the dips in the trail, the low bushes and brush that cling to my legs.

My heart is pounding. Not from the run. From panic. She's out here. Alone. In the dark. And she's terrified of the dark.

I remember that night we played the game in her cabin. And now she's not just in the dark, she's in a storm, soaked to the bone, scared, and probably freezing. And I'm not there with her.

"Come on, baby. Answer me." The words are barely audible over the rain hammering the canopy above.

The light catches on something, just a broken branch. I press forward, dodging limbs, slipping in mud, ignoring the sting of wet leaves slapping my face. She has to be close. She has to be. I shout again, louder this time. "KINSLEY!"

But only thunder answers. *Damn it.* I sweep the light around again. My hands are shaking, not from the cold, but from imagining her out here, hurt, crying, holding that damn cat, trying to be brave even though she's scared out of her mind. I have to find her.

I pick up the pace, mud sucking at my boots, rain dripping from my hair, my clothes soaked and clinging to me. Every flash of lightning gives me just enough visibility to know I'm not seeing her. And every second that passes without a response knots my gut tighter.

"Please." I whisper to the dark. "Please be okay." And then I shout again, voice hoarse and desperate. "KINSLEY!"

I keep searching, my flashlight beam darting through the dense forest, illuminating nothing but trees and rain. I glance down at my phone, on 1;00 a.m. She's been gone almost three hours maybe longer. I don't know when she chased the cat. *Goddamn it Kinsley! Why didn't you come get me?* I'm not angry, I'm scared.

My thumb hovers over the screen, about to dial for help, but the "No Service" icon mocks me from the corner. *Of course.* I'm too deep under the trees. I grit my teeth, rip a strip from the hem of my shirt, and tie it to a low branch, a marker in case I need to come back.

I turn and move fast, pushing back through the wet underbrush toward the house. Every step is agony. I can't stop picturing her soaked, scared. And now it's pitch black, and she's alone.

As I break through the tree line, I scan the yard, praying for movement. Nothing. I yank my phone out again, step into the open, and finally, one bar. I dial 911 with shaking hands.

"911, what's your emergency?"

"I need search and rescue at Davison Farms. My girlfriend is lost in the forest. She ran after my cat during the storm or before. I've been searching for three hours."

"We're dispatching a team now. Stay by your phone, units will be on scene in fifteen minutes."

I let out a shaky breath. "Okay. Thank you."

I hang up and head for the house, boots squishing in the wet grass. I scrub the rain from my face, rake my hands through my soaked hair, and pull my phone out again. Reed.

He picks up on the first ring. "What's wrong?" His voice is sharp, knowing I wouldn't call this late otherwise.

"It's Kinsley," I say, trying to stay calm. "She chased the cat into the woods hours ago. She hasn't come back."

"Shit. Are you sure?"

"She's not in the house, her phone's still in the kitchen and the cat's gone, too. I've searched everywhere."

"Okay. I'm calling the station and getting the department in route. We'll find her." The line clicks as he hangs up.

I don't hesitate, next is Judy.

"Miles?" She answers on the first ring.

"She's in the forest," I manage. "Lost. I can't find her."

"Oh, my Lord! I'll be there in two minutes."

The call ends, and I head back inside. I spot her phone on the counter and grab it, hoping for some kind of clue, but it's locked. I don't even know her parents' names to call them.

Just as I'm about to pace a hole in the floor, headlights cut across the yard. I rush out the front door as Judy barrels up the porch steps. "How sure are you she's in the woods?" she asks, out of breath.

I swallow hard. "The cat's gone, too. If she'd gone out the front, I would've seen her, I was outside. But out back? That's the only direction I didn't have eyes on."

Judy presses a hand to her chest, eyes glistening. "Okay. Then let's find her."

"I don't want you in those woods." I pull open the coat closet and yank out my jacket. "Stay here, just in case she finds her way out. Direct everyone when they arrive."

Thunder cracks again, sharp and violent, rattling the porch windows. Judy flinches, her hand flying to her mouth. "Miles, please." Her voice trembles. "Wait until help gets here. Don't go back out there alone."

I shake my head, already slipping into the jacket. "I know these woods. I'll be fine."

She steps forward like she might grab my arm, but she stops herself. She knows I won't stay put. Just as I open the front door, headlights cut through the rain. Reed's truck barrels down the driveway, tires sliding in the mud. He doesn't even park properly, just throws it in gear and jumps out, sprinting through the downpour toward the porch.

I step outside to meet him, the wind whipping rain sideways across the yard. My boots splash in the puddles as I jog forward. Reed meets me halfway, both of us soaked within seconds.

"You, okay?" He looks past me, already scanning the tree line.

"No. She's out there. We're wasting time."

Reed gives one solid nod, his jaw set. We turn together, stepping towards the woods, just as another pair of headlights slices through the rain-soaked dark.

A state police cruiser rolls to a stop. The door creaks open, and a trooper steps out, his posture already screaming annoyance at having to be out in this weather. He hunches against the wind, climbing the steps to the porch where Judy waits. Reed and I turn back, joining her. Judy takes the lead, explaining the situation quickly.

The officer turns to me, frowning. "She's your girlfriend?"

"Yes," I say, without a second of hesitation.

He glances toward the trees, then back at me, skeptical. "You think she went into the woods, during this storm?" His tone's more accusation than question.

"I was out locking things down before it hit. When I came back, she was gone. Her phone was in the kitchen. And the cat's missing, too. If she ran, Kinsley would've gone after her."

The officer exhales through his nose, not convinced. "Hard to believe she'd chase a cat into a storm like this. Does she have any enemies? Exes? Anyone who might want to hurt her?"

I clench my fists, fighting the frustration rising. "She's a divorce attorney from Seattle. I'm sure she's pissed off a few people. But she didn't run off. She's out there."

"She have any angry exes?"

Before I can speak, Judy cuts in. "There's a man named Ben. He showed up at the potluck last week uninvited. Caused a scene."

I try not to cut her off, but I can't help myself. "We're wasting time talking about her damn ex. She's in the woods."

Reed steps forward, resting a hand on my shoulder. His voice is steady. "If my brother says she's out there, then she's out there.

We've already contacted the fire department. They're gathering volunteers and gear. Should be here in a few hours."

The officer finally nods, backing off a few steps to radio for additional support. I'm already turning toward the woods again.

"Let's go." Urgency sharpens my voice as my eyes flick to the darkened woods. I can't stand here another second, not while she's still out there.

37

Barefoot and Brave

Kinsley

I've been wandering through the dark for hours, cold sinking deeper with every step. Miss Dashworth's still tucked inside my shirt, her tiny body trembling against me. My feet are torn up. I can feel every sting, every throb, but I can't see well enough to check. And even if I could, what would I do?

Another flash of lightning tears across the sky followed by a deafening crack. It sounds like it hit something close, maybe a tree, but I can't see through the curtain of rain and thick canopy.

I stumble to a stop beneath a pine tree, its branches thick enough to block some of the downpour. It's not much, but it's a small relief. I crouch low, carefully pulling the cat free for a second, checking her over. She's wet, scared and wide-eyed but safe.

"Shhh." I can't even hear my own whisper over the roar of rain pounding on the leaves above us.

I sit down, legs trembling, and rest my back against the tree. For a few seconds, I let myself breathe, closing my eyes. My fingers are numb. My teeth won't stop chattering. Everything aches.

I gently rub the bottoms of my feet, trying to soothe the burning and stinging. I'm not even sure if I'm helping or hurting, but it's something to do, something to keep from falling apart completely.

"I just need to keep going," I murmur to the cat. "We'll get out of this." But even as I say it, doubt claws at me. Because the truth is, I have no idea where I am. And I'm so, so tired.

After a few more minutes of rest, I force myself back to my feet. Every muscle protests, especially my legs. They feel like wet sandbags, but I can't stop now. The storm hasn't let up, and the longer I stay in one spot, the colder I get.

The rain still slices through the trees like needles, and each gust of wind rattles the forest, making it groan and creak like it's alive. Water drips steadily from the branches overhead, pooling in the hollows of my collarbones.

I glance around. The trees all look the same, dark silhouettes smudged against a deeper black. Moss-covered trunks, slick rocks, tangled roots. There's no sign of a trail. No familiar landmarks. Just the endless, wet woods and the low, distant growl of thunder. But I keep moving, because stopping feels worse.

Miles has to know by now. He's smart. He'd come back inside, see I'm not there, see my phone on the counter. He'd notice the cat's missing. He'd put it together. *God, I hope he does. I hope he's already looking.*

I step over a fallen branch, my foot slipping out from under me on the slick forest floor. I fall fast, instinctively clutching the cat with both hands, twisting midair to keep her safe. The impact knocks the wind out of me as I land hard on my hip, the jolt radiating up my side.

"Damn it," I hiss, rain splattering across my face as I stare up at the canopy above. Cold water drips from the branches, mixing with the sting of pain blooming along my ribs. I lie there for a moment, catching my breath, trying not to cry. Then, with a groan, I roll onto my side and slowly push myself upright. My legs shake beneath me, and I wince as I press my palm to the sore spot at my hip. That's definitely going to bruise.

The rain finally starts to let up, easing from a pounding torrent to a soft, steady drizzle. The wind dies down, too, no longer howling through the trees but whispering, like the storm is finally catching its breath.

It's still dark, but the edge of the sky is beginning to shift, the deep black softening into murky gray. Morning is coming. I've made it through the night. The realization hits me hard. I've been out here for hours. Wet. Cold. Lost. I shiver violently. I don't know what hurts worse; my feet, my ribs, or the ache in my chest from how long it's been since I've seen a light.

I press my back against a tree trunk, trying to get my bearings. Everything looks the same, but at least now I can see a little better. My body is so tired it feels hollow, like I've burned through everything I had just to keep moving. My thoughts feel just as slow. But I know one thing for sure: I can't stay still. I need to keep moving.

I rub a hand over my face, wiping water from my eyes, and whisper to the cat. "Just a little longer, okay? He's looking for us. I know he is."

I keep walking. The sky continues to lighten, streaks of pale gold pushing back the gray. My eyes burn with exhaustion, my body's so tired I feel like I could lie down and sleep right here on the forest floor. The rain finally stopped, but I'm still soaked, my clothes clinging to me like ice. Every step feels heavier than the last.

Up ahead, I catch sight of a break in the trees, a small clearing where the canopy thins just enough to let sunlight touch the ground. Desperate for warmth and hoping the sun might help dry me off, I limp toward it. I sink to the wet ground in the center of the sunbeam, too tired to care about how cold or muddy it is. Miss Dashworth squirms against me, trying to wriggle out of my shirt, but I don't have the strength to chase her if she gets away again. That's when an idea hits me.

I reach under my shirt to my waistband and tug the drawstring free from my sweatpants. Carefully, I pull Miss Dashworth out, still holding her tight. I loop the string around her like a makeshift leash and set her down. She tries to run, but the string stops her, and I let out a huff.

I take a moment to finally look at my feet. They're a mess; scraped, cut, filthy. I can't even tell where the dirt ends, and the bruises begin. My hands tremble as I wipe them on my shirt. I tilt my face up toward the soft morning sun and whisper a prayer. "Please, let someone find me soon."

The little warmth from the sun helps. Just enough to ease the tremble in my limbs. I lie back, too tired to see straight, my body curled around Miss Dashworth. I loop the drawstring leash around my wrist so she can't wander off, then let myself rest. I don't sleep long. A tug at my wrist and the soft rustle of movement wakes me. I blink my eyes open, squinting into the light. Miss Dashworth is pawing at the string, and nearby, a squirrel scurries up a tree, its tiny claws scratching bark.

I watch it for a while, half in a daze, until an idea hits me. If I can climb a tree, get high enough, I might be able to see a road, a clearing, anything that can point me toward help. I glance down at the cat and carefully tie her leash to a small, sturdy tree.

"Don't move," I murmur, like she will actually listen.

I scan the trees until I spot one with low, thick branches. It's not huge, but it might be enough. I step up, my legs trembling, and place a hand on the bark. *This is a bad idea.* If I fall, I could break something. No one would know. No one would help. But what choice do I have? Swallowing my fear, I tighten my grip and begin to climb.

I start the climb, gripping the rough bark with both hands, testing each branch before I trust it with my weight. About halfway up, my foot slips. I gasp and scramble to hold on, my arm scraping hard down the trunk. Pain flashes hot and sharp across my skin, but I don't let go. I cling tighter, pressing my cheek to the tree as I catch my breath. *Don't look down.* My heart's pounding. My arm stings.

But I keep climbing. Each branch gets thinner, the wind stronger. My knuckles are white where I grip the wood. Higher and higher. Every movement is careful, deliberate.

Then the memory hits. That summer when I was eight. Trying to climb the huge maple tree in our backyard. Getting cocky, losing my grip. The crack of the branch, the sickening rush of falling. The pain. The hospital. The months in a sling after I shattered my collarbone.

My breathing grows shallow, my hands slick with sweat despite the cold, but I keep going. I have to. Finally, I reach as high as I can go. The branch beneath me creaks, swaying under my weight. I wrap both arms around it, pressing my chest to the bark and slowly turn my head. All I can see is trees. A sea of green and brown stretching forever in every direction. The sky above me is bright and blue, like last night's storm never happened. Like it hadn't just tried to drown me.

I bite down on the inside of my cheek, fighting back the sting in my eyes. The disappointment sinks like a stone in my stomach. My arms tremble from exhaustion. I press my forehead against the bark, letting out a shaky breath. Nothing. Just trees and sky. No signs of life. No hints of a path. No way to tell where I am. I let myself sit there for one more minute, then I know I have to climb down.

Going down is worse. Way worse. Because now…now I have to look. I glance over my shoulder, and the ground is so far below it makes my stomach drop. My legs tremble, and for a second, I freeze, gripping the branch like my life depends on it. Because it does.

I try to steady my breathing. One step at a time. I ease my foot down, searching blindly for the next branch. My scraped arm aches as I lower myself, fingers shaking as they close around the cold bark. The wind shifts the tree again, and I squeeze my eyes shut, willing it to stop. Another branch down. Then another. But I'm slower now. Every step feels like a risk. My foot slips again, just enough to jolt my body and nearly send me toppling. A choked cry leaves my throat as I cling to the tree, hugging it like a lifeline.

The tears I've been holding back sting my eyes, but I don't have the luxury of crying. I keep going, swallowing my panic, even when my toes are numb and my muscles are on fire. Finally, after what feels like an eternity, my bare feet hit the ground. I slump against the tree trunk, arms shaking. My legs buckle, but I catch myself and slide to the damp earth. I look over. The cat's still pacing in tight circles, leash stretched taut. I reach out, untying the drawstring from the sapling and pull her into my lap. She curls up, trembling like I am.

"I'm trying." I hold her close. "I'm really trying." I close my eyes for just a second, letting myself feel the cold ground beneath me and the growing dread that this nightmare isn't over yet. But I survived the climb.

I sit there for what feels like ten minutes, maybe more. It's hard to tell anymore. Finally, I force myself to stand. My sweatpants hang low, soaked and heavy, dragging against my legs. I bend down and tuck both feet into the elastic cuffs, using the pant legs like makeshift socks to protect my torn-up soles. It's not perfect, but it's something.

Miss Dashworth tugs at the drawstring leash, clearly over this entire adventure. I give the line a gentle tug back, and after a few stubborn seconds, she starts to move with me. Reluctantly.

This time, I'm more careful. I watch the trees, scanning for anything unique; a strange-shaped trunk, a mossy boulder, anything I might recognize if I pass it again. I try to leave a mark on the occasional tree, scraping bark with a sharp stick as I go. Just in case.

My body is stiff and sore, and every step sends a dull ache through my hips and feet. But it's my mind that wanders the most, back to my conversation with my mom. Back to what she said about Miles. I should've told him how I felt. I should've said something before this. Before I was lost in the woods with a cat and a bunch of regrets weighing heavier than the storm ever did. I sigh, the sound lost in the silence of the trees.

I keep walking. It feels like hours. My clothes are still damp and cling to my skin in patches. I'm thirsty, so thirsty, and my stomach growls, angry and empty.

Then something crashes out of the brush ahead of me. A deer, startled from its hiding place, bolts across the trail just feet in front of me. I scream. Miss Dashworth hisses and tries to run after it, but the drawstring leash tugs her back. She yowls in protest.

My heart's still hammering when I take another step, and that's when it happens. A searing pain shoots up my leg. I scream again and collapse, catching myself just before I land on the cat. The makeshift leash slips through my fingers but catches on my wrist. I breathe hard, reaching for my foot, afraid to look.

A jagged stick, half-buried in the soft earth, has torn a deep gash across the bottom of my foot. It's not quite deep enough to need stitches, I think. But it's bleeding, and bad.

I grab the hem of my T-shirt, rip it and use the fabric to wipe away the blood, hissing through my teeth as I press it against the wound. Then I tuck my foot back into the pant leg, using the soaked fabric to protect it from the dirt.

A few tears fall, hot against my already chilled cheeks. I swipe them away with the back of my hand. Not now. Not here. I breathe deep and look around the forest. The sky above is brighter now, but I'm still lost. Still hurting. Still alone. But I'm not giving up. I push myself back up and start walking again.

After a while, I spot another patch of sunlight breaking through the canopy. I limp toward it and sink down in the middle, soaking up every bit of warmth I can. Miss Dashworth curls up beside me, finally calm. I lie back on the damp ground, eyes fluttering closed, just hoping to rest.

I know when night falls, the cold will come back sharp and cruel, and I'll need to keep moving just to stay warm. But for now, I'm still. Just for a minute. Surprisingly, I drift off.

It can't be long before the chill creeps in again, waking me with a shiver that runs deep. My whole body aches, my teeth chatter. I open my eyes, and the first thing I notice is the fading light. Night is coming. I sit up slowly, pressing my palms to my face, trying to breathe through the fear clawing at my throat. *Another night out here. Alone.*

The thought sends a wave of dread through me. I don't want to do this again. I don't want to be cold or scared or lost anymore. I want to be in Miles' arms, safe and warm, his breath in my hair, his chest steady against mine. All I want is to go home. Because I think, I really think, I might love him.

38

Rallied the Troops

Miles

After hours of searching, through thunder, lightning, wind and sheets of rain, Reed and I finally make our way back toward the house. My legs are soaked and caked in mud, my flashlight barely cutting through the gloom. The storm has started to break, but the weight in my chest hasn't.

As we step out from the tree line, the sight nearly brings me to my knees. The entire property is lit up like a damn emergency scene. Dozens of people are moving around, some gathered under white canopies set up around folding tables, others stuffing supplies into backpacks and waterproof bins. There's a rhythm to the chaos, organized, urgent. Headlamps bob in the dark. Radios crackle. Help is here.

As we move closer to the house, a few familiar faces stand out through the blur of activity; Dylan, Luke, Naya, even Floyd. They're all here, and I know Judy called them all. Luke's got a clipboard in his hands, barking orders to a group of volunteers. Dylan is checking gear, flashlights, tarps, ropes, his usual smirk replaced with a look of quiet focus. Naya's pacing, phone in hand, eyes red-rimmed but determined. Floyd stands back near one of the canopies, arms crossed, watching it all unfold like he's been through this kind of thing before.

They all stop when they see us. I give a tired nod. "Anything?"

Naya shakes her head and walks up to me quickly. "Not yet."

The whole group circles around us, Judy included. "What do you need?"

I want to say Kinsley, but I swallow it down. "I need everyone to start searching."

Just then, Fire Chief Sanford joins the group. He shakes Reed's hand and claps me on the back. "We're just about ready to begin. Everyone will be searching in pairs, one experienced person per team. We only have enough handheld radios for one per group, so stay close to your partner."

Naya shoots her hand up like we're in school and doesn't wait to be called on. "Are we using search dogs?"

Chief Sanford sighs. "Unfortunately, our county only has two. One is injured and the other is already deployed on another case."

"What about drones?" Dylan asks, his brow furrowed in concern.

"No funding for that yet. Sorry."

Judy pinches the bridge of her nose. "Has anyone contacted her family?"

The chief glances around. "Good question. Has anyone?"

I let out a long sigh. "Her phone's locked, and I don't have their number."

I turn to Luke. "Can you get into her phone?"

"Yes," he says simply. Without hesitation, I step back into the house and return with Kinsley's phone. I hand it to Luke. The fire chief watches us closely but doesn't say a word.

Luke steps away and pulls his own phone from his pocket. He reads off Kinsley's number to someone, then slides the back off her phone to reveal the serial number. A few seconds later, the phone pings with a notification. Luke taps the screen and unlocks it.

"Who do you want me to call?" Luke asks, already scrolling through Kinsley's phone.

Chief Sanford looks surprised but doesn't say a word. If anyone could get into her phone, it's Luke. I've always known he had his ways, he's hinted at it enough, but what he actually does for a living, none of us really know.

"Call her parents and her best friend, Raelynn." I pull out my wallet and hand the whole thing to him. "Book them flights. Get them a driver to bring them here, please."

"You got it," Luke replies. "Also, I've got two high-tech drones arriving as soon as possible. Just in case."

This time, the fire chief actually chuckles, shaking his head. "I'm not even going to ask."

Luke grins. "Good. Because I wouldn't have told you."

Even with everything going on, I can't help the small smile that tugs at my lips.

I turn to Judy and Floyd, meeting both of their eyes. "I need you two to stay here, organize food, keep traffic under flowing. And when her family gets here, please set them up in the guest rooms." They both nod, and Judy immediately turns to start organizing whatever task she decides needs doing. Honestly, I don't care what it is, if it keeps her away from the woods. Floyd, as always been capable, but the man's nearly eighty. I'm not risking him out there, either.

"Alright, let's get started."

The fire chief nods and steps forward, raising his voice to the gathered crowd. "I need everyone's attention." The murmurs quiet instantly.

"If you're familiar with the forest, please move to the right. If not, move to the left."

Reed, Dylan, Luke and I step to the right. Naya crosses to the left with a few others.

"I want one person from each side to partner up," the chief instructs. "Half of the teams will head out now. The other half will rest and take over once the first wave comes back. We'll rotate, keep everyone sharp and safe."

People begin pairing off, exchanging a few quiet words and nods. I head straight for Naya. I'm not letting her go out there without someone I trust watching her back, and right now, that someone is me.

Once everyone's paired up, the fire chief starts calling out the first wave of search teams. I step forward before he can say a word, not asking, but telling. The look in my eyes says everything: I'm going, and there's no talking me out of it.

He reads me right and gives a small nod. Reed steps up beside me. "I'm in too."

Dylan and Luke hang back, waiting for the next rotation. Luke volunteers to stay behind this round. Someone has to keep coordinating things, and he's still handling arrangements with Kinsley's family.

I grab a handheld radio from the charging block snag two fresh flashlights, and shoulder one of the supply backpacks; first aid kit, bottled water, snacks, the basics. I hand the radio to Naya, and she clips it to her waistband without saying a word, eyes fierce. With flashlights in hand, our group sets off.

We fan out into the forest, far enough apart that we can't see each other, only hear faint voices calling her name through the trees.

"Kinsley! Kinsley!" Each shout feels like it punches through my ribs.

As Naya and I step into the forest, I stop and turn to face her, making sure I have her full attention.

"If you need a break, just say so. And if you're ready to head back at any point, I'll take you. No questions."

She nods. I can see the nerves in her eyes, but there's no hesitation. She's scared, but there's no way in hell she'd sit this out.

I nod back. "I already covered this area earlier, so we're going to keep our eyes open but move fast until we get to where I left off."

Naya squares her shoulders and faces the dense, dark woods, her voice firm despite the fear. "Let's go." Moving forward, flashlights slice through the shadows, scanning every inch of the forest, with one goal in mind.

We walk for nearly two hours, following the route I took earlier. When we finally reach the spot where I'd turned back, I stop and glance around.

"From here on, we need to be sharp. The sun's starting to come up, so visibility's better, but the ground's uneven. Watch your step."

We move slower now, more deliberate, calling Kinsley's name every few minutes. The woods are still damp, heavy with silence except for the occasional rustle of leaves or the snap of a branch beneath our boots.

After a while, Naya breaks the quiet. "Miles, can you tell me again what happened? I just...I'm trying to understand why she'd come out here."

It's the fourth time I've told the story, but I don't mind. If repeating it helps her feel closer to Kinsley, I'll tell it a hundred more. I explain everything again; Miss Dashworth, the storm, the back porch, and how I pieced it all together.

Just as I finish, there's a sharp rustle to our left. I freeze, flashlight up, sweeping the area. A bird shoots out from a low nest, wings flapping wildly. It must've fallen from a tree during the storm. I exhale hard, tension leaving my shoulders.

"Miles." Naya's voice is soft, hesitant. "They told me not to say anything, but I feel like you should know."

I turn to her, dread climbing up my spine. If they're hiding something from me, it can't be good. "What is it?"

She places a hand gently on my shoulder before speaking. "Cabin number two, it was destroyed in the storm. A tree came down on it."

I blink, then exhale, relieved. "That's okay. As long as no one was hurt."

"You're not mad?" she asks, puzzled.

"I'm upset Kinsley's still out here. The cabin? That can be replaced. I've got insurance on it."

She gives me a small, sad smile. "You really are a good man. I can see why Kinsley loves you."

Her words stop me cold. I look at her, searching her face. No teasing, no hesitation. Just truth. I swallow the knot in my throat and nod.

Then I turn, flashlight in hand, and we keep going. More determined than ever to find her, I start moving faster. Naya keeps pace beside me without complaint.

After a few hours, we stop to catch our breath. The rising sun filters through the trees now, no more need for flashlights. I take a long drink from my water bottle, then turn to her. "You good to keep going?"

"Absolutely." She snaps the lid closed and tucks it back in the bag. The radio clipped to her hip has been quiet the entire time. No news. Which means she still hasn't been found.

We push forward, but the undergrowth thickens, vines and fallen branches tangling around our boots. Each step gets harder. Just ahead, the terrain dips sharply. A deep slope, slick with mud and leaves.

"We'll take it slow," I tell her, already picking my way down. But the moment we try, the ground gives beneath us. Naya lets out a sharp squeal as we both lose our footing and go down hard, sliding fast. I throw my arm out and catch her just in time, keeping her from slamming into a tree. At the bottom, I quickly scramble to my feet and help her up. "You okay?" I ask, brushing mud from my sleeves.

"Yeah, I think so. I'm sure I'll feel it tomorrow." She smears mud off her pants with a grimace.

I pat her shoulder and look around, heart still pounding. Then I point ahead. "Let's keep going. That way." We continue in silence for hours, the only sound besides our footsteps is the occasional call of Kinsley's name echoing through the trees.

The forest looks different in the late afternoon light. Shadows stretch across the ground, golden beams filtering through the thinner canopy above. It should feel peaceful, even beautiful, but nothing about this feels calm. The air is thick with the smell of wet pine and damp earth. Our boots squish through patches of mud, snag on hidden roots and crunch over fallen branches. Ferns brush our legs.

Naya walks just a few feet beside me, her eyes constantly scanning the underbrush, lips pressed into a tight line. Every now and then, one of us calls out Kinsley's name. Still nothing. No response. Not even a hint of movement in return. My throat is raw from shouting.

We stop for a moment, and I shrug the backpack off my shoulders, digging out a granola bar and a stick of beef jerky. I hand them to Naya without a word. She takes them, peeling the wrapper back as we both catch our breath.

With her mouth full, she glances at me. "You're not eating?"

I shake my head. "Not right now."

The truth is, I can't. Not while Kinsley's still out here, possibly hungry. The thought of chewing through a granola bar while she might be cold and hungry makes my stomach turn. I know it's irrational. I know it's not going to help her if I run myself into the ground. But guilt's louder than reason right now.

Once Naya finishes, we push forward again. We stop caring about the scratches on our skin, the bruises forming under our clothes. The sweat running down our backs is constant. It's not warm, maybe fifty degrees, but the movement, the backpack weight and our jackets keep us from getting chilled. I keep wondering if Kinsley had time to grab hers. If she's even wearing shoes. That thought alone makes me sick.

A few minutes later, the handheld radio crackles. We both freeze, holding our breath for good news. It's Chief Sanford. "Naya, Miles, status check."

Naya clicks the button. "We're fine."

"Copy. You're the last of the first wave still out."

I exhale through my nose. "Tell him we're on our way back. It'll take a couple hours to get there." She relays the message, and I tie a strip of yellow marker tape to the nearest tree before turning back the way we came. We're quiet for a while until Naya finally speaks, not looking at me. "Why are we heading back?"

I glance at her, steady. "Because I don't want you pushing past your limit. You need a break, and if you rest now, you'll be ready to go back out later."

She nods, and we keep moving, every step taking us further from where I want to be.

As we finally break through the trees, the murmur of voices reaches us, a low hum of conversation and movement. The temperature hits us almost immediately; it's easily ten degrees warmer near the house. For a moment, it feels like a different world than the one we just came from.

Naya and I walk side by side toward Reed, who's standing with the fire chief. "Welcome back. Your replacements went out about forty-five minutes ago." Reed pats my shoulder and heads out to a truck that just pulled in with more supplies.

Naya sets the handheld back on the charger without a word, and I shrug the pack off my back, my muscles aching with relief. I turn to her, placing a hand briefly on her shoulder. "Get some rest. Couch is open. Just go inside."

She nods, eyes tired, and heads toward the house without arguing. I grab a fresh radio and a new pack, slinging it over my shoulder. The fire chief watches me, brow furrowed. "What are you doing?"

I stare at him, deadpan. "I'm going back out."

He sighs, already shaking his head. "You can't go alone."

I open my mouth to tell him exactly why I can, but a voice interrupts from behind me.

"I'll go with him."

I turn. Raelynn stands there, chin set, shoulders squared despite the exhaustion in her face. And beside her, two people I've never seen before but would recognize anywhere. The woman looks just like Kinsley. Her mother, no doubt. Her father stands close by, both of them with puffy eyes and expressions carved from worry.

"Okay," I say, nodding. I hand Raelynn the spare handheld and pack two flashlights into the new backpack. Then I turn to her, eyes serious.

"We'll be out past dark. You sure you want to go?"

She grips the strap of the radio and meets my gaze, unwavering. "She's my best friend. I NEED to go."

I turn to face Kinsley's parents, my throat tight with guilt and words I don't know how to say. What do you even say to the people whose daughter you lost? That it was my stupid cat she ran after?

That I should've known sooner, should've figured it out faster? Maybe if I had, she wouldn't have gotten so far?

"Hi, Mr. and Mrs. Brighton," I start, voice low. "I'm Miles. I'm so sorry, I…"

But Kinsley's mom gently reaches out and places her hand on my arm. The simple gesture freezes me. I glance down at her hand, then up into her eyes. She's calm…calm in a way that reminds me of Kinsley. There's no blame in her face, just quiet strength.

"Don't apologize," she says softly. "You did nothing wrong. Judy told us everything. And if it weren't for you, no one would've realized she was out there at all."

She picks up a bottle of water from the table beside her, pressing it into my hand. "Now, you get back out there and find our girl."

I open my mouth, but no words come out. I turn to leave. All I can think is, *yes. She is my girl.*

39

Even If It Hurts

Kinsley

The air feels sharper now, colder with every passing minute as the sun dips below the horizon. Night is coming fast. Again.

I can't stop moving, not if I want to stay warm. My feet are raw, my legs ache and Miss Dashworth is dragging behind me, her tiny frame clearly over it. She lets out a low, tired meow and tries to sit, but I give the leash a gentle tug.

"I know," I whisper hoarsely. "I'm tired too."

But I can't stop. If I sit, I'll freeze. If I rest, I'll fall asleep. The thought alone makes my heart race.

The second night out here is somehow more terrifying than the first. Everything feels heavier. The darkness. The silence. The fear. I know Miles is out there somewhere, looking for me, I have to believe that. But a tiny voice in my head keeps whispering: *What if he doesn't find you? What if you've wandered too far?"* And worst of all... this is all my fault. I should've been more careful when I opened the door. I should've asked him for help when the cat ran out. I should've listened to the voice in my head that told me not to go chasing after her. I should've never stepped into these woods alone.

I stop walking. The weight of it all crashes into me like a wave. My shoulders hunch. My hands rise to cover my face, and I finally let go. The tears spill fast and hot, cutting down my cold cheeks as a sob racks through me. I bury my face in my palms and cry, silent, shaking, broken.

When there's nothing left, I wipe my face with the edge of my shirt and force myself to keep walking. Miss Dashworth is done. She's dragging her feet, leash taut, clearly ready for someone to carry her. I sigh, scoop her up and cradle her against me. Her fur is damp but warm, offering the faintest comfort.

Just ahead, something moves. I freeze. A flicker of shape, too large to be anything good. I squint through the fading light, my pulse thudding in my ears. A bear.

My breath catches. My whole body stiffens. I duck behind the nearest tree, pressing my back to the rough bark as gently as I can. My heart feels like it's pounding out of my chest. I cover my mouth with one hand, trying to muffle each shaky breath. I don't dare move. I don't dare breathe too loudly. Every muscle in my body is locked tight, trembling.

Finally, when I'm sure I'll pass out from the tension, I risk peeking around the tree. It's gone. I stay still a moment longer, just to be sure. But the bear is nowhere in sight. I can't keep going that way. I need to put distance between us, fast.

I step away from the tree slowly, carefully, and begin tiptoeing through the underbrush. Each step is deliberate, my focus narrowed to the placement of my feet. I'm holding my breath without meaning to, and it only makes my heart race harder.

Eventually, I start to move quicker, glancing down often to watch the terrain. Then something in me snaps and I break into a run, reckless and frantic. The cat clings to me, her claws gripping my shirt, holding on for dear life. It's not graceful. It's desperate and panicked. I glance over my shoulder, checking for movement behind me. Another mistake. Because when I turn back, it's too late.

I trip over a thick branch, and time seems to slow as I fall. Instinct takes over, I twist my body and throw out my free arm to protect the cat. I hit the ground hard, landing on my wrist with a sickening jolt. Pain explodes up my arm, from wrist to elbow, like fire under my skin.

I roll onto my back, gasping. The cat squirms free and darts a few feet away, but I can't move. I clutch my wrist to my chest, silent screams ripping through me, tears slipping past clenched eyelids. The pain is blinding. I can't breathe, can't think, just lie there on the cold ground, crying as quietly as I can. Because screaming will only lead the bear my way.

I force myself to breathe through the pain. It pulses, sharp and hot, possibly broken. I shift onto my knees, wincing as every movement sends new waves of ache through my arm and feet. My fingers fumble for the makeshift leash. The cat isn't trying to run anymore. She just watches me, too exhausted to protest.

The pain dulls slightly, enough for me to think. I stay kneeling, letting the weight off my raw, aching foot as I reach down and tug the leash under it to keep it secure. Then, with one shaky hand and my teeth, I tear another strip from the bottom of my shirt. My movements are clumsy, but I manage to wind the fabric around my swelling wrist, yanking it tight enough to hold. The throb intensifies under the pressure, but it's a necessary pain. I suck in a sharp breath, blink past the sting in my eyes, and sit back for a second. Then, slowly, I rise.

My legs wobble beneath me, weak and sore. My wrist screams with every shift in balance. But I manage to scoop Miss Dashworth back into my arms, and I keep going.

It's fully dark now. The last threads of light vanished hours ago, and with them went whatever adrenaline had been carrying me. Now it's just me, the cold and the pain.

The air feels sharp, like it has teeth. Every inhale burns my throat, every exhale fogs out in front of me like a warning. If I make it out of this, I swear I'm signing up for a wilderness survival class. I want to know how to start a damn fire with sticks.

I shuffle forward, slower than before. Each step is a dull punch to the soles of my feet. The bottom of my sweatpants has started to rip, the elastic no match for the abuse. The fabric bunches and drags, loose and torn, doing little to protect my feet anymore.

Everything inside me aches, but I can't stop moving. If I stop, the cold will settle in deeper, and I might not get back up. One shaky step at a time, I walk through the darkness and the fear.

I whisper into the quiet night, just to remind myself I still have a voice. "Just a little further," I murmur. "Just a little longer." And I pray, silently, desperately, that someone is still looking. That Miles is still out there. That I'm not already too far gone.

The forest is alive with sounds I'd normally never notice too soft, too subtle. But out here, in this kind of silence, everything echoes. A distant creak of shifting branches. The patter of water dripping from leaves overhead. A sudden flutter of wings in the trees makes my heart leap. I pause, listening hard, but it's gone. Every sound could be danger. Every noise might be something watching.

The smell is wet earth and bark, mossy, thick and oddly metallic. The scent of rotting leaves clings to the air, sharp and rich and layered with something else, animal maybe. Mixing with the scent of mud caked to my legs.

It's so dark I can't see beyond a few feet. The trees blend together, their trunks nothing more than shadows stacked on shadows. Without light, my other senses scream to compensate. Every brush of wind feels like a whisper against my skin. Every crunch underfoot jolts through my spine like a gunshot. The hair on my arms rises without warning, reacting to things I can't see, only feel.

The cold is everywhere now. It's not just on the outside anymore. It's in my bones. My fingers feel thick, uncoordinated, like they're no longer mine. My jaw aches from chattering, and my shoulders hunch tighter with every cool breeze.

My mouth is dry, painfully so. My tongue sticks to the roof, my throat rough with every swallow. My lips are cracked, split at the corners. I rub them with the back of my hand, but it only makes it worse. I'd give anything for a drink of water. Or better yet, that bowl of mac and cheese I made. I'd been so proud of it, creamy, perfectly golden on top. I can practically taste it now, and the thought brings tears to my eyes. Stupid, how something so small can feel like such a loss. But I'd give anything for that warmth, that comfort. For a real meal, a blanket, a hand to hold.

It's as if God himself has shown me mercy. My foot splashes into a shallow puddle. I drop to my hands and knees, frantically feeling for the edges I can't see. I scoop a handful, bringing it to my nose first. All I smell is dirt and moss. It's water. Muddy, gritty, awful, but water.

I sip carefully. It tastes like earth, like rot and rain, but I drink it anyway. I might be from the city and know nothing about survival, but I do know the human body can only last three days without water. I keep drinking until my hands scrape the damp ground. I stand and wipe my mouth as I continue to walk.

I don't know how long I've been walking. Time's slippery out here, like everything else. My legs move on autopilot through the dark, but my mind? My mind starts to slip.

What if no one finds me? The thought lands hard. Heavy. It echoes in my mind like thunder. *What if no one ever finds me?*

I try to shake it off, but it sticks, digging deeper with every frozen step. My family, they'll wait a few days. Call. Text. Get annoyed when I don't respond. My mom will panic. She always said she had a "mother's intuition." She'll know something's wrong.

My dad, he'll be furious. Not at me, but at the world. He won't know where to put the anger, so he'll carry it. Quiet and heavy.

And Raelynn? She'll blame herself. She'll replay every conversation. She'll cry. She'll shut down. And then she'll get angry, because that's how she copes. And she'll hate herself for being angry, like somehow that makes her a bad friend.

Miles? If no one finds me, he'll never forgive himself. I know that without a doubt. Even if it's not his fault, he'll make it his fault. He'll think he should've come after me sooner. That he should've realized I was missing faster. That he should've known where I went. He'll carry it. And I can't stand that. I can't stand the thought of him blaming himself. Of him walking through life with that guilt like a weight around his neck. I think of his arms around me. The way he looked at me like I was something precious. Like I was his.

I never told him how I felt. I never told him that I wanted more. That I wanted him. And now… now he might never know.

Tears blur what little I can see. For a second I might actually collapse. My knees wobble, my breath stutters. The weight of what-ifs presses down so hard I feel like I might crack open from the inside out.

I stop walking, too tired to move. I press my forehead to the rough bark of a nearby tree and just breathe shallow, shaking breaths. "I don't want to die out here," I whisper.

I press my forehead harder into the tree, grounding myself in its rough bark. My breath still trembles, but something shifts. Maybe it's the cold, maybe it's the ache in my wrist, or maybe it's just the raw, bitter truth: I am NOT dying out here. I don't care how tired I am, how lost, how cold. I don't care if my feet are shredded or if my bones feel like glass. This forest does not get to win.

I lift my head, jaw tight, breath fogging the air in front of me. "You don't get to take me," I whisper, voice hoarse but clear. I wrap my arm tighter around Miss Dashworth, feel her warmth, her steady little heartbeat under all that damp fur. "We are getting out of here. You hear me?" My voice cracks, but I don't back down.

Step by step. That's all it takes. And I take one. Then another. The wind moans through the trees like it's trying to talk me out of it, but I keep walking. My feet drag, my body protests with every movement, but I move anyway. I won't stop. I won't quit.

Just when I feel like I might crumble again, I glance through the trees ahead, barely visible past the twisted limbs and thick canopy. The sky is lighter. Not light. Not day. But lighter. A dull grayness blooming at the edge of black. Dawn. The first breath of morning. It might be an illusion. It might still be hours away. But I can see it. I can feel it. Suddenly, it's enough. Enough to push me forward. Enough to keep my legs moving. Enough to pull me through just a little bit longer.

40

A Hunger No Food Can Fix

Miles

The trees thin, and the first burn of sunlight stabs through the branches ahead. I squint into the pale morning haze as we finally break through the edge of the forest. My boots covered in mud, every muscle in my body aching, my pack dragging heavy on my shoulders. The house comes into view like some kind of mirage, white canopy tents glowing faintly in the dawn light, silhouettes of people shifting beneath them. We're back. But we don't have her.

Raelynn stumbles beside me, wiping at her face with a dirt-smeared sleeve. She's been crying off and on since the last break we took, quiet sobs that she tried to hide at first, but eventually gave up on. Now, her eyes are red-rimmed and swollen, lips trembling. She hasn't said a word in the last hour, but she didn't have to. Her silence said everything.

Three nights. Kinsley's been out here for three whole nights.

I don't even know how she's surviving at this point. The thought makes my stomach turn, acid rising in my throat. The cold alone could kill someone. That's not even considering injury, hunger, or animals. I force myself to stop. I can't let my brain go there. Not yet. Not when she's still out there somewhere. Not when I haven't seen her face.

Raelynn lets out a sound, half sob, half breath, as we approach the tents. Her steps are slower now, the adrenaline clearly burned out of her system. That's the only reason I finally agreed to turn back. Not because I wanted to. Not because I believed we'd searched enough. But because I could see it in her posture, the way she tripped more often, how she leaned heavier on her flashlight even when it was barely needed anymore. She wouldn't quit. Not unless I made her. And I couldn't risk her collapsing out there.

The assistant fire chief's voice crackled through the radio just before dawn, saying the next shift was ready to head out. But Raelynn and I didn't respond right away. I let her keep going until I saw her pace drop. That's when I said it. "Let's head in." She didn't argue. She just cried.

I adjust my grip on the radio and unclip it from my belt. I signal in our return, my voice low and tight. "Heading back."

Static answers me for a second, then a clipped, "Copy that. We'll regroup."

Raelynn steps past me, her shoulders slumped. She just heads straight for the house like she's running out of strength to pretend she's holding it together.

I glance toward the canopy tents where a small crowd's gathered. Judy is there, moving between people with paper plates in her hands, trying to keep everyone fed and moving forward. When her eyes find mine, her expression softens. She grabs a plate, scrambled eggs, toast, something warm, but I shake my head before she can even open her mouth. She doesn't argue. Just nods like she understands and turns to offer the plate to someone else.

I move toward the supply table, stocked with bottled water, radios, flashlights and first-aid kits. My fingers work on autopilot as I unzip my pack and start refilling it. A roll of gauze. Trail mix I have no intention of eating. Every motion is mechanical, like if I stop moving for one second, I'll break.

Reed steps up beside me, his voice low. "Judy says you haven't eaten this entire time. I'll get you a plate."

"No," I snap, not even looking up.

"Miles."

"I don't want any fucking food," I growl, slamming the pack shut.

He opens his mouth to say something else, probably something reasonable, something like "what good will you be if you're too hungry to keep going," but I don't let him get that far. I pick up my water bottle and hurl it at the side of the house with everything I've got. The hollow thud echoes louder than it should and heads turn, but I don't care.

"You think I give a shit about food right now?" I shout, voice shaking with rage. "I don't want rest! I don't want eggs! I don't want comfort! I want her!"

My chest heaves as the words tear out of me, and for a moment, there's nothing but silence. Then Reed steps in, his voice cutting through the air like a blade.

"You're being stubborn," he snaps. "Hard-headed and reckless. You think this is helping anyone?"

I lose it. "Fuck you!" I bellow, grabbing the nearest chair and hurling it across the yard. It crashes against the supply table, skidding into the grass with a loud crack.

Before he can say another word, I shove him. Hard. "You think I care about what you think?! You think I'm going to stand here while she's out there, cold, scared, alone, and do nothing?!" He stumbles back but doesn't move from in front of the table. "I dare anyone to try and stop me!"

Judy rushes forward, arms half-raised, her voice trembling. "Miles, honey, please…"

355

"Stop, Judy!" I snap, not even looking at her. "Don't!" She freezes in place, tears in her eyes.

I turn back, hands balled at my sides. Reed's still there. Blocking the gear. Blocking me. I step forward, about to swing, anger blinding me. But then, a gentle touch. A soft hand on my arm. My gaze snaps down to the hand, delicate and calm. And then up to her face.

It's not Kinsley, but it might as well be. The shape of her eyes, the calm curve of her brow, even the sadness in her expression. Kinsley's mother stands there, not flinching, not afraid.

"You love her?" she asks, her voice steady, soft, a whisper in the middle of a storm.

The question cuts deeper than anything else could. All the rage, all the fire in me collapses in on itself. I look down, swallowing hard, and then nod. "Yes." My voice cracks. "Yes."

Her eyes don't leave mine, full of something fierce, maternal and achingly familiar. "Then take two hours to rest, and eat. Because if you love her, Miles, you have to survive this, too."

I can't speak. I just keep nodding like it's the only thing tethering me to the ground. Reed steps closer again, quieter this time. "I'll go in your place," he offers. "Let me cover the next shift."

I look at him, jaw clenched, something hot burning behind my eyes. Then I drop my head, shoulders sagging. "Two hours," I mutter. "After that, I don't care. I'm going back out."

He nods. For the first time in days, I let someone else take the lead, because I have to find her. When I do, I need the strength to bring her home.

I grab a radio off the table, shoving it into the side pocket of my pack. Just in case. In case they find her while I'm forced to take this damn break. In case someone tries to keep it from me.

I head inside, ignoring the pull of the stairs that lead to my bedroom. I can't go in there. Not without her. The couch will have to do. I drop down onto it, stiff and aching, and pull my phone from my pocket. I set an alarm for exactly two hours, not a minute more. Then I toss the phone on the side table and close my eyes for half a second.

The door creaks open again. I don't look up until I catch the soft scent of cinnamon and eggs. Judy steps in, plate in hand. She doesn't speak. Just offers it out gently. I take it without protest this time. "Thanks," I mutter, barely above a whisper. She pats my shoulder once warmly and leaves without saying word. The back door clicks shut behind her.

I stare at the plate for a long moment. It's probably still warm, but I don't taste much when I finally force a few bites down. My stomach turns with every chew, guilt crowding out my hunger. When I can't pretend anymore, I set the plate aside and lie back, one arm slung across my chest hoping it will stop the ache. The silence in the room is deafening. I close my eyes, but my mind doesn't quiet. I picture her out there, alone, cold and scared. I picture her curled up under a tree, hurt or crying or… *no I can't go there.*

My hand tightens into a fist. Two hours. I just have to make it two hours. Then I'm going back out.

My alarm drags me out of a half-sleep that never really felt like rest. I sit up, heart pounding like I've already been running. I grab my already packed bag and sling it over my shoulder.

When I push open the back door, Luke is standing there, arms crossed, his expression unreadable. "Exactly two hours." He glances at his smartwatch before lifting his eyes to meet mine. There's no judgment in his voice, just quiet knowing. He never expected me to stay longer.

"I'm heading back out." I step past him toward the porch steps.

"The drones will be here in twenty. You should know, though, it's not a guarantee I'll see anything. Heavy tree cover. Limited heat signature."

I nod once. "If you do, radio me."

"I will but take someone with you. Reed's still out there."

I turn, scanning the small camp. Raelynn's curled up on the porch swing, finally asleep. I won't wake her, not after the night she had. Judy's occupied under the tents with Kinsley's parents. Dylan's probably still with Reed. Everyone who could go, already is.

"I'm coming." Naya steps forward. Her hair's pulled back in a messy ponytail, eyes shadowed with exhaustion but sharp with something else. Resolve.

"You sure."

"Let's go."

I don't say another word. I grip my radio tighter, pull the strap on my pack and head back into the trees.

As we walk the long two-plus hours back to where we left the last marker, a bit of the pressure in my chest starts to ease, not much, but enough to breathe. Being out here again, moving, searching, it quiets some of the rage. It gives the pain somewhere to go.

Naya walks beside me in silence for a while, then says quietly, "I heard you earlier." I glance at her, but she's looking straight ahead, her expression unreadable.

"You love her."

She wants to hear me say it.

I face forward again, step over a fallen branch, and exhale. "I do."

She sniffs, wiping her nose on her sleeve. "We're going to find her. I know it. I feel it." A moment of silence passes between us. "When we do, you need to tell her. Ask her to stay."

My throat tightens, but I nod. "I know." Because I've known it for days. Maybe even longer. I just have to get to her first.

"She loves you, too, you know." She tells me again.

I glance at her, eyebrows pulled together, heart kicking up in my chest. "Did she tell you that?" I stop for a second, skeptical but hopeful.

We start moving again, stepping over tangled roots and ducking under low-hanging branches. Naya lets out a soft chuckle. "She didn't need to. How drunk she got the other night, trying to forget the fact that she's supposed to leave? That girl was wrecked over it."

I don't say anything, but my mind flashes to that night, the morning after, the two of us tangled together on the couch.

Naya keeps going, her voice gentle but sure. "I think she feels like she has to go back to Seattle. Like it's the smart move, the responsible choice. But she doesn't. The only thing she really needs is to be happy." She glances sideways at me. "You make her happy, Miles."

My jaw clenches. I swallow hard. "Thank you, for saying that."

But inside, I'm still unsure. I want to believe it. *God, I need to believe it.* But what if Naya's wrong? I force the thought out of my head and shift the focus.

I keep my eyes ahead as we maneuver around a thicket of underbrush. "Who's running the bakery with you out here?"

She smiles a little, adjusting the strap of her bag. "My mom's holding down the fort. She kicked me out when she found out what happened. Said I wasn't allowed to come home until we brought Kinsley back."

I huff a small laugh through my nose, just as the radio clipped to Naya's hip crackles to life. We both freeze.

The assistant chief's voice cuts through the static. "All teams check in. Repeat, all teams check in."

She lifts it to her mouth. "This is Naya. Miles and I are fine."

One by one, the other teams begin to respond. Dylan and Reed. Then Luke and someone from the fire department. Everyone's accounted for. But none of them have found her.

We finally make it back to the marker, the exact spot where Raelynn and I turned back this morning. My boots crunch over the underbrush, the silence between us tense but focused, until a sudden rustling in the brush to our left freezes us both. I instinctively throw my arm out in front of Naya, stepping slightly in front of her.

"Kinsley?" she breathes, eyes wide, voice soft with hope. She stares into the trees where the noise came from.

Then a deer bursts through the foliage, startled by our presence. It freezes for a heartbeat right in front of us, equally surprised, then bolts in the opposite direction, disappearing into the trees with a snap of branches and thundering hooves.

Naya exhales sharply and clutches her chest. "That scared the hell out of me."

I nod once, but I'm not shaken by the deer. Not really. What rattles me is that it wasn't Kinsley. I let out a long, slow breath, forcing the disappointment down. We keep moving, scanning high and low, calling her name. Hours pass as the sun starts to dip lower behind the trees, the shadows stretch long and the forest starts to dim.

My stomach knots. I check my phone. We don't have much daylight left. "Radio in," I mutter, jaw tight. "Tell them we're heading back."

Naya turns to me, concern flickering in her eyes. "Are you sure? I can keep going."

360

I shake my head, firm. "Yes. I need you to get back and rest. We still have a few hours of walking ahead of us, and I'll take someone else next round."

She hesitates but doesn't argue. Her exhaustion is written across her face, even if she's too stubborn to admit it. I reach for the radio, but she beats me to it, lifting it to her mouth with a quiet sigh.

"This is Naya. We're heading back in. No sign yet." My heart aches at the word...yet. And it nearly breaks at the realization that Kinsley is alone another night in these woods.

41

Until I Couldn't

Kinsley

I might have rested for a few hours. Maybe less. Maybe more. Time doesn't feel real anymore. Just patches of light and dark, just cold and colder.

The small patch of sunlight I found earlier has long since faded, but I stayed anyway, curled up with Miss Dashworth beside me, trying to soak in whatever warmth I could. My body doesn't even shiver now. I'm so cold I don't feel cold anymore. That's not a good sign.

I blink slowly, my eyes dry and burning. My lips crack more every time I move them, splitting with a sting that feels like tiny blades dragging across dry skin. I run my tongue across them, but my mouth is like cotton.

Miss Dashworth stirs in my arms, and I stroke her fur, but even that feels distant, like my fingers are wrapped in thick gloves. Except they're not. I look down at my hands. They're pale. Trembling. I think they're starting to go numb. So are my thoughts.

I force myself to stand, legs wobbling underneath me like they've forgotten how to work. Everything aches. My hip, my wrist, the soles of my feet, raw and torn, but I push up anyway.

I look around, turning slowly, trying to take in my surroundings. But everything blends together. Trees and shadows. Green and brown and black. It's getting darker again, and the sun… God, the sun's setting again.

My head swims. I'm having trouble stringing thoughts together. I know I need to move. But I can't remember where I was going. Everything's jumbled and twisted.

I wrap my arms tighter around Miss Dashworth and whisper, my voice is barely audible, hoarse and brittle like dry leaves. "Find Miles." I press a kiss to the top of her tiny head, clinging to her for a second longer than I should, like letting go might shatter me. The thought of sending her off alone guts me, but it's the only choice I have left. My chest tightens with the weight of it…of goodbye. Then, with hands that barely work, I kneel down and fumble with the knotted drawstring leash. Every part of me screams in protest, but I get it loose. As much as I need her right now, need her warmth, her presence, someone to talk to, I know I have to let her go. She might be my only hope now. A small part of me aches at the thought of being even more alone out here.

"Go," I whisper, gently nudging her. "Go find home." She doesn't move at first. Just stands there, paws shifting in the cold dirt. But after a long, tense second, she takes a few hesitant steps forward. Then another. Then she runs.

I try to follow. I really do. I take a few steps, my hands outstretched, but the pain is too much. My feet are raw and throbbing with every step. My wrist feels like it's caught in a vice. I can't keep up. I stop and watch as her tiny form disappears into the shadows between the trees.

Tears burn hot in my eyes and spill over, blurring my vision as I press a fist to my mouth to keep from sobbing. *God, I hope she makes it. I hope someone sees her. Follows her. Finds me.*

I take a breath. Shaky. Shallow. The air feels like knives now, sharp and thin. My chest heaves with the effort. I blink back the tears clouding my vision and force myself to move.

So, I walk. Or shuffle, really. One slow, dragging step at a time. The tattered ends of my pants hang around my ankles, dragging in the dirt, damp and torn. My feet, bloody, blistered, raw, scream with every step, each one more painful than the last. Every inch of my body hurts, but I don't stop.

Clouds roll in overhead, heavy and low, blotting out what little moonlight I had. The darkness thickens until it's hard to tell where the trees end and the shadows begin. The cold sinks deeper into my skin. I wrap my arms around myself, trying to hold in what little warmth I have left.

The silence wraps around me like a noose. I'm completely alone. Without Miss Dashworth padding along beside me, it's so much worse. The cat may have been small, but her presence had been something, someone. Now there's nothing. I miss her more than I thought possible. But I had to let her go.

A soft whimper slips out of me before I can stop it. My body trembles. I wipe my face on my arm. My mouth is dry, so dry it hurts to swallow. The taste of blood faint and metallic on my tongue.

My stomach growls, low and desperate. The ache of hunger pulses with each heartbeat, sharp and steady.

A sound cracks through the quiet, just a step, a crunch of something behind me, and my pulse leaps into my throat. I freeze, ears straining, my body tensed like a deer about to bolt. But then, nothing. It's my own footstep. I let out a breath that feels more like a sob.

I press my good hand against a nearby tree and use it to keep myself upright. My legs barely work now, stiff with cold and exhaustion. I limp forward, leaning on every tree I pass to keep from falling, from giving in.

Every inch of me wants to curl up and stop. To give up. Just melt into the earth and disappear. But somehow, I don't. Somehow, I survive the longest, coldest, most agonizing night of my life.

When the first birds begin to chirp in the distance, I pause, barely daring to believe it. Their soft, hopeful songs pierce through the silence like tiny beams of light. I blink slowly, realizing the sky is starting to shift. Morning.

The sun will be up soon. It gives me the smallest sliver of peace, a reprieve, no matter how brief. I'm still alive. Still here.

When the light is strong enough to see more than just shadows, I start to count anything, everything. Trees. Red leaves. The speckles of moss clinging to bark. Anything to give my brain something to focus on, something to hold.

Twenty-one red leaves. Fifty-seven trees with twisted roots. Eighty-two tree trunks with holes. Somewhere around one hundred, I lose track.

That's when my legs finally give out. My knees slam into the dirt, my body pitching forward. My hands hit the ground, my wrist screams in protest, pain tearing through my arm so sharp and violent it steals my breath.

I scream. I scream so loud and raw it feels like it could split me in two. Frustration. Rage. Fear. Hopelessness. All of it breaks free in one desperate, broken sound that echoes into the trees. Then I press my forehead to the cold ground and breathe, shaking, heart pounding, not sure if I'm going to cry or throw up. I don't know how much longer I can keep doing this.

Five days. I've managed to survive out here. No food. No clean water. No shelter. No warmth. I know, deep in my bones, I don't have much time left.

My body aches in ways I didn't know were possible. Everything stings. Everything throbs. But I force myself to stand, muscles screaming in protest, legs trembling beneath me. I limp forward, one breath at a time. Just keep moving. Just keep going.

That's when I hear it. A heavy rustle behind me, too loud to be wind, too heavy to be anything small. I turn slowly, stomach dropping, heart thundering. And there it is.

A massive black bear, twenty feet away, staring me down. I scream, my voice scratchy and weak, barely more than a croak. I throw my arms out wide, legs spread, trying to make myself as big as I can, just like Judy told me to. But the bear doesn't flinch. Doesn't blink.

He lifts up on his hind legs, taller than any living thing has a right to be, and takes a step forward. I back away slowly, inching left, trying to put a tree between us. My heartbeat is so loud I can hardly hear the rain pattering on the leaves above. Maybe I'm near its den. Maybe it smells how weak I am.

It drops back onto all fours and starts moving faster. Straight for me. I scream again and turn to run, legs barely functioning, my body dragging behind my will to survive. I weave through the trees, using them like a shield, a desperate obstacle course to buy time. But the bear is fast. Too fast.

I push harder, slipping in the mud. My foot catches on a root. I go down, tumbling hard. My body slams into the ground, and I roll, coming to a stop on my back. I blink once, and the bear is there. Towering over me. I can smell it, earth and wet fur and musk and death. It rears back again and lets out a roar that splits the air. I raise my arms, curl into a ball, trying to protect my head, bracing for the blow. Its paw crashes down, raking across my arm. I scream, hot pain tearing through my shoulder and elbow as skin splits. I feel the gush of blood instantly. I sob, waiting for the next blow.

But it doesn't come. Because suddenly, out of nowhere, I hear a snarl. Then tiny, feral, miraculous Miss Dashworth launches herself at the bear. She clings to its back, yowling and clawing like a demon, her fur puffed and wild, pure instinct and rage.

Tears flood my vision. I use the distraction, her sacrifice, to crawl, to scramble, to run. I don't know where I'm going. I don't stop to think. I just move. Run. Bleeding and limping and crying as the forest blurs around me.

When I finally slow, panting so hard it hurts, I duck behind a tree. I press my back against the bark and slide down, gasping, shaking. "Please be okay," I whisper. "Please be okay, Miss Dashworth."

I look down at my arm and nearly vomit. One gash is superficial, two are deeper, but the fourth...the fourth is bad. Blood pours from it, soaking the edge of my T-shirt, running down my forearm and dripping to the leaves below. I can see the layers, muscle, fat, maybe even bone.

I clench my jaw. Squeeze my eyes shut. My hands tremble. With teeth gritted, I bend and grab the hem of my pant leg. I rip it upward, pain blooming so intense I nearly black out. I bite down on my lip so hard I taste blood, stifling the scream threatening to tear free.

Hands shaking, I wrap the strip of fabric tight around my arm, trying to slow the bleeding. When it's done, I press the back of my head to the tree and cry, not loud, not wild. Just broken, numb, gutted, spent. I don't know if Miss Dashworth is alive. I don't know if I'm going to be.

I pull myself up, body trembling, legs shaking, my breath coming in quick bursts. The makeshift wrap around my arm is already soaked through, dark red and useless. Blood trickles from beneath it, running in rivulets down to my fingers, dripping off my knuckles.

Panic builds again, rising up like bile in my throat. I grit my teeth and press my other hand over the worst of it, gripping tight, trying to stanch the bleeding. I hiss in pain, but it seems to work. The blood slows. The flow no longer steady.

I need to move. I can't stay here, not with the scent of blood fresh in the air, not with a bear still somewhere behind me. I glance down at the spot where I'd been crouched, stained red, the leaves sticky and dark.

I turn away. And I start walking. Every step is agony, but I welcome it. Pain means I'm still alive. Pain means I can keep going.

My heart, still thudding, starts to settle into something steadier, a rhythm that almost feels like hope. It's faint, fragile, but it pulls me forward, tethering me to the idea that maybe I'm not done yet. I take in the sun, high now and burning bright through the thinning trees. It bathes the world in light, but I barely feel its warmth. I'm too far gone for that.

I walk. And walk. And walk. My vision blurs. My mouth is dry, tongue thick. My legs drag, my balance unsteady. I've lost feeling in the fingers of one hand. The arm I wrapped is throbbing, bone-deep, like something inside me is breaking.

Then, I fall. My knees hit the forest floor hard, jarring everything. My arms collapse under me, and I slump forward into the dirt. My cheek presses to the earth, cold, wet, unyielding. I can't move. Not anymore.

A tear breaks free, raw and hopeless, and I cry, quiet, heaving sobs that wrack my already broken body. My limbs are done. My chest feels like it's caving in. My vision fades in and out, blackness creeping along the edges.

I know what this is. I'm slipping. And I don't think I'm getting back up. Through my tears, I whisper one last thing, "Please…" And then everything goes still.

42

Every second matters

Miles

When Naya and I make it back to the house, the place feels quieter, emptier. Fewer people walk around now. Some are sitting in folding chairs with their heads in their hands. Others are clustered in silent, tired groups near the tents and supply tables. The energy is different, lower, heavier.

Reed meets me near the table of gear, his face unreadable. "Is everyone still out searching?" I ask, already grabbing a fresh water bottle.

He shakes his head slowly. "No. A few people went home."

I pause, glance up at him, then look back down at my hands as I zip the bag shut. I can feel the anger start to rise, tight in my throat, but I shove it down.

He doesn't stop talking. "The chief said the official search ends tomorrow evening."

My jaw clenches so tight it aches. I don't even try to hide it. I stare past him at nothing in particular and force my voice to stay level. "I'm going back out. I'm not stopping until she's found."

Dylan walks up behind him, his expression serious but softer than Reed's. "No one's asking you to stop, Miles. We're not giving up either. A lot of people are still volunteering to help. It just won't be as coordinated. But Luke's taking over organizing things from the house."

He nods over his shoulder toward the porch where Luke is standing in front of a laptop, focused on a live feed from one of the drones circling overhead. I follow his gaze for a moment.

"Okay." I swing the pack onto my back.

Reed throws his pack over his shoulder. "I'm going with you this time. Dylan's taking a couple volunteers to the south side."

I nod once, and we move. The clouds are heavy and low. I don't say it out loud, but I pray they don't break open. We don't need more rain. Not now.

We reach the edge of the forest in silence. Dylan and his team veer right. Reed and I head left, back to the same stretch I've been scouring again and again. The path is worn now, the brush trampled underfoot from how many times I've come this way. I know every tree, every bend. It still feels useless.

We move fast through the dense woods. No talking. Just the steady rhythm of boots crunching the forest floor and the occasional squawk of the handheld radios.

After a while, we hit the marker I carved and pause for water. I take a long pull from my bottle and swipe sweat from my forehead.

Reed shifts beside me, his voice low. "I know you don't want to hear this…"

I cut him off without looking at him. "Then don't say it." Because I already know what he's about to say. I can see it in his damn face. That we might not find her. That if we do, it might be too late. That she's been out here too long. That no one survives this long.

The thought alone makes my heart hurt to the point I might scream. Or break something. Anything to not feel this helpless. But I keep walking instead.

Reed and I split up, keeping about fifty feet between us, something I couldn't risk when the girls were with me. I didn't want to worry about them getting too far out of reach. But now I need to cover more ground.

It's sprinkling again, but the dense canopy shields most of it. Only every now and then do droplets build up and spill over, slapping the forest floor in soft, cold splashes that echo through the silence.

We move steadily, careful but fast, combing the forest as the last of the night hangs heavy around us. My flashlight beam flickers over roots, broken branches. Nothing that leads to her.

The forest shifts, gradually softening as the first signs of daybreak stir in the trees. There's no full sunrise, not yet, but the darkness eases, giving way to the gray light of early morning.

My radio crackles. "Miles." Luke's voice cuts through, alert and steady.

I yank the radio from my pocket, heart thudding. "Yeah," I answer quickly, hope flaring like a struck match.

Reed walks over from the left, his eyes on the sky. He lifts a finger, pointing up through the branches. Above us, barely audible over the rustle of leaves, the drone hovers. Just high enough that you can hear the hum if you listen for it.

Luke's voice continues through the speaker. "Dylan and two other volunteers are about fifteen minutes from your position, headed east to join your search grid."

I exhale, slow and heavy, letting go of the breath I hadn't realized I was holding. "Copy that. We'll wait here for them."

371

I slide the pack off my shoulders, feeling the tension ease slightly from my back. Reed does the same, and we both stand there, eyes trained on the trees to the west, watching.

The quiet is thick but not uncomfortable. It's the silence of men who understand what's at stake, who don't need to speak to know they're thinking the same thing.

Exactly fifteen minutes later, three figures appear through the woods, Dylan out front, a volunteer on either side. Their faces are lined with exhaustion, but no one complains. No one asks to rest.

Dylan steps in beside me. "Let's move. Everyone spread out, put about a hundred feet between us. We'll sweep this area clean."

We all nod silently and begin to fan out, spreading wide across the forest floor. With this many eyes and this much distance between us, we can cover a lot more ground. It's not perfect, but it's something. And right now, something is everything.

I tighten the straps on my pack again, grip the radio in one hand and press forward into the woods, heart pounding, jaw set.

We search for a while, eyes scanning, calling Kinsley's name every few minutes. It's quiet, the kind that makes your skin crawl.

Then, slicing through the quiet like a blade, Luke's voice snaps through the radio, sharp and fast. "Miles. Reed." Before I can even hit the button to respond, the radio crackles again, louder this time. "You've got a bear heading your way."

I freeze. My head jerks up, eyes darting through the trees. I search for Reed, he's about thirty feet away, and Dylan's further out, flanked by the two volunteers.

I press the radio to my mouth, keeping my voice low but steady. "Where?"

Reed meets my eyes across the clearing, his body already stiff with alertness. Dylan turns, slowly making his way back toward us, motioning the volunteers in with tight, controlled hand signals.

"To your left!" Luke barks. I can hear it in his voice now, urgency, tight and tense. "It's close!"

I move slowly, backing away to the right, toward Reed and the others. One by one, we close the distance, drawing in tight in the small opening between trees. Every sound becomes louder now; the creak of branches above, the shift of boots in the dirt, the soft click as Reed flicks the safety off his handgun. And then the trees part.

A massive black bear steps out from the brush, angrily, snarling under its breath. Its eyes sweep across us, ears pinned back. It doesn't bolt. It doesn't run. It's pissed, and it's staring straight at us.

Reed raises his gun, both hands steady. The bear snorts and moves closer, and with every heavy step, the ground seems to vibrate.

Then it rises, huge, up on its back legs. And Reed fires. The crack of the shot rips through the trees like a lightning strike. The bear lets out a roar, earsplitting and full of rage. It drops back onto all fours, sways, then collapses.

The weight of it hits the forest floor like thunder. No one moves. No one breathes.

My heart pounds in my ears, every nerve on fire. Reed keeps the gun raised another beat, watching for movement, until he's sure it's down. Only then does he lower the weapon.

"Jesus Christ!" Dylan bellows, breaking the silence.

We stand there in the stillness that follows, shaken but alive. I glance back toward the bear, then over at Reed.

"Nice shot."

He nods once, jaw tight. "Let's just hope that's the only one."

"Holy shit!" Luke's voice crackles over the radio, breathless with disbelief.

Despite everything, the fear, the exhaustion, the ache in every part of my body, we all laugh. It's the kind of laugh that borders on hysteria, the kind that erupts when the pressure breaks just enough to let something else in. It's short, tired, a little unhinged, but real. And for a brief second, it feels like air after drowning.

"Thanks for the warning." I glance up and wave toward the drone, its dark silhouette gliding silently above the trees.

"Anytime," Luke replies, and I know he means it. He's been behind that screen for hours, eyes wide open, holding this whole operation together.

Dylan steps forward and pats Reed on the shoulder. "Good job, man."

Reed gives a tight nod, and walks over, and cautiously approaching the bear. He squats beside it, looking for the slow rise and fall of its chest. After a second, he stands again. "It's gone." There's no pride in his voice, just the quiet heaviness that comes with having no other choice. None of us wanted to kill it. It was just doing what wild things do. But it was us or the bear, and out here, that line gets real clear, real fast.

We linger for a moment, all of us quiet. The gravity settles again. The adrenaline starts to fade, leaving behind exhaustion.

I adjust the trap on my pack. "We keep moving." No one argues.

We separate again, spreading out, eyes scanning every inch of the forest floor. Reed to the left, Dylan to the right, the volunteers fanning wider. The trees close in around us, thick and shadowed, but the sky is lighter now, the morning haze lifting bit by bit.

Overhead, the drone hums eastward, gliding ahead of us like a silent scout.

We search for hours, spread wide but moving slow, eyes locked on the ground, every snapped twig and bent blade of grass pulling our focus. My legs ache from the steady pace, but I don't slow down. I can't.

374

Then, something catches my eye. A dark stain, low against the base of a tree, just ahead on the left. I step toward it, heart pounding. My boots crunch over the underbrush as I crouch, ignoring the way my knees scream at the movement. Blood. A lot of it.

My stomach flips, bile rising into my throat, a sharp surge of terror and guilt hitting me all at once. *What if we're too late? What if this is all that's left of her?* It's pooled in the dirt, smeared across a patch of moss, soaking into the forest floor. Not fresh but not old either.

I fumble for the radio in my pocket, thumb pressing the button hard. "Reed, come here."

Seconds later, he jogs through the trees and drops beside me, scanning the ground with sharp eyes. He doesn't say anything at first, just studies it, jaw tight.

"You think it's human?"

Please, let it be anything else.

Reed slowly reaches down, dipping two fingers into the edge of the bloodstain. He rubs it between his thumb and forefinger, brows furrowing.

"I can't tell. It's starting to dry, but it's not completely crusted over." He looks up at me, something grim flashing in his eyes. "Could be hers."

I swallow hard and look down again. The blood trail continues, thin droplets scattered just beyond the tree, leading off deeper into the woods.

My heart thunders. "If it is," I say, rising to my feet, "she's close. She has to be."

Reed nods silently and stands, following my gaze. We don't need to speak. We're already moving. We follow the droplets, bright against the forest floor, smeared along the edges of leaves and broken branches, until they disappear into nothing. I stare at the last faint splash of red, hoping for more, but there's nothing. Just dirt.

Reed steps up beside me and gently pats my shoulder before veering off to the right, widening the gap between us again to keep covering more ground. I look down at the blood one last time before pushing forward.

Then Luke's voice cuts through the radio, urgent. "Miles."

I snatch the radio up fast. "Yeah?"

"About a half mile north of your position. I see something." He pauses. "I can't tell what it is, but whatever it is, it's moving. Slow. If at all."

My heart drops into my stomach. A jolt of something raw and electric rips through me. I don't ask for confirmation. I don't wait for Reed. I just bolt.

"Got it," I bite out into the radio and take off, pushing through branches, dodging under limbs, the pack on my back slamming against me with every step.

Every second matters. She's close. I know it.

43

On the Edge of Gone

Kinsley

Everything around me fades. The forest hushes, even the wind quiets, and for a moment, it feels like the world is letting me go. But then, I hear something. A sound. Distant. Barely more than a breath.

My eyes flutter open. Heavy. Too heavy. I blink against the light, trying to focus, but I see nothing. Just shapes. Shadows. My lids fall again. I imagined it, I want it too badly. Then, the voice again, low, strained and threaded with urgency, like a lifeline thrown across a chasm.

Faint. Far. But unmistakably real. "Kinsley."

My head jerks up an inch. A ragged, broken breath escapes me. I try to sit forward, my muscles screaming in protest. That voice. It's not my mind. It's not a hallucination. It's him.

"Miles," I croak. The sound barely makes it past my lips.

I roll to my hands and knees, my body shaking so violently I nearly collapse. I brace myself against the tree behind me, pushing until I'm upright. My vision blurs. My legs are jelly beneath me, but I don't care. I have to move.

377

Another voice, closer now. "Kinsley!"

I try to scream again, but it's hoarse, shredded. Nothing but air. Still, I move, stumbling one step, then two. My leg buckles. I fall hard, landing on my injured arm. Pain explodes up to my shoulder as the wound rips open again. Warm blood spills down my wrist, soaking the shredded fabric of my makeshift wrap.

I cry out, this time louder. And when I lift my head, I see him. Miles. He's standing a few yards away, wide-eyed, scanning the trees. His face is slack with disbelief.

I manage one last burst of strength. "Miles," I whisper again.

His eyes snap to me. He runs. He yells something over his shoulder to someone, but I only see him. Every inch of him. His face is pure panic, pure relief...eyes wide and frantic. His whole body leans forward, straining toward me, as if seeing me saves us both. Then he's there. Arms wrapping around me as I collapse forward, unable to hold myself up anymore.

He lowers me gently to the ground, cradling me like I might break, and I might. "I'm here, baby," he breathes, voice cracking. His hands cup my cheeks, thumbs brushing the dirt and tears from my face. Relief crashes into me so hard I sob.

He presses his forehead to mine. "Stay with me, Kinsley. Please. Open your eyes."

But I'm so tired. My body wants to stop. It's done. I try to hold on, for him, but everything is heavy again. Fading. Footsteps pound the earth behind him. I blink through the haze, and I see Reed, breathless and pale.

Miles looks at my arm and swears under his breath. His hands are shaking. "Baby, look at me. You're okay. I've got you."

I try to smile, to say something, but the words don't come. I just look at him. And even though my body is giving up, my heart finally feels safe.

"Look at me, Kinsley."

I do, blinking hard, trying to keep my eyes open. Everything's blurry. Distant. But I can just make out Reed opening his backpack and handing Miles something.

I watch as Miles unwraps my arm. The moment he sees it, horror stretches across his face. His jaw clenches tight. He doesn't say a word. Just starts wrapping the wound with fresh gauze, his hands firm but careful.

The sting is instant and brutal. I flinch, a raw scream ripping from my throat, but the sound is muffled, like it's underwater.

"I know, baby," he murmurs. "I have to stop the bleeding."

My head falls back, darkness pulling at the edges. The pain, the cold, the exhaustion. I'm slipping. Then I feel his arms around me, strong and steady.

"Radio Luke," Miles orders. "Tell him to have an ambulance waiting at the edge of the forest. And tell her parents."

My eyes flicker open at his words. *My parents?* Then everything dims.

I'm weightless, floating somewhere between sleep and pain. Everything around me is a blur, tree branches, sky, the sound of feet pounding against dirt.

"Come on, Kinsley. Stay awake." Miles whispers, his voice raspy. "Keep your eyes open, baby. Come on, just a little longer."

I try. God, I try. My eyes flutter, but they don't want to stay open. They're so heavy.

"Do you need a break?" someone asks, maybe Reed, maybe Dylan, I can't tell.

"No," Miles snaps. "I've got her." And I believe him. Now that he's found me, I know he won't let go. Not for anything.

The world jolts as he moves faster, then suddenly stops. His arms adjust around me, and he kneels, holding me tighter.

"Kinsley," he says, sharper now, pulling me back from the edge. "Open your eyes. I need you to take a drink. Can you do that?"

My lips are cracked. My throat feels like sandpaper. But I manage a slight nod, or maybe it's just a twitch. Either way, he takes it as a yes.

I feel the cool press of a water bottle against my mouth. His hand cradles the back of my head, tipping just enough. A trickle of water hits my tongue, and I gasp. It's cold, pure, real.

"That's it. Good girl. Just a little more. You're doing so good. Stay awake, ok? Just one more drink."

Scooping me back up he doesn't slow down. Not once. His grip on me is unrelenting, solid, sure. Like if he lets up even for a second, I'll slip away.

I drift in and out, darkness tugging me under, but his voice keeps finding me.

"Stay with me. Open your eyes, Kinsley. We're almost there."

My body's too heavy, my skin on fire, but I crack my eyes open just enough to find his jaw tight with determination, sweat mixing with rain on his brow.

"Miles," I whisper, my voice barely there.

"I'm here. I've got you."

I want to tell him I love him. I want to tell him about Miss Dashworth, that she stayed with me and she saved me. I want to tell him I'm sorry for worrying him, for disappearing, for everything. But the words won't come.

My lips tremble. My breath hitches. The tears start falling, silent, helpless. I cry because I'm scared, because I'm grateful, because I'm alive and he found me. He feels it. He pulls me in tighter.

"Shh," he murmurs. "Save your energy baby, don't cry."

I rest my head on his chest, right over his heart. The steady, thundering beat of it anchors me, a sharp contrast to the chaos still spinning inside my head. It's the one sound that cuts through the fear. It's the only thing in this world I trust right now. Step after step, he carries me through the mud, over branches, across uneven ground, never once faltering. I hear someone offer to take over again.

"I said I've got her," Miles growls. He won't stop. He won't put me down. Not until he gets me out.

Then, through the trees, I see it. A break in the forest where golden light spills through the branches. I hear the distant murmur of voices, the rustle of movement and the faint glint of something metallic. Warmth floods through me, fragile and flickering, but real. Rescue. Light. Movement. Shapes of people rushing forward. The edge. We made it. I blink up at him, tears still sliding down my cheeks.

He doesn't look at me, he's locked in, focused, but I feel the shift in his body. The slight tremble in his arms, not from weakness, but from the overwhelming force of relief.

Miles steps out of the tree line, and the sky is brighter here. The canopy breaks, letting in slivers of sunlight that make the moment feel too big, too real. My eyes flutter closed, and I turn my face into his chest, breathing him in. The scent of him, sweat, rain, earth, wraps around me like a safety net.

Then the voices come. All at once. My mother's cry slices through the air. "Kinsley!"

I blink my eyes open just enough to see her face, crumpled in anguish, tears streaking down her cheeks. My dad's hand comes to his mouth as he exhales a heavy, trembling breath. Relief. They crowd Miles, desperate to reach me, but he doesn't stop. Not for anyone. He walks straight to the waiting gurney, focused and relentless, barely noticing the people parting around him. Hands reach out, his name whispered, questions asked, but he doesn't stop. He's locked in, every ounce of his energy aimed at getting me to safety.

When he tries to lower me onto it, I panic, my fingers grip the front of his shirt with what little strength I have left. I can't let go. Not yet. He feels it.

"It's okay. I'll be right behind you."

But when my body touches the gurney, I still don't let go. My hand is locked to his shirt like it's the only thing keeping me alive. He leans in, threading his fingers through mine.

"Look at me, baby."

I do. I look into his eyes, and it's all there, everything he's feeling.

"I'll be right behind you," he repeats gently. "Do you understand?"

I nod, just barely, and let go. That's when Raelynn appears at my side, breathless from running. Her eyes are wide, face pale and streaked with worry.

"Kins, oh my God! I'm going to follow the ambulance, okay? I love you!"

The paramedic straps me in, checking vitals, calling something over the radio. My mom climbs in beside me, brushing hair from my forehead, whispering prayers between sobs. As the doors start to close, I look one last time just long enough to see him. Miles, standing in the clearing, soaked and scraped and unmoving. Watching. Waiting.

The doors slam shut behind us, and the siren kicks to life, wailing into the wind as the ambulance jolts forward. I feel the motion only vaguely, like I'm floating again, but then the paramedic's voice pulls me back down. "I'm starting fluids now. Her temperature's dropping, she's at eighty-two. I'm wrapping her in a thermal blanket."

I feel it then, cool plastic against my skin, crinkling and strange. It sounds like aluminum foil, but it holds in the heat like a second skin.

My mother holds my hand the entire time, her grip reassuring, her other hand smoothing my hair back as if she can soothe me with touch alone. Her eyes are red, her face pale, and her lips move in silent prayer even as she tells me, over and over, "You're okay. You're safe."

Then the paramedic reaches for my arm. The injured one. "We need to look at this," he says, not unkindly, but focused, clipped. "I'm unwrapping it." The moment the gauze peels away, pain rips through me. I scream. The sound is raw, primal, broken. I thrash instinctively, the pain too sharp, too much to bear.

"Hold her still!" the paramedic barks.

My mother leans over me, tears spilling from her eyes. "It's okay, it's almost over."

"It's alright, sweetheart," the paramedic says, his tone softening as he works quickly. "We're almost there. You're doing good."

But I can't breathe. Can't see. The pain is a wave crashing through me again and again. I squeeze my mother's hand with all I have left. Then her voice reaches me again, barely a whisper through the storm of pain.

"Miles is right behind us. He's coming. Just hang on, Kinsley. Just a little longer."

That's the last thing I remember. My mother's voice. "Miles is right behind us." The pain surges one final time, like the tide pulling back. The voices around me fade, the siren grows distant and my body stops fighting. My eyes slip closed. Darkness takes me again.

44

On My Knees

Miles

The ambulance doors slam shut, and I feel it in my chest like a
gunshot. My breath stutters, knees threatening to buckle, but I lock
them straight and just keep staring after it. She's in there. The siren
wails as the engine roars to life, kicking up dirt and grass as it pulls
away down the narrow road, red lights flashing through the trees
until it's swallowed up by the bend. I don't take my eyes off it. Not
for a second.

People start clapping shoulders behind me, congratulating
Reed, thanking Dylan, shaking Luke's hand.

"Hell of a job."

"We got her."

"Couldn't've done it without you guys."

They try to include me. Hands pat my back, someone even
grabs my arm and gives it a squeeze. I don't remember who. All I do
is watch the ambulance until it disappears from sight.

I hear Reed answering questions, Luke already talking
logistics, people coordinating rides back to town. I hear the chief's

voice saying something about wrapping up the site. But I can't move. I just can't.

Everyone slowly filters toward their cars, boots crunching in the gravel, engines starting, doors slamming shut. Relief hangs heavy in the air, earned and real, but none of it reaches me. Because she's gone. Not gone forever but gone from my arms. I don't know what's waiting on the other side of that ambulance ride.

I close my eyes for a second and see her face again, bloody, pale, broken, but still trying to smile for me. Still gripping my shirt when I tried to let go. "I'll be right behind you," I'd said.

I force my legs to move, dragging myself toward the house. My body's running on fumes, but I don't stop. Inside, everything is still. I step into the kitchen and grab my keys off the counter, and that's when it hits me. The wave of worry, relief, pain and love. All of it crashes over me at once, and I can't hold it back anymore.

My knees hit the floor. Hands cover my face. And for the first time, I cry.

I cry for the fear, for the hours lost in the woods, for the sound of her screams when I touched her arm, for the image of her on the ground, cold and bleeding. I cry because I found her. Because I almost didn't. Because I love her, and I almost lost her.

Then, softly, a hand touches my shoulder. I don't have to look to know it's Judy. She doesn't say a word. She just stands there beside me, rubbing my shoulder gently, steady as ever. Letting me fall apart without judgment. Letting me feel it.

Eventually, I catch my breath. My shoulders stop shaking. I wipe my face on my sleeve and slowly rise to my feet. Judy steps in front of me and cups my face, her palms warm and grounding.

She finally speaks. "Love is worth it, Miles. Go get your girl."

I nod, still unable to speak. But she's right. I'd do this a thousand times if it meant getting the chance to love her. I lean down and kiss Judy's cheek, then turn and step out the door.

When I reach my truck, Reed is leaning against the passenger door, waiting for me, his arms crossed and face drawn with exhaustion. There's relief in his eyes, but also something unspoken, worry maybe, or the weight of everything we just lived through. Neither of us says anything as we climb in. The silence feels earned. I start the engine and pull away, driving faster than I should. I glance over just in time to see Reed reach for his seatbelt and yank it tighter.

"Thanks for believing me," I say after a moment. "And…I'm sorry I snapped on you."

Reed turns toward me and shrugs. "That's what brothers are for, Miles. I'll have your back till the day we die."

"I know." My voice cracks, rough with emotion. "I love you."

He pulls a face, groaning like he's in physical pain. "Okay, now you went too far."

I chuckle, and for the first time all day, it feels normal.

But then he softens and says, quieter. "I love you too, man."

I glance over. "Yeah, you're right. That was too much."

We both laugh, a brief moment of light in the middle of the wreckage.

Then Reed's phone rings. He answers, voice clipped. "Hello? Yeah, okay. I'll tell him." He hangs up and looks over at me. "That was Dylan. He and Luke are behind us, trying to keep up. He said, and I quote, 'Tell Miles to slow the fuck down before we lose him.'"

I grunt, easing up on the gas just a little. But not much.

We pull into the hospital parking lot, tires screeching just a little as I cut into a space near the emergency room doors. A second later, Dylan and Luke pull in beside us. They climb out fast, no time wasted and fall into step beside me. None of us say a word. We don't need to.

The automatic doors slide open, and the cold fluorescent lights hit like a wall. That antiseptic smell, the quiet tension in the air, I feel it all settle deep inside me.

Naya's waiting just inside, pacing, arms crossed tightly. The second she sees us, she rushes forward. "They took her back right away." Her eyes are wide with worry but trying to stay calm. "The paramedics said her vitals were weak. They're working on her now."

My jaw tightens. Naya reaches out and lightly grabs my arm. "We're in the waiting room. Come on, this way." She leads us through the sterile maze of hallways, past nurses at their stations and a few other families hunched in chairs, whispering, crying, waiting.

I step into the lounge and take it all in at once. Her parents sit side by side, clinging to each other like if they let go, they'll fall apart. Raelynn is pacing the floor, eyes red. Dylan and Luke settle into chairs next to each other, drained and silent.

But I can't stay here. I can't sit and watch this. I can't be still. I back out of the room into the hallway. My boots echo softly against the linoleum as I start to pace. Up and down. Over and over. Every second feels like forever.

Reed stays with me. Doesn't say anything, just stands there, leaning against the wall, a quiet steady presence like he always is. Time stretches. I lose count of how many times I've walked the same twenty feet.

Finally, the door to the waiting room opens, and a doctor steps inside. Everyone goes still. Even from the hallway, I feel the shift. I stop pacing. My heart kicks hard.

The doctor steps forward, clipboard in hand, face composed but tired. Everyone rises, Raelynn stops pacing, her parents stand, Judy and Naya go quiet, and I freeze just outside the doorway, unable to breathe.

387

He clears his throat and begins. "She's stable. She came in with severe dehydration, mild hypothermia and several lacerations. She has about forty stitches in her arm, another eight on the bottom of her foot and fractured left wrist."

I feel every word like a strike to the ribs.

"We have her under heat blankets now. Her core temperature is slowly rising, which is a good sign."

Everyone exhales, but no one really relaxes.

"The biggest concern right now is infection. We're watching her vitals closely, especially for signs of fever. But she's young, strong, and she made it out. That says a lot."

Her mom presses a hand to her chest and sinks back into her chair. Her dad wraps an arm around her shoulders. Raelynn quietly starts to cry again.

"She's not awake yet," the doctor continues, "but we expect her to be soon. When she is, we'll allow visitors, but please, keep it quiet and short. She's going to be very weak for a while."

Then he scans the room, glancing at each face until his eyes land on me, standing just beyond the threshold. "Who's Miles?"

My throat tightens. I take a step forward. "I am," I say, barely trusting my voice.

The doctor nods slowly. "She's been asking for you."

For a second, I don't know how to breathe. She's in pain, drugged, broken, and still, she's asking for me. "Okay," I manage, because it's the only word I can get out.

He gives me a small smile. "We'll let you in first. Give us a few minutes to finish checking her over."

I nod again, silent, hands clenched at my sides. Because after everything, she still wants me. The doctor walks away, and for a moment, no one moves. We all just stand there, letting his words settle over us like dust. Slowly, conversation picks back up, soft voices, cautious hope.

Then, a few minutes later, a nurse steps out from the hallway. "Miles?" she asks scanning the room.

I step forward immediately.

"Come with me."

I follow behind her, heart pounding, but just before I reach the door, I pause and turn back. My eyes find Kinsley's mom. She hasn't stopped shaking since the doctor spoke. Without thinking, I reach out and take her hand. She looks at me, startled, and I nod once. "You should be there, too. You're her mom."

Her fingers tighten around mine. No words. Just a trembling squeeze. We walk together, side by side, through the sterile hallway. Past rooms filled with machines and soft murmurs, with patients lying still under dim lights.

Then we reach hers. The nurse pushes the door open. I step in and nearly stagger back. There are wires everywhere. Tubes. Machines. A silver metallic blanket drawn up over her chest like something out of a sci-fi movie. The monitors beep steadily, each sound a painful reminder of how close I came to losing her. She looks so small.

Her mother circles the bed and takes her hand, gently rubbing her head. I move to the other side, my heart breaking all over again. I lean down, so close my lips nearly touch her ear. "I'm here, baby," I whisper.

I lean back slightly, just enough to see her face. Her eyes flicker open, groggy and slow. They struggle to focus, then finally land on me. So quiet I almost miss it, she whispers, "You found me."

Then her eyes close again, drifting off before I can answer. "I did, baby," I whisper, brushing the back of her hand gently.

God, I want to crawl into that bed with her. I want to wrap her in my arms, hold her close, tell her I love her over and over again until it sinks in. Instead, I pull a chair up next to her and sit down, resting my head beside her shoulder, close enough to hear her breathe. To listen to the rhythm of the machines keeping her safe.

At some point, exhaustion wins. My eyes slip shut, and I doze off, finally letting myself rest, finally letting go of the fear. Because she's going to be okay. When I wake, the light is softer. Raelynn's sitting where Kinsley's mom had been.

She gives me a small smile. "Her parents went to the cafeteria to grab something to eat."

I sit up and stretch. "You should eat, too."

"I will, but I wanted to talk to you first in the hallway." She glances toward Kinsley's sleeping form.

We step out into the quiet hall, and she turns to face me, arms folded tight.

"The day before I got the call," she starts, voice a little shaky, "my soon-to-be ex-husband was served with the divorce papers. When I told him about Kinsley, he freaked out. Tried to stop me from coming. We had a huge fight and…" she trails off.

My jaw clenches. My fists curl at my sides. "Did he hit you?"

She shakes her head slowly. "He just grabbed me. Pushed me into the wall. I grabbed my bag and ran out the door."

Rage simmers to the surface, but I breathe through it.

"Judy offered me Cabin 5. I hope that's okay. I don't really have anywhere else to go. And I don't want to leave Kinsley."

"Raelynn, you don't even have to ask. You're more than welcome to stay as long as you need. We'll figure it all out."

She exhales, some of the tension slipping from her shoulders.

390

"Just so you know, I plan on asking her to stay with me. For good."

Her eyes soften, and for the first time in days, I see a small, genuine smile cross her face. "I'll go grab something to eat with her parents. Let her rest."

"Thanks." I watch her walk down the hall and disappear around the corner.

I step back into the hospital room. It's quiet again, just the low hum of machines, the soft beeping of monitors and Kinsley's steady breathing. I cross the room slowly and sink back into the chair beside her. She hasn't moved much, but there's a little more color in her face now. The silver thermal blanket still covers her, wires trailing from her arms, her wrist in a soft brace, but somehow, she looks more at peace.

I reach for her hand, gently, so I don't disturb the IV, and lace my fingers through hers.

"I meant what I said," I murmur. "I found you. And I'm not letting go."

She doesn't respond, but I stay there anyway, watching her sleep. Her skin's warm again. That's enough for now.

I brush my thumb across her knuckles and lean forward, resting my forehead beside her hand on the bed. "I love you," I whisper, barely louder than a breath.

I rest my head beside her on the mattress. My body gives out before my mind does. Every muscle aches, every nerve has frayed to the edge. For the first time since she went missing, I let myself fully rest, not because the fear is gone, but because hope has finally taken its place. My Eyes close and slowly, I drift off, her hand still wrapped in mine.

45

I Know Now

Kinsley

When I wake, the room is dim and quiet. My body feels heavy, but not nearly as broken as I remember. The last thing I can recall is doctors standing over me, barking orders, moving fast. I asked for Miles. *Where is he?* I blink slowly and turn my head toward the movement beside me. It's my mom.

She straightens in the chair when she sees me stir, her lips parting with a shaky sigh. "Kinsley, welcome back, sweetheart."

"Hi, Mom," I manage. My voice is rough, but it doesn't hurt to talk. I feel better. Stronger. "Am I okay?" I try to piece together what's real and what's a dream. "How long have I been here?"

She reaches for my hand, her eyes glassy. "Yes, honey, you're going to be okay. You got here yesterday."

I glance down at my arm, lifting it slowly. A thick bandage and a light cast wrap around my wrist and arm. I should be in pain, but I barely feel it. "Must be on the good stuff," I mutter, and she gives me a soft smile. I try to sit up. She helps me with a hand behind my back. "Where's Miles?"

She adjusts the blanket around me. "He just stepped out to use the bathroom."

My heart's already beating faster. I need to see him.

She hesitates. "Kinsley...I was wrong."

My brow pulls together, confused. "About what?"

She takes a moment, then meets my eyes. "Miles. Do you love him?"

I look away, just for a second. Then back at her. "Yes." That's all I say. Because I want him to be the first one to really hear it.

My mom nods slowly, tears rising again in her eyes, but this time, they aren't from fear. They're from something else.

"Then you should stay," she says, her voice trembling but sure. "Because what I saw him do, the sacrifice he made. The fight to find you. It told me everything I needed to know about him." She pauses, like she's letting the truth settle in her own heart. "He will do anything for you, Kinsley. Anything."

My throat tightens. "Tell me," I whisper. "Tell me everything that happened while I was gone."

She does. She tells me about the search party. About the storm. About how Miles refused to stop when others wanted to call it for the night. How he barely slept, barely ate. How he kept pushing himself and everyone else through the worst of it.

She tells me how Luke organized the volunteers and tried to keep everything running from the house. How Reed and Dylan never stopped. How Raelynn and Naya never gave up. How Judy took care of everybody.

But it was Miles who led the charge into the forest. She describes how he carried me out of the woods himself, refused to let anyone else take me, even when they offered. How he wouldn't stop walking until I was in the back of that ambulance. And how, when the doors shut, he didn't celebrate. He just stood there. Quiet. Still.

393

Like his whole soul had gone with me. By the time she finishes, my cheeks are wet. I don't remember starting to cry. I just know that I love him.

I take a few minutes after my mom finishes, wipe my cheeks and take a deep breath. The truth of everything she told me, what Miles did, how far he went to find me. It wraps around me like a second blanket. Full of love.

I'm still holding onto that when the door opens. I lift my eyes just as Miles steps into the room. He stops cold. I'm sitting up now, pale and bandaged, sure, but awake. Alert. The look on his face, it shatters me in the best way. His whole body goes still. His lips part like he doesn't trust what he's seeing. Then slowly, a smile tugs at the corner of his mouth, small, soft, and so him. He crosses the room, not rushing, like he's afraid to wake me from a dream. He leans down, kisses my forehead, and murmurs, "Welcome back, City Girl."

That one sentence makes my heart ache in a way that has nothing to do with pain or injury. I rest my head back against the pillow, my eyes never leaving his.

"I missed that voice," I whisper.

My mom stands, brushing hair from my face before leaning down and kissing my cheek. "I'll give you two a minute."

Then she turns to Miles, pausing just long enough to shoot him a quick wink, before slipping out the door.

Miles sits on the edge of the bed beside me, his presence grounding, solid in a way that makes my heart full. I reach for his hand. He takes it instantly.

Our fingers tangle together like they've always belonged that way. I stare at them for a moment, then take a deep breath. "I have to tell you what happened to me while I was out there."

He shakes his head softly, his thumb brushing across mine. "Kinsley, you don't have to. Not right now."

394

"No, Miles," I say gently. "I do."

He meets my eyes, and I see it clear as day. The pain. The quiet pleading that wants to protect me from having to relive it, but I need him to understand. To know why I'm sitting here and how I made it back.

So, I begin. I tell him about the cat, how I chased her into the woods. I tell him about the storm hitting. I tell him about the first night. Then the second. And the third and so on. The way I slept curled up with Miss Dashworth pressed against my side. The way she stood between me and a bear, her tiny body shaking but fierce.

"She saved me." Tears slip down my cheek before I can stop them.

Miles reaches up and wipes them away, his touch as gentle as his eyes are stormy. Still, he says nothing, just listens.

I tell him how I started losing hope. How I could barely move. How I was almost ready to let go, and then I heard him. "I heard your voice," I say, swallowing.

He doesn't look away. Not once. His hand never leaves mine.

"I thought about you the whole time, Miles," I whisper. "Every day. Every night. About how I was going to get back to you."

Silence settles between us. Full of everything we've both been carrying. "I have to tell you one more thing." But before I can say the words, before I can tell him I love him, tell him I want to stay, the door bursts open.

Raelynn steps in first, a bunch balloons floating behind her like she's trying to throw a unicorn-themed birthday party in a hospital room, complete with glitter balloons and sparkly streamers that don't quite fit the sterile walls. Naya's right behind her, cradling a glass vase filled with wildly colorful flowers; sunflowers, roses, daisies, and something bright purple that looks entirely made up. Bringing up the rear is Mel, clutching a teddy bear and already crying.

Raelynn starts tying ballons to the bed. "Okay, it's way too quiet in here for a girl who just survived the forest like some badass mountain queen."

Mel leans in kissing my face, hugging me gently like she afraid I'll break, tears streaking her cheeks. "I'm so sorry," she chokes out. "I didn't know until yesterday. I got the first flight out. I'm so happy you're okay. You scared the hell out of me, Kins."

"Thanks, Mel." I hug her back as tight as I can with one good arm. "I'm glad you're here."

Then Naya steps forward, carefully placing the vase of flowers on the rolling table next to me. She sits on the edge of the bed and leans in, eyes bright with emotion but her grin unmistakable. "So, I brought flowers. I figured it was either that or tequila, and they were weirdly against me smuggling alcohol into a hospital."

I let out a soft laugh, the first real one in what feels like forever. "You made the right call. Tequila would've clashed with my IV drip."

"That's what I told them," She rolls her eyes. "Apparently, patient survival is, like, super important." We all laugh, even Mel, wiping at her tears.

The room is filled with flowers, balloons and the soft hum of voices and laughter when the door opens again. Judy walks in first, holding a tote bag that's probably filled with snacks, magazines and something lavender-scented. My mom follows close behind with a fresh coffee in one hand and a warm, relieved smile.

Miles stands up as they enter, his hand still tangled in mine. He leans over and presses a soft kiss to my cheek, his scruffy jaw brushing my skin. "Well, looks like you've got a full-on girls' night happening in here. I'm officially outnumbered and underqualified."

The room chuckles, and even Judy snorts. "Smart man."

He leans in again, closer this time, his lips brushing the shell of my ear. "I'll be right outside," he whispers, the words a promise more than reassurance.

I nod, my heart doing that fluttery thing I've only ever felt around him. He gives my hand one last squeeze, then steps out of the way, letting the women crowd in around me like a force of nature.

My mom takes the seat Miles had just vacated, settling gently beside me with her coffee in hand. Naya stands up without hesitation, giving up her spot so Judy can sit on the other side of me. I glance around, heart full.

My three best friends, loud, ridiculous, loving, are all here. They're talking over each other, teasing, laughing, and somehow making this sterile hospital room feel like the coziest place on earth. I lean back against the pillows, just watching, soaking it in.

Then, thirty minutes later, the door opens, and everything goes still.

A doctor steps in, clipboard in hand, and immediately, everyone freezes. Raelynn stops mid-sentence, Naya straightens in her seat and Mel sets down the cup she was about to sip from. Miles is right behind him.

He must've been standing just outside the door, waiting, because there's no way he just happened to walk in at the same time. His eyes find mine instantly, and even in the quiet tension, I feel steadier having him there.

The doctor's brows lift at the sight of the very full room. "Ms. Brighton." His eye sweep over the crowd before landing on me. "Well, you've certainly drawn a crowd."

Everyone chuckles softly, but no one says a word. He flips through the chart, nodding as he reviews. "I'm happy to report you've shown steady improvement. Barring any complications overnight, you'll be discharged tomorrow morning."

Relief ripples through the room. "But…" His gaze moves deliberately around the group, a silent warning in his expression. "There will be restrictions. No physical activity for at least two weeks. Keep resting, take your antibiotics exactly as prescribed and I want to see you back here for a follow-up in one week. No excuses."

All my friends suddenly become very interested in the floor. I manage a smile. "Yes, sir."

"Good." He gives a small nod. "We'll have discharge paperwork ready in the morning." Then he turns and walks out, already pulling out his pager as the door clicks shut behind him.

Miles lingers in the doorway, his hand resting lightly on the frame, a small smile pulling at the corner of his mouth. "You have more visitors waiting." His voice is laced with amusement.

The girls all pick up on the hint. One by one, they step up to my bed, hugging me gently, brushing hair from my face, kissing my cheek, whispering soft promises to bring food, comfort and gossip. Naya straightens the flowers one last time like she needs to do something with her hands. Mel fluffs my pillow. Raelynn lingers a beat longer, squeezing my hand and mouthing, 'love you.' Then they're gone, filing out with Judy and Naya linking arms.

My mom is the last to stay. She settles into the chair beside me and takes my hand, her thumb brushing gently over my knuckles. Her eyes linger on mine, full of emotion, but there's calm there now. Peace.

"Your dad and I are going to head home tonight. I know you're in good hands here."

She glances toward Miles, and he straightens slightly, giving her a respectful nod. "I'll take care of her."

I squeeze her hand, and she leans in to hug me. We hold each other for a long time, longer than usual, and when she finally pulls back, she cups my face with both hands and kisses my forehead.

"Your dad will be in shortly."

My throat's thick with emotion as I watch her walk out. For a moment, the room is still. But only for two minutes.

The door swings open again, and in comes Reed, Dylan, Luke and my dad. It's like the air shifts at once. More footsteps. More voices. More them. I can't help but smile.

46

Where She Belongs

Miles

The door swings open and the room fills up fast, boots scuffing tile, laughter already bubbling up before anyone even says a word.

Reed walks in first, holding a bag of vending machine snacks like it's a care package. Dylan follows, grinning like he's got a joke locked and loaded. Luke's got his usual calm, cool look, until he sees Kinsley and his whole face softens. Her dad brings up the rear, quieter than the rest, but you can see the emotion in his eyes the second he looks at her. They all crowd around her bed like she's the guest of honor at some backwoods award ceremony.

"Well, well," Reed drawls, tossing a pack of sour candy onto her table. "Look who survived the wilderness and lived to tell the tale."

"She probably just curled up under a fern and waited for room service," Dylan adds with a wink.

Kinsley rolls her eyes, but the smile on her face is real. She's glowing, even under hospital lights.

Luke steps forward, shaking his head. "You had half the county out looking for you."

"Oh come on," Reed grins. "She just wanted Miles to come rescue her. You should've seen him, Kins. Man wouldn't eat. Barely slept. Damn near bit my head off when I said he needed to eat."

I groan. "Alright, alright. Let's not make me sound too dramatic."

But Kinsley's looking at me now, quiet, soft-eyed, and I can tell she doesn't think any of it was too much.

Her dad steps closer, his voice low and full of something deeper. "Thank you, boys. Every one of you."

They all go still for a second, the weight of her dad's words hanging in the air.

The guys don't stay long after that. One by one, they say their goodbyes, soft see you laters, gentle shoulder squeezes, teasing comments toned down now by the exhaustion and the gratitude.

Her dad lingers the longest. He leans down, presses a kiss to her forehead. "I love you, sweetheart."

Then he straightens and turns to me. He holds out his hand. I take it.

"Thanks for saving my girl."

I want to say OUR girl, but I hold it back. I want to get her home first.

He glances back at her one last time before walking out the door. The soft click of it closing leaves the room in silence. It's just us now. She slowly lays back, shifting her body with care, then slides over a few inches and pats the bed beside her.

I lower the rail and climb in, careful not to jostle anything. I stay on the edge, giving her space, but she doesn't hesitate, she shifts closer, nestling into my side. I wrap my arm around her, pulling her gently into my chest. She exhales, a soft sigh against my shirt.

"You must be tired. Get some sleep," I whisper.

401

"Are you going to stay with me tonight?"

I rest my head next to hers. "I'm not going anywhere."

A few minutes later, her breathing deepens. I watch her as long as I can, until my eyes grow heavy and I finally let them close, holding her safely in my arms.

I sleep without moving, completely drained, body and soul worn thin from the last several days. It isn't until I feel her fingers gently combing through my hair that my eyes flicker open.

She's sitting up, looking at me with that soft smile that always knocks the wind right out of me.

"You want to spend another night here," she says, holding up her discharge papers, "or do you want to take me home?"

I stretch, rubbing my face with one hand. "I thought you'd never ask."

She chuckles, quiet and raspy.

I slide out of the bed, grabbing my hoodie from the chair. "I don't know, though. I was really starting to like the vibe here. Fluorescent lights. Bland food. Beeping machines every ten seconds. Very romantic."

"Oh yeah," she chuckles. "Super cozy. Five stars. Ten, if they gave me extra pudding cups."

The nurse steps in with a clipboard in one hand and a kind smile. She walks over and checks Kinsley's temp, then removes the IV with a practiced flick, replacing it with a small bandage on her hand.

"There you go. You're officially free. But per hospital policy, I have to roll you down in a wheelchair."

Kinsley gives her a dramatic nod. "Is my chariot ready?"

The nurse laughs. "Yes, Your Highness. I'll be right back."

Kinsley looks over at me, grinning. "You think they'll let you push the chair?"

"Oh, definitely not. But I'm doing it anyway."

I push the wheelchair through the sliding doors of the emergency room and into the bright morning light. As soon as we're clear, I set the brakes and jog across the lot to grab the truck, pulling it up as close to the curb as I can.

By the time I hop out and circle back around, the nurse is already helping Kinsley to her feet. Her legs wobble at first, unsteady beneath her, but she doesn't fall. After a few tentative steps, she straightens. Finds her footing, then she walks. Step by step.

She might be moving slow, but she's upright. Moving forward. Watching her make her way toward my truck, her hand gripping the doorframe, her hair a little messy and her hospital bracelet still clinging to her wrist. She might be the strongest woman I've ever known. With fire still in her eyes, like she'd dared the wilderness to break her and came out stronger. What she survived, the pain, the cold, the thirst, the hunger, it would've broken most people. But not her.

I help her into the truck carefully, steadying her as she climbs in. Then I move around to my side and slide behind the wheel.

"You ready, baby?"

She turns her head toward me, eyes bright. "More than you know."

We drive the twenty minutes back, the kind of quiet ride where everything feels lighter, like the weight has finally started to lift. We talk and laugh about how many people will probably stop by once they hear she's home.

I tell her about Raelynn and how she's already settled into Cabin 5.

"I'm happy she's here." Her smile falters just a little. "But I'm sad she has to go through this."

"I know, but she's tough. Like someone else I know."

As we pull into the driveway, something hits me, hard.

Memories. The flashing red lights. The ambulance pulling away. The way my hands wouldn't stop shaking after they took her. That hollow feeling in my chest like I'd already lost her.

I stop the truck near the front steps and hop out quickly, circling around to her side. I open the door and help her down. We start toward the house slowly.

Then she stops. Dead in her tracks. Tears spill from her eyes before I can even ask what's wrong.

"Kinsley? Are you in pain?"

She doesn't answer, just lifts her hand and points toward the porch, her voice caught somewhere in her throat.

I follow her gaze.

There, curled up right in front of the door is Miss Dashworth.

Kinsley lets out a broken sound, halfway between a laugh and a sob. She climbs the porch steps slowly. The second she's close enough, Miss Dashworth bolts to her. Kinsley drops to her knees carefully and scoops her up, burying her face in soft gray fur. She cries, not loudly, not with words, but with that deep, silent ache that only someone who's survived will understand.

My heart aches watching her because I know that's not just about the cat. That's about everything. Kinsley stands, Miss Dashworth tucked under her chin. I reach around her and open the door.

The moment it swings open, Miss Dashworth jumps down and bolts inside, beelining straight for her food dish. Kinsley chuckles softly behind me. "She's hungry and probably thirsty. You might want to make her a vet appointment, have her checked out."

"I'll do it tomorrow."

I head into the kitchen, grab the bag of kibble from the cabinet and pour it into her dish. She immediately digs in, and I crouch down beside her, running a hand gently down her back.

"Thanks for saving her," I whisper. "I owe you treats for life, you little hero."

When I return to the living room, Kinsley's sitting on the couch, looking worn but peaceful, the kind of tired that settles in when you're finally safe.

I can't wait any longer. I walk over and drop to my knees in front of her. Her eyes widen slightly, searching mine, and I take her hands in mine.

"I love you," I say, voice rough with everything I've been holding in. "I should've said it sooner. I love you. I want to build a life with you. Right here. But if you don't want to stay, if your heart's still in Seattle, I'll move. I'll pack up tomorrow. Just say the word."

Tears gather in her eyes and slide down her cheeks. "Miles," she whispers, her voice shaking, "I would never ask you to give this up." She gestures softly around the room. "This, all of this, it's you. It's part of who you are."

Then she touches my face softly and leans in. "I love you, too, and I want this life with you."

I cup her face in my hands, brushing away the last of her tears with my thumbs. Her eyes search mine, wide and full of everything we've been through.

Then I lean in and kiss her. The first time in days. It's not rushed or hungry. It's not about need. It's a promise. To love her. To protect her. To find her, every damn day. The way her lips move against mine, soft and certain, I feel her promise too. To stay. To trust me. To love me back.

When we finally part, she rests her forehead against mine, both of us holding on like the world outside the house doesn't exist. For the first time in what feels like forever... It doesn't have to.

Epilogue
Starting Over, Together

Kinsley

One week later, I almost feel like myself again. My wrist is healing, the bruises are fading and the nightmares don't come quite as often. What hasn't faded is Miles' extreme commitment to following the doctor's orders. He won't touch me. Not really. I miss him. That deep, aching kind of miss, the kind that blooms under your skin. But I know it's getting to him, too. I can tell when his jaw ticks and he groans curse words under his breath. Every time I lean in or try to tempt him with a kiss that lingers too long, he just smirks and mutters something like, "Doc said no strenuous activity." Like I'm made of glass. Like I might break. He won't even let me lift a gallon of milk without hovering nearby like I'm about to deadlift a tractor engine. It's sweet. It's maddening. It's so Miles.

So, what do I do? I lay it on thick. Reach over him a little too slowly. Brush my hips against him in the kitchen. Cook in nothing but an apron. He still won't cave. I catch the way his eyes darken, the slight hitch in his breath, the way he grips the edge of the counter a little too tight, but he holds the line. Barely.

Today we're driving back to Seattle. Miles, Raelynn and me. Raelynn's in the back seat, singing off-key to the radio, boots

407

propped on the center console, already listing off everything she's packing first. She talks fast when she's anxious. I let her. It's comforting, the sound of her voice filling the cab of the truck as we head toward the city.

Behind us, Naya's driving her Jeep, following close in the rearview. She's insisted on coming along, partly to help, partly because she doesn't trust me to take it easy. Judy's riding shotgun with her, a shoebox full of homemade snacks clutched in her lap because, in her words, "Seattle doesn't know how to feed people properly." There's carrot cake, deviled eggs and something wrapped in foil that I'm pretty sure is some kind of meat. She keeps unwrapping things and offering them to Naya, who's too excited to care. She hasn't stopped smiling since we told her I was staying.

As the city skyline comes into view, it doesn't feel like mine anymore. It feels like something I once wore that doesn't quite fit now. There's no sadness in that. Just clarity. I never fully unpacked when I moved in, so it should be easy, just pack up the remnants and let the movers take care of the rest. After a lot of thinking, and a surprise offer, the associates at my firm bought me out. They heard what happened to me. They knew I wouldn't be coming back.

I'm opening my own firm. Right there in Cranberry Ridge. Mel's agreed to come on board when the time's right. She didn't hesitate. Just said, "Tell me when," and that was that. Every town needs a family lawyer. I can't think of a better place to start over.

Raelynn's headed back to gather what's left of the life she's walking away from. Her soon-to-be ex is out of town for work, and the moment he left, she packed fast. I sat on the edge of her bed while she filled boxes with folded clothes. Every drawer closed with a kind of finality that made the air feel free. Some things she tossed without a second thought. Others, photos, books, a few old mugs, she packed. Not because she wanted to keep them, but because she couldn't let them go just yet.

She smiled through most of it. Laughed at old receipts. Cursed at tangled chargers. When she zipped up her last bag, she sat down beside me and cried. Not because she regrets leaving, but because mourning what could've been is its own kind of grief.

Tomorrow, she and I will walk into court together and file for legal separation. Side by side. No more secrets. No more fear.

Miss Dashworth didn't make the trip to Seattle. She stayed behind with Reed, being spoiled and checked in on like she was recovering from trauma, too. Reed sent daily updates, complete with photos of her stretched out on the bed or perched at the windowsill like a sentry. The day after I got back from the hospital, we took her to the vet, just to be sure, and she checked out fine. Healthy. Steady. Unbothered.

Miles decided she needed a bath after that, and let's just say... it did not go well. She went feral the second her paws hit the water. Tried to assassinate him mid-shampoo with the rage of a thousand wet cats. Then spent the next three hours glaring at him from atop the fridge.

She hasn't left my side until now. She follows me everywhere, room to room. Sleeps curled against my ribs. Sits on the tub while I shower. She watches me, like she's guarding the weight of a memory only she carries.

Back in Cranberry Ridge, the rhythm is different. Slower. Steadier. Real. Raelynn's staying in Cabin 5 for now. It's close enough I could reach her in two minutes flat, but far enough that she can breathe. She keeps to herself mostly, taking long walks along the lake, curling up in the rocking chair on the front porch with a blanket. We talk but not too much. I let her have the quiet. I know what it means to need silence, to sort through everything inside without having to explain it to someone else. I leave her space. And when she's ready, I'll be right here.

Apparently, Miles already signed me up for wilderness first aid, navigation and self-defense. He didn't ask. Enrolled me twice a week for the next month. And honestly? I love him for it.

Because loving Miles isn't soft. It's solid. It's late-night flashlight checks. Hands that hold steady. Eyes that see everything.

A heart that never once asked me to be less. He loves me. I know it. In the quiet moments. In the way he won't leave my side. In the unspoken promise that he will never let me walk through darkness alone again.

***

Miles

Today makes two weeks. Two weeks since I carried her out of the woods. Two weeks since the hospital. Two weeks of healing, holding back, sleeping beside her without touching her the way I've wanted to.

Her things were delivered this morning, boxes from Seattle now stacked in the spare rooms. Clothes in my closet. Her scent on every pillow. No more Seattle. She's home.

We're having chicken stir fry and wine for dinner, something she picked out. I can see it in her eyes, no more restrictions. She knows it and so do I. She sits across from me at the table, a little smile on her face. The same thing she's been doing for the last week. Flirting, brushing across my body, kissing me deeper. Driving me crazy with want and bending my control.

I barely touch dinner because I can't think straight with her this close. In this house. In this body I haven't touched in two weeks. Too long.

She slowly licks a bit of sauce from her thumb, eyes flicking up to catch me watching. That's it! I snap.

The chair scrapes behind me as I stand. Kinsley's eyes widen, smile curling deeper, but she doesn't move. "Get over here," I say, my voice low, rougher than I mean it to be.

She rises slowly, sauntering around the table with that subtle sway in her hips she knows drives me insane. The second she's within reach, I grab her hips, spin her, and lift her straight onto the

410

dining table, plates shifting, silverware clinking. She gasps, gripping the edge behind her.

"Miles!" She giggles.

"You think I've been sleeping next to you every night without losing my mind?" I growl, pushing her knees apart, skirt around her waist. "You think I forgot how sweet you taste? How you fall apart for me?"

I don't wait for an answer. I drop to my knees, dragging her closer by the hips. I rip the thin lace from between her legs, letting it fall to the floor. My mouth on her before she can say another word.

She gasps, head tipping back, thighs already trembling. Her fingers thread into my hair, gripping tight as I work my tongue over her clit. I push two fingers in her opening, slow at first, then rougher stretching her for my waiting cock.

"Oh my God. Miles please!" She begs.

"You've waited two weeks for this. Come so I can give you my cock," I mutter, mouth slick. She does. Hard.

Her body arches off the table, her moan echoing off the walls, legs locked around my head. I suck and lick every shudder, every breathless cry out of her.

When she goes still, chest heaving, I rise. Her eyes are half-lidded, hair a mess, cheeks flushed.

Mine. All mine.

I flip her gently, bending her over the table, hands braced against the wood. She lets out a breathy sound as I grip her hips.

"You ready for this?" I murmur against her neck. "Because I'm not holding back."

"Please," she whispers. "Don't."

I inch inside her, slow at first, I groan when I feel the tightness and heat wrap around my tip. Unable to take much more I slam into her. She cries out my name.

"God, you feel like heaven," I hiss, dragging my hands up her spine and down. Gripping her waist as I move, rougher, every thrust driving weeks of want straight into her. She's moaning again, her back arching, nails scraping across the wood.

"You missed this, didn't you?" I breathe into her ear. "Missed the way I ruin you?"

"Yes, Miles, yes."

She takes all of it, meeting me with the same hunger. I pump harder, my rhythm steady. I feel it building low in my spine.

"Come baby. Let me hear who you belong to," I growl between thrusts. I reach my hand around her, my fingers slipping between her legs. Sliding over her wet bud circling, pressing, driving her to the edge.

She falls apart, loud, breathless, "I'm yours!" She screams, head falling forward, body shuddering around me.

I follow with a groan, my pace slowing, grinding deep as I spill inside her, milking every drop, burying myself to the hilt. The sound of her moans still echoing as I breathe through the aftershocks, not ready to let go just yet. We collapse to the floor, tangled and spent, the wood cool against our bare skin. I pull her into my arms, pressing my forehead to hers.

She's still catching her breath when she whispers, "That was worth the wait."

I smile, kissing her softly now, slow, reverent. "No more waiting, Not ever again."

She falls asleep on my chest not long after. Like her body finally believes we're safe. Like mine finally remembers what it means to stay still and just be. I just lay there, holding her, breathing her in. Skin warm, body soft, hair stuck to her cheek. It still knocks the wind out of me sometimes, how close I came to losing her. But I didn't. She's here. She's whole. And every day, I get to watch her heal.

There's a strength in her now that wasn't there before. Not a loud one. Not something she talks about. It's in the way she walks down to the lake barefoot in the morning, coffee in hand. The way she checks in on Raelynn without hovering. The way she lets herself rest without guilt. She laughs more. Sleeps deeper. When she looks at me, there's something in her eyes that wasn't there before either. Peace.

We've still got things to do. She needs a car, for one. I've been driving her around like she's royalty, and I don't mind a bit, but she's itching for independence again. Then there's cabin two. Total loss after the storm. Roof gone, water damage everywhere. We'll rebuild it in the spring. I've got ideas. She's got Pinterest boards. We'll figure it out.

But for now, this, her in my arms, our life unfolding one quiet moment at a time, it's enough. Hell, it's everything.

Author's Note

When I started writing Cabin 6, I thought I was telling a simple love story, just a woman burned out from the city and a man grounded in the quiet rhythms of the land. But somewhere along the way, it became something more. A story about coming home to yourself. About learning to rest, to risk and to love without apology.

Kinsley and Miles showed up in my mind fully formed, stubborn, sharp, tender in all the best and worst ways. They pulled me through their story one page at a time, and I was just smart enough not to get in their way. If you saw a bit of yourself in them, whether it was Kinsley's need to let go, or Miles' quiet need to hold on I hope this story gave you a place to breathe.

Cranberry Ridge is full of messy, beautiful people, and Cabin 6 is only the beginning. There's more to tell, more stories tucked into lakeside cabins and meddling aunts, more healing, more heartbreak, and of course, more love.

Thank you for taking a chance on these pages. I hope you'll come back.

With love,

P. L. Wellisley

Acknowledgments

This book began as a quiet whisper in the back of my mind and somehow turned into a full-blown love story with a beating heart and muddy boots.

To the family who listened to me ramble about fictional characters as if they were real, thank you. You nodded patiently, asked follow-up questions and didn't run when I explained the emotional significance of a canoe scene. That's real love.

To the late-night coffee, early-morning doubt, and the playlist that got me through the hard chapters, you were the unsung heroes.

To the one who told me to keep going when I almost didn't (you know who you, MJ), I heard you. I needed you. I'm still writing because of you. Love your Face.

To every reader who sees themselves in Kinsley's fire or Miles' quiet steadiness, this one's for you. You're not alone in the wilderness.

And finally, to whoever needs the reminder: your story matters, even if you're still living through the messy middle of it.

With love and way too many sticky notes,

P. L. Wellisley

Coming Soon

Book Two of the Cranberry Ridge Series

Cabin 5: Raelynn & Reed's story begins…

About the Author

P. L. Wellisley is a small-town romance author with a soft spot for emotionally messy characters, slow-burn chemistry, and the kind of love that sneaks up on you and stays a while. She lives in rural Michigan with her husband and their four mostly grown kids, all of whom still think she knows where everything is in the house, and she probably does.

A stay-at-home mom turned storyteller, P. L. has always found comfort in creating things, whether it's a handcrafted project, a heartfelt scene, or a fictional town full of second chances. When she's not writing or wrangling household chaos, you can usually find her knee-deep in craft supplies and quietly rooting for fictional couples to get their act together.

Her debut novel, Cabin 6, is the first in the Cranberry Ridge series, a cozy, emotionally rich world where lakeside cabins, hometown secrets, and long looks across bonfires set the stage for unforgettable love stories. As a nod to her Michigan roots, every character in the series carries the last name of a real town or city in the state, a hidden detail she included as a personal love letter to the place that shaped her.

She writes for readers who crave a good ache before the payoff, who understand that healing doesn't happen in a straight line, and who believe, deep down, that love is always worth the risk.